A DEAL
AT THE ALTAR

BY

LYNNE GRAHAM

First published in Great Britain 2012
by Mills & Boon, an imprint of Harlequin (UK) Limited.
Large Print edition 2012
Harlequin (UK) Limited, Eton House,
18-24 Paradise Road, Richmond, Surrey TW9 1SR

© Lynne Graham 2012

ISBN: 978 0 263 22598 3

Harlequin (UK) policy is to use papers that are natural, renewable and recyclable products and made from wood grown in sustainable forests. The logging and manufacturing process conform to the legal environmental regulations of the country of origin.

Printed and bound in Great Britain
by CPI Antony Rowe, Chippenham, Wiltshire

CHAPTER ONE

'WHAT do I want to do about the Royale hotel group?' The speaker, a very tall and well-built Greek male with blue-black hair, raised an ebony brow and gave a sardonic laugh. 'Let's allow Blake to sweat for the moment...'

'Yes, sir.' Thomas Morrow, the British executive who had asked the question at the behest of his colleagues, was conscious of the nervous perspiration on his brow. One-on-one encounters with his powerhouse employer, one of the richest men in the world, were rare and he was keen not to say anything that might be deemed stupid or naive.

Everybody knew that Sergios Demonides did not suffer fools gladly. Unfortunately, priding himself on being a maverick, the Greek billionaire did not feel the need to explain the objectives behind his business decisions either, which could make life challenging for his executive team. Not so long ago the acquisition of the Royale hotel group at any price had seemed to be the goal and there was even a strong rumour that Sergios might be planning to marry the exquisite Zara Blake, the daughter of the man who owned the hotel chain. But after Zara had been pictured in the media in the arms of an Italian banker that rumour had died and Sergios's curious staff had not noticed their boss exhibiting the smallest sign of annoyance over the development.

'I took the original offer to Blake off the table. The price will come down now,' Sergios pointed out lazily, brilliant black eyes glittering at that prospect for more than anything else in life he liked to drive a hard bargain.

Purchasing the Royale group at an inflated price would have gone very much against the grain with him, but a couple of months ago

Sergios had been prepared to do it and jump through virtually any hoop just to make that deal. *Why?* His beloved grandfather, Nectarios, who had started his legendary business empire at the helm of the very first Royale hotel in London, had been seriously ill at the time. But, mercifully, Nectarios was a tough old buzzard, Sergios thought fondly, and pioneering heart surgery in the USA had powered his recovery. Sergios now thought that the hotel chain would make a timely little surprise for his grandfather's eightieth birthday, but he no longer had any intention of paying over the odds for the gift.

As for the wife he had almost acquired as part of the deal, Sergios was relieved that fate had prevented him from making that mistake. Zara Blake, after all, had shown herself up as a beautiful little tart with neither honour nor decency. On the other hand her maternal instincts would have come in very useful where his children were concerned, he conceded grudgingly. Had it not been for the fact that his cousin's premature death had left Sergios responsible for his three young children, Sergios would not even have considered taking a second wife.

His handsome face hardened. One catastrophe in that department had been quite sufficient for Sergios. For the sake of those children, however, he had been prepared to bite the bullet and re-marry. It would have been a marriage of convenience though, a public sham to gain a mother for the children and assuage his conscience. He knew nothing about kids and had never wanted any of his own but he knew his cousin's children were unhappy and that piqued his pride and his sense of honour.

'So, we're waiting for Blake to make the next move,' Thomas guessed, breaking the silence.

'And it won't be long. He's over-extended and under-funded with very few options left,' Sergios commented with growling satisfaction.

'You're a primary school teacher and good with young kids,' Monty Blake pointed out, seemingly impervious to his eldest daughter's expression of frank astonishment as she stood in his wood-panelled office. 'You'd make the perfect wife for Demonides—'

'No, stop right there!' Bee lifted a hand to physically emphasise that demand, her green eyes bright with disbelief as she used her other hand to push the heavy fall of chestnut-brown hair off her damp brow. Now she knew that her surprise and disquiet that her father should have asked her to come and see him were not unfounded. 'This is me, not Zara, you're talking to and I have no desire to marry an oversexed billionaire who needs some little woman at home to look after his kids—'

'Those kids are not his,' the older man broke in to remind her, as though that should make a difference to her. 'His cousin's death made him their guardian. By all accounts he didn't either want or welcome the responsibility—'

At that information, Bee's delicately rounded face only tightened with increased annoyance.

She had plenty of experience with men who could not be bothered with children, not least with the man standing in front of her making sexist pronouncements. He might have persuaded her naive younger sister, Zara, to consider a marriage of convenience with the Greek shipping magnate, but Bee was far less impressionable and considerably more suspicious.

She had never sought her father's approval, which was just as well because as she was a mere daughter it had never been on offer to her. She was not afraid to admit that she didn't like or respect the older man, who had taken no interest in her as she grew up. He had also badly damaged her self-esteem at sixteen when he advised her that she needed to go on a diet and dye her hair a lighter colour. Monty Blake's image of female perfection was unashamedly blonde and skinny, while Bee was brunette and resolutely curvy. She focused on the desk photograph of her stepmother, Ingrid, a glamorous former Swedish model, blonde and thin as a rail.

'I'm sorry, I'm not interested, Dad,' Bee told him squarely, belatedly noticing that he wore an undeniable look of tiredness and strain. Perhaps he had come up with that outrageous suggestion that she marry Sergios Demonides because he was stressed out with business worries, she reasoned uncertainly.

'Well, you'd better get interested,' Monty Blake retorted sharply. 'Your mother and you lead a nice life. If the Royale hotel group crashes so that Demonides can pick it up for a song, the fallout won't only affect me and your stepmother but *all* my dependants...'

Bee tensed at that doom-laden forecast. 'What are you saying?'

'You know very well what I'm saying,' he countered impatiently. 'You're not as stupid as your sister—'

'Zara is *not*—'

'I'll come straight to the point. I've always been very generous to you and your mother...'

Uncomfortable with that subject though she

was, Bee also liked to be fair. 'Yes, you have been,' she was willing to acknowledge.

It was not the moment to say that she had always thought his generosity towards her mother might be better described as 'conscience' money. Emilia, Bee's Spanish mother, had been Monty's first wife. In the wake of a serious car accident, Emilia had emerged from hospital as a paraplegic in a wheelchair. Bee had been four years old at the time and her mother had quickly realised that her young, ambitious husband was repulsed by her handicap. With quiet dignity, Emilia had accepted the inevitable and agreed to a separation. In gratitude for the fact that she had returned his freedom without a fuss, Monty had bought Emilia and her daughter a detached house in a modern estate, which he had then had specially adapted to her mother's needs. He had also always paid for the services of a carer to ensure that Bee was not burdened with round-the-clock responsibility for her mother. While the need to help out at home had necessarily restricted Bee's social life from a young age, she was painfully aware that only her father's financial support had made it possible for her to attend university, train as a teacher and actually take up the career that she loved.

'I'm afraid that unless you do what I'm asking you to do the gravy train of my benevolence stops here and now,' Monty Blake declared harshly. 'I own your mother's house. It's in my name and I can sell it any time I choose.'

Bee turned pale at that frank warning, shock winging through her because this was not a side of her father that she had ever come up against before. 'Why would you do something so dreadful to Mum?'

'Why should I care now?' Monty demanded curtly. 'I married your mother over twenty years ago and I've looked after her ever since. Most people would agree that I've more than paid my dues to a woman I was only married to for five years.'

'You know how much Mum and I appreciate

everything that you have done for her,' Bee responded, her pride stung by the need to show that humility in the face of his obnoxious threatening behaviour.

'If you want my generosity to continue it will *cost* you,' the older man spelt out bluntly. 'I need Sergios Demonides to buy my hotels at the right price. And he was willing to do that until Zara blew him off and married that Italian instead—'

'Zara's deliriously happy with Vitale Roccanti,' Bee murmured tautly in her half-sister's defence. 'I don't see how I could possibly persuade a big tough businessman like Demonides to buy your hotels at a preferential price.'

'Well, let's face it, you don't have Zara's looks,' her father conceded witheringly. 'But as I understand it all Demonides wants is a mother for those kids he's been landed with and you'd make a damned sight better mother for them than Zara ever would have done—your sister can barely read! I bet he didn't know that when he agreed to marry her.'

Stiff with distaste at the cruelty of his comments about her sister, who suffered from dyslexia, Bee studied him coolly. 'I'm sure a man as rich and powerful as Sergios Demonides could find any number of women willing to marry him and play mummy to those kids. As you've correctly pointed out I'm not the ornamental type so I can't understand why you imagine he might be interested in me.'

Monty Blake released a scornful laugh. 'Because I know what he wants—Zara told me. He wants a woman who knows her place—'

'Well, then, he definitely doesn't want me,' Bee slotted in drily, her eyes flaring at that outdated expression that assumed female inferiority. 'And Zara's feistier than you seem to appreciate. I think he would have had problems with her too.'

'But you're the clever one who could give him exactly what he wants. You're much more practical than Zara ever was because you've never had it too easy—'

'Dad…?' Bee cut in, spreading her hands in a silencing motion. 'Why are we even having this insane conversation? I've only met Sergios Demonides once in my life and he barely looked at me.'

She swallowed back the unnecessary comment that the only part of her the Greek tycoon had noticed had appeared to be her chest.

'I want you to go to him and offer him a deal— the same deal he made with Zara. A marriage where he gets to do as he likes and buys my hotels at the agreed figure—'

'*Me*…go to *him* with a proposal of marriage?' Bee echoed in ringing disbelief. 'I've never heard anything so ridiculous in my life! The man would think I was a lunatic!'

Monty Blake surveyed her steadily. 'I believe you're clever enough to be convincing. If you can persuade him that you could be a perfect wife and mother for those little orphans you're that something extra that could put this deal back on the table for me. I need this sale and I need it now or everything I've worked for all my life is going to tumble down like a pack of cards. And with it will go your mother's security—'

'Don't threaten Mum like that.'

'But it's not an empty threat.' Monty shot his daughter an embittered look. 'The bank's threatening to pull the plug on my loans. My hotel chain is on the edge of disaster and right now that devil, Demonides, is playing a waiting game. I can't afford to wait. If I go down you and your mother will lose everything too,' he reminded her doggedly. 'Think about it and imagine it—no specially adapted house, day-to-day responsibility for Emilia, no life of your own any more...'

'Don't!' Bee exclaimed, disgusted by his coercive methods. 'I think you have to be off your head to think that Sergios Demonides would even consider marrying someone like me.'

'Perhaps I am but we're not going to know until you make the approach, are we?'

'You're crazy!' his daughter protested vehemently, aghast at what he was demanding of her.

Her father stabbed a finger in the air. 'I'll have a For Sale sign erected outside your mother's house this week if you don't at least go and see him.'

'I couldn't…I just *couldn't*!' Bee gasped, appalled by his persistence. 'Please don't do this to Mum.'

'I've made a reasonable request, Bee. I'm in a very tight corner. Why, after enjoying all my years of expensive support and education, shouldn't you try to help?'

'Oh, puh-lease,' Bee responded with helpless scorn at that smooth and inaccurate résumé of his behaviour as a parent. 'Demanding that I approach a Greek billionaire and ask him to marry me is a *reasonable* request? On what planet and in what culture would that be reasonable?'

'Tell him you'll take those kids off his hands and allow him to continue enjoying his freedom and I think you're in with a good chance,' the older man replied stubbornly.

'And what happens when I humiliate myself and he turns me down?'

'You'll have to pray that he says yes,' Monty Blake answered, refusing to give an inch in his desperation. 'After all, it is the *only* way that your mother's life is likely to continue as comfortably as it has done for years.'

'Newsflash, Dad. Life in a wheelchair is not comfortable,' his daughter flung at him bitterly.

'And life without my financial security blanket is likely to be even less comfortable,' he sliced back, determined to have the last word.

Minutes later, having failed to change her father's mind in any way, Bee left the hotel and caught the bus home to the house she still shared with her mother. She was cooking supper when her mother's care assistant, Beryl, brought Emilia back from a trip to the library. Wheeling into the kitchen, Emilia beamed at her daughter. 'I found a Catherine Cookson I haven't read!'

'I won't be able to get you off to sleep tonight now.' Looking down into her mother's worn face, aged and lined beyond her years by illness and suffering, Bee could have wept at the older woman's continuing determination to celebrate the smallest things in life. Emilia had lost so much in that accident but she never ever complained.

When she had settled her mother for the night, Bee sat down to mark homework books for her class of seven-year-olds. Her mind, however, refused to stay on the task. She could not stop thinking about what her father had told her. He had threatened her but he had also told her a truth that had ripped away her sense of security. After all, she had naively taken her father's continuing financial success for granted and assumed that he would always be in a position to ensure that her mother had no money worries.

Being Bee, she had to consider the worst-case scenario. If her mother lost her house and garden it would undoubtedly break her heart. The house had been modified for a disabled occupant so that Emilia could move easily within its walls. Zara had even designed raised flower beds for the back garden, which her mother could work at on good days. If the house was sold Bee had a salary and would naturally be able to rent an apartment *but* as she would not be able to afford a full-time carer for her mother any more she would have to give up work to look after her and would thus lose that salary. Monty Blake might cover the bills but there had never been a surplus or indeed a legal agreement that he provide financial support and Emilia had no savings. Without his assistance the two women would have to live on welfare benefits and all the little extras and outings that lightened and lifted her mother's difficult life would no longer be affordable. It was a gloomy outlook that appalled Bee, who had always been very protective of the older woman.

Indeed when she thought about Emilia losing even the little things that she cherished the prospect of proposing marriage to a very intimidating Greek tycoon became almost acceptable. So what if she made a fool of herself? Well, there was no 'if' about it, she would make a colossal fool of herself and he might well dine out on the story for years! He had seemed to her as exactly the sort of guy likely to enjoy other people's misfortunes.

Not that he hadn't enjoyed misfortunes of his own, Bee was willing to grudgingly concede. When her sister had planned to marry Sergios, Bee had researched him on the Internet and she had disliked most of what she had discovered. Sergios had only become a Demonides when he was a teenager with a string of petty crimes to his name. He had grown up fighting for survival in one of the roughest areas of Athens. At twenty-one he had married a beautiful Greek heiress and barely three years later he had buried her when she died carrying their unborn child. Yes, Sergios Demonides might be filthy rich and successful, but his personal life was generally a disaster zone.

Those facts aside, however, he also had a name for being an out-and-out seven-letter-word in business and with women. Popular report said that he was extremely intelligent and astute but that he was also famously arrogant, ruthless and cold, the sort of guy who, as a husband, would have given her sensitive sister Zara and her cute pet rabbit, Fluffy, nightmares. Fortunately Bee did not consider herself sensitive. Growing up without a father and forced to become an adult long before her time as she learned to cope with her mother's disability and dependence, Bee had forged a tougher shell.

At the age of twenty-four, Bee already knew that men were rarely attracted to that protective shell or the unadorned conservative wrapping that surrounded it. She wasn't pretty or feminine and the boys she had dated as she grew up had, with only one exception, been friends rather than lovers. She had never learned to flirt or play girlie games and thought that perhaps she was just too sensible. She had, however, for a blissful few months been deeply in love and desperately hurt when the relationship fell apart over the extent of her responsibility for her disabled mother. And while she couldn't have cared less about her appearance, she *was* clever and passing so many exams with distinction and continually winning prizes did, she had learned to her cost, scare off the opposite sex.

The men she met also tended to be put off when Bee spoke her mind even if it meant treading on toes. She hated injustice or cruelty in any form. She didn't do that fragile-little-woman thing her stepmother, Ingrid, was for ever flattering her father with. It was hardly surprising that even Zara, the sister she loved, had grown up with a healthy dose of that same fatal man-pleasing gene. Only her youngest sister, Tawny, born of her father's affair with his secretary, resembled Bee in that line. Bee had never known what it was to feel helpless until she found herself actually making an appointment to see Sergios Demonides…such a crazy idea, such a very pointless exercise.

Forty-eight hours after Bee won the tussle with her pride and made the appointment, Sergios's PA asked him if he was willing to see Monty Blake's daughter, Beatriz. Unexpectedly Sergios had instant recall of the brunette's furious grass-green eyes and magnificent breasts. A dinner in tiresome company had been rendered almost bearable by his enticing view of that gravity-defying bosom, although she had not appreciated the attention. But why the hell would Blake's elder daughter want to speak to him? Did she work with her father? Was she hoping to act as the older man's negotiator? He snapped his long brown fingers to bring an aide to his side and requested an immediate background report on Beatriz before granting her an appointment the next day.

The following afternoon, dressed in a grey

trouser suit, which she usually reserved for interviews but which she was convinced gave her much-needed dignity, Bee waited in the reception area of the elegant stainless-steel and glass building that housed the London headquarters of SD Shipping. That Sergios had used his own initials to stamp his vast business empire with his powerful personality didn't surprise Bee at all. Her heart rate increased at the prospect that loomed ahead of her.

'Mr Demonides will see you now, Miss Blake,' the attractive receptionist informed her with a practised smile that Bee could not match.

Without warning Bee was feeling sick with nerves. She was too intelligent not to contemplate the embarrassment awaiting her without inwardly cringing. She was quick to remind herself that the Greek billionaire was just a big hulking brute with too much money and an inability to ignore a low neck on a woman's dress. She reddened, recalling the evening gown with the plunge neckline that she had borrowed from a friend for that stupid meal. While his appraisal had made Bee blush like a furnace and had reminded her why she usually covered up those particular attributes, she had been stunned by his apparent indifference to her beautiful sister, Zara.

When Beatriz Blake came through the door of Sergios's office with a firm step in her sensible shoes, he instantly recognised that he was not about to be treated to any form of charm offensive. Her boxy colourless trouser suit did nothing for her womanly curves. Her rich brown hair was dragged back from her face and she wore not a scrap of make-up. To a man accustomed to highly groomed women her lackadaisical attitude towards making a good impression struck him as almost rude.

'I'm a very busy man, Beatriz. I don't know what you're doing here but I expect you to keep it brief,' he told her impatiently.

For a split second Sergios Demonides towered over Bee like a giant building casting a long tall shadow and she took a harried step back, feeling crowded by his sheer size and proximity. She had forgotten how big and commanding he was, from his great height to his broad shoulders and long powerful legs. He was also, much though it irritated her to admit it, a staggeringly handsome man with luxuriant blue-black hair and sculpted sun-darkened features. The sleek unmistakeable assurance of great wealth oozed from the discreet gleam of his thin gold watch and cufflinks to the spotless white of his shirt and the classy tailoring of his dark business suit.

She collided with eyes the colour of burnished bronze that had the impact of a sledgehammer and cut off her breathing at its source. It was as if nerves were squeezing her throat tight and her heart started hammering again.

'My father asked me to see you on his behalf,' she began, annoyed by the breathlessness making her voice sound low and weak.

'You're a primary school teacher. What could

you possibly have to say that I would want to hear?' Sergios asked with brutal frankness.

'I think you'll be surprised…' Bee compressed her lips, her voice gathering strength as reluctant amusement briefly struck her. 'Well, I *know* you'll be surprised.'

Surprises were rare and even less welcome in Sergios's life. He was a control freak and knew it and had not the smallest urge to change.

'A little while back you were planning to marry my sister, Zara.'

'It wouldn't have worked,' Sergios responded flatly.

Bee breathed in deep and slow while her white-knuckled hands gripped the handles of her bag. 'Zara told me exactly what you wanted out of marriage.'

While wondering where the strange dialogue could possibly be leading, Sergios tried not to grit his teeth visibly. 'That was most indiscreet of her.'

Discomfiture sent colour flaming into Bee's

cheeks, accentuating the deep green of her eyes. 'I'm just going to put my cards on the table and get to the point.'

Sergios rested back against the edge of his polished contemporary desk and surveyed her in a manner that was uniquely discouraging, 'I'm waiting,' he said when she hesitated.

His impatient silence hummed like bubbling water ready to boil over.

Beneath her jacket, Bee breathed in so deep her bosom swelled and almost popped the buttons on her fitted blouse and for a split second Sergios dropped his narrowed gaze there as the fabric pulled taut over that full swell, whose bounty he still vividly recalled.

'My father utilised a certain amount of pressure to persuade me to come and see you,' she admitted uncomfortably. 'I told him it was crazy but here I am.'

'Yes, here…you…are,' Sergios framed in a tone of yawning boredom. 'Still struggling to come to the point.'

'Dad wanted me to offer myself in Zara's place.' Bee squeezed out that admission and watched raw incredulity laced with astonished hauteur flare in his face while hot pink embarrassment surged into hers. 'I know, I told you it was crazy but he wants that hotel deal and he thinks that a suitable wife added into the mix could make a difference.'

'Suitable? You're certainly not in the usual run of women who aspire to marry me.' Sergios delivered that opinion bluntly.

And it was true. Beatriz Blake was downright plain in comparison to the gorgeous women who pursued him wherever he went, desperate to attract his attention and get their greedy hands on, if not the ultimate prize of a wedding ring, some token of his wealth. But somewhere deep in his mind at that instant a memory was stirring.

'Homely women make the best wives,' his grandfather had once contended. 'Your grandmother was unselfish, loyal and caring. I couldn't have asked for a better wife. My home was kept like a palace, my children were loved, and my word was law. She never gave me a second of concern. Think well before you marry a beauty, who demands more and gives a lot less.'

Having paled at that unnecessary reminder of her limitations, Bee made a fast recovery and lifted her chin. 'Obviously I'm not blonde and beautiful but I'm convinced that I would be a more appropriate choice than Zara ever was for the position.'

A kind of involuntary fascination at the level of her nerve was holding Sergios taut. His straight black brows drew together in a frown. 'You speak as though the role of being my wife would be a job.'

'Isn't it?' Bee came back at him boldly with that challenge. 'From what I understand you only want to marry to have a mother for your late cousin's children and I could devote myself to their care full-time, something Zara would never have been willing to do. I also—'

'Be silent for a moment,' Sergios interrupted,

studying her with frowning attention. 'What kind of pressure did your father put on you to get you to come here and spout this nonsense?'

Bee went rigid before she tossed her head back in sudden defiance, wondering why she should keep her father's coercion a secret. Her pride demanded that she be honest. 'I have a severely disabled mother and if the sale of the Royale hotel chain falls through my father has threatened to sell our home and stop paying for Mum's care assistant. I'm not dependent on him but Mum is and I don't want to see her suffer. Her life is challenging enough.'

'I'm sure it is.' Sergios was unwillingly impressed by her motivation. Evidently Monty Blake was crueller within his family circle than Sergios would ever have guessed. Even Nectarios, his grandfather and one of the most ruthless men Sergios had ever met, would have drawn the line at menacing a disabled ex-wife. As for Beatriz, he could respect her honesty and her family loyalty, traits that said a lot about the kind of woman she was. She wasn't here for his enviable lifestyle or his money, she was here because she didn't have a choice. That was not a flattering truth but Sergios loathed flattery, having long since recognised that few people saw past his immense wealth and power to the man behind it all.

'So, tell me why you believe that you would make a better wife than your sister?' Sergios urged, determined to satisfy his curiosity and intrigued by her attitude towards marriage. A wife as an employee? It was a new take on the traditional role that appealed to him. A businessman to the core, he was quick to see the advantages of such an arrangement. A paid wife would be more likely to respect his boundaries while still making the effort to please him, he reasoned thoughtfully. There could be little room for messy human emotion and misunderstanding in such a practical agreement.

'I would be less demanding. I'm self-sufficient, sensible. I probably wouldn't cost you very much either as I'm not very interested in my appearance,' Bee pointed out, her full pink mouth folding as if vanity could be considered a vice. 'I'm also very good with kids.'

'What would you do with a six-year-old boy painting pictures on the walls?'

Bee frowned. 'Talk to him.'

'But he doesn't talk back. His little brother keeps on trying to cling to me and the toddler just stares into space,' Sergios told her in a driven undertone, his concern and incomprehension of such behaviour patent. 'Why am I telling you that?'

Surprised by his candour, Bee reckoned it was a sign that the children's problems were very much on his mind 'You thought I might have an answer for you?'

With a warning knock the door opened and someone addressed him in what she assumed to be Greek. He gave a brief answer and returned his attention to Bee. Something about that assessing look made her stiffen. 'I'll think over your proposition,' he drawled softly, startling her. 'But be warned, I'm not easy to please.'

'I knew that the first time I looked at you,' Bee countered, taking in the sardonic glitter of his eyes, the hard, uncompromising bone structure and that stubborn sensual mouth. It was very much the face of a tough guy, resistant to any counsel but his own.

'Next you'll be telling me you can read my fortune from my palm,' Sergios retorted with mocking cool.

Bee walked out of his office in a daze. He had said he would consider her proposition. Had that only been a polite lie? Somehow she didn't think he would have given her empty words. But if he was seriously considering her as a wife, where did that leave her? Fathoms deep in shock? For since Bee had automatically assumed that Sergios Demonides would turn her down she had not, at any stage, actually considered the possibility of becoming his wife…

CHAPTER TWO

FOUR days later, Bee emerged from the gates of the primary school where she worked and noticed a big black limousine parked just round the corner.

'Miss Blake?' A man in a suit with the build of a bouncer approached her. 'Mr Demonides would like to offer you a lift home.'

Bee blinked and stared at the long glossy limo with its tinted windows. How had he found out where she worked? While wondering what on earth Sergios Demonides was playing at, she saw no option other than to accept. Why queue for a bus when a limo was on offer? she reflected ruefully. Had he come in person to deliver his negative answer? Why would he take the trouble to do that? A man of his exalted status rarely put himself out for others. As a crowd of colleagues and parents parted to give Bee and her bulky companion a clear passage to the opulent vehicle self-conscious pink warmed her cheeks because people were staring.

'Beatriz,' Sergios acknowledged with a grave nod, glancing up from his laptop.

As Bee slid into the luxury vehicle she was disturbingly conscious of the sheer animal charisma that he exuded from every pore. He was all male in the most primal sense of the word. Smell the testosterone, one of her university friends would have quipped. The faint tang of some expensive masculine cologne flared her nostrils, increasing her awareness. She felt her nipples pinch tight beneath her bra and she went rigid, deeply disconcerted by her pronounced awareness of the sexual charge he put out. Her shielded gaze fell on his lean masculine profile, noting the dark shadow of stubble outlining his angular jaw. He was badly in need of a shave. It was the only sign in his otherwise immaculate appearance that he was nearing the end of his working day rather than embarking on its beginning. Aware that her hair was tossed by the breeze and her raincoat, skirt and knee-high boots were more comfortable than smart, she was stiff and awkward and questioning why because as a rule her sole concern about her appearance was that she be clean and tidy.

As the limousine pulled away from the pavement Sergios flipped shut his laptop and turned his arrogant head to look at her. His frown was immediate. She was a mess in her unfashionable, slightly shabby clothing. Yet she had flawless skin, lovely eyes and thick glossy hair, advantages that most women would have made the effort to enhance. For the first time he wondered why she didn't bother.

'To what do I owe the honour?' Bee enquired, watching him push the laptop away. He had beautiful shapely hands, she registered, and then tensed at that surprising thought.

'I'm leaving for New York this evening and I would like you to meet my children before I go.'

'Why?' Green eyes suddenly wide with confusion, Bee stared back at him. 'Why do you want me to meet them?'

A very faint smile curled the corners of his wide sensual mouth. 'Obviously because I'm considering you for the job.'

'But you *can't* be!' Bee told him in disbelief.

'I am. Your father played a winning hand sending you to see me,' Sergios fielded, amused by her astonishment, which was laced with a dismay that almost made him laugh out loud. She was a refreshing woman.

Her well-defined brows pleated and she frowned. 'I just don't understand…you could marry anybody!'

'Don't underestimate yourself,' Sergios responded, his thoughts on the enquiries and references he had gathered on her behalf since their last meeting. He had vetted her a good deal more thoroughly than he had vetted her flighty sister,

Zara. 'According to my sources you're a loyal, devoted daughter and a gifted and committed teacher. I believe that you could offer those children exactly what they need—'

'Where did you get that information from?' Bee asked angrily.

'There are private investigation firms which can offer such details within hours for the right price,' Sergios fielded with colossal calm. 'Naturally I checked you out and I was impressed with what I learned about you.'

But I wasn't *seriously* offering to marry you, she almost snapped back at him before she thought better of that revealing admission and hastily swallowed it back. After all her father's threat still hung over her and his financial security was integral to her mother's support system. Take away that security and life as her mother knew it would be at an end. Suddenly Bee was looking down a long, dark, intimidating tunnel at a future she could no longer predict and accepting that if Sergios Demonides decided that he did want to marry her, she would be in no position to refuse him.

'If your cousin's children are disturbed, I have no experience with that sort of problem,' Bee warned him quietly. 'I have no experience of raising children either and I'm not a miracle worker.'

'I don't believe in miracles, so I'm not expecting one,' Sergios said very drily, resting sardonic golden eyes on her strained face. 'There would also be conditions which you would have to fulfil to meet my requirements.'

Bee said nothing. Still reeling in shock at the concept of marrying him, she did not trust herself to speak. As for his expectations, she was convinced they would be high and that he would have a very long list of them. Unhappily for her, Sergios Demonides was unaccustomed to settling for anything less than perfection and the very best in any field. She dug out her phone and rang her mother to warn her that she would be late home. By the time she finished the call the

limousine was already filtering down a drive-
way adorned with silver birch trees just coming into leaf. They drew up outside a detached
house large and grand enough to be described
as a mansion.

'My London base.' Sergios shot her a rapier-
eyed glance from level dark eyes. 'One of your
duties as my wife would be taking charge of my
various homes and ensuring that the households
run smoothly.'

The word 'wife', allied to that other word,
'duties', sounded horribly nineteenth century
to Bee's ears. 'Are you a domestic tyrant?' she
enquired.

Sergios sent her a frowning appraisal. 'Is that
a joke?'

'No, but there is something very Victorian
about mentioning the word wife in the same sentence as duties.'

His handsome mouth quirked. 'You first referred to the role as a job and I prefer to regard
it in the same light.'

But Bee very much liked the job she already had and registered in some consternation that she was literally being asked to put her money where her mouth was. She had done what her father had asked her to do without thinking through the likely consequences of success. Now those consequences had well and truly come home to roost with her. As she accompanied Sergios into a sizeable foyer, he issued instructions to the manservant greeting him and escorted Bee into a massive drawing room.

'Unlike your sister, you're very quiet,' he remarked.

'You've taken me by surprise,' Bee admitted ruefully.

'You look bewildered. Why?' Sergios breathed, his bronzed eyes impatient. 'I have no desire for the usual kind of wife. I don't want the emotional ties, the demands or the restrictions, but on a practical basis a woman to fulfil that role would be a very useful addition to my life.'

'Perhaps I just don't see what's in it for me—

apart from you buying my father's hotels which would hopefully ensure my mother's security for the foreseeable future,' Bee volunteered frankly.

'If I married you, *I* would ensure your mother's security for the rest of her life,' Sergios extended with quiet carrying emphasis, his dark deep drawl vibrating in the big room. 'Even if we were to part at a later date you would never have to worry about her care again, nor would she have to look to your father for support. I will personally ensure that your mother has everything she requires, including the very best of medical treatment available to someone with her condition.'

His words engulfed her like a crashing burst of thunder heralding a brighter dawn. Instantly Bee thought of the expensive extras that could improve Emilia Blake's quality of life. In place of Bee's home-made efforts, regular professional physiotherapy sessions might be able to strengthen Emilia's wasted limbs and something might be found to ease the breathing difficulties that sometimes afflicted her. Sergios, Bee appreciated suddenly, was rich enough to make a huge difference to her mother's life.

A young woman in a nanny uniform entered the room with a baby about eighteen months old in her arms and two small children trailing unenthusiastically in their wake.

'Thank you. Leave the children with us,' Sergios instructed.

Set down on the carpet the youngest child instantly began to howl, tears streaming down her little screwed-up face, a toddler of about three years old grabbed hold of Sergios's trousered leg while the older boy came to a suspicious halt several feet away.

'It's all right, pet.' Bee scooped up the baby and the little girl stopped mid-howl, settling anxious blue eyes on her. 'What's her name?'

'Eleni…and this is Milo,' Sergios told her, detaching the clinging toddler from his leg with difficulty and giving him a little helpful prod in

Bee's direction as if he was hoping that the child would embrace her instead.

'And you have to be Paris,' Bee said to the older boy as she crouched down to greet Milo. 'My sister Zara told me that you got a new bike for your birthday.'

Paris didn't smile but he moved closer as Bee sank down on the sofa with the baby girl in her arms. Milo, clearly desperate for attention, clambered up beside her and tried to get on her lap with his sister but there wasn't enough room. 'Hello, Milo.'

'Paris, remember your manners,' Sergios interposed sternly.

With a scared look, Paris extended a skinny arm to shake hands formally, his eyes slewing evasively away from hers. Bee invited him to sit down beside her and told him that she was a teacher. When she asked him about the school he attended he shot her a frightened look and hurriedly glanced away. It did not take a genius to guess that Paris could be having problems at school. Of the three children, Milo was the most normal, a bundle of toddler energy in need of attention and entertainment. Paris, however, was tense and troubled while the little girl was very quiet and worryingly unresponsive.

After half an hour Sergios had seen enough to convince him that Beatriz Blake was the woman he needed to smooth out the rough and troublesome places in his life. Her warmth and energy drew the children and she was completely relaxed with them where her sister had been nervous and, while friendly, over-anxious to please. Bee, on the other hand, emanated a calm authority that ensured respect. He called the nanny back to remove the children again.

'You mentioned conditions…' Bee reminded him, returning to their earlier conversation and striving to stick to necessary facts. Yet when she tried to accept that she was actually considering marrying the Greek billionaire the idea seemed so remote and unreal and impossible that her thoughts swam in a sea of bemusement.

'Yes.' Poised by the window with fading light gleaming over his luxuriant black hair and accenting the hard angles and hollows of his handsome features, Sergios commanded her full attention without even trying. His next words, however, took her very much by surprise.

'I have a mistress. Melita is not negotiable,' Sergios informed her coolly. 'Occasionally I have other interests as well. I am discreet. I do not envisage any headlines about that aspect of my life.'

The level of such candour when she had become accustomed to his cool reserve left Bee reeling in shock. He had a mistress called Melita? Was that a Greek name? Whatever, he was not faithful to his mistress and clearly not a one-woman man. Bee could feel her cheeks inflame as her imagination filled with the kind of colourful images she did not want to have in his vicinity. She lowered her lashes in embarrassment, her rebellious brain still engaged in serving up a creative picture of that lean bronzed body of his entangled with that of a sinuous sexy blonde.

'I do not expect intimacy with you,' Sergios spelt out. 'On the other hand if you decide that you want a child of your own it would be selfish of me to deny you that option—'

'Well, then, there's always IVF,' Bee broke in hurriedly.

'From what I've heard it's not that reliable.'

Bee was now studying her feet with fixed attention. He had a mistress. He didn't expect to share a bed with her. But where did that leave her? A wife who wasn't a wife except in name.

'What sort of a life am I supposed to lead?' Bee asked him abruptly, looking up, green eyes glinting like fresh leaves in rain.

'Meaning?' Sergios prompted, pleased that she had demonstrated neither annoyance nor interest on the subject of his mistress. But then why should she care what he did? That was exactly the attitude he wanted her to take.

'Are you expecting me to take lovers as well…

discreetly?' Bee queried, studying him while her colour rose and burned like scalding hot irons on her cheeks and she fought her embarrassment with all her might. It was a fair question, a sensible question and she refused to let prudishness prevent her from asking it.

His dark eyes glittered gold with anger. 'Of course not.'

Bee was frowning. 'I'm trying to understand how you expect such a marriage to work. You surely can't be suggesting that a woman of my age should accept a future in which any form of physical intimacy is against the rules?' she quantified very stiffly, fighting her mortification every step of the way.

Put like that her objection sounded reasonable but Sergios could no more have accepted the prospect of an unfaithful wife than he could have cut off his right arm. Features taut and grim, his big powerful length rigid, he breathed with the clarity of strong feeling, 'I could not agree to you taking lovers.'

'That old hypocritical double standard,' Bee murmured, strangely amused by his appalled reaction and not even grasping why she should feel that way. So what was good for the goose was not, in this case, good for the gander? Yet she could barely believe that she was even having such a discussion with him. After all, she was a twenty-four-year-old virgin, a piece of information that would no doubt shock him almost as much as the idea of a wife with an independent sexual appetite.

In response to that scornful comment, Sergios shot her a seething appraisal, his dark eyes flaming like hot coals. 'Don't speak to me in that tone...'

Lesson one, Bee noted, he has a very volatile temper. She breathed in deep, quelling her wicked stab of amusement at his incredulous reaction to the idea of an adulterous wife. 'I asked you a reasonable question and you did not give me a reasonable answer. How long do you expect this marriage to last?'

'At least until the children grow up.'

'My youth,' Bee remarked without any emotion, but it was true. By the time the children acquired independence her years of youth would be long gone.

Sergios was studying her, recalling those lush violin curves in the evening gown she had worn at their first meeting. Full pouting breasts, generous womanly hips. He was startled when that mental picture provoked the heavy tightness of arousal at his groin.

'Then we make it a real marriage,' Sergios fielded with sardonic bite, blanking out his physical response with male impatience. 'That is the only other possible option on the table. If you want a man in your bed you will have me, no other.'

The flush in Bee's cheeks swept up to her brow and her dismayed eyes skimmed away from the intrusion of his. 'I don't really wish to continue this discussion but I should say that while you have other women in your life I would not be willing to enter an intimate relationship with you.'

'We're wasting time with this nonsense and we're adults. We will deal with such problems as and when they arise,' Sergios delivered curtly. 'There will be a pre-nuptial contract for you to sign—'

'You mentioned your homes and your, er… mistress. What other conditions are you planning to impose?'

'Nothing that I think need concern you. Our lawyers can deal with the contracts. If you choose to argue about terms you may do so through them,' Sergios completed in a crushing tone of finality. 'Now, if you will excuse me, I will have you driven home. I have business to take care of before I leave for New York.'

Bee, who had had a vague idea that he might invite her to stay to dinner, learned her mistake. She smoothed down her raincoat and rose slowly upright. 'I have a condition as well. You would have to agree to be polite, respectful and considerate of my happiness at all times.'

As that unanticipated demand hit him Sergios froze halfway to the door, wondering if she was criticising his manners. Since he had reached eighteen years of age before appreciating that certain courtesies even existed, he was unusually sensitive to the suggestion. He turned back, brooding black eyes glittering below the lush fan of his lashes. 'That would be a tall order. I'm selfish, quick-tempered and often curt. I expect my staff to adapt to my ways.'

'If I marry you I won't be a member of your staff. I'll be somewhere between a wife and an employee. You will have to make allowances and changes.' Bee studied him expectantly, for it would be disastrous if she allowed him to assume that he could have everything his way. She had no illusions about the fact that she was dealing with a very powerful personality, who would ride roughshod over her needs and wishes and ignore them altogether if it suited him to do so.

Sergios was taken aback at her nerve in challenging him, viewing him with those cool assessing green eyes as though he were an intellectual puzzle to be solved. His stubborn jaw line squared. 'I may make some allowances but I will call the shots. If we're going ahead with this arrangement, I want the wedding to take place soon so that you can move in here to be with the children.'

Consternation filled Bee's face. 'But I can't leave my mother—'

'You're a teacher, good at talking but not at listening,' Sergios chided with a curled lip. '*Listen* to what I tell you. Your mother will be taken care of in every possible way.'

'In every possible way that facilitates what *you* want!' Bee slammed back at him with angry emphasis.

He raised a brow, sardonic amusement in his intent dark gaze. 'Would you really expect anything different from me?'

CHAPTER THREE

LIFE as Bee knew it began to change very soon after that thought-provoking parting from Sergios.

Indeed Bee came home from school the very next day to find her mother troubled by the fact that her father had made an angry phone call to her that same afternoon.

'Monty told me that you're getting married,' Emilia Blake recounted with a look of frank disbelief. 'But I told him that you weren't even seeing anyone.'

Bee went pink. 'I didn't tell you but—'

Her mother stared at her with wide, startled eyes. 'My goodness, there is someone! But you only go out twice a week to your exercise classes—'

Bee grimaced and reached for her mother's frail hands. Not for anything would she have told the older woman any truth that might upset her. Indeed when it came to her mother's peace of mind, Bee was more than ready to lie. 'I'm sorry I wasn't more honest with you. I do want you to be happy for me.'

'So, obviously you weren't at classes all those evenings,' Emilia assumed in some amusement while she studied her blushing daughter with fond pride in her shadowed eyes. 'I'm so pleased. Your father and I haven't set you a very good example and I know you haven't had the same choices as other girls your age—'

'You still haven't told me what my father was angry about,' Bee cut in anxiously.

'Some business deal he's involved in with your future husband hasn't gone the way he hoped,' Emilia responded in a dismissive tone. 'What on earth does he expect you to do about it? Take my advice, don't get involved.'

Dismayed by her explanation, Bee had tensed. 'Exactly what did Dad say?'

'You know how moody he can be when things don't go his way. Tell me about Sergios—isn't he the man you met at that dinner your father invited you to a couple of months ago?'

'Yes.' So, although the marriage was going ahead, it seemed that her father was not to profit as richly as he had expected from the deal. Clearly that was why the older man was angry, but Bee thought there was a rare justice to the news that her sacrifice was unlikely to enrich her father: threats did not deserve a reward.

'My word, you've been having a genuine whirl-wind romance,' Emilia gathered with a blossom-ing smile of approval. 'Are you sure that this Sergios is the man for you, Bee?'

Bee recalled Sergios Demonides's assurance that she would never again have to look to her father to support her mother. She remembered the fearless impact of those shrewd dark eyes and although she was apprehensive about the future she had signed up for she did believe that Sergios would stand by his word. 'Yes, Mum. Yes, I'm sure.'

Sergios phoned that evening to tell her that a member of his personal staff would be liaising with her over the wedding arrangements. He suggested that she hand in her notice immediately. His impatience came as a surprise when he had seemingly been content to wait several months before taking her sister Zara to the altar. He then followed that bombshell up with the news that he expected her to move to Greece after the wedding.

'But you have a house here,' Bee protested.

'I will visit London regularly but Greece is my home.'

'When you were planning to marry Zara—'

'Stop there—you and I will reach our own arrangements,' Sergios cut in deflatingly.

'I don't want to leave my mother alone in London.'

'Your mother will accompany us to Greece—

but only after we have enjoyed a suitable newly married period of togetherness. I have already issued instructions to have appropriate accommodation organised for her. Have you heard from your father yet?'

In shock at the news that he was already making plans for her mother to accompany them to Greece, Bee was in a complete daze, her every expectation blown apart. On every issue he seemed to be one step ahead of her. 'I believe he was annoyed about something when he was talking to my mother today,' she admitted reluctantly.

'Your father did not get the deal he wanted,' Sergios informed her bluntly. 'But that is nothing to do with you and so I told him on your behalf.'

'Did you indeed?' Bee questioned with a frown, her hackles rising at the increasingly authoritarian note in his explanations. Acting as chief spokesperson for the women in his life evidently came very naturally to Sergios. If she wasn't careful to keep his controlling streak within bounds, Bee thought darkly, he would soon have her behaving with all the self-will of a glove puppet.

'You are the woman I'm going to marry. It is not appropriate for your father to speak of either you or your mother with disrespect and I have warned him in that regard.'

Bee's blood ran cold in her veins, for she could picture the scene and the warning with Monty Blake raging recklessly and Sergios cold as ice and equally precise in his razor-sharp cutting edge. Her father was outspoken in temper but Sergios was altogether a more guarded and as-tute individual.

'How soon can you move into my London house?' Sergios pressed. 'It would please me if you could make that move this week.'

'*This* week?' Bee exclaimed in dismay.

'The wedding will be soon. I'm out of the country and the domestic staff are in charge of the children right now. If possible I would prefer you to be in the house while I'm away. If you're concerned about your mother being alone, you need not be—I've already requested a live-in companion for her from a vetted source.'

Bee came off the phone feeling unusually harassed as she accepted that regardless of how she felt about it, her life was about to be turned upside down. Although she could not fault Sergios for his wish that she become involved with the children as soon as possible, she felt very much like an employee having her extensive duties listed and held over her head. As she had already told her mother about the three orphaned kids in Sergios's life, Emilia Blake was quick to understand her daughter's position.

'You really *must* put Sergios and those children first, Bee,' the older woman instructed worriedly. 'You mustn't make me more of a burden than I already am. I'll manage, I always have.'

Bee gently squeezed her parent's shoulder. 'You've never been a burden to me.'

'Sergios expects to come first and that's normal for a man who wants to marry you,' Emilia told her daughter. 'Don't let me become a bone of contention between you.'

Having drawn up innumerable lists and tendered her letter of resignation, for it was the last day of the spring term, Bee attended her evening pole exercise class and worked up a sweat while she tried not to fret about the many things that she still had to do. The list grew even longer after a visit from Annabel, the glossily efficient PA Sergios had put in charge of the wedding.

'I'm to have a consultation with a personal stylist and shopper?' Bee repeated weakly, staring down at the heavy schedule of appointments already set up for her over the Easter break that began that weekend. As well as a consultation with an upmarket legal firm concerning the prenuptial agreement, there was a day-long booking at a famous beauty salon. 'That's ridiculous. That's got nothing to do with the wedding.'

'Mr Demonides gave me my instructions,' Annabel told her in a steely tone.

Bee swallowed hard and compressed her lips.

She would argue her case directly with Sergios. Possibly he thought a makeover was every woman's dream but Bee felt deeply insulted by the proposition. Her mother's new live-in companion/carer arrived that same evening and Bee chatted to her and helped her to settle in before she packed her own case ready for her move into Sergios's house the next morning.

When she arrived there she was shown upstairs into a palatial bedroom suite furnished with every possible necessity and luxury, right down to headed notepaper on a dainty feminine desk. The household seemed to operate just like an exclusive hotel. A maid came to the door to offer to unpack for her. Overcoming her discomfort at the prospect of being waited on by the staff, Bee smiled in determined agreement and went off to find the children instead.

Only Eleni, the youngest, however, was at home. Paris was at school and Milo was at a play group, the nanny explained. A rota of three nannies looked after the children round the clock. Bee found out what she needed to know about the children's basic routine and got down on her knees on the nursery carpet to play with Eleni. Initially when she was close by and utilised eye contact the little girl was more responsive but her attention was hard to hold. When the wind caught the door and it slammed shut Bee flinched from the loud noise but noted in surprise that Eleni did not react at all.

'Has her hearing been checked?' Bee asked with a frown.

The newly qualified nanny, who had replaced someone else and only recently, had no idea. During the preceding months the children had suffered several changes in that line and had enjoyed little continuity of care. Having tracked down the children's health record booklets and drawn another blank, Bee finally phoned the medical practice to enquire. She discovered that Eleni had missed out on a standard hearing check-up a couple of months earlier and she made a fresh appointment for the child. When she returned to the nursery the nanny was engaged in conducting her own basic tests and even to the untrained eye it did seem as though the little girl might have a problem with her hearing.

Milo, who was indiscriminately affectionate with almost everybody, greeted her as though they were long-lost friends. She was reading a picture book to the little boy as he dropped off for a nap when Paris appeared in the nursery doorway and frowned at the sight of her with his little brother.

'Are you looking after us now?' Paris asked thinly.

'For some of the time. You won't need so many nannies because I'll be living here from now on. Sergios and I will be getting married in a few weeks.' Bee explained, striving to sound much calmer than she actually felt about that event.

Paris shot her a resentful glance and walked past into his own room, carefully shutting the door behind him to underline his desire for privacy. Resolving to respect his wishes until she had visited his school and met his teacher, Bee suppressed a rueful sigh. She was a stranger. What more could she expect? Establishing a relationship with children who had lost their parents, their home and everything familiar only months before would take time and a good deal of trust on their part and she had to hope that Sergios was prepared for the reality that only time would improve the situation.

Forty-eight hours later, it was a novelty for Sergios to return to a house with a woman in residence and not worry about what awaited him. He could still vividly remember when he had never known what might be in store for him when he entered his own home. That experience had left him with an unshakable need to conserve his own space. Bee didn't count, he told himself irritably, she was here for the kids, not for him personally and she would soon learn to respect his privacy. He was taken aback, however, when his housekeeper informed him that Bee had gone out. He was even less impressed when he rang her cell phone and she admitted that she was travelling back on public transport.

'I wasn't expecting you back this soon…I was visiting my mother,' she told him defensively.

When Bee finally walked back into the mansion, she was flushed and breathless from walking very fast from the bus stop and thoroughly resentful of the censorious tone Sergios had used with her on the phone. Didn't he think she had a right to go out? Was she supposed to ask for permission first? Was her life to be entirely consumed by his? Heavy dark brown hair flopping untidily round her face, she stepped into the echoing hall.

Sergios appeared in a doorway and she lost her breath at that first glimpse, his impact thrumming through her like a sudden collision with a brick wall. He was still dressed in a black business suit and striped shirt, his only hint of informality the loosening of his tie. He looked like an angry dark angel, lean strong features taut, stubborn jaw line squared and once again he needed a shave. Stubble suited him though, sending his raw masculine sex appeal right off the charts, she conceded numbly, reeling in shock from the sudden loud thump of her heartbeat in her ears and the dryness of her mouth.

Sergios subjected his flustered bride-to-be to a hard scrutiny. From her chaotic hair to her ill-fitting jeans she was a mess. He realised that he was eager for the makeover to commence. 'I gave orders that if you went out you were to use a car and driver,' he reminded her flatly.

Bee reacted with a pained look. 'A bit much for a girl used to travelling by bus and tube.'

'But you are no longer that girl. You are the woman who is to become my wife,' Sergios retorted crisply. 'And I expect you to adapt accordingly. I am a wealthy man and you could be targeted by a mugger or even a kidnapper. Personal security must now become an integral part of your lifestyle.'

The reference to kidnapping cooled the heated words on Bee's ready tongue and, although she had stiffened, she nodded her head. 'I'll remember that in future.'

Satisfied, Sergios spread wide the door behind him. 'I want to talk to you.'

'Yes, we do need to talk,' Bee allowed, although in truth she wanted to run upstairs to her bedroom and stay there until her adolescent hormonal reaction to him died a natural death and stopped embarrassing her. Her face felt hot as a fire. It had been such a long time since a man had had that effect on her. When it had happened in his office she had assumed it was simply the effect of nerves and mortification but this time around she was less naive and ready to be honest with herself. As a physical specimen, Sergios Demonides was without parallel. He was absolutely gorgeous and few women would be impervious to his powerful attraction. That was all it was, she told herself urgently as she walked past him, her head held high, into a room furnished like an upmarket office. He had buckets of lethal sex appeal and all her body was telling her was that she had a healthy set of hormones. It was that simple, that basic, nothing to fret about. It certainly did not mean that she was genuinely attracted to him.

Sergios asked Bee about the children and she relaxed a little, telling him that Eleni had performed very poorly at her hearing test and the doctor suspected that she was suffering from glue ear. The toddler was to be examined by a consultant with a view to receiving treatment. Bee went on to talk about the picture that Paris had drawn on his bedroom wall. She considered his depiction of his once-happy family complete with parents and home to be self-explanatory. He had no photos of his late parents and Bee asked Sergios if there was a reason for that.

'I thought it would be less upsetting that way— he has to move on.'

'I think Paris needs the time to grieve and that family photos would help,' Bee pronounced with care.

'I put his parents' personal effects into storage. I'll have them checked for photo albums,' Sergios proffered, surprising her by accepting her opinion.

'I think that all that is wrong is that the children have endured too many changes in a short space of time. They need a settled home life.'

Sergios expelled his breath with a slight hiss, his expression grim. 'I've done my best but clearly it wasn't good enough. I know nothing about children. I don't even know how to talk to them.'

'The same way you talk to anyone else—with interest and kindness.'

A grudging smile played at the corners of his sardonic mouth. 'Not my style. I'm more into barking orders, Beatriz.'

'Call me Bee…everyone does.'

'No, Bee makes you sound like a maiden aunt. Beatriz is pretty.'

Bee almost winced at that opinion. 'But I'm not.'

'Give the beauty professionals a chance,' Sergios advised without hesitation.

At that advice, Bee took an offended stance, her spine very straight, her chin lifting. 'Actually that's what I wanted to discuss with you.'

With veiled attention, Sergios watched the buttons pull on her shirt, struggling to contain the full globes of her breasts. He wanted to rip open the shirt and release that luscious flesh from captivity into his hands. More than a comfortable handful, he reckoned hungrily, his body hardening. Startled by the imagery, he decided that he had to be in dire need of sexual fulfilment. Clearly he had waited too long to release his desire. He did not want to look on his future wife in that light.

Lost in her own thoughts, Bee breathed in deep and spoke with the abruptness of discomfiture. 'I don't want a makeover. I'm happy as I am. Take me or leave me.'

Sergios was not amused by that invitation. His clever dark eyes rested on her uneasy face. 'You must appreciate that when it comes to your appearance a certain amount of effort is required. Right now, you're making no effort at all.'

Incensed by that critical and wounding statement, Bee threw her slim shoulders back. 'I'm not going to change myself to conform to some outdated sexist code.'

Sergios released an impatient groan. 'Leave the feminism out of it. What's the matter with you? Why don't you care about your appearance?'

'There's nothing the matter with me,' Bee answered with spirit. 'I'm just comfortable with myself as I am.'

'But I'm not. I expect you to smarten up as part of the job.'

'That's too personal a request…beyond your remit,' Bee spelt out in case he hadn't yet got the message. 'I have already given up my home, my job…surely how I choose to look is my business.'

His brilliant dark eyes flamed gold, dense black lashes lowering over them to enhance the flash-fire effect. 'Not if you want to marry me, it's not.'

Bee flung her head back, glossy chestnut strands trailing across her shoulders, an angry flush across her cheekbones. 'That's ridiculous.'

'Is it? I find you unreasonable. It's normal for a woman to take pride in her appearance. What happened to you that made you lose all interest?' Sergios demanded starkly.

The silence hummed like a buzz saw against Bee's suddenly exposed nerves. She very nearly flinched, for that incisive question had cut deep and hit home hard. There had been a time when Bee had taken great interest in her personal appearance and had chosen her clothes with equal care. But it was not a period she cared to recall. 'I don't want to talk about this. It's absolutely none of your business.'

'The makeover is not negotiable. There will be public occasions when I expect you to appear by my side. There is no longer any excuse for you to go around in unflattering clothes with your hair in a mess,' Sergios asserted with derisive cool.

Rage surged up through Bee like lava seeking a vent. 'How dare you speak to me like that?'

'I'm being honest with you. Come over here,' Sergios urged, a firm hand at her elbow guiding her across to the mirror on the wall. 'And tell me what you see...'

Forced to acknowledge a reflection that displayed windblown hair, an old shirt and baggy jeans, Bee just wanted to slap him. Her teeth gritted. 'It doesn't matter what you say or what you want. I'm not having a makeover and that's that!'

'No makeover, no marriage,' Sergios traded without a second of hesitation. 'It's part of the job and I will not compromise on my expectations.'

Trembling though she was with the force of her emotions, Bee slung him a look of loathing and lifted and dropped her hands in a gesture of finality. 'Then there'll be no marriage because we need to get one thing straight right now, Sergios—'

Sergios lifted a sardonic black brow. 'Do we?'

'You are not going to rule over me like this! You are *not* going to tell me what I do with my hair or what I should wear,' Bee launched back furiously at him, green eyes pure and bright as emeralds in sunshine. 'You're a domineering guy but I won't stand for that.'

Her magnificent bosom was heaving. Was he, at heart, a breast man? he suddenly wondered, questioning his preoccupation with those swelling mounds and seeking an excuse for his strange behaviour. Her eyes were astonishingly vivid in colour. Indeed she looked more attractive in the grip of temper than he had ever seen her but he would not tolerate defiance. 'It is your choice, Beatriz,' Sergios intoned coldly. 'It has always been your choice. At this moment I am having second thoughts about marrying you because you are acting irrationally.'

Assailed by that charge, Bee quivered with

sheer fury. '*I'm* being irrational?' she raked back at him incredulously. 'Explain that to me.'

His face set in forbidding lines, Sergios opened the door for her exit instead. 'This discussion is at an end.'

Bee stalked up the stairs in a tempestuous rage. She had never stalked before and she had definitely never been so mad with anger but Sergios Demonides had made her see red. Rot the man, rot him to hell, she thought wildly. How dared he criticise her like that? How dared he ask what had happened to make her lose interest in her appearance? How dared he have that much insight into her actions?

For something traumatic *had* happened to Bee way back when she was madly in love with a man who had ultimately dumped her. That man had replaced her with a little ditsy blonde whose looks and shallow personality had mocked what Bee had once foolishly believed was a good solid relationship. After that devastating wake-up call, the fussing with hair, nails and make-up, not to mention the continual agonising over which outfits were most becoming, had begun to seem utterly superficial, pathetic and a total waste of time. After all, given a free choice Jon had gone for a woman as physically and mentally different from Bee as he could find. For months afterwards, Bee had despised herself for having slavishly followed the girlie code that insisted that a woman's looks were of paramount importance to a man. That code had let her down badly for in spite of all her efforts she had still lost Jon and ever since then she had refused to fuss over her appearance and compete with the true beauties of the world.

And why should she turn herself inside out for Sergios Demonides? He was just like every other man she had met from her father to Jon. Sergios might have briefly flattered her by telling her that she was a loyal daughter and a gifted teacher, but regardless of those qualities he was still judging her by her looks and ready to dump her for failing to meet his standards of feminine beauty. Well, that didn't matter to her, did it?

No, *but* it would certainly matter to her mother, a little voice chimed up quellingly at the back of Bee's brain and she froze in consternation, recalled to reality with a vengeance by that acknowledgement. If Bee backed out of the marriage, Emilia Blake would most probably lose her home, for Bee was convinced that her angry father would try to punish Bee for his failure to get the price he wanted for the Royale hotel group. Monty Blake was that sort of a man. He always needed someone else to blame for his mistakes and losses and Bee and her mother would provide easy targets for his ire.

And if Bee didn't marry Sergios, Paris, Milo and Eleni would suffer yet another adult betrayal. Bee had encouraged the children to bond with her, had announced that she was marrying Sergios and had promised to stay with them. Paris had looked unimpressed but Bee had guessed that he wanted her to prove herself before he took the risk of trusting her. Her sister Zara had already let those children down by winning their acceptance and then vanishing from their lives when she realised that she couldn't go through with marrying their guardian because she had fallen for another man. Was Bee willing to behave in an equally self-centred fashion?

All over the prospect of a visit to a beauty salon and some shopping trips? Wasn't walking out on Sergios because of such trivial activities a case of overkill? He had too much insight though, she acknowledged unhappily. When he had asked her what had happened to her to make her so uninterested in her appearance he had unnerved her and hurt her pride. That was why she had lost her head. He had mortified her when he marched her over to that mirror and forced her to see herself through his eyes. And unhappily Bee had not liked what she saw either. She had seen that her hair needed a decent cut and her wardrobe required an urgent overhaul and that she was being thoroughly unreasonable when she expected a man of his sophistication and faultless grooming to accept her in her current au naturel state.

Bee tidied her hair before descending the stairs at a much more decorous pace than she had raced up them. A mutinous expression tensing her oval face, she lifted a hand as if she was about to knock on the door and then she thought better of the gesture and simply walked back unannounced into his home office.

Sergios was at his desk working on his laptop. His head lifted and glittering dark eyes lit on her, his expression hard and unwelcoming.

It took near physical force for Bee to rise above her hurt pride and part her lips to say, 'All right, I'll do it…the makeover thing.'

'What changed your mind?' Sergios pressed impassively, his expression not softening in the slightest at her capitulation.

'My mother's needs…the children's,' she admitted truthfully. 'I can't walk out on my responsibilities like that.'

His hard cynical mouth twisted. 'People do it every day.'

Bee stood a little straighter. 'But I don't.'

Sergios pushed away his laptop and rose fluidly upright, astonishingly graceful for a man of his height and powerful build. 'Don't fight me,' he told her huskily. 'I don't like it.'

'But you don't always know best.'

'There are more subtle approaches.' He offered her a drink and she accepted, hovering awkwardly by his desk while she cradled a glass of wine that she didn't really want.

'I'm not sure I do subtle,' Bee confided.

He was suddenly as remote as the Andes. 'You'll learn. I won't be easy to live with.'

And for the first time as she tipped the glass to her lips and tasted an expensive wine as smooth and silky as satin, Bee wondered about Melita. Was he different with his mistress? Was she blonde or brunette? How long had she been in his life? Where did she live? How often did he see her? The torrent of questions blazing a mortifying trail through her head made her redden as she attempted to suppress that flood of unwelcome curiosity. It was none of her business and she didn't care what he did, she told herself squarely. She was to be his wife in name only, nothing more.

'We will drink to our wedding,' Sergios murmured lazily.

'And a better understanding?' Bee completed.

Sergios dealt her a dark appraisal. 'We don't need to understand each other. We won't need to spend that much time together. After a while we won't even have to occupy the same house at the same time…'

Chilled to the marrow by that prediction, Bee drank her wine and set the glass down on the desk. 'Goodnight, then,' she told him prosaically.

And as she climbed the stairs she wondered why she should feel lonelier than she had ever felt in her life before. After all, had she expected

Sergios to offer her his company and support? Was he not even prepared to share parenting responsibilities with her? It seemed that in his head the parameters of their relationship were already set in stone: he didn't love her, didn't desire her and, in short, didn't need her except as a mother to the children. Being his wife really would be a job more than anything else…

CHAPTER FOUR

BEE stepped out of the spacious changing cubicle and up onto the dais to get the best possible view of her wedding dress in the mirrored walls of the showroom.

Although it galled her to admit it, Sergios had done astonishingly well. She had had a sharp exchange of words with him when he had startled her with the news that he had actually selected a gown for her.

'What on earth were you thinking of?' Bee had demanded on the phone. 'A woman looks forward to choosing her wedding dress.'

'I was at a fashion show in Milan and the model came down the catwalk in it and I knew immediately that it was *your* dress,' Sergios had drawled with immense assurance.

She had wanted to ask him whom he had accompanied to the fashion show, for she did not believe that he had attended one alone, but she had swallowed back the nosy question. Ignorance, she had decided, was safer than too much information in that department. What she didn't know couldn't hurt her, she told herself staunchly, and not that she was in any danger of being hurt. She could not afford to develop silly notions or possessive feelings towards a man who would not even share a bed with her. Although he had *offered*, she reminded herself darkly, preferring to sacrifice himself if she decided that she could not live without sex rather than allow her to engage in an extra-marital affair.

Now she posed in the wedding gown Sergios had chosen for her, noting how the style showcased her voluptuous cleavage while emphasising her small waist. The neckline was lower than she liked but the fitted bodice definitely flattered her fuller figure. Apparently, Sergios hadn't earned his notorious reputation with women without picking up some useful fashion tips along the way. Bee would have been the first to admit that her appearance had already undergone a major transformation. Her chestnut hair now curved in a sleek layered shoulder-length cut that framed her face, all the heaviness gone. Cosmetics had helped her rediscover her cheekbones and accentuate her best features while every inch of her from her manicured nails to her smooth skin had been waxed, polished and moisturised to as close to perfection as a mortal woman was capable of getting. The irony was that, far from feeling exploited or belittled by the beauty makeover, she was enjoying the energising feel of knowing she looked her very best.

In thirty-six hours it would be her wedding day, Bee acknowledged, breathing in deep and slow to steady her nerves. That afternoon she had a final appointment to sign the pre-nuptial agreement, which had already been explained to her in fine detail during her first visit to the upmarket legal firm employed by Sergios to protect her interests. Her mother's long-term care was comprehensively covered, but she had had to request the right of regular access to the children in the event of their marriage breaking down. Bee was more concerned that Sergios might refuse that demand than she was by the fact that divorce would leave her a wealthy woman. The more time she spent with Paris, Milo and Eleni the more they felt like *her* children.

As Bee left the showroom, elegant in a grey striped dress and light jacket, a bodyguard was by her side and within the space of a minute a limousine was purring up to the kerb to pick her up. She was getting used to being spoilt, she registered guiltily, as she emerged again directly outside the lawyer's plush offices. After only three weeks she was already forgetting what it was like to walk in the rain or queue for a bus.

She was seated in the reception area when she saw a familiar face and she was so shaken by the resulting jolt of recognition that she simply stared, her heartbeat thumping very loudly. It was her ex-boyfriend, Jon Townsend, and more than three years had passed since their last meeting. Now, without the smallest warning, there he was only ten feet away, smartly clad in a business suit and tie. He was slim, dark-haired and attractive, not particularly tall but still taller than she was. As she struggled to overcome her shock she wondered if perhaps he worked for the firm because he had just qualified in law when she first met him.

Jon turned his head and recognised her at almost the same moment as the receptionist invited her to go into Mr Smyth's office. Blue eyes full of surprise, Jon crossed the foyer with a frown. 'Bee?' he queried as though he couldn't quite believe that she was physically there in front of him.

'Jon…sorry, I have an appointment,' Bee responded, rising to her feet.

'You look terrific,' Jon told her warmly.

'Thanks.' Her smile was a mere stretch of her

tense lips, for she had not forgotten the pain he had caused her and all her concentration was focused on retaining her dignity. 'Do you work here?'

'Yes, since last year. I'll see you after your appointment and we'll chat,' Jon declared.

Her fake smile dimmed at that disconcerting prospect and she hastened into Halston Smyth's office with a peculiar sense of both relief and anticipation. What could Jon possibly want to chat to her about? It might have happened three long years ago but he *had* ditched her, for goodness' sake. Did they even have any old times to catch up on? Having lost contact with mutual friends after they broke up, she did not think so. He was married now—or at least so she had heard—might even have children, although when she had known him he had not been sure he wanted any. Of course he had been equally unsure he was the marrying kind until he had met Jenna, Bee's little blonde bubbly replacement, the daughter of a high-court judge. A most useful connection for an ambitious young legal whiz-kid, her more cynical self had thought back then.

Mr Smyth ran through the pre-nup again while a more junior member of staff hovered attentively. On her first visit, Bee had realised that as the future wife of a billionaire she was considered big business and they were eager to please. As soon as she realised that her desire to retain contact with the children in the event of a divorce had been incorporated in the agreement, she relaxed. In spite of all the warnings to carefully consider what she was doing she signed on the dotted line while wondering how soon she could book physiotherapy sessions for her mother.

Mr Smyth escorted her all the way to the lift and at the last possible minute before the doors could close Jon stepped in to join her and her bodyguard.

'There's a wine bar round the corner,' Jon informed her casually.

Her brow furrowed. 'I'm not sure we have much to talk about.'

'Well, I can't physically persuade you to join me with a security man in tow,' he quipped with a familiar grin.

'Do you know this gentleman, Miss Blake?' her bodyguard, Tom, asked, treating Jon to an openly suspicious appraisal.

Meeting Jon's amused look, Bee almost giggled. 'Yes. Yes, I do,' she confirmed. 'I can't stay long, though.'

Curiosity had to be behind his request, Bee decided. After all, three years ago when Jon had been with her she had been a final-year student teacher from a fairly ordinary background. While her father might be wealthy, Bee had never enjoyed a personal allowance or, aside of the occasional family invite, an entrée into Monty Blake's exclusive world. Jon was most probably aware that she was on the brink of marrying one of the richest men in Europe and wondering how that had come about. She suppressed a rueful smile over the awareness that few people would believe the truth behind that particular development.

In the bar her bodyguard chose a seat nearby and talked on his phone. Jon ordered drinks and made light conversation. She remembered when his smile had made her tummy tighten and her heart beat a little faster and crushed the recollection.

'Jenna and I got a divorce a couple of months ago,' Jon volunteered wryly.

'I'm sorry to hear that,' Bee said uncomfortably.

'It was an infatuation.' Jon pulled a rueful face. 'I lived to regret leaving you.'

'Never mind about that now. I don't hold grudges,' Bee interposed, feeling a shade awkward beneath the earnest onslaught of his blue eyes.

'That's pretty decent of you. Now let me get to the point of my invite and you are, of course, welcome to tell me that I'm a calculating so-

and-so!' Jon teased, extracting a leaflet from his pocket and passing it across the table to her. 'I would be very grateful if you would consider becoming a patron for this charity. It does a lot of good work and could do with the support.'

Bee was taken aback, for the Jon she recalled had been too intent on climbing the career ladder to spend time raising money for good causes. Maturity, it seemed, had made him a more well-rounded person and she was impressed. He was a trustee for a charity for disabled children, similar to one she had volunteered with when she was a student. 'I doubt that I could do much on a personal basis because I'll be based in Greece after the wedding.'

'As the wife of Sergios Demonides, your name alone would be sufficient to generate a higher profile for the organisation,' Jon assured her with enthusiasm. 'And if you were to decide to get more involved the occasional appearance at public events would be very welcome.'

Bee was relieved then that it appeared Jon's

desire to see her was professional rather than personal. She very much appreciated the fact that he studiously avoided asking her anything about Sergios. They parted fifteen minutes later but before she could turn away, Jon reached for her hand.

'I meant what I said earlier,' he stressed in an undertone. 'I made a colossal mistake. I've always regretted losing you, Bee.'

Green eyes turning cool, Bee was quick to retrieve her hand. 'It's a little late in the day to tell me that, Jon.'

'I hope you'll be happy with Demonides.' But the look on his face told her that he didn't think she would be.

Unsettled by that exchange, Bee travelled back to Sergios's house to have tea with the children. Sergios had been jetting round the world on business for over two weeks and their only contact had been by phone. After their meal Bee supervised Paris's homework assignment and bathed Milo and Eleni before tucking them into bed.

In a month's time, Eleni was scheduled for surgery to have grommets inserted in both ears to resolve her hearing problems. Having consulted Paris's teacher, Bee had learned that the boy was struggling to make friends at school and she had tried to improve the situation by inviting some of his classmates over to play after school. Paris was beginning to find his feet and as he did so he had become more receptive to Bee and less suspicious of her.

Just before Bee went to bed, Sergios called from Tokyo. 'Who was the man you accompanied to the wine bar?' he demanded.

Bee stiffened defensively. 'So, Tom's a spy, is he?'

'Beatriz…' Sergios growled impatiently, forceful as a lion roaring a warning to an unwary prey.

'He was just an old friend I hadn't seen since university.' Bee hesitated but decided to say nothing more, feeling she didn't owe Sergios any more of an explanation.

'You'll find that plenty of old friends will come scurrying out of the woodwork now that you're marrying me,' Sergios replied cynically.

'I find that offensive. This particular friend is asking me to get involved with a children's charity. You can scarcely find fault with that.'

'Is that why he was holding hands with you?'

Bee flushed scarlet. 'He grasped my hand—big deal!'

'In public places I expect you to be discreet.'

Her anger rose. 'You always have to have the last word, don't you?'

'And I'm always right, *latria mou*,' Sergios agreed equably, not one whit disturbed by the accusation.

That night Bee lay in her big luxurious bed and played the game of 'what if' with Jon in a starring role. Well, she was only human and naturally she could not help wondering what might have happened had she met her charming ex when she was not on the brink of getting married to another man. Probably nothing would have happened, she decided ruefully, for had it not been for the pressure Sergios had put on her she would have looked like a real Plain Jane and Jon would have been less than impressed. In any case, Sergios was much better looking and had a great deal more personality...

Now where on earth had that thought come from? Bee wondered in confusion. There was no denying that Sergios was a very, very handsome guy but he was not *her* guy in the way Jon had once seemed to be and he never would be. Bee decided that she was far too sensible to indulge in 'what if' dreams. Besides she had long since worked out that if Jon had truly loved her he would never have dumped her because she had a mother who would always need her support. Jon's rejection had shattered the dream of family, which Bee valued most.

'That's a very romantic dress,' Tawny commented, studying her half-sister with frankly curious eyes, for the fitted lace gown with the flowing skirt was exceedingly feminine and not in Bee's usual conservative style. 'And a very thoughtful choice for a guy entering a very practical marriage of convenience.'

Bee went pink, wishing her other sister, Zara, had not been quite so frank with their youngest sister, who thoroughly disapproved of what Bee was doing in marrying a man she didn't love. She also wished Zara had not chosen to avoid what might have been an uncomfortable occasion for her by pleading her reluctance to travel while pregnant. 'Sergios isn't romantic and neither am I.'

'Granted the kids are cute,' Tawny conceded, her coppery head held at a considering angle, blue eyes troubled. 'And Sergios, on the outside he's sex on a stick, but only for an adventurous woman and you're as conventional as they come.'

'You never know,' Bee quipped, lifting her bouquet.

'If I was the suspicious type I would suspect

that you're doing this for your mother's benefit,' Tawny commented with a frown, revealing a glimpse of wits that were sharp as a knife.
'You'd do anything for her and she's a lovely
woman.'

'Yes, isn't she? My mother is also very happy
for me today,' Bee slotted in with a pointed
glance. 'Please don't spoil that for her by giving her the wrong idea about my marriage…'

'Or even the *right* idea,' Tawny muttered half
under her breath, not being that easy to silence.
'Just promise me that if he's awful to live with
you'll divorce him.'

Bee nodded instant agreement to soothe her
half-sibling's concerns and descended the stairs
with care in her high heels. She was in her
mother's house for she had spent the last night
of her single life there at the older woman's request. Tawny was not acting as a bridesmaid
because Bee had drawn the line at taking the
masquerade of her wedding that far.

'But I know you, you won't do it if it means

leaving those cute kids behind.' Tawny sighed. 'You'll be like faithful Penelope, stuck with him for ever, and I bet he plays on it when he realises what a softy you are.'

Bee had no intention of being a pushover, convinced as she was that Sergios would happily tread a softy right into the ground and walk on without a backward glance. He was tough, so she had to be even tougher. She reminded herself of that fact when her scowling father extended his arm to her at the mouth of the church aisle and fixed a social smile to his face. Monty Blake had recently been trodden on by Sergios and his ego and his pockets were still stinging from the encounter. She thought it said even more about Sergios's intimidating influence that her father was still willing, however, to play his part at their wedding.

Full of impatience, Sergios wheeled round at the altar to watch his bride approach. His face unreadable, he studied her and started to frown. She had had her long hair cut back to her shoulders. Whose very stupid idea had that been? But aside from that, Beatriz looked…luscious, he finally selected after a long mental pause while he ran his brooding dark gaze from the sultry peach-tinted fullness of her mouth down to the generous curves he never failed to admire. He wondered absently if men developed a taste for larger breasts when they reached a certain age. He was thirty-two, not fifty-two though. But as he saw the burgeoning swell of those plump creamy mounds so beautifully displayed in that neckline there was no denying that he was spell-bound. The model on the catwalk in Milan had had nothing to show off but an expanse of flat bony chest. In her place, however, Beatriz would have been a show-stopper. He frowned at that thought.

Determined not to be cowed by the fact her bridegroom was glowering at her, Bee lifted her chin. Even the most critical woman would have had to admit that Sergios did look spec-tacularly handsome in a beautifully cut morning suit. Encountering those hard eyes trained on her, she felt briefly dizzy and breathless. The minister of her church was inclined to ramble a little, but he soon controlled the tendency after Sergios urged him in an impatient undertone to 'speed it up'. Affronted by her bridegroom's intervention, Bee reddened to the roots of her hair. Had Sergios no idea how to behave in church? Well, it was never too late for a man to learn, although she suspected he would fight learning anything from her every step of the way. He thrust the wedding ring onto her finger with scant ceremony. She rubbed her hand as though he had hurt her, although he had not.

'You were rude to the minister,' she said on the way down the aisle again.

A brow lifted. 'I beg your pardon?'

'You heard me. There are some occasions when you just have to be patient for the sake of good manners and a wedding service is one of those occasions.'

In the thunderous silence that now enfolded the

bridal couple, Milo wriggled like an eel off his nanny's lap and rushed to Bee's side to clutch her skirt. She patted his curly head to quieten him and took his hand in hers.

'He was repeating himself,' Sergios breathed harshly, but, watching the toddler beam his big trusting smile up at Bee, he restrained the outrage her impertinence had sent hurtling through him. After little more than two weeks abroad he had returned to his London home and noticed a distinct change for the better in his cousin Timon's children. All the kids had calmed down. Milo had become less frantic in his need for attention, the little girl was smiling and even Paris was occasionally venturing into shy speech.

Sergios had never had a best friend but had he done so Timon would have come the closest, although on the surface serious, steady and quiet Timon would have appeared to have had little in common with Sergios's altogether more aggressive extrovert nature. But the bond had been there all the same and it was a matter of honour to Sergios to see Timon's children thrive in his care. Beatriz, it seemed, had the magic touch in that department.

A line of cameras greeted their emergence from the church. As Bee's eyes widened and she froze with the dismay of someone unaccustomed to media attention Sergios took immediate advantage of the moment. He swung her round into the circle of his arms and, with one hand braced to the shallow indentation of her spine to draw her close, he bent his head and kissed her, instinctively righting the status quo in the only way available to him.

Shock crashed through Bee and made her knees shake at that first breath-taking instant of physical contact. She had never been less prepared for anything and impressions hit her in a flood of overwhelming sensuality: the exotic tang of his designer cologne, the uncompromising strength and power of that lean, muscular body crushing her softer curves, the hard, demanding pressure of his erotic mouth on hers.

And while at the back of her mind a voice was shrieking no and urging her to pull back her body was singing entirely another song. There was a wildly addictive fire to the taste of him. She wanted more, she wanted *so* much more she trembled with the astonishing force of that wanting. His raw masculine passion sliced through her every defence and roused a surge of naked hunger within her. The plunge of his tongue into the sensitive interior of her mouth made her body tremble, while heat pooled between her thighs and her breasts swelled, pushing against the lace of her bra so that it felt too tight for comfort.

'You're not supposed to taste that good, *yineka mou*,' Sergios breathed in a roughened undertone, drawing back, his brilliant dark eyes cloaked and cool, his face taut.

Dragging her clinging hands from his broad shoulders, Bee was aghast and she turned blindly to pose for the cameras, her head swimming, her treacherous body torn by silent anguish as she struggled to suppress that monstrous hunger he had awakened. She had never felt like that in her life before, not even with Jon. It was as if Sergios had called up something she hadn't known existed within her and that treacherous loss of control had embarrassed the hell out of her. My goodness, she had *clung* to him, pushed her breasts into his chest like a wanton hussy and kissed him back with far too much gusto. She could not bring herself to look at him again and inside she was dying of mortification. Obviously he had planned to give her a social kiss for the benefit of the cameras but she had flung herself into it as though she were sex-starved.

Teeth gritted behind his determined smile, Sergios willed his arousal into subjugation and reminded himself forcefully that sleeping with his wife would curtail his freedom and deprive him of the choices that any intelligent man would value. One woman was much like another; all cats were grey in the dark. He repeated that oft-considered mantra to himself with rigorous determination: he had no plans to bed his bride, no

need to do so either. To think otherwise was to
invite chaos into his head and home. Breaking
the rules of his marriage would cost him and
why take that risk? Unless he was very much
mistaken, and when the subject was women
Sergios was rarely mistaken, his mistress would
push out every sexual stop to impress him on
his next visit. Satisfaction could be had without complications and wasn't that all that really
mattered?

The reception was staged at an exclusive hotel
where security staff vetted every arriving guest.

'Zara was such a fool,' Bee's stepmother,
Ingrid Blake, remarked in her brittle voice. 'It
could have been her standing here in your place
today.'

Features austere, Sergios settled an arm to his
bride's rigid spine. 'There can be no comparison. Beatriz is…special,' he murmured huskily.

Bee went pink at the unexpected compliment,
although the apparent slur on Zara embarrassed
her and as the older woman moved out of ear-

shot Bee muttered, 'Ingrid has a wasp's tongue but I could have managed her on my own.'

'I will never stand in silence while my wife is being insulted,' Sergios asserted. 'But only the most foolish would risk incurring my wrath.'

'Ingrid is a sourpuss but she's my father's wife and a member of the family,' Bee reminded him gently.

Noting the anxious light in her gaze, Sergios laughed out loud. 'You can't protect everyone from me.'

His vital laugh, so full of his essential energy, ironically chilled her, reminding her how much ruthless power and influence he had in the world and how much he took it for granted. She thought of her father walking her down the aisle even though it would have been more in character for the older man to express his resentment by refusing to take part in the wedding. Monty Blake's submission to her husband's wishes had shaken Bee and shown her the meaning of true supremacy. She had no doubt that if she ever dared to cross Sergios he would become her most bitter enemy.

'I understood that your grandfather was planning to come today,' Bee admitted.

'He has bronchitis and his doctor advised him to stay at home. You'll meet him tomorrow when we arrive in Greece. I didn't want him to take the risk of travelling.'

It was not a particularly large wedding: Sergios equated small with the privacy and discretion with which he liked to separate his private life from his public one. Although there were only fifty guests everybody on Sergios's list was a *somebody* in the business world. He seemed to have very few actual relatives, explaining that his grandfather had had only two children, both of whom had died relatively young.

'Was he looking for an heir when he discovered you?'

'No. In those days he had Timon. Social services discovered my connection to Nectarios and informed him about me. He didn't know I even existed before that. He came to see me when I was seventeen. I needed a decent education, he offered the opportunity,' Sergios admitted tautly.

She wanted to ask him more about his parentage but his reluctance to discuss his background was obvious and it seemed neither the time nor the place to probe further. Tense at being so much the centre of attention, she ate a light meal. A celebrity group entertained them. Bee noticed a beautiful female guest casting lascivious eyes in Sergios's direction and felt her fingers flex like claws ready to scratch. She didn't like other women looking at him in that speculative sexual way as if trying to imagine what he would be like in bed. It was that wretched kiss, it had changed everything, even the way she thought about him, Bee conceded unhappily.

She had not known that a mere kiss could make her feel hot and hungry and frantic for another. In fact she had always believed that she wasn't that sexual, and even when she was in love with Jon keeping him at arm's length had not proved much of a challenge for her. She had longed for some sign of commitment from him before she slept with him, had wanted sexual intimacy to mean something beyond the physical. With hindsight she suspected that she had always sensed that Jon was holding back as well and reluctant to get in too deep with her.

'This day seems endless,' Sergios breathed tersely as he checked his phone for the hundredth time, fingers tapping a restive tattoo on the table.

'It'll be over soon,' Bee said calmly, for she had guessed at the church that he found almost every aspect of their wedding day a demanding challenge. It made her wonder what his first wedding and his first wife had been like. Was he reliving disturbing memories? Had his first wedding been a day of love and joy for him? How could she not wonder? Yet Sergios didn't strike her as the kind of guy likely to have buried his heart with his dead wife and unborn child in the grave eight years earlier. He was too pragmatic and abrasive and far too fond of female company.

'Let's get the dancing over with,' Sergios breathed abruptly, springing upright and extending a hand to her.

'I love your enthusiasm,' Bee riposted, smiling brightly as her mother beamed at her. Emilia Blake was a happy woman and Sergios had not only visited her before the wedding but had also made the effort to sit down and talk that afternoon to her, which Bee appreciated. Emilia believed that her son-in-law was the sun, the moon and the stars and not for worlds would Bee have done or said anything to detract from that positive impression.

This marriage *had* to work, she reflected anxiously. If her mother came out to live in Greece their relationship would be on constant display, so she had to ensure from the start that the marriage worked for both of them. She would have to be practical, even-tempered and tolerant…for he was neither of the last two things.

Sergios shifted his lean powerful length against her as he danced with a fine sense of rhythm and all those rational uplifting thoughts left her head in one bound for suddenly all she was conscious of were the tightening prominence of her nipples and the smouldering dark gold of his eyes as he gazed moodily down at her. Heat and butterflies rose and fluttered in the pit of her tummy. Desire, she recognised as the twisty sensation stirring up hunger in her pelvis, was digging talon claws of need into her.

'*Theos*…you move well,' Sergios husked, whirling her round and admiring both her energy and the pert stirring curve of her derriere as she wriggled it in time to the music.

'After years of dance classes, I ought to.'

From there the day seemed to speed up. Moving from table to table, group to group, they spoke to all their guests. Bee was impressed that Sergios put on such a good show. He did not strike her as a touchy-feely guy, but the whole time he was by her side he maintained physical contact with either an arm or a hand placed on her. The children got tired and the nannies took them back to the house. Within an hour of their departure Sergios decided they could leave as well and they climbed into a waiting limousine and were carried off. From below her feathery lashes, Bee glanced covertly at her new husband, recognising his relief that the occasion was over.

'Is it all weddings you don't like or just your own?'

'All of them,' he admitted, his handsome mouth hardening. 'I can't stand the starry eyes and the unrealistic expectations. It's not real life.'

'No, it's hope and there's nothing wrong with the fact that people long for a happy ending.'

Sergios shrugged a big broad shoulder in what struck her as the diplomatic silence of disagreement. He sprawled back into the corner of the leather seat, long powerful thighs splayed in relaxation. 'Do you long for a happy ending, Beatriz?'

'Why not?' Bee fielded lightly.

'It won't be with me,' he promised her grimly. 'I don't believe in them.'

Well, that was certainly telling her, she thought ruefully as the limo drew up outside the London house that had become her new home. They mounted the splendid staircase together and were traversing the landing to head off in different directions when Sergios turned to Bee, his face impassive. 'I'm getting changed and going out. I'll see you at the airport tomorrow.'

And with that concluding assurance delivered with the minimum of drama he strode down the corridor where his bedroom suite lay and vanished from view. A door thudded shut. Bee had fallen still and she was very pale. She felt as if he had punched her in the stomach, winding her so that she couldn't catch her breath. It was the first day of their marriage, their wedding night, and he was going out, leaving her at home on her own.

And why should he not? This was not a normal marriage, she reminded herself doggedly.

It was not his duty to keep her company, was it? But was he going to see another woman? Why should that idea bite as if an arrow tipped with acid had been fired into her flesh? She didn't know why, she only knew it hurt and she felt horribly rejected. It felt humiliating to ask one of the maids for her assistance in getting out of her wedding finery. Yet, she knew that had he even been available she would not have approached Sergios for the same help. Still feeling gutted and furious with herself for a reaction she could not understand, Bee went for a shower to remove the last remnants of bridal sparkle from her body. Sergios wasn't her husband, not really her husband, so what was the matter with her?

Did Melita live in London or was she here visiting for a prearranged meeting? Or could it be that Sergios was rendezvousing with some other woman? Presumably he would be having sex with someone else tonight. Her tummy muscles tightened as if in self-defence and perspiration dampened her brow, leaving her skin clammy.

There was no point being prudish or naive about the emptiness of her marriage, she told herself in exasperation. Right from the start Sergios had demanded the freedom to get naked and intimate with other women on a regular basis. According to the media and those ladies who, when he was younger, were anything but discreet about his habits in the bedroom, he was very highly sexed.

And what exactly did she have to complain about? Sergios was doing only what he had said he would do and by loathing what he was doing *she* was the one breaking the rules by getting too personally involved! It was time she was more honest with herself, she reasoned irritably. In the normal way a man of Sergios's dazzling good looks and wealth would never be attracted to a woman as ordinary as she was. She should not forget that his first wife, Krista, had been gorgeous, similar to Zara with her fragile blonde loveliness. Bee had won Sergios as a husband solely by agreeing to allow him to retain his freedom within the marriage and be a mother to his cousin's children. That was how it was and that was the reality that she had to learn to live with.

A knock sounded on the door and she called out. Paris, clad in his superhero pyjamas and slippers, peered in, a photo album tucked snugly beneath one arm. 'I saw Uncle Sergios going out. Do you want to see my photos?'

'Why not?' Bee said with resolute good cheer, for a regular appraisal of photos of his parents and his baby years had become quite a feature of the little boy's life in recent days. He would show Bee the pictures and explain who the people were and where and when he thought they were taken and she would *ooh* and *aah* with appreciation and ask questions while he worked through his sadness for a period of his life that was now gone.

'Would you like a hot drink to help you sleep?' she prompted, deciding that this was a wedding night that she would never forget.

And if Bee blinked back tears while she sat on

the side of her bed with an arm anchored comfortingly round Paris's skinny little body and a mug of cocoa in her other hand, her companion was too intent on sharing his photo album to notice.

CHAPTER FIVE

Two nannies, Janey and Karen, were accompanying Bee and the children to Greece. Shown around Sergios's incredibly large and opulent private jet by an attentive stewardess late the next morning, Bee saw the entire party settled in the rear cabin, which was separate from the main saloon. Armed with enough toys, magazines and films to while away a much longer flight, the young women were thrilled by their deluxe surroundings.

In a lighter mood, Bee would have found it equally difficult not to be seduced by her newly luxurious mode of travel, but she had too much on her mind. She had slept badly and had been forced to out-act a Hollywood film star with her good cheer over the breakfast table, for she had been keen to soothe the boys' nervous tension. After all, Paris and Milo were apprehensive about making yet another move for they had already had to adjust to so much change in their short lives. Paris, however, was quick to address the steward in Greek and Milo's head tipped to one side and his brow furrowed as though he too was recalling the language of his very first words. Although they would not be returning to their former home in Athens, they were heading back to the country of their birth and they might well find Sergios's home on the island of Orestos familiar, for they had often visited it with their parents.

Having ensured that everyone was comfortable, Bee returned to the main saloon and took a seat to leaf through a magazine that she couldn't have cared less about. Having teamed a green silk top and cardigan with white linen trousers, she felt both smart and comfortable. Her hand shook a little when she heard voices outside and her fingers clenched tightly into the publication in her hand, her body tensing, her heartbeat literally racing as she heard steps on the metal stairs. Sergios was tearing her in two, she suddenly thought in frustration. One half of her could barely wait to lay eyes on him while the other half would have preferred to never see him again.

'*Kalimera*…good morning, Beatriz,' Sergios intoned, as tall, dark and gloriously handsome as an angel come to earth, perfect in form but exceedingly complex in nature.

And with her breath convulsing in her dry throat, she both looked at him and blanked him at one and the same time so that their eyes did not quite meet, a polite smile of acknowledgement on her lips combined with an almost inaudible greeting. Why was she embarrassed? Why the hell was she embarrassed? Enraged by her ridiculous oversensitivity, Bee glanced up at him unwarily and collided with golden eyes full of energy and wariness. She *knew* it, he was no fool, and indeed he was just waiting for her to say or do something she shouldn't, to react in some inappropriate way to his departure the night before. Keeping her smile firmly in place, Bee was determined to deny him that satisfaction and she dropped her attention resolutely back to her magazine.

And there her attention stayed…throughout take-off, a visit to the children, lunch and the remainder of the flight. Sergios shot her composed profile a suspicious appraisal. She had said not one word out of place, not one word. He could not understand why he was not pleased by the fact, why indeed he felt almost affronted by her comprehensive show of disinterest and detachment. He did not like and had even less experience of being ignored by a woman. But Beatriz was very much a lady and he appreciated that trait. The acknowledgement sparked a recollection and he dug into his pocket to remove a jewel box.

'For you,' he murmured carelessly, tossing the little box down on the table between them.

Her teeth gritted. She lifted the box almost as though she were afraid it might soil her in some way, flipped up the lid, stared down at the fabulous diamond solitaire ring, closed the lid and set it aside again. 'Thank you,' she pronounced woodenly with anything but gratitude in her low-pitched voice.

Too clever not to work out that the denial of attention was some form of challenge and punishment, Sergios was becoming tenser because his brand-new bride was already revealing murky depths he had not known she possessed. Frustration filled him. Why did women *do* that? Why did they pretend to be straightforward and then welch on the deal with a vengeance? He knew she was strong-willed, stubborn and rather set in her conventional ways but he had not foreseen any greater problem and had by his own yardstick done what he could to cement their relationship.

'Aren't you going to put it on?' Sergios prompted flatly.

Bee opened the box again, removed the ring and rammed it roughly down over the third finger of her right hand with a lack of ceremony or appreciation that was even more challenging than her previous behaviour. She then returned to perusing her magazine with renewed concentration. She was so furious with him she could neither trust herself to speak to or look at him. If she did look, she would only end up picturing him cavorting in a messy tangle of bed sheets with some sinuous, sexy lover to whom she could never compare in looks or appeal. Yet until that very day looks or sex appeal had never seemed that important to Bee, who had been happier to put a higher value on her health and peace of mind. Unfortunately marrying Sergios appeared to have destroyed her peace of mind.

After a long moment of disbelief, for no woman had ever accepted a gift from him with such incivility before, dark temper stirred in Sergios. Simmering, he studied her, catching the jewelled glint of defiance in her green eyes as she sneaked a glance at him from below her curling lashes and bent her head. Shining chestnut hair fell against the flawless creamy skin of her cheek and her voluptuous pink mouth compressed. That fast he went taut and hard, sexual heat leaving him swallowing back a curse under his breath as he imagined what she might do with those full pouting lips if he got her in the right mood, and Sergios had never once doubted his ability to get a woman in the right mood.

'Excuse me,' Bee said without expression, breaking the tense silence. She was on her feet before he was even aware she was about to move. Seconds later she disappeared into the rear cabin and he heard Milo yell out her name in welcome.

Almost light-headed with relief at escaping the fraught atmosphere in the saloon, Bee sat down to amuse the children. The younger nanny, Janey, caught her hand and gasped at the huge diamond on her finger. 'That ring is out of this world, Mrs Demonides!' she exclaimed, impressed to death.

No, that ring is the price of lust, Bee could have told her. Bee was deeply insulted. He had had sex with another woman and it had meant so little to him that he had betrayed not a shred of discomfiture in Bee's presence. He was, as always, beautifully dressed and immaculate without even a hint of another woman's lipstick or perfume on him. That he was as cool as ice as well offended her sense of decency. She had wanted to throw that ring back at him and tell him to keep it. She had had to leave the saloon before she did or said something that she would live to regret.

Why couldn't she start thinking of him as a brother or a friend? Why was she burdened with this awful sense of possessiveness where Sergios was concerned? Why did she have to be so hatefully attracted to him? It was an appalling admission to make but she already knew that she couldn't bear the idea of Sergios with another woman in an intimate situation. Had she developed some kind of silly immature crush on him? She cringed at the suspicion but what else could be causing all these distressingly unsuitable feelings?

She had to reprogramme her brain to view him in the light of a brother, an asexual being, she instructed herself firmly. That was the only way forward in their relationship. That was the only way their marriage of convenience could possibly work for all of them. She had her mother's happiness to think about as well as that of Paris, Milo and Eleni. This marriage was not all about *her* and her very personal reactions to Sergios were a dangerous trap that she could not afford to fall into.

After all, Sergios was not all bad. He was tough, ruthless, arrogant and selfish, but while he might have the morals of an alley cat he had been remarkably kind to her mother. Without even being asked to do so, he had behaved as though theirs was a normal marriage for Emilia Blake's benefit. Although he appeared to have little interest in his cousin's kids or kids in general, he had still retained guardianship of the troubled trio and had married Bee on their behalf. Yet he could more easily have shirked the responsibility and retained his freedom by paying someone else to do the job of raising them for him.

The jet landed in Athens and the entire party transferred to a large helicopter to travel to the island of Orestos. Conscious of the cool gleam in Sergios's appraisal, Bee went pink and pretended not to notice while peering out of the windows to get a clear view of the island that was to be her future home. Orestos was craggy and green with a hilly interior. Pine forests backed white sand beaches that ran down to a violet blue shining sea and a sizeable small town surrounded the harbour.

'Gorgeous, just like a postcard!' one of the nannies commented admiringly.

'Has the island been in your family for long?' Bee asked Sergios.

'My great-grandfather accepted it in lieu of a bad debt in the nineteen twenties.'

'It looks like a wonderfully safe place for children to run about,' the other nanny remarked approvingly to her companion.

Bee thought of the far from safe and tough inner city streets where Sergios had grown up. Perhaps it was not that surprising that he was so hard and uncompromising in his attitude to the world and the people in it, she conceded reluctantly. The helicopter landed on a pad within yards of a big white house adorned with a tall round tower. Surrounded by the pine forest, it could not be seen except from the air. Sergios jumped out and spun round to help her leave the craft. Laughing uproariously in excitement, Milo jumped out too and would have run off had Sergios not clamped a restraining hand into the collar of his sweatshirt.

'There are dangers here with such easy access to the sea and the rocks,' he informed the hovering nannies. 'Don't let the boys leave the house alone.'

The warning killed the bubbly holiday atmosphere that had been brewing, Bee noted. Janey and Karen looked intimidated.

'The children are going to love it here but they'll have to learn new rules to keep them safe,' Bee forecast, stepping into the uneasy silence.

The housekeeper, Androula, a plump, good-natured woman with a beaming smile, came out to welcome them with a stream of Greek. Sergios came to a sudden halt as if something she had said had greatly surprised him.

'Nectarios is here,' he said in a sudden aside, his ebony brows drawing together in a frown.

'I assumed that your grandfather lived with you.'

'No, he has his own house across the bay. Androula tells me that his home suffered a flood during a rain storm, rendering it uninhabitable,' he said with the suggestion of gritted teeth. 'This changes everything.'

Bee had no idea what he was talking about. Androula swept them indoors and a tall, broad-shouldered and eagle-eyed elderly man came out to meet them. Paris rushed eagerly straight to his white-haired great-grandfather's side, Milo trailing trustingly in his brother's wake. Keen dark eyes set below beetling brows rested on Bee and she flushed, feeling hugely self-conscious.

'Introduce me to your bride, Sergios,' the old man encouraged. 'I'm sorry to invade your privacy at such a time.'

'You're family. You will always be a welcome guest here,' Bee declared warmly, some of the strain etched in her face dissipating. 'Look how pleased the boys are to see you.'

'Beauty and charm,' Nectarios remarked softly to his grandson. 'You've done well, Sergios.'

Bee did not think she was beautiful, but she thought it was very kind of the old man to pretend otherwise. At that very moment her make-up had worn off and she was wearing creased linen trousers stained by Milo's handprints. Eleni was whinging and stretching out her arms to her and she took the child and rested her against her shoulder, smoothing her little dark head to soothe her. The children were getting tired and cross and she took advantage of the fact to leave the men and follow Androula to the nursery. While the boys enthused over toys familiar from previous visits, Bee asked Androula to show her to her room. Her accommodation was in the tower and her eyes opened very wide when she entered the huge circular bedroom with full-height French windows opening out onto a stone balcony with the most fabulous view of the bay. It was a spectacular and comparatively new addition to the house and her eyes only opened wider when she was taken through the communicating door to inspect a luxurious en suite and matching dressing rooms. Purpose-built accommodation for two and her cheeks warmed. Naturally the household would be expecting Sergios and his bride to share this amazing suite of rooms.

Assured that she had time before dinner, Bee scooped up the wrap she glimpsed in one of her open cases and left the maids to unpack while she went for a bath. She was just in the mood to soak away her stress. Leaving her clothes in an unusually untidy heap and anchoring her hair to the top of her head to keep it dry, she tossed scented bath crystals into the water and climbed in, sinking down into the relaxing warmth with a sigh of appreciation.

A knock sounded on the door and she frowned, recalling that she had not locked it. She was in the act of sitting up when the door opened without further warning to frame Sergios.

Bee whipped her arms over her breasts and roared, 'Get out of here!'

'No, I will not,' Sergios responded with thunderous bite.

CHAPTER SIX

THE smouldering gold of anger in Sergios's stunning eyes dimmed solely because he was enjoying the view.

There Beatriz was, all pink and wet and bare among the bubbles. Her fair skin was all slippery and his hands tingled with the need to touch. Those breasts he had correctly calculated at more than a handful were topped by buds with the size and lushness of ripe cherries. Erect at that tempting vision within seconds, Sergios was deciding that the need to share facilities might not be quite the serious problem and invasion of privacy that he had gloomily envisaged. In fact it might well pay unexpected dividends of a physical nature.

Outraged green eyes seethed at him. 'Go!' Bee yelled at him.

Instead, Sergios stepped into the bathroom and closed the door to lean back against the wood with infuriating cool. 'Don't raise your voice to me. The maids are unpacking next door and we're supposed to be on our honeymoon,' he reminded her huskily. 'For someone so hung up on good manners you can be very rude. I knocked on the door—you chose not to answer!'

'You didn't give me the chance.' Bee said resentfully before she reached for a towel, fed up with huddling like some cowed Victorian maiden in the water and all too well aware that her hands didn't cover a large enough expanse of flesh to conceal the more sensitive areas. As she got up on her knees she deftly used the towel as cover and slowly stood up, keen not to expose anything more.

Fully appreciating the rolling violin curve visible between her waist and hip, Sergios treated her to a wolfish grin of amusement. 'You need a bigger towel, Beatriz.'

And just like that Beatriz became instantly aware of the fact she was large and clumsy rather than little and dainty. Equally fast she was recalling her size zero sister, Zara, whom Sergios had initially planned to marry, not to mention his equally tiny first wife. That was the shape of woman that was the norm for her Greek husband. On his terms she *was* a big girl.

'Or you could just drop the towel altogether, *yineka mou*,' Sergios continued huskily, his dark deep drawl roughening round the edges at that prospect.

'If I wasn't so busy trying to knot this stupid towel I would slap you!' Beatriz countered, assuming that he was teasing her, for by no stretch of the imagination could she even picture circumstances in which she might deliberately stand naked in front of a man, even if he was the one whom she had married.

Sergios tossed her a much larger towel from

the shelf on the wall and she wrapped it round her awkwardly. 'We have to share this suite,' he spelt out, suddenly serious.

Her brow indented. 'What are you talking about?'

'My grandfather is staying and I want him to believe that this is a normal marriage. He won't believe that if we occupy separate rooms and be-have like brother and sister,' he said with a sar-donic curl to his wide sensual mouth. 'We don't have a choice. We'll just have to tough it out and hope our acting skills are up to the challenge.'

'You're expecting me to share that bedroom with you…even *the bed*?' Bee gasped. 'I won't do it.'

'I didn't offer you a choice. We have an ar-rangement and it includes providing cover for each other.' Eyes dramatised by black spiky lashes raked her truculent face in an unashamed challenge. 'We do what we have to do. I don't want to upset Nectarios just as you didn't want to worry your mother. He needs to believe that this is a real marriage.'

'But I am not willing to agree to share a bed with you,' Bee repeated with clarity. 'And that's all I've got to say on the subject apart from the fact that if you sleep out there, I'll have to sleep somewhere else.'

His eyes glittered as bright as stars in the night sky. 'Not under my roof—'

Bee felt somewhat foolish and at a disadvantage swaddled in her unflattering towel for if she looked large without it how much larger must she look engulfed within its capacious folds? And had a towel the size of a blanket been a deliberate choice on his part or a coincidence?

'I'll get dressed for dinner,' Bee announced, waiting for him to step aside and let her out of the bathroom. *Not under my roof?* He could be as threatening as a sabre-toothed tiger but she was not about to change her mind: she was entitled to her own bed.

Eyes narrowed with brooding intensity, Sergios

lounged back against the door frame like the lean, powerful predator that he was and the atmosphere was explosive. As she moved past he rested a hand on the bare curve of her shoulder and she came to a halt.

'I want you,' Sergios declared, using his other hand to ease her back against him and run his fingers lightly up from her waist to her ribcage.

In the space of a moment Bee froze and stopped breathing, panic gripping her. *I want you?* Since when?

'That's not part of our agreement,' she said prosaically, standing as still as a statue as if movement of any kind might encourage him.

Above her head, Sergios laughed, the sound full of vitality and amusement. 'Our agreement is between adults and whatever we choose to make of it—'

'Trust me,' Bee urged. 'We don't want to muddy the water with sex.'

'This is the real world. Desire is an energy, not something you can plan or pin down on paper,' he intoned, and his hands simply shifted position to cover her towel-clad breasts.

Even beneath that light pressure, her heartbeat went crazy. Boom-boom-boom it went in her ears as he boldly pushed the fabric down out of his path and closed his hands caressingly round the firm globes, teasing the stiffly prominent nipples between his fingers. A startled gasp escaped from Bee. She looked down at those long fingers stroking the swollen pink peaks, flushed crimson and then shut her eyes tight again, her legs trembling beneath her. She should push him away, she should push him away, tell him to stop, *insist* that he stop.

Sergios swept her up off her feet while she was still struggling to reclaim her poise and strode into the bedroom to lay her down on the big wide bed. He hit a button above the headboard and she heard the door lock and she sat up, wrenching the towel back up over her exposed flesh.

'You're not going anywhere…' Sergios husked

with raw masculine assurance, coming down to the bed on his knees and reaching for her.

'This is not a good idea,' Bee protested in a voice that without the slightest warning emerged as downright squeaky.

'You sound like a frightened virgin!' Sergios quipped, using one hand to tip up her chin and kiss her with hard, hungry fervour, his teeth nipping at her full lower lip, his tongue plunging in an erotic raid on her tender mouth. With his other hand he stroked the straining sensitive buds on her breasts and it was as if he had jerked a leash to pull her in, for instead of pushing back from him she discovered that she only wanted to go one way and that was closer.

'Sergios…' she cried against the demanding onslaught of his sensual mouth.

'*Filise me*…kiss me,' he urged, his strong hands roaming. 'I love your breasts.'

As sweet tempting sensation executed its sway over her treacherous body, Bee felt her lack of fight travelling through her like a debilitating disease. In a sudden move of desperation she flung herself sideways off the bed. She fell with a crash that bruised her hip and jolted every bone in her body and Sergios sat up to regard her with a look of bewilderment. He reached down to help her up again. 'How did you do that?' he questioned. 'Are you hurt?'

'No, but I had to stop what we were doing,' Bee volunteered jerkily, hauling at the towel again and feeling remarkably foolish.

'Why?' Sergios countered in frank astonishment.

Bee veiled her eyes and shut her mouth like a steel trap. 'Because I don't want to have sex with you.'

'That's a lie.' Smouldering eyes came to a screeching halt on her. 'I can tell when a woman wants me.'

Sitting on the wooden floor on a rug that did not make the floor any more comfortable, Bee marvelled that she did not simply scream and launch herself at him like a Valkyrie. He was like a dog with a bone; he wasn't going to give it up without a fight. 'I forgot myself for a moment…a weak moment. It won't happen again. You said you didn't want intimacy—'

'I've changed my mind,' Sergios admitted without skipping a beat.

Bee very nearly did scream then in frustration. 'But I haven't—changed my mind, that is.'

An utterly unexpected grin slanted his beautiful shapely mouth, lending a dazzling charisma to his already handsome features that no woman could have remained impervious to. He lounged fluidly back on the bed and shifted a graceful hand. 'So, then we deal, *yineka mou*—'

'*Deal?*' Bee parroted in a tone of disbelief.

'You're so uptight, Beatriz. You need a man like me to loosen you up.'

Tousled chestnut hair tumbling round her wildly flushed oval face, Bee stood up still clutching the towel. 'I don't want to loosen up. I'm quite happy as I am.'

Sergios released his breath in an impatient

hiss. 'You can get pregnant if you want,' he proffered with a wry roll of his stunning dark eyes as if he were inviting her to take two pints of his blood. 'We're already saddled with three kids—how much difference could another one make?'

Her eyes wide with consternation at that shockingly unemotional appraisal, Bee backed away several feet. 'I think you're crazy.'

Sergios shook his arrogant dark head. 'Think outside the box, Beatriz. I'm trying to make a deal with you. As you're not in business, I'll explain—I give you what you want so that you give me what I want. It's that simple.'

'Except when it's my body on the table,' Bee replied in a tone of gentle irony. 'My body is not going to figure as any part of a deal with you or anybody else. We agreed that there would be no sex and I want to stick to that.'

'That is not the message your body is giving me, *latria mou*,' Sergios drawled softly.

'You're reading the signals wrong—maybe it's your healthy ego misleading you,' Bee suggested thinly as she hit the button he had used to lock the door to unlock it again.

As Bee leant across him Sergios hooked his fingers into the edge of the towel above her breasts. Immobilised, she looked up at him and collided with his dazzling eyes enhanced by ridiculously long lush lashes. Her heart seemed to jump into her throat.

'It's *not* my ego that's talking,' Sergios purred like a prowling big cat of the jungle variety.

'Yes, it is. Even though you don't really want me and I'm not your type.'

'I don't go for a particular type.'

'Zara? Your first wife? Let me remind you— *slim, glamorous*?' Bee stabbed without hesitation, watching his face tauten and pale as though she had struck him. The hand threatening the closure of the towel fell back and Bee was quick to take advantage of his uncharacteristic retreat. 'That's your type. I'm not and never could be.'

Sergios dealt her a steely-eyed appraisal. 'You don't know what turns me on'

'Don't I? Something you've been told you can't have. A challenge—that's all it takes to turn you on!' Bee hissed at him, fighting to hide the depth of her outrage. 'And I accidentally made myself seem like a challenge this evening. You're so perverse. If I was throwing myself at you, you would hate it.'

'Not right at this moment, I wouldn't,' Sergios purred in silken contradiction, running a hand down over the extended stretch of one long powerful thigh and by doing so drawing her attention to the tented effect of his tailored trousers over his groin. 'As you can see, I'm not in any condition to say no to a reasonable offer.'

As he directed her gaze to the evidence of his arousal Bee could feel a tide of mortified heat rush up from her throat to her hairline and she did not know where to look even as a kernel of secret heat curled in her pelvis. 'You're disgusting,' she said curtly and knew even as she said it that she didn't mean it. The knowledge that lust for her had put him in that state was strangely stimulating and there was something even more satisfying in that unsought but graphic affirmation of her femininity.

'Over dinner, think about what you want most,' Sergios advised lazily. 'And remember that there's nothing I can't give you.'

Consternation in her eyes, Bee stepped back from the bed, her oval face stiff with angry condemnation. 'Are you offering me money to sleep with you?'

Sergios winced. 'You're so literal, so blunt—'

'You just can't accept the word no, can you?' Bee launched at him in a furious flood. 'You even sank low enough to try and use a baby as a bargaining chip!'

'Of course you want a baby—I've watched you with my cousin's kids. Nobody could be that way with them if they didn't want one of their own,' Sergios opined with assurance. 'I've had enough experience with women to know that at some point in our marriage you will decide that you want a child of your own.'

'Right at this very moment,' Bee told him shakily, 'I'm wondering how I can possibly stay married to such a conniving and unscrupulous man!'

'Your mother, the kids, the fact that you don't like to fail at anything? You're not a quitter, Beatriz. I admire that in a woman.' Straightening his tie and finger-combing his black hair back off his brow, Sergios sprang off the bed, his big powerful body suddenly towering over her. 'But I do have one small word of warning for you,' he murmured in a tone as cool as ice. 'I don't talk about my first wife, Krista...*ever*, so leave her out of our...discussions.'

Shell-shocked from that spirited encounter and that final chilling warning, Bee got back into her cooling bath and sat there blinking in a daze. When he had touched her, a tide of such longing had gripped her that she had almost surrendered. But she wasn't stupid, and even though she had never been so strongly affected before by a man she had always accepted that sex and the cravings it awakened could be very power-ful and seductive. Why else did the lure of sex persuade so many people to succumb to temp-tation and get into trouble over it? It might be a sobering discovery but she had only learned that she was as weak as any other human being.

After Krista's death—she who must not be mentioned—Sergios had become a notorious playboy. He had to be a very experienced lover and he knew exactly how to pull her strings and extract ladies who ought to have known better from towels, she allowed in growing chagrin. Well, he hadn't got the towel the whole way off, she told herself soothingly. With a male as fe-rociously determined and untamed as Sergios even the smallest victory ought to be celebrated.

It was silly how it actually hurt her pride that Sergios didn't *really* desire her. He was annoyed that his grandfather's presence in his home would force them to live a lie to conceal the re-ality that their marriage was a fake. His ego was challenged by the prospect of having to share a bed with a woman he had agreed not to touch, so he was trying to tear up the terms of their agreement by whatever means were within his power. Even so, she reckoned it had to be a very rare event for a man to try to seduce a woman by offering to get her pregnant.

Sergios could certainly think on his feet. Indeed he was utterly shameless and callous in pursuit of anything he wanted. But he was also, Bee thought painfully, extremely clever and far too shrewd for comfort. He had sensed the softy hiding below her practical surface and made an educated guess that the prospect of having her own child would have more pulling power with her than the offer of money or diamonds. And he had guessed right, *so* right in fact that she wanted to scream in frustration and embarrassment.

How could he see inside her heart like that? How could he have worked out already what she had only recently learned about herself? Only since she had been in daily contact with Paris,

Milo and Eleni had Bee appreciated just how much she enjoyed being a mother. Out on a shopping trip she had bought baby clothes for Eleni and found herself drawn to examining the even tinier garments and the prams, newly afflicted by a broodiness that she had heard friends discuss but until then had never experienced on her own behalf.

But common sense warned her that right now she had to stand her ground with Sergios. If she allowed him to walk over her so early in their marriage she would be the equivalent of a cipher within a few years, enslaved by her master's voice. He had to respect the boundaries they had set together. After all, he had Melita and other women in his life and she had no wish to join that specific party. The reflection tightened her muscles and made her head begin to ache as she appreciated that she truly was caught between a rock and a hard place with a man who attracted her but whom she could not have. She stretched back against the padded headrest, desperate to shed her tension and troubled thoughts. Sergios was an absolute menace to her peace of mind. He kept on moving the goalposts to suit himself. He was like a pirate on the high seas, always in pursuit of an advantage or a profit. But when it came to fencing with Bee he was just as likely to run aground on the rocks hidden beneath her deceptively calm surface.

When Sergios strolled into the bedroom, Bee was putting the finishing touches to her appearance. Her full-length blue evening dress fitted her like a glove without showing a surplus inch of flesh. His brilliant eyes narrowing, she watched in the mirror as Sergios subjected her to a considering appraisal.

'Sexy,' he pronounced approvingly.

Bee stiffened defensively. 'It's high at the neck and it doesn't even show my legs,' she argued.

Her immediate protest at his comment made amusement curl the corners of his handsome mouth. He scanned the lush swell of breast and derriere so clearly defined by the clinging fabric and said nothing at all. No skin might be on show but the dress hugged her every curve and those she had in abundance.

He touched the end of a straying strand of her dark hair where it lay on her shoulder. 'Grow your hair again. I liked it longer.'

'Are you used to women doing what *you* like with their appearance?' Bee prompted a tad sourly.

'Yes,' Sergios proclaimed without a shred of discomfiture.

'Any other orders, boss?' Bee could not resist the crack.

'Smile and relax,' he urged. 'Nectarios is already very taken with you. He sees a big improvement in his great-grandsons—'

'My goodness, it's not down to my influence. I've only been with the children a few weeks—'

'But they didn't see that much of their own mother, so your attention means a great deal to them.'

'Why didn't they see much of their mother?'

'She was a popular TV presenter and rarely at home. Timon adored her.'

Suddenly she wanted to know if Sergios had adored Krista but she found that she couldn't imagine him in thrall to a woman, eager to impress and please. There was a bone-deep toughness and a reserve to Sergios that suggested that nothing less than pole position in a relationship would satisfy him. Yet he had only been twenty-one when he wed Krista and to marry so young he must have been a good deal less cynical about the institution of marriage. Comparing that to his attitude at their wedding the day before, Bee could only assume that he had got badly burned by Krista in some way. Of course there was the alternative view that losing Krista and their unborn child had hurt him so much that he had resolved never to fall in love or marry again.

Suddenly irritated by her curiosity, she asked herself why she should care. He had married her purely for the sake of Timon's children and she needed to remember that. This afternoon he had wanted to bed her and the motivation for that staggering turnaround was not that hard to work out, Bee reflected ruefully. How many other sexual options could this little Greek island offer Sergios? He was supposed to be on his honeymoon and if he wanted his grandfather to believe that it was a normal marriage he could scarcely ditch his bride and rush off to seek satisfaction in some other woman's bed. So, for the present, Sergios was trapped in a masquerade and Bee had become miraculously desirable through a complete absence of competition. Right now she was the only option her sensual Greek husband had. It was an acknowledgement that would certainly ensure she didn't develop a swollen head about the precise nature of her attractions.

Dinner was served on a terrace outside the formal dining room. The sun was going down over the sea in fiery splendour and the food was delicious. Bee ate with relish while Nectarios entertained her with stories about the history of the island and family ownership. As the two men finally succumbed to catching up on business, it amused her to recognise how alike Sergios and his grandfather were in looks and mannerisms and she told them she would not be offended if they switched to talking in Greek. She would have to learn the language and quickly, she recognised, grateful that learning languages came relatively easily to her, for it was essential that she be able to communicate effectively with the staff and the children. She did not want to be shut out of half of the conversations going on around her.

She contemplated Sergios over her fresh fruit dessert. The low lights gleamed over his cropped black hair and cast shadows on his strong bronzed profile. He was extraordinarily handsome and even the way he moved was sensual, she thought abstractedly, her eyes following the elegant arc inscribed by an eloquent hand as he spoke. When she glanced up and realised that Nectarios was watching her watch Sergios she went pink. A few minutes later she said it was time she looked in on the children and she left the table.

Having checked on the kids and agreed to take Paris down to the beach in the morning, Bee walked past the door of the main bedroom and on up the final flight of stairs to the bedroom at the top of the tower. Earlier that evening she had found the room and had decided that it would do her nicely as a bolthole. Hadn't she read somewhere recently that it was fashionable for couples with sufficient space in their homes to pursue a better night's sleep by occupying different bedrooms? Separate beds need not mean that anyone's relationship was on the rocks and that was what she would tell Sergios if he tried to object.

She slid on a light cotton nightdress that was far from glamorous, for she had disdained the silk and satin lingerie the personal shopper had directed her towards in London. She climbed into her big comfortable bed and lay with her cooling limbs splayed in a starfish shape to let all her tension drain away. In time this house and the new life she was leading would feel familiar and comfortable, she told herself soothingly.

The door opened and she jerked in surprise, lifting her head several inches off the pillow to peer across the room. The light from the stairwell fell on Sergios's lean strong features and glimmered over his bare, hair-roughened chest and the towel that appeared to be all he was wearing. Bee's short-lived relaxation dive-bombed and her limbs scissored back together again as she sat up and switched on the light.

'What are you doing in here?'

'As you've deserted the marital bed so must I. Wherever we sleep, we stay together,' Sergios spelt out with hard dark eyes and an unyielding angle to his jaw line.

Bee was intimidated by the amount of naked masculine flesh on view. He was tall and broad and, stripped, his big strong shoulders, powerful torso and tight flat stomach were distinctly imposing. 'Don't you dare take off that towel!' she warned him thinly.

'Don't be such a prude,' Sergios told her impatiently. 'I sleep naked. I always have.'

'I can't treat you like a brother if I've seen you naked!' Bee snapped back in embarrassment.

Sergios, engaged in wondering why she would want to treat him like a brother when his own intentions had roamed so far from the platonic plane, threw up both hands in a sudden gesture of exasperation. 'You must've seen loads of guys naked!'

'Oh, is that a fact?' Bee hissed, insulted by that assumption. 'You think I've slept with a lot of men?'

'I've had quite a few women. I'm not a hypocrite,' Sergios said drily.

Bee was seething. 'FYI some of us are a little more particular.'

'Did they all wear pyjamas?' Sergios asked, unable to resist that crack as his wondering gaze took in the full horror of the nightdress she wore: a baggy cotton monstrosity edged with fussy lace.

Bee cringed inwardly. 'There hasn't actually been anyone yet,' she admitted, hoping dismay at her inexperience would persuade him that she really did need her privacy.

Sergios came to an abrupt halt about ten feet from the foot of the bed. A frown had drawn his brows together. 'You can't mean that you've never had a lover…'

Bee reddened but she lifted and dropped both shoulders in a dismissive shrug as though the subject did not bother her at all. 'I haven't.'

Momentarily, Sergios was transfixed by the concept. He had believed virgins had died out around the same time as efficient contraception was developed. He had certainly never expected to find one in his bed. He swung on his heel and strode back out of the room without another word. Released from stasis, Bee breathed in slow and deep and switched out the light. Well, that news had certainly cooled his jets, she conceded.

She had fallen out of the challenge category into the sort of unknown territory he evidently had no desire to explore.

But in that conviction Bee was wrong for the bedroom door opened again, startling her, and she raised herself on her elbows with a frown. Sergios was back, minus the towel and clad in a pair of black boxers, which did spectacularly little to conceal the muscular strength and bronzed beauty of his powerfully masculine body.

Sergios got into the far side of the bed in silence. A *virgin*, he was thinking with unholy fascination, a novelty calculated to appeal to even the most jaded palate.

Bee's toes encountered a masculine leg and she pulled hurriedly away as if she had been burned by the contact. His persistence in doing exactly what he wanted to do, regardless of her objections, was beginning to wear down even her nerves of steel.

'I've never gone to bed with a virgin before...'

Sergios informed her in his deep drawl. 'In to-day's world you're as rare as a dinosaur.'

And at that astonishing assurance a bubble of unquenchable mirth formed and swelled in Bee's chest and then floated up into her throat to almost choke her before she finally gave vent to her laughter.

Sergios snaked out an arm and hauled her close. 'I wasn't trying to be funny.'

'Try to picture yourself as a d-dinosaur!' Bee advised, shaking with a hilarity she could not restrain. 'I just hope you weren't thinking of a T-Rex.'

Her laughter was even more of a surprise to a man who took life very seriously and sex more seriously still. He held her while wave after wave of uncontrollable amusement rippled through her curvy body and rendered her helpless. Her breasts rubbed his chest, her thighs shifted against his and he breathed in the soapy scent of her, picturing her equally helpless from passion in his arms. Desire roared through him afresh with a savagery that took even him aback.

Knotting one hand into the fall of her hair to hold her steady, Sergios dipped his tongue between her parted lips with erotic heat. All lingering amusement left her in the space of a moment as he plundered her ready response, nibbling and suckling at her full lower lip, skating an exploration over the sensitive roof of her mouth until her toes were curling and she was stretching up to him helpless in the grip of her need for more.

'Sergios…' she framed in vague protest when he let her breathe again.

'You'll still be a virgin in the morning,' Sergios murmured. 'I promise, *yineka mou.*'

CHAPTER SEVEN

BEE was trembling, insanely conscious of every erogenous zone on her body, but that saying that curiosity had killed the cat was playing in the back of her mind as well. Sergios was playing a game with her and she didn't know the rules, was convinced that she would live to regret letting down her defences. But there was a tightening sense of pressure at the heart of her that pulled tighter with every insidious flick of his tongue against hers and she could not resist its sway.

He inched the nightdress down over her slim shoulders, trapping her arms at the same time as he exposed her generous breasts. In the moonlight pouring through the filmy drapes those high round swells were the most tempting he had ever seen. He kneaded them with firm hands, closed his mouth hungrily to a rigid pink nipple and teased with his lips and his teeth while her back arched and she whimpered beneath his attentions. He switched his focus to her other breast, treating her to one tantalising caress after another, steadily utilising more pressure and urgency on her increasingly sensitised flesh.

It was like being taken apart and put together again in a different sequence, Bee acknowledged in an agony of uncertainty that did nothing to stop the raging hunger that controlled her. She might never be the same again yet she still could not summon the will power to pull back or insist that he stop touching her. Her clenching fingers delved into his luxuriant hair while he stroked deliciously at her pointed nipples and kissed and licked his passage across the creamy slopes of her breasts before possessing her mouth again, drinking deep from her. She was wildly, seethingly aware of the brimming heat and moisture between her thighs and the ache of longing that had her hips digging into the bed beneath her. Her hands shifted back and forth across his satin-smooth shoulders as the knot of tension at the heart of her built and built. She pushed up to him desperate for more powerful sensation and she couldn't stay still then, couldn't find her voice, couldn't stop the gasps emanating from her throat either. And then suddenly it was all coalescing into one explosive response and she was arching and jerking and crying out in ecstasy as her body took her soaring onto another plane and there was nothing she could do to control any of it.

Afterwards, Bee wanted to leap out of the bed and run but there was nowhere to run to. The thought of cowering behind the bathroom door was not appealing. Still in his arms, she lay like a stone that had been dropped from a height, insanely conscious of her ragged breathing and racing heartbeat, not to mention the feel of his potent arousal against her hip. Dear heaven, what had she done?

'That was interesting,' Sergios purred with dark amusement. 'Definitely an ice breaker.'

'Er…you…?' Bee mumbled unevenly, conscious that events had been distinctly one-sided.

'I'll have a cold shower,' Sergios said piously.

Her face burning, Bee was relieved by the get-out clause. She knew it was selfish to be relieved but she was out of her depth and feeling it. She hadn't known, hadn't even guessed that she could reach a climax that way and she was not pleased that he had put her on that path of sexual discovery.

'You're a very passionate woman, *moli mou*,' Sergios intoned as he vaulted out of bed. 'Obviously Townsend wasn't the right guy for you.'

Bee went rigid. 'What do you know about Jon?'

Sergios paused in the doorway of the bathroom and swung back. 'More than you were prepared to tell me,' he admitted unrepentantly. 'I had him checked out.'

'You did...what?' Bee was righting her night-dress and trying to get out of bed at one and the same time, the simultaneous actions resulting in a clumsy manoeuvre that only infuriated her more. 'Why on earth did you do that? I *told* you he was a friend of mine—'

'But he wasn't—he was your ex, which made the little get-together in the bar rather less inno-cent, *moli mou*,' Sergios intoned, studying her furious face with level dark eyes. 'But, as I see it, since you never slept with him he doesn't re-ally count.'

'If you ever touch me again I'll scream.'

'No complaints on that score. I love the way you scream in my arms,' Sergios traded with silky sardonic bite and shut the bathroom door.

Bee knotted her hands into furious fists and contemplated throwing something at that closed door. It would be childish and she was *not* child-ish. But she had let herself down a bucketful by succumbing to his sexual magnetism. A tide of irritation swept through her then. No wonder he had called her a prude. She might feel mortified but they had hardly done anything in terms of sex. She was taking it all far too seriously and it would be much cooler to behave as though nothing worthy of note had happened.

But, without a doubt, Sergios was lethal between the sheets. The minute he got in she should have got out because compared with him she was a total novice and certain to come off worse from any encounter. And why had he checked Jon Townsend out after her single trivial meeting with her former boyfriend? Didn't Sergios trust anybody? Obviously not. How often had he been betrayed to become that suspicious of other human beings? It was a sobering thought and, although he had not been in love with her sister, Zara had agreed to marry him and then let him down. Perhaps had Bee chosen to be more honest with him he might have had more faith in her.

Around that point of self-examination, Bee must have drifted off to sleep because she wakened when Sergios stowed her into a cold bed. 'Er….what…where…*Sergios*?'

'Go back to sleep, Beatriz,' he intoned.

Her eyes fluttered briefly open on a view of the circular main bedroom in the moonlight and she simply turned over and closed her eyes again, too exhausted to protest. She woke alone in the morning, only the indent on the pillow across from hers telling her that she had had company. After a quick shower she put on Bermuda shorts and a sapphire-blue tee for the trip to the beach she had promised the boys. Nectarios was reading a newspaper out on the terrace where Androula brought Beatriz tea and toast.

'Sergios is in the office working,' his grandfather told her helpfully, folding his paper and setting it aside. 'What are you planning to do today?'

'Take the boys to the beach,' Bee confided.

'Beatriz…this is your honeymoon,' the elderly Greek remarked thoughtfully. 'Let the children take a back seat for a while and drag my grandson out of his office.'

Her imagination baulked at the image of getting Sergios to do anything against his will, but she could see that Nectarios was already picking up flaws in their behaviour as a newly married couple. He asked her about her mother and said he was looking forward to meeting her. Having eaten, Bee went off to find Sergios, although after their intimate encounter the night before she would have preferred to avoid him.

Sergios was working on a laptop in a sunlit room while simultaneously talking on the phone. Her troubled gaze locked to his bold bronzed profile. No matter how angry he made her she could never deny that he was drop-dead beautiful to look at any time of day. Finishing the call, he turned his sleek dark head, brilliant eyes welding to her, and her colour fluctuated wildly while her mouth ran dry at the impact of his gaze. 'Beatriz...'

'I'm taking the children to the beach. You

should come with us. Nectarios is surprised that you've already gone back to work.'

'I don't do kids and beaches,' Sergios replied with a suggestive wince at the prospect of such a family outing.

Bee threw back her slim shoulders and spoke her mind, 'Then it's time you learned. Those kids need you…they *need* a father as well as a mother.'

'I don't know how to be a father. I never had one of my own—'

'That doesn't mean you can't do better for your cousin's children,' Bee cut in, immediately dismissing his argument in a manner that made his stubborn jaw line clench. 'Even an occasional father is better than no father at all. My father wasn't interested in me and I've felt that lack all my life.'

Under attack for his views, Sergios had sprung upright. He shrugged a broad shoulder and raked an impatient hand through his hair. His wide sensual mouth had taken on a sardonic curve. 'Beatriz—'

'No, don't you dare try to shut me up because I'm saying things you don't want to hear!' Beatriz shot back at him in annoyance. 'Even if you can only bring yourself to give the kids an hour once a week it would be better than no time at all. One *hour*, Sergios, that's all I'm asking for and then you can forget about them again.'

Sergios studied her grimly. 'I've told you how I feel. I married you so that you could take care of them.'

'Was that our "deal"?' Bee queried in a tone of scorn. 'I was just wondering. As you've already changed the terms on my side of the fence, why do you have to be so inflexible when it comes to your own?'

Sergios raised a brow. 'If I come to the beach will you share a room without further argument?'

Bee sighed in frustration. 'Relationships don't work like deals.'

'Don't they? Are you saying that you don't believe in give and take?'

'Of course, I do but I don't want to give or take sex like it's some sort of service or currency,' Bee told him with vehement distaste.

'Sex and money make the world go round,' Sergios jibed.

'I'm better than that—I'm worth more than that and so should you be. We're not animals or sex workers.'

Her love of frankness was peppered with an unexpected penchant for drama that amused him and he marvelled that he could ever have considered her plain or willing to please. With those vivid green eyes, that perfect skin and ripe pink mouth she was the very striking image of natural beauty. He could still barely believe that she was the only woman he had ever met to have refused him. While rejection might gall him her unattainability was a huge turn-on for him as well and when she had admitted she was a virgin he had understood her reluctance a great deal better and valued her all the more.

Recognising the tension in the atmosphere, Bee stiffened. He gave a look, just a look from his smouldering dark golden eyes and her nipples tightened, her tummy flipped and moist heat surged between her thighs. Colouring, she hastily fixed her eyes elsewhere, outraged that she could have so little control over her own body.

'All right,' she said abruptly, spinning back to deal him a withering look that almost made him laugh. 'If you do the hour a week with the children without complaining, I won't argue about sharing a room any more. Over breakfast I realised that your grandfather doesn't miss a trick and he is suspicious.'

'I said a long time ago that I would never marry again and he knows me well. Naturally he's sceptical about our marriage.'

'See you down at the beach,' Bee responded a touch sourly, for she was not pleased that she had had to give way on the bedroom issue.

Unfortunately her previous attempts to persuade Sergio to get involved with his cousin's children had proved fruitless and if there was anything she could do to improve that situation she felt she had to make the most of the opportunity.

Karen was on duty and the children were already dressed in their swimming togs while a beach bag packed with toys and drinks awaited her. Paris led the way down through the shady belt of pine forest to the crisp white sand. They were peering into a rock pool when Sergios arrived. Wearing denim cut-offs with an unbuttoned shirt and displaying a flat and corrugated muscular six-pack that took Bee's breath away, Sergios strode across the sand to join them. The boys made a beeline for him, touchingly eager for his attention. Paris chattered about boy things like dead crabs, sharks and fishing while Bee held Milo and Eleni's hands to prevent them from crowding Sergios. She paddled with the toddlers in the whispering surf to amuse them.

When Paris began building a sandcastle, Milo and Eleni ran back to join their brother.

Sergios walked across to Bee.

'Thirty-two minutes and counting,' she warned him in case he was thinking of cutting his agreed hour short.

An appreciative grin slashed his handsome mouth. 'I haven't got a stopwatch on the time.'

'What happened to your father?' she asked in a rush before she could lose her nerve.

As he looked out to sea his eyes narrowed. 'He died at the age of twenty-two trying to qualify as a racing driver.'

'You never knew him?'

'No, but even if Petros had lived he wouldn't have taken anything to do with me.' Sergios volunteered that opinion with telling derision. 'My mother, Ariana, was a teenage reception-ist he knocked up on one of the rare days that he showed up to work for Nectarios.'

'Did your mother ever tell him about you?' Bee prompted.

'He refused her calls and got her sacked when she tried to see him. She didn't know she had any rights and she had no family to back her up. Petros had no interest in being a father.'

'It must have been very tough for so young a girl to get by as a single parent.'

'She developed diabetes while she was pregnant. Her health was never good after my birth. I stole to keep us,' he admitted succinctly. 'By the age of fourteen I was a veteran car thief.'

'From that to...*this*...' Her spread hands encompassed the big opulent house beyond the forest and the island owned by his grandfather. 'Must have been a huge step for you.'

'Nectarios was very patient. It must've been even harder for him. I was poorly educated, bitter about my mother's death and as feral as an animal when he first employed me. But he never gave up on me.'

'You were probably a more worthwhile investment of his time than the father you never met,' Bee offered.

Sergios surveyed her steadily, his stunning gaze reflecting the sunlight as he slowly shook his arrogant head in apparent wonderment at that view. 'Only you would think the best of me after what I've just told you about my juvenile crime record, *yineka mou*.'

Bee coloured, noticed that Milo was approaching the sea with a bucket and sped off to watch over the little boy. But it was Sergios who stepped from behind her and scooped up Milo as he teetered uncertainly ankle deep in the surging water, swinging the child up in the air so that he laughed uproariously before depositing him and, thanks to Bee's efforts, a filled bucket of water back beside the sandcastle.

Eleni her silent companion, Bee spread the rug and Sergios threw himself down beside her. As she knelt he closed a hand into her chestnut hair and lifted her head, searching her oval face with brooding eyes. She gazed back at him with a bemused frown. 'What do you want from me?' she questioned in frustration.

'Right now?' Sergios released a roughened laugh that danced along her taut spine like trailing fingertips. 'Anything you'll give me. Haven't you worked that out yet?'

He crushed her mouth under his, tasting her with an earthy eroticism that fired up every skin cell in her quivering body. Hunger rampaged through her like a fire burning out of control and the strength of that hunger scared her so much that she thrust him back from her, her attention shooting past him to check that the children were still all right. Paris had been watching them kiss and he turned away, embarrassed by the display but no more so than Bee was. Sergio rested back on an elbow, one raised thigh doing little to conceal the bold outline of his arousal below the denim. Suddenly as hot as though she were roasting in the fires of hell, Bee dragged her gaze from him and watched the children instead.

'You're trying to use me because I'm the only

woman available to you right now,' she con-
demned half under her breath.

Sergios ran a fingertip down her arm and she
turned her head reluctantly to collide with his
glittering dark eyes. 'Do I really strike you as
that desperate?'

Her full mouth compressed. 'I didn't say *desperate.*'

'I can leave the island any time I like to scratch
an itch.'

'Not if you want to convince your grandfather
that you're a happily married man.'

'I could easily manufacture a business crisis
that demanded my presence,' Sergios countered
lazily. 'You have a remarkably low opinion of
your own attraction.'

'Merely a realistic one. Men have never beaten
a path to my door,' Bee admitted without concern. 'Jon was special for a while but once he
realised that my mother and I were a package
he backed off.'

'And married a wealthy judge's daughter. He's

ambitious, not a guy with a bleeding heart,' Sergios commented, letting her know how much he knew and making her body tense with resentment over the professional snooping that had delivered such facts. 'Doesn't it strike you as odd that he should now be approaching you as the representative of a children's charity?'

Bee ignored the hint that Jon was an opportunist because she did not intend to adopt Sergios's cynicism as her yardstick when it came to judging people's motives. 'No. As your wife I could be of real use to the charity.'

'And as my ex-wife you could be of even more use to Jon,' Sergios completed with sardonic bite. 'Be careful. You could be his passport to another world.'

'I'm not stupid.'

'Not stupid, but you are naive and trusting.' He studied her with amusement. 'After all, you ignored all the warnings and married me.'

'If you treat me with respect I will treat you

the same,' Bee swore. 'I don't lie or cheat and I don't like being manipulated.'

Sergios laughed out loud. 'And I'm a very manipulative guy.'

'I know,' Bee said gravely. 'But now you've got me in the same bed that's as far as it goes.'

His curling black lashes semi-concealed his stunning eyes. 'That would be such a waste, Beatriz. We have the opportunity, the chemistry.'

'With all due respect, Sergios,' Beatriz murmured sweetly, cutting in, 'that's baloney. You only want to bed me because you believe it'll make us seem more intimate and therefore more of a couple for your grandfather's benefit. And while I think he's a lovely old man, I don't want to go that far to please.'

'I can make you want me,' Sergios reminded her smooth as silk but it was the tough guy talking, his dark eyes hard as ebony, his strong bone structure taut with controlled aggression.

'But only in the line of temporary insanity. It

doesn't last,' Bee traded, longing for the smile and the laughter that had been there only minutes earlier and suddenly recognising another danger.

It would be so easy to fall for this man she had married, she grasped with a sudden stab of apprehension. He wasn't just gorgeous to look at, he was an intensely charismatic man. Unfortunately he had very few scruples. If she let him, he would use her and discard her again without thought or regret. Where would she be then? Hopelessly in love with a guy who didn't love her back and who betrayed her with other women? She suppressed a shudder at that daunting image, and her heart, which he had made beat a little faster, steadied again.

A ball suddenly thumped into her side and the breath she was holding in escaped in a startled huff. Instantly Sergios was vaulting upright and telling Paris off, but Bee was relieved by the interruption and quick to intervene. She threw the ball back to the boys, retrieved Eleni from the shells she was collecting and joined in their game.

Unappreciative of the fact that she was using the children as a convenient shield, Sergios was equally challenged by the idea that she could so easily discard the idea of becoming a proper wife. He thought of the countless women who had gone to extraordinary lengths to get him to the altar and failed and then he looked at Beatriz, distinctly unimpressed by what he had to offer in bed or out of it. He was out of his element with a woman who put a value on things without a price. He didn't do feelings, fidelity or…virgins. Basically he operated on the belief that women were all the same, money greased the wheels of his affairs and he had few preferences. That ideology had carried him along a safe smooth path after his first marriage right up to the present day. But nothing in that credo fitted Beatriz Blake. In her own quiet way she was a total maverick.

A manservant came down to the beach to tell

Sergios about an important call. He departed and Bee tried not to care that he had gone, leaving behind a space that absolutely nothing else could fill. It was impossible to be unaware of a personality and a temperament as larger than life as Sergios Demonides. When Bee trekked up from the beach late afternoon with two tired little boys and an equally tired and cross little girl, she was damp and sandy and pink from the sun in spite of her high factor sun cream.

Having fed Eleni and spent some time cuddling the little girl while chatting with the nannies about the child's upcoming surgery that would hopefully improve her hearing, Bee left the nursery and went for a shower before changing for dinner. In the bedroom she found several boxes of exclusive designer nightwear on the bed in her size, items fashioned to show off the female body for a man's benefit and not at all the sort of thing that Bee wore for comfort and cosiness. She could barely believe Sergios's nerve in ordering such items for her but it was certainly beginning to sink in on her that he was a very determined man. When she returned to the bedroom, clad in her own light robe, Sergios was there and she stiffened, unaccustomed to the lack of privacy entailed in sharing a bedroom. Engaged in tying the sash on the robe to prevent it from falling open, she hovered uncomfortably.

'Did you order those nightgowns for me?' she pressed.

'Yes. Why not?'

'They're not the sort of thing I would wear.'

Sergios shrugged off the assurance. 'My grandfather has decided to return to his home.'

'I thought it was uninhabitable.'

'Two rooms are but it's a substantial property. I think that was an excuse to allow him to check us out,' Sergios confided wryly. 'He's taking the children and their nannies back with him.'

Her head flew up, green eyes wide with surprise and bewilderment 'Why on earth would he take the kids with him?'

'Because it's a rare newly married couple

who want three children around on their honeymoon,' Sergios drawled, his face impassive. 'Don't make a fuss about this. It's a well-meant offer and he is their grandfather—'

'Yes, I know he is *but*—'

'Objecting isn't an option,' Sergios sliced in with sudden impatience. 'It's a done deal and it would look strange if we turned him down.'

Bee could not hide her consternation at the arrangement that had been agreed behind her back. He had married her to act as a mother to those children but it seemed that she was not entitled to the rights or feelings of a mother if they conflicted with his wishes. 'Yes, but the children are just getting used to me. It's unsettling for them to be passed around like that.'

'You can go over and see them every day if you like.' His beautiful wilful mouth took on a sardonic slant. 'First and foremost you are my wife, Beatriz. Start acting like one.'

Bee reddened as though she had been disci-

plined for wrongdoing, her temper flaring inside
her. 'Is that an order, sir?'

'*Ne*...yes, it is,' Sergios confirmed without hesitation or any hint of amusement. 'Let's keep it
simple. I tell you what I want, you do it.'

Those candid words still echoing in her ears,
Bee vanished back into her bathroom to do her
make-up. Being ordered around when she was
naked below a wrap didn't feel right or comfortable. But then she never had liked being told
what to do. In addition she was very angry with
him. He had encouraged her to act like a mother,
only to snatch the privilege back again when it
no longer suited him. *Act like a wife?* If she did
that he wouldn't like it at all...for a wife would
make demands.

CHAPTER EIGHT

CLEARLY in no mood to make the effort required to convince the staff that he was an attentive new husband, Sergios did not join Bee at the dinner table until she was halfway through her meal and the silence while they ate together screamed in her ears like chalk scraping down a blackboard.

'I didn't think you'd be the type to sulk.'

'Am I allowed to shout at you, sir?'

'Enough already with the sir,' Sergios advised impatiently.

Her appetite dying, Bee pushed her plate away.

'I'll take you out sailing tomorrow morning,' he announced with the air of a man expecting a round of applause for his thoughtfulness.

'Lucky me,' Bee droned in a long-suffering voice.

'Later this week, I'll take you over to Corfu to shop.'

'I hate shopping—do we have to?'

The silence moved in again.

'When I married you I believed you were a reasonable, rational woman,' Sergios volunteered curtly over the dessert course.

'I believed you when you said you wanted a platonic marriage,' Bee confided. 'Just goes to show how wrong you can be about someone.'

'Do you think your own mother will be fooled by the way we're behaving into believing that this is a happy marriage?'

Hit on her weakest flank by that question, Bee paled.

'Don't wait up for me,' Sergios told her as he too pushed away his plate, the food barely touched. 'Last month I took over my grandfather's seat on the island council and it meets tonight. I'll stay for a drink afterwards.'

Frustrated by his departure when nothing between them had been resolved, Bee phoned her mother and lied through her teeth about how very happy she was. She then tried very hard to settle down with a book but her nerves continued to zing about like jumping beans and at well after ten that evening she decided that, as she wasn't the slightest bit tired, vigorous exercise might at least dispel her tension. At her request a pole had been fitted in the house gym and she had politely ignored Sergios's mocking enquiry as to what she intended to do with it. Like all too many people Sergios evidently assumed that pole dancing was a lewd activity best reserved for exotic dancers in sleazy clubs. Clad in stretchy shorts and a crop top, Bee did her warm-up exercises to loosen up before putting on her music.

Sergios was resolutely counting his blessings as he drove back along the single-track road to his home. Unhappily a couple of drinks and all the jokes with his colleagues on the island council that had recognised his status as a newly married man hadn't taken the edge off his mood. In fact he was engaged in reminding himself that being married was by its very nature tough. Learning how to live with another person was difficult. Nobody knew that better than him, which was why he had cherished his freedom for so long. Indeed the lesson of having once lost his freedom was engraved on his soul in scorching letters, for Sergios never forgot or forgave his own mistakes. He knew he should be grateful that Beatriz was so very attached to children who were not her own. She was a good woman with a warm heart and strong moral values. He knew he should be appreciative of the fact that if he came home unexpectedly he was highly unlikely to walk into a wild party…

When he walked into the lounge, however, he was vaguely irritated to find that Beatriz had not waited up for him, thereby demonstrating her concern for his state of mind and their marriage. He was hugely taken aback to recognise that he actually *wanted* her to do wifely things of that nature. That she had just taken herself off to bed was definitely not a compliment. It was hardly surprising, he acknowledged in sudden exasperation, that Beatriz should be confused about what he wanted from her when he no longer knew himself.

The bedroom, though, was also empty and Androula, plump and disapproving in her dressing gown, answered his call and informed him that Beatriz was in the gym. Having dispensed with his tie and his jacket, Sergios followed the sound of the music but what he saw when he glanced through the glass doors of the gymnasium brought him to a sudden stunned halt.

Beatriz was hanging upside down on a pole. By the time he got through the door she was doing a handstand and swirling round the pole, legs splaying in a distinctly graphic movement that he would not have liked her to do in public. He was astonished by how fit she was as she went through an acrobatic series of moves. That stirring display was so unexpected from such a quiet conservative woman that it made it seem all the more exciting and illicit. He watched her kick, toes pointed, slender muscles flexing in a shapely leg and in a rounded, deliciously plump derriere. Around that point he decided simply to enjoy the show. As she undulated sexily against the pole, full breasts thrust out, hips shifting as though on wires, he was hard as a rock and her sinuous roll on the floor at the foot of the pole was frankly overkill.

'Beatriz?' Sergios husked.

In consternation at the sound of his voice, Bee flipped straight back upright, wondering anxiously for how long she had had an audience. Brilliant dark eyes welded to her, Sergios was by the door, tall, darkly handsome and overwhelmingly masculine. Lifting her towel to dry the perspiration from her face, she paused only to switch off the music.

'When did you get back?'

'Ten minutes ago. How long have you been doing that for?'

'About three years,' she answered a little breathlessly, drawing level with him. 'It was more fun than the other exercise classes.'

His gaze smouldering, he bent his dark head and crushed her parted lips hotly beneath his, ravishing her mouth with the staggering impact of a long, drugging kiss. A shiver of sensual shock ran through her as his arms came round her and she felt the hard urgency of his erection against her stomach.

'*Se thelo*…I want you,' he breathed raggedly. 'Let's make this a real marriage.'

Taken aback by that proposition, Bee tried to step back but Sergios had a strong arm braced to her spine as he walked her down the corridor. 'We need to think about this,' she reasoned, struggling to emerge from that potent kiss, which had made her head swim.

'No, I believe in gut instinct. We've been thinking far too much about things,' Sergios fired back with strong masculine conviction. 'You're not supposed to agonise over everything you do in life and look for all the pitfalls, Beatriz. Some things just happen naturally.'

He thrust open their bedroom door, whirled her round and devoured her mouth hungrily beneath his again, his tongue darting into the tender interior of her mouth, setting up a chain reaction of high voltage response inside her. This, she registered, was the sort of thing he believed should happen naturally, but from Bee's point of view there was nothing natural about the fact that she was trembling and unable to think straight. The force of his passion knocked her off balance while a raging fire leapt up inside her to answer it. Locked together, they stumbled across the room and down on the bed, his hands smoothing over her Lycra-clad curves with an appreciative sound deep in his throat.

'I don't want anyone else seeing you dance like that,' Sergios spelt out. 'It's too sexy—'

'But that's how I keep fit—it's only exercise.'

'It's incredibly erotic,' Sergios contradicted, wrenching off the shorts with impatient hands.

'We really ought to be discussing this,' she told him anxiously.

A heart-breaking smile slashed his beautiful mouth. 'I don't want to talk about it…we've talked it to death.'

That smile made her stretch up to kiss him again, her fingertips smoothing over a hard cheekbone and delving into his silky black hair with a licence she had never allowed herself before. If they made love he would be hers as no other man had ever been and she wanted that with every fibre of her being and a strength of longing she had not known she was capable of feeling. Unbuttoning his shirt, she pulled it off his shoulders and he cast it off, laughing at her impatience. Standing up, he dispensed with the rest of his clothing at efficient speed and a tingling hum of arousal thrummed through her as she looked at his powerfully aroused body. He was ready for her.

Sergios pulled her up and peeled her free of the crop top and the sports bra she wore beneath. With a groan of sensual satisfaction he cupped the creamy swell of her breasts and licked and stroked the swollen pink tips until she shivered. 'Perfect,' he husked.

Liquid heat pooled between her legs as he located the damp stretch of fabric between her legs and eased a finger beneath it to trace her delicate centre. She twisted beneath his touch and lifted her hips as he took off her knickers. He kissed a trail down over her writhing length until he found the most truly sensitive spot of all. As he lingered there to subject her to the erotic torment of his skilled mouth and hand, she had to fight her innate shyness with all her might.

Had she been in control it would have been wrenched from her by the power of her response. As it was, she was free to abandon herself to sensation and she did, her head moving restively back and forth on the pillow, shallow gasps escaping her throat as her hips rose and fell on the bed. She was at the very height of excitement before he came over her and entered her in one effortless stroke. Even so there was still a stark moment of pain and she cried out as he completed his possession, driving home to the very core of her. The discomfort swiftly ebbed even as his invasive hard male heat awakened and stimulated her need again.

'Sorry,' he sighed with intense male pleasure. 'I was as gentle as I could be.'

'You're forgiven,' she murmured, very much preoccupied as she arched her spine and lifted her hips to accept more of him, desire driving her to obey her own needs.

'You're so tight,' he breathed with earthy satisfaction, rising up on his elbows and withdrawing only to thrust back deeper into her receptive body in a movement that was almost unbearably exhilarating.

Her breath catching in her throat, her heart thundering with growing fervour she shut her eyes, revelling in the feel of him inside her. She writhed beneath him as he drove deeper with every compelling thrust and his fluid rhythm increased, plunging her into an intoxicating world of erotic and timeless delight. The excitement took over until all she was aware of was him and the hot, sweet pleasure gathering stormily at the heart of her. She reached an explosive climax and plunged over the edge into ecstasy, gasping and writhing in voluptuous abandon.

Shuddering over her, Sergios cried out with uninhibited fulfilment gripped by the longest, hottest climax of his life. As her arms came round him to hold him he pulled back, however, releasing her from his weight. He threw himself back against the pillows next to her, enforcing a separation she was not prepared for at that most intimate of moments.

'That was unbelievably good, *yineka mou*,' Sergios savoured, breathing in a lungful of much-needed air. 'Thank you.'

Thank you? Bee blinked in bewilderment at that polite salutation and reached for his hand, closing her fingers round his and turning over to snuggle into his big powerful body, spreading her fingers across a stretch of his warm muscular torso. He stiffened at the contact.

'I don't do the cuddling thing, *glikia mou*.'

'You're not too old to learn,' Bee told him dreamily, dazed by what they had just shared but also happy at the greater closeness she sensed between them. 'You just persuaded me to do something spontaneous and that's not usually my style.'

Recognising the truth that Beatriz almost always had a smart answer for everything, Sergios made no comment. Instead he settled curious dark golden eyes on her flushed face. 'I hurt you. Are you sore?'

Bee gave a little experimental shift of her hips and winced. 'A little.'

'Shame,' he pronounced with regret, a sensual curve to his firm mouth. 'Right now, I would love to do it all over again but I'll wait until tomorrow.'

'You didn't use a condom,' Bee remarked, her surprise at that oversight patent.

'I'm clean. I have regular health checks. Hopefully we'll get away with it this once on the contraception front. I don't keep condoms here,' he admitted bluntly. 'I don't bring women to my home. I never have done.'

There were so many questions brimming on her lips but she wouldn't let herself ask them. She liked the fact that the room and bed had not been used by other women. But she did want to know about his first wife—there was not even a photo of Krista on display in the house. Then there was his mistress, and where Bee and Sergios were to go from here, but that thorny question would be a case of too much too soon for a guy who had fought so hard to retain his freedom and keep his secrets. He wasn't going to change overnight, she told herself ruefully.

Let's make this a real marriage, he had said in the gym. Had he truly meant it? Or had a desire for sex momentarily clouded his judgement when her dancing awakened his libido? Could he simply have told her what he thought she wanted to hear? Uneasy at that suspicion, Bee tensed but refused to lower herself to the level of asking him if he was genuinely committed to their marriage. Expressing doubt, after all, might just as easily encourage what she most feared to come about.

'We'll put a pole up in the bedroom so that you can exercise in here where nobody else can see you,' Sergios informed her lazily.

Bee could not believe her ears. His persistence on that subject was a revelation. He had not been joking in the gym when he said he didn't want anyone else to see her dancing. 'I didn't think you would be such a prude.'

'You're my wife,' Sergios reminded her, but his face was taut, as if giving her that label pained him.

Looking up into those darkly handsome features, Bee could already see the wheels of intellect turning as he questioned their new intimacy.

How did he really feel about that? She lowered her lashes, refusing to agonise over something she had no control over. Living with Sergios would be a roller-coaster ride and as he did not suffer anything in silence she had no doubt that she would soon know exactly how he felt.

'I'll be late back tonight,' Sergios told her, sinking down on the side of the bed. He hesitated for a split second before he grasped the hand that she had instinctively extended to stop him leaving the room.

Still half asleep, for it was very early, Bee studied him drowsily, noting the brooding tension etched into his face while loving the warmth of his hand in hers and the golden intensity of his gaze. 'Why?'

'It's the anniversary of Krista's death today. I usually attend a memorial service with her parents and dine with them afterwards,' Sergios explained, his intonation cool and unemotional.

Taken aback, for although they had been married for six weeks he still never ever mentioned his first wife, Bee nodded and belatedly noticed the sombre black suit that he wore.

'It's an annual event,' he said with an uneasy shrug. 'Not something I look forward to.'

She bit back the comment that some people regarded a memorial service as an opportunity to celebrate the life of the departed. 'Would you like me to go with you?' she asked uncertainly.

'That's a generous offer but I don't think Krista's parents would appreciate it. She was their only child. I get the impression that they don't want to be reminded that my life has moved on,' Sergios commented, compressing his handsome mouth with the stubborn self-discipline that was so much a part of his character.

Her ignorance of what he was feeling troubled Bee for the rest of the day. But then she was madly, hopelessly in love with Sergios and prone to worrying about what was on his mind. Although the sexual chemistry they shared was indisputably fantastic, that wasn't what had awakened more tender feelings in her heart. It was while Bee was busily working out what made Sergios tick that she had fallen head over heels in love with him.

When he was away on business she felt as though she were only half alive. Deprived of his powerful and often unsettling charismatic presence, she would watch her phone like a lovesick adolescent desperate for his call, count the hours until he came home and then lavish attention on him in bed until he purred like a big jungle cat. He was in her heart as though he had always been there, strong and stubborn and infuriatingly unpredictable.

In learning to love him she had also recognised his vulnerabilities. He was unsure how to behave with the children because his mother's ill health had deprived him of a carefree childhood. Although Bee had come from a similar background the burden of caring had been lightened in her case by her mother's deep affection. Sergios's mother, however, had been very young and immature and might possibly have resented the adverse impact of a child on her life and health. For whatever reasons, Sergios had not received the love and support he had needed to thrive during his formative years.

Within days of being removed to their grand-father's home on the other side of the bay Paris, Milo and Eleni had made it clear how much they were missing Bee and Sergios had swiftly ac-cepted the inevitable and agreed to their return. With Bee's support since then Sergios had grad-ually spent more time with his cousin's kids, getting to know them so that he no longer froze when Milo hurled himself at him or looked un-easily away when Eleni opened her arms to him. Bridges were being built. Paris turned to Sergios for advice, Milo brought his ball and Eleni smiled at him when he risked getting close. Sergios was slowly learning how to accept af-fection and how to respond to it.

Bee had been relieved when she received the proof that their unprotected lovemaking on the first night they had spent together had not led to her conceiving a child. In her opinion an unplanned pregnancy would have been a disaster for their marriage. Sergios was very much a man who needed to make the decision that he wanted to be a father for himself. Yet when she had told him that he need not worry on that score, he had shrugged.

'I wasn't worrying about that,' he had insisted. 'If you had conceived we would have coped.'

But Bee would not have been happy while he merely 'coped'. She only wanted to have a baby with a man who was actively *keen* for her to have his baby. She did not want Sergios to make the best of an accidental conception or to offer her the option of a pregnancy because she was broody: she wanted him to make a choice that he wanted a child with her, a child of his own.

The weeks they had shared on the island had not been only about the children. Bee had stopped fretting about the future and had lived for the moment and Sergios had made many of those moments surprisingly special. He had proudly given her a tour of the wheel-chair-friendly cottage in the grounds where her mother was to live. A carer whom Emilia would choose for herself from a list that had already been drawn up would come in every day to help her cope. Bee could hardly wait to see the older woman's face when she enjoyed her first cup of tea on the sunny terrace with its beautiful view of the bay.

Sergios had also flown Bee to Corfu for a week. The busy streets lined with elegant Italianate buildings, sophisticated shops and art studios had delighted her and one afternoon when Sergios had briefly lost her in the crowds he had anchored his hand to hers and kept it there for the rest of the day. He had bought her a beautiful silver icon she admired and they had had drinks on The Liston, an arcaded building modelled on the Rue de Rivoli in Paris. By the time they had returned to their designer hotel she was giggly and tipsy and he had made passionate love to her until dawn when she fell asleep in his arms. Opening her eyes again on his handsome features in profile as he worked at his laptop, getting some work out of the way before the day began, she had seen into her own heart and had known in the magic of that moment that she loved him. Loved him the way she had never thought she would ever love any man, with tenderness and appreciation of both his flaws and his strengths.

They had enjoyed numerous trips out and about on Orestos. He had shown her all over the island, had taken her swimming and sailing and snorkelling, letting the children join in whenever possible. He had enjoyed the fact that she was energetic enough to share the more physical pursuits with him. She also now knew that he was very competitive when it came to building sandcastles or fishing and that he was crazy about ice cream. He also loved it when she and the children were there to greet him when he came home from a trip. There was an abyss of loneliness deep inside Sergios that she longed to assuage.

With such uneasy thoughts dominating her mind about Krista's memorial service and what those memories might mean to her husband, Bee could not settle that afternoon. She received another text from Jon Townsend, who had stayed in surprisingly regular contact with her since her arrival in Greece, and suppressed a sigh. Her ex-boyfriend had sent her reams of information about the charity he was involved with and was keen to set up a meeting with her during her approaching visit to the UK.

On such a beautiful day it had seemed a good idea to collect Milo from his playgroup in town on foot rather than drive there as she usually did. The summer heat, however, was intense and by the time she picked up Milo Bee was questioning the wisdom of having trudged all the way along the coast road, particularly when she had no alternative other than to walk back again. Milo, in comparison, hopped, jumped and skipped along by her side with the unvarnished energy that was his trademark.

She was walking through the town square with Eleni dozing below a parasol in her pushchair when Nectarios waved at them from a table outside the taverna. He wore his faded peaked cap, and only a local would have recognised him as the powerful business tycoon that he still was even in semi-retirement. She guessed by his clothing that he had been out sailing in the small yacht he kept at the harbour and she crossed to that side of the street.

'What are you doing here on foot?' he asked with a frown, spinning out a chair for her and snapping his fingers for the proprietor's attention.

'Milo was at his playgroup. It didn't seem quite so warm when I left the house.'

'My lift will be here in ten minutes. You can all ride back with me.' The old man ordered drinks for Bee and the children while calmly allowing Milo to clamber onto his lap and steal his cap to try it on and then treat it like a frisbee.

While they sat there enjoying the welcome shade of the plane tree beside the terrace various passers-by came over to chat to Nectarios. Bee was daily picking up more Greek words and she understood odd snatches of the conversations about fishing trips, weddings and christenings. Tomorrow she was returning to London, where Eleni would have surgery on her ears, and when they came back to the island her mother would be travelling with her. She was helping Eleni with her feeding cup when she became aware of a flutter of whispers around her. Glancing up, Bee noticed the statuesque blonde walking through the square. She wore a simple figure-hugging white dress and she had that swaying walk and brash confidence that men almost always seemed to find irresistible. Certainly every man in the vicinity was staring in admiration.

'Who's that?' she asked the man beside her,

who had faltered into a sudden silence. 'Is she a tourist?'

The woman looked directly at them with big brown eyes and a sultry smile on her red-tinted lips, her attention lingering with perceptible curiosity on Bee.

Nectarios gave the blonde a faint nod of acknowledgement. 'That's Melita Thiarkis.'

That familiar first name struck Bee like a slap but she would have thought nothing of it if Nectarios had not looked distinctly ill at ease.

'And she's…*who*?' she pressed, hating herself for her persistence in the face of his discomfiture.

'A fashion designer in Athens, but she was born on the island and maintains a property here.'

That fast Bee's stomach threatened to heave and she struggled to control her nausea with perspiration beading her brow and her skin turning unpleasantly clammy. The blonde *had* to be Sergios's mistress, Melita. There could not be such a coincidence. Indeed Nectarios's embarrassment at her appearance had confirmed the fact. But Bee was in shock at the news that Melita was actually staying on the island. That possibility had not even occurred to her and she had naively assumed that Orestos offered Sergios no opportunity to stray. But how many evenings had he left her alone for several hours while he attended island council meetings? Or to visit his grandfather's home? Lately there had been several such occasions and she had thought nothing of them at the time. Had she been ridiculously naive?

'May I offer you some advice?' Nectarios enquired as the four-wheel drive that had picked them up raised a trail of dust on the winding, little-used road back to the big white house with the tower on the headland.

Bee shot him a glance from troubled eyes. 'Of course.'

'Don't put pressure on my grandson. Give him the time to recognise what you have together.

His first marriage was very unhappy and it left deep scars.'

The old man was the product of another generation in which men and women were not equal and women expected and even excused male infidelity. Bee had no such guiding principle to fall back on and she could not excuse what she could not live with. And she knew that she would never be able to live in silence with the suspicion that Sergios might have laid lustful hands on another woman while he was sharing a bed with Bee.

Oh, how the mighty had fallen, Bee conceded wretchedly. Now she had to face up to the reality that she had allowed Sergios to run their marriage *his* way rather than hers. They had not renegotiated the terms of their original marriage plan. There had been no earnest discussions, no agreements and no promises made on either side. For almost two months they had coasted along without the rules and boundaries that she had feared might make Sergios feel trapped. Take things slowly, Bee had thought in her innocence, eager to pin her husband down, but too sensible not to foresee the probable risks of demanding too much from him upfront.

Now she was paying the price of not frankly telling him that he could not have her *and* a mistress. Strange how she had no doubt that he would angle for that option if he thought he could get away with it. Bee was well aware of how ruthless Sergios could be. In any confrontation he was hardwired to seek the best outcome that he could. Sometimes he manoeuvred people into doing what he wanted purely as a means of amusement. She had stood on the sidelines of his life watching him, learning how he operated and monitoring her own behaviour accordingly. Although she loved him she didn't tell him that and she certainly didn't cling to him or cuddle him or flatter him or do or say any of the things that would have given her true feelings away. She had decided that she was happy to give him time to come to terms with their new relationship…as long as he was faithful.

The thought that he might not have been, that he might already have betrayed her trust in another woman's arms, threatened to tear Bee apart. In the circumstances he might even try to persuade her that he had assumed that their original agreement that he could have other women still held good. After all, Sergios thought fast on his feet and was, she reckoned ruefully, liable to fight dirty if she pushed him hard enough.

But Melita Thiarkis was a different kettle of fish. She was an islander, a local born and bred on Orestos, so Sergios had probably known her for a very long time. A fashion designer as well—no wonder he was so hung up on even his wife being stylish. There would be ties between Melita and Sergios stronger than Bee had ever wanted to consider. Melita was strikingly attractive rather than beautiful but very much the hot, sexy type likely to appeal to Sergios's high-voltage libido. The blonde was also confident of her place in Sergios's life, Bee recognised worriedly, recalling the way the other woman had looked her over without a shade of discomfort or concern. Melita, Bee reflected wretchedly, did not seem the slightest bit threatened by the fact that Sergios had recently got married. And what did that highly visible confidence signify? Had Sergios slept with his mistress since he had become Bee's husband?

As for the confirmation from Nectarios that Sergios's first marriage had been unhappy, Bee had long since worked that out for herself. The fact that there were no photos of Krista and her name was never mentioned had always suggested that that had been anything but a happy marriage. But Sergios, even though given every opportunity to do so, had still not chosen to confide that truth in Bee.

On the other hand, Bee reminded herself doggedly, she *had* been really happy and contented until she laid eyes on Melita Thiarkis and realised that temptation lived less than a mile from their door. Sergios, after all, had been remarkably attentive since they had first made love, but how could Bee possibly know what he got from his relationship with Melita? That he had insisted Melita was a non-negotiable feature of his life even *before* their marriage suggested the blonde had very good reason to be confident.

He did have a thing for blondes even though he wouldn't admit it, Bee thought bitterly as she peered at her dark brown locks in the bedroom mirror and tried to imagine herself transformed into a blonde. It would be sad to dye her hair just for his benefit, wouldn't it? Just at that moment of pain and stark fear she discovered that she didn't care if it was sad or not and she decided that she might well return from London with a mane of pretty blonde hair.

CHAPTER NINE

'I THOUGHT you would be in bed,' Sergio admitted when he landed in a helicopter after eleven that evening and strolled into the house. His tie was loosened and he was unshaven, his stunning eyes shadowed with tiredness. His sense of relief at being home again was intense and it startled him. 'It's been a long day and we have an early flight to London tomorrow morning.'

Bee glanced at him in surprise. 'You're coming with us?'

'Eleni's having surgery,' he reminded her with a frown. 'Of course I'm coming. Didn't you realise that?'

'No, I didn't.'

Delighted by his readiness to be supportive, Bee resisted the urge to immediately dredge up

Melita's presence on the island. After all, if the blonde had a home and relatives on Orestos, she had a perfect right to visit and it might have nothing to do with Sergios. Was that simply wishful thinking? Bee asked herself as she put together a light supper in the big professional kitchen. She saw no need to disturb the staff so late when she was perfectly capable of feeding Sergios with her own fair hands.

He came out of his bathroom with a towel wrapped round his hips and sat down at the small table she had set up for his use. With his black hair flopping damply above his face and clean shaven, he looked less weary.

'Was it a difficult day?' Bee prompted uncertainly.

'It's always difficult.' Sergios grimaced and suddenly shrugged, acknowledging that it no longer felt reasonable to continue to keep Beatriz in the dark when it came to the touchy subject of his first marriage. 'Krista's parents remember a young woman I never knew, or maybe the young woman they talk about is the imaginary daughter they would have *liked* to have had—she certainly bears no resemblance to the woman I was married to for three years.'

Bee was confused. 'I don't understand…'

'Krista was a manic depressive and she loathed taking medication, didn't like what the prescribed tablets did to her. I didn't know about that when I married her. To be fair I hardly knew her when I asked her to marry me,' Sergios confided with a harsh edge to his dark deep drawl. 'I was young and stupid.'

'Oh.' Bee was so shattered about what his silence on the subject of his first wife had concealed that she could think of nothing else to say. A manic depressive? That was a serious condition but treatable with the right medical attention and support.

'I fell in love and rushed Krista to the altar, barely able to believe that the girl of my dreams was mine. Unfortunately the dream turned sour for us both,' he volunteered grittily, his face grim. 'As she refused medication there was no treatment that made an appreciable difference to her moods. For most of our marriage she was out of control. She took drugs and threw wild parties before crashing drunk at the wheel of one of my cars. She died instantly.'

'I am so sorry, Sergios,' Bee whispered with rich sympathy, her heart truly hurting for him. 'So very sorry you had to go through that and lose your child into the bargain.'

'The baby wasn't mine. I don't know who fathered the baby she was carrying at the time of her death.' His handsome mouth twisted. 'By then we hadn't shared a bed for a long time.'

'I wish you'd shared this with me sooner.' Bee was still struggling to accept his wounding admission of how much he had loved Krista, for she had convinced herself that Sergios didn't know *how* to love a woman. Now she was finding out different and it hurt her pride.

'I've always felt guilty that Krista died. I should've been able to do more to help her.'

'How could you when she wouldn't accept that her condition needed treatment?' Bee prompted quietly as she got into bed and rested back against the pillows. 'Didn't her parents have any influence over her?'

'She was an adored only child. They were incapable of telling her no and they refused to recognise the gravity of her problems. Ultimately they blamed me for her unhappiness.'

Striding restively about the room, his stunning eyes bleak with distressing memories and his strong jaw line clenched, he finally told her what his life had been like with Krista. When he came home to the apartment he had shared with his late wife in Athens back then he had never known what would greet him there. Violent disputes and upsetting scenes were a daily occurrence, as were his wife's periods of deep depression. Krista had done everything from shopping to partying to excess. On various occasions he had found her in bed with other men and high as a kite on the illegal drugs that she was convinced relieved her condition better than the proper medication. Staff walked out, friends were offended, the apartment was trashed and valuable objects were stolen. For three long years as he struggled to care for his deeply troubled wife Sergios had lived a life totally out of his own control and the love he had started out with had died. Bee finally understood why he had been so determined to have a businesslike marriage, which demanded nothing from him but financial input. He had put everything he had into his first marriage and it had still failed miserably. Krista had betrayed him and hurt him and taught him to avoid getting too deeply attached to anyone.

'Now you know why I never mention her,' Sergios murmured ruefully, sliding into bed beside her. 'I let her down so badly.'

'Krista was ill. You should forgive her and yourself for everything that went wrong,' Bee reasoned. 'You did your best and that's the most that anyone can do.'

Eyes level, Sergios lifted a hand and traced the full curve of her lower lip with a considering fingertip. 'You always say the right thing to make people feel better.'

Insanely conscious of his touch as she was, her heart was galloping and her mouth had run dry. 'Do I?' she asked gruffly.

'When Paris asked you if his mother was in heaven you said yes even though you know she was an atheist, *moli mou*.'

'She still could have made it there in the end,' Bee reasoned without hesitation. 'Paris was worrying about it. I wanted him to have peace of mind.'

'I should've told you about Krista a long time ago but I hate talking about her—it feels wrong.'

'I understand why now and naturally you want to be loyal to her memory.' Melita's name was on the tip of her tongue but she could not bring herself to destroy that moment of closeness with suspicion and potential conflict. That conversation about Krista was quite enough for one evening.

'So sweet, so tactful…' Sergios leant closer, his breath fanning her cheek, and pried her lips apart with the tip of his tongue. With one kiss he could make her ache unbearably for the heat and hardness of his body.

'Someone round here has to be,' she teased, her breath rasping in her throat.

His tongue explored her tender mouth in an erotic foray and her nipples tingled into prominence. Desire slivered through her then, sharp as a blade. He freed her of the silk nightdress, cupping her breasts with firm hands, stroking the prominent pink crests with ravishing skill. She gasped beneath his mouth as he found the heated core of her and he made a sound of deep masculine satisfaction when he discovered how ready she was.

He turned her round and rearranged her, firm hands cupping her hips as he plunged into her velvety depths with irresistible force and potency. He growled with pleasure above her head and pulled her back hard against him as he slowly rotated his hips to engulf her in an exquisite wash of sensation. While he pumped in and out of her he teased her clitoris with expert fingers. A soul-shattering climax gripped Bee as the tightening knot of heat inside her expanded and then exploded like a blazing star. Shaking and sobbing with pleasure, she fell back against him, weak as a kitten and drained of every thought and feeling.

'Go to sleep,' Sergios urged then, both arms still wrapped round her damp, trembling body. 'You'll exhaust yourself fretting about Eleni tomorrow.'

That he should know her so well almost made her laugh but she was too tired to find amusement in anything. Worry about Melita and Eleni and the passion had exhausted her and she fell heavily asleep.

Her first night back in London, Bee spent with her mother, who was both excited and apprehensive about her approaching move to Greece. Eleni was admitted to hospital the next morning. Both a nurse and the surgeon had talked Bee through every step of the entire procedure, which was likely to take less than an hour to complete, but Bee remained as nervous as a cat on hot bricks on Eleni's behalf, particularly because the little girl was too young to be prepared for the discomfort that might follow the surgery.

'We've already discussed all this,' Sergios reminded Bee firmly, very much a rock in the storm of her concern and anxiety. 'There is very little risk attached to this procedure and she will recover quickly from it. It may not improve her hearing but she is falling so far behind with her speech that it is worth a try.'

Cradling Eleni's solid little body in her lap with protective arms, Bee blinked back tears that embarrassed her for she had long since decided that surgery was currently the best treatment available. 'She's just so little and trusting.'

'Like you were when you married me,' Sergios quipped with a rueful grin, startling her with that light-hearted sally. 'You really didn't have a clue what you were signing up for but it hasn't turned out too bad for you, has it?'

'Ask me that in a year's time,' Bee advised, in no mood to stroke his ego.

'What a very begrudging response when I'm trying so hard to be the perfect husband!' he mocked.

Bee looked up at his handsome face and felt her heart leap like a dizzy teenager's. The perfect husband? Since when? And why? She had made no complaints, so it could not be her he was trying to influence. Most probably he was trying to please his grandfather, who was openly keen to see his only surviving grandson settling down with a family. But she didn't want Sergios putting on an act purely to impress Nectarios. Anything of that nature was almost certain to make Sergios feel deprived of free choice and she did not want their marriage to feel like an albatross hanging round his neck.

Bee accompanied Eleni to the very doors of the operating theatre and then waited outside with Sergios. He had taken the whole day off, which really surprised her. It was true that he stepped out several times to make and receive phone calls and that a PA brought documents for his signature, but it was so unusual for him to put work second that she was very appreciative of his continuing support.

The surgery was completed quickly and successfully and Bee took a seat by Eleni's bed. By that stage the little girl was already regaining consciousness. While she was groggy she was not, it seemed, in pain and, reassured by Bee's presence at her bedside, she soon drifted off to sleep. One of the nannies arrived to sit with the child while Sergios took Bee out for a meal and a much-needed break.

'You're exhausted. Why do I employ a team of nannies only to find you in this state? Come home with me,' Sergios urged when Bee's head began to nod towards the latter stages of their meal.

Her eyes widened and she studied him ruefully. 'I should be there if Eleni wakes up again and there is a bed in the room for me to use,' she reminded him. 'I won't have an entirely sleepless night.'

'Sometimes you should put yourself first,' Sergios reasoned levelly.

Bee tensed at that declaration and lost colour. Would he tell himself that when he felt the need for something a little more exotic than the marital bed could offer him? Would boredom or lust be his excuse? Would he even need an excuse or was sex with Melita already so familiar that it would not feel like a betrayal of his marital vows? She studied his features: the level line of his brows, the stunning dark golden eyes above those blade-straight cheekbones and the wide carnal mouth that could transport her to paradise. Her cheeks burned as she tore her attention from him. She should challenge him about Melita. Why wasn't she doing that? When would there ever be a *right* moment for such a distressing confrontation?

When Eleni was lying in a hospital bed was definitely not the right time, she decided unhappily. That conversation was not something she wanted to plunge blindly into either. She needed to know exactly what she planned to say and right at that instant it felt like too emotive a subject for her to maintain a level head. She didn't want to shout or cry. She was determined to retain her dignity. After all she was in love with him and at the end of the day dignity might be all she had left to embrace, along with the empty shell of her marriage as they both retired behind their respective barriers. Would they ever share a bed again after that conversation?

'What's wrong?' Sergios demanded abruptly. 'You look haunted. Eleni's going to be fine. Stop doing this to yourself. It was a straightforward procedure and it went perfectly.'

'I know…I'm sorry. I think I'm just tired,' Bee muttered evasively, embarrassed that he could read her well enough to know that she was currently existing in a sort of mental hell. Melita was a sexy stunner; there was no getting round that hard fact. Every man in the taverna between fifteen and eighty-odd years had been staring appreciatively at the racy blonde. Just at that instant Bee could not forget, humiliatingly, that she had had to get half naked and swing provocatively round a pole to tempt her highly sexed and sophisticated husband into making their marriage a real one.

'You worry far too much about stuff.' Sergios shook his handsome dark head in emphasis. 'It's like you're always on the lookout for trouble.'

Bee was back by Eleni's bed when her cell phone vibrated silently in receipt of a text and she took it out of her jacket pocket, wondering wearily if it would be Jon Townsend again. Once he knew she would be over in London he had asked her to lunch with key charity personnel.

Too concerned about Eleni's needs to spare the time for such an occasion, Bee had hedged. But it was not Jon texting her this time…

I'm in London. I would like to meet you in private. *Melita.*

Aghast at the idea while noting that the word private was emphasised, Bee looked at her phone as though it had jumped up and bitten her. Her husband's mistress was actually texting her? Was it for real? But for what possible reason would anyone try to set Bee up with a fake text purporting to be from Melita? Assuming the text was genuine, how on earth had Melita Thiarkis got Bee's phone number? Had she taken it from Sergios's phone? It was the most likely explanation and as such hit Bee's spirits hard because it was not long since she had got a new number and if Melita was in possession of it, it suggested very recent contact between Sergios and the other woman.

Bee got little sleep that night although Eleni slept like a little snoring log. Sergios put in an appearance on his way into his London office. Bee was in the corridor and noticed the ripple of interest that her extraordinarily good-looking husband excited among the nursing staff. With his tall, wide-shouldered, long-legged frame encased in a charcoal-grey designer suit, Sergios looked spectacular. Eleni was equally impressed and whooped with glee when he came through the door and held out her arms.

An odd little smile softened the hard line of Sergios's mouth as he set down the package in his hand. Bending down, he scooped the little girl gently out of her bed, addressing her in Greek as he did so.

And for the very first time Eleni answered, looking up at him with big dark eyes. The words were indistinct and the sentence structure nonexistent, but it was a response she would not have attempted before the surgery.

'I noticed she was more attentive to what I was saying from the minute she woke up this morning,' Bee told him with forced brightness. 'She's definitely able to hear more. Her eyes don't wander the same way when you're speaking to her either.'

Bee helped Eleni unwrap the wooden puzzle that Sergios had brought and pulled up the bed table for the little girl's use. A ward maid popped her head round the door and offered them a cup of coffee.

'Not for me, thanks,' Sergios responded. 'I have an early meeting.'

'If her consultant thinks everything is in order, Eleni will be released later this afternoon,' Bee revealed.

'Good. The boys missed you last night,' Sergios told her.

If he had told her that *he* had missed her she would have thrown herself into his arms like a homing pigeon, but no such encouraging declaration passed his lips. Nor would it, Bee reflected wretchedly. Sergios didn't say sentimental stuff like that or make emotional statements. She loved a guy who would never ever tell her he loved her back. And why would he settle solely for Bee's charms when he already had a woman like Melita and countless other discreet lovers eternally on offer to him? He was an immensely wealthy tycoon and, when it came to women and sex, spoilt for choice and it would always be that way. Somehow, she didn't know yet *how*, she would have to come to terms with the reality of their marriage. Possibly meeting Melita Thiarkis in the flesh would be a sensible first step in that much-needed process.

That decision made, Sergios had barely left the building before Bee texted the other woman to set up the requested meeting. After all, what did she have to lose? Sergios wouldn't like the idea of them meeting at all but why should that bother her? He would never find out, would he? Had he chosen to be more frank about the relationship, however, Bee would probably have ignored the text from his mistress. Melita replied immediately and asked Bee to meet her in the bar of her Chelsea hotel mid-morning. Wary of staging such a delicate encounter in a public place, Bee suggested she come to her room instead.

Bee would very much have liked her entire designer wardrobe on hand to choose from before she met up with Melita. But, travelling direct from the hospital, that was not possible and Bee, not only had very little choice about what to wear, but despised the vain streak of insecurity that had prompted such a superficial thought. She could hardly hope to top a fashion designer in the style stakes, she told herself wryly as she freshened up her make-up and left Eleni with her nanny for company. Pausing only to tell her security team of two that she did not require them, she walked out of the hospital.

The receptionist sent her straight up to Melita's room on the first floor. She knocked only once on the door before it opened to frame the strikingly attractive woman, who even at that point impressed Bee as being vastly overdressed for morning coffee in her low-cut glittering jacket, narrow skirt and very high heels.

'Beatriz…' Melita murmured smoothly. 'I'm so grateful that you agreed to come, but let's not tell Sergios about this. Men hate it when we go behind their backs.'

CHAPTER TEN

BEE took due note of the fact that her husband's mistress, Melita, was more scared of consequences than she was. As Bee had no intention of keeping their meeting a secret unless it suited her to do so, she did not reply.

Melita already had a pot of coffee waiting in her opulent hotel room with its black and white designer chic decor. She sat down opposite Bee, a process that took a good deal of cautious lowering and wriggling in six-inch heels and a black skirt so tight it would split if put under too much pressure. Melita walked a thin line between sexy and tarty.

'I didn't think that Sergios would ever marry again,' the Greek woman said plaintively. 'But we're adults. There's no reason why we can't be, er…distant friends.'

Only one, Bee completed inwardly. *If you sleep with my husband I might try to murder you.*

'Sergios and I have been very close for a great many years,' Melita informed her with a self-satisfied smile.

Not a muscle moving on her taut face, Bee compressed her lips and pretended to sip at the too-hot coffee that Melita had poured for her. 'I guessed that.'

'I have no intention of poaching on your territory,' Melita declared importantly. 'I've never wanted to be a wife or a mother, so I don't covet what you have.'

'But you do covet Sergios,' Bee heard herself say helplessly.

'*Any* woman would covet him,' the other woman fielded, her sultry eyes widening in amused emphasis. 'But there's no reason why we can't share him.'

'Just one,' Bee murmured flatly. 'I *don't* share.'

Melita's pencilled brows drew together in surprise at that bold statement. 'Is that a declaration of war?'

'It's whatever you choose to make of it. Why did you invite me here?' Bee enquired drily.

'I wanted to reassure you that I have no desire to damage your marriage. Sergios really does need a wife to do wifely things like looking after his houses and his children. Naturally I'm aware that it is a marriage of…shall we say…' Melita looked unconvincingly coy for a moment '…mutual convenience?'

'Oh, dear…is that what Sergios told you?' Bee asked, wincing with an acting ability she had not known she possessed, for she refused to cringe at the apparent level of Melita's knowledge about Sergios's reasons for marrying her. 'Men can be so reluctant to break bad news. I'm afraid our marriage is rather more than one of convenience.'

'If by that you mean that Sergios shares your bed, I expected that. After all you're there when

I can't be and he's a man, very much a man,' Melita purred with glinting eyes of sensual recollection.

For a split second Bee felt so sick that she almost ran into the en suite and lost her sparse hospital breakfast. She could not bear to think of Melita naked and intimately wound round Sergios. That *hurt*, that hurt like a punch in the stomach. Nor could she bear to consider herself a sexual substitute, a sort of cheap and available fast-food option instead of the grand banquet of thrilling sensuality that she imagined Melita might offer.

'You do realise, I hope, that your husband is still shagging me every chance he gets!' Dropping the civilised front with a resounding crash, Melita surveyed Bee with angry, resentful dark eyes. 'He was with me on your wedding night and I have no intention of giving him up.'

'Whatever,' Bee framed woodenly, setting down the cup with precise care and rising to her feet again with all the dignity she could muster.

'I think we've shared a little too much for comfort. If you contact me again I'll tell Sergios.'

'Don't you dare threaten me!' Melita ranted furiously.

Bee walked out and she didn't look back or breathe until she was safe inside the lift again. Sergios was still sleeping with his mistress and had been from the first night of their marriage. Why was she so shocked? What else had she expected? That a man with a notoriously active libido would suddenly turn over a new leaf on entering a platonic marriage? That had never been a possibility. Before their marriage she had agreed to him maintaining his relationship with Melita. He had said upfront that Melita was not a negotiable facet of his life. Having received that warning, she had chosen to ignore it by allowing their marriage to become much more real than either of them had ever envisaged.

Leaving the hotel, Bee was blank-eyed, her mind in chaos and emotions raging through her in horribly distressing waves. She didn't know where she was going but she knew she couldn't return to the hospital in such a state, nor would she involve her mother when she was so upset. Her cell phone was ringing and she checked it. It was Jon Townsend. Heaving a sigh, but in a strange way grateful for the distraction, Bee answered his call. He invited her to join him at his apartment for lunch with the charity's PR woman. It was somewhere to go, something to do in a world rocking on its foundations, and she agreed and boarded a bus, too wrapped in her own unhappy thoughts to notice that she was being followed.

Sergios had already cancelled appointments and left his office, planning to meet with Beatriz at the hospital. The news that she had met up with Melita had hit him like a torpedo and almost blown him out of the water. Where had that come from? How had that happened? What had he done to deserve that outcome? Nourishing a strong sense of injustice along with the suspicion that he was being royally stitched up, Sergios was in no mood to receive the bodyguard's second piece of news: Beatriz had entered an apartment owned by Jon Townsend?

'Beatriz...' From the minute Bee stepped through the door, she began regretting having agreed to lunch. Jon was alone, the PR lady apparently having been held up in traffic. Unfortunately her host's effusive welcome made Bee feel even more awkward.

Bee toyed with the salad on her plate and for the third time attempted to steer their conversation back to the subject of the charity and away from the past times that Jon seemed much more eager to discuss.

'We were so close back then.' Jon sighed fondly.

'Not as close as I thought at the time. We *were* still very young,' Bee pointed out lightly.

'I didn't realise how much you meant to me until it was too late and I'd lost you,' Jon said baldly.

'It happens.' Her attempted smile of acknowledgement was a mere twist of her lips, for she was in no frame of mind to deal tactfully with Jon's evident determination to resurrect their shared past. 'If you had been happy with me you wouldn't have strayed.'

Jon brought a hand down on top of hers and she was so irritated with him that she very nearly lifted her other hand to stab him with the fork. 'Jenna—'

Bee lifted a hand to silence him. 'Stop right there. I really don't want to hear about your marriage, Jon. It's none of my business.'

'Perhaps I want to make it your business.'

'More probably you're barking up the wrong tree—I'm in love with my husband,' Bee responded impatiently. 'And now I think it's time I went. I want to get back to the hospital.'

As she got up Jon leapt up as well and the doorbell went in one long shrill shriek as if the caller's finger had accidentally got stuck to the button.

'A shame your PR lady is arriving so late,' Bee remarked.

'That was just a ruse, Bee,' Jon snapped, his fair features twisting with bad temper and momentarily giving him the aspect of a disgruntled little boy.

'Evidently, Sergios was right to tell me that I'm too trusting,' Bee was saying as Jon angrily yanked open the front door, annoyed by the timely interruption.

Bee was totally shattered to see Sergios poised on the doorstep. 'What are you doing here?' she asked in astonishment. 'How did you find out where I was?'

His eyes had a smouldering glitter and were welded to Jon's discomfited face. 'Why did my wife say that I was right to call her too trusting?'

Bee really couldn't be bothered with Jon at that moment. The whole silly lunch set-up had thoroughly irritated her, but she didn't want Sergios to thump him. And that, she sensed, very much aware of the powerfully angry aggression Sergios exuded, was quite likely if she didn't act to defuse the tension.

'I was just joking. We were discussing a charity dinner—'

Sergios closed a hand round her wrist and drew her out of the apartment as if he couldn't wait to remove her from a source of dangerous contagion. His face hard as iron, he studied Jon, who was pale and taut. 'Leave my wife alone,' he instructed with chilling bite. 'What's mine stays mine. Try not to forget that.'

What's mine stays mine. Bee could have been very sarcastic about that assurance had she not been outraged by Sergios's intervention and sexist turn of phrase.

'Sometimes you're very dramatic,' she commented lamely, recognising that quality in him for the first time and surprised by the discovery.

'What were you doing in Townsend's apartment alone with him?' Sergios shot at her, visibly unrepentant.

'None of your business.'

As the lift doors opened on the ground floor

Sergios shot Bee an arrested look. 'Explain yourself.'

'Are we going to pick up Eleni?' Bee enquired coldly instead, picturing Melita with her smug cat-got-the-cream smile. Nausea pooled in her tummy again and turned her skin clammy.

'Eleni was released an hour ago. Karen phoned me and I told her to take Eleni home.'

'Oh.' Bee made no further comment, stabbed by guilt that she had forgotten the little girl was due to leave hospital that afternoon. She felt drained by the emotional storm of the past couple of hours. The man she loved had a mistress whom he regularly slept with and would not give up. Where did she go from there? Did she really want to lower herself to the level of arguing about Melita? Did she want to run the risk of exposing how deep her own feelings went for him?

Or did she do the sensible thing? Take it on the chin and move on? Obviously no more sharing of marital beds. That kind of intimacy was out of the question with Melita in the picture. But she had signed up to a long-term relationship for the sake of her mother and for the children. Every fibre of her being might be urging her to make some sort of grand gesture like walking out on her marriage, but too many innocent people would be hurt and damaged by her doing that. Even Sergios had said that she wasn't a quitter and he had been right on that score. She gave her word and, my goodness, she stuck to it through thick and thin.

Even through Melita? Could she still stick to her word in such circumstances? Pain slivered through Bee and cut deep like a knife. They had roamed so far from their original agreement. Far too many tender feelings had got involved. Stepping back from that intimacy, learning to be detached again would be a huge challenge, she acknowledged wretchedly. Had she really once believed that she could treat Sergios like a rather demanding employer? Looking at Sergios's beloved face now, she was no longer sure that she had the strength to stand by her promise and survive the sacrifices that that would demand.

How could she bear to turn her back on what she had believed they had and know that Melita was replacing her in every way that mattered? From now on it would be Melita he kissed awake in the morning, Melita he took to dine in cosy little restaurants where nobody recognised him, Melita he bought whopping big diamonds for. How could Bee live with knowing that he had only made love to her because she was there when more tempting sexual prospects were not? What had meant so much to her had evidently meant very little to him. A cry of anguish was building up inside Bee. She felt as though she were being ripped apart.

The limo came to a halt. White-faced, she got out without even looking to see where she was going and came to a sudden bemused halt once she realised that they had not alighted at the mansion that was their London home but outside an apartment building she had never seen before. 'Where are we?'

'I own an apartment here.'

'Oh…do you?' she queried drily, wondering if this was where he had come on their wedding night to make love with his Greek blonde. She was ready to bet that he had not had to nudge Melita towards the sexy lingerie. Gut instinct warned her that Melita already had that kind of angle covered, or uncovered, as regarded his preference, she thought bitterly. Had she seriously considered dying her hair blonde? Had she really been that pathetic? Where had her pride and her independence gone?

Love had decimated those traits, she decided painfully, standing, lost and sick to the soul, in the lift on the way up to the apartment she had not known he possessed. Love had made her hollow and weak inside. Love had made her want to cling and dye her hair and wear the fancy lingerie if that was what it took to hold him. But her brain told her that that was nonsense and that those were only superficial frills, not up to the challenge of keeping a doomed relationship afloat. And a relationship between plain, ordinary, sensible Bee Blake and rich and gorgeous Sergios Demonides had always been doomed, hadn't it? A union between two such different people was unlikely to be a marriage that ran and ran against all the odds...unless you believed in miracles and wild dreams coming true. And Bee had so *badly* wanted to believe that she could have the miracle, the dream.

Virtually blind to her surroundings while that ferocity of emotion remained in control of her, Bee preceded Sergios into a spacious lounge that had that slightly bare, unlived in quality of a property not in daily use. 'So this is where you and Melita—'

Sergios froze in front of her as though she had said a very bad word, his face clenching hard, sensual mouth compressing. 'No, not here. My grandfather uses this place when he visits

London—he likes his independence. It's a company property.'

Bee nodded and her spine relaxed just a jot. She had conceived a loathing for Melita Thiarkis, everywhere the other woman had ever been with Sergios and everything to do with her that was excessive to say the least.

'She's never been here—she has her own apartment,' Sergios breathed abruptly as if he were attuned to Bee's every thought.

Never having had quite so many mean, malicious thoughts all at once, Bee seriously hoped that he was not that attuned. Her disconcerted face was hot, her complexion flushed to the hairline with embarrassment and the distress she was fighting to conceal. Suddenly unable to bear looking at him, she spun away and faked an interest in the view.

'Whatever it takes I want to keep you,' Sergios breathed with startling harshness. 'I hope you appreciate the fact that I didn't knock Townsend's teeth down his throat the way I would've liked to have done.'

'You can be such a caveman.' In a twisty way that appealed to the dark side of her temperament, she was painfully amused that despite his own extra-marital interests he could still be so possessive of *her*. The logic of his attitude escaped her. But, of course, he wanted to keep her as a wife: he needed her for the children. They loved her and she loved them. Now there had to be a compromise found that she and Sergios could both live with. Some magical solution that would provide a path through the messy swell of emotion currently blurring her view of the world.

'Look at me...' Sergios urged.

'I don't want to,' Bee said truthfully, but she turned round all the same.

She wondered why it was that she could now see that Jon sulked and pouted like a spoilt little boy when he didn't get his own way, but that in spite of what she had learned about Sergios she still could not see a visible flaw in him. He remained defiantly gorgeous from his stunning dark golden eyes to his slightly stubbled and shadowed chin.

'That's better,' he murmured, scrutinising her with an intensity that made her uncomfortable.

'Why did you bring me here?'

'If we're going to argue, if there's going to be dissension between us, I didn't want the children as an audience,' Sergios admitted flatly, features grave.

'My word, you think of everything!' Bee was all too wretchedly aware that she would not have considered that danger until it was too late.

'They deserve better from us—'

'Is that you reminding me of my duty?' Bee prompted tightly, her throat suddenly thickening with tears.

'Whatever it takes I want to hold onto you.'

'You already said that.'

'It's more than I've ever said to a woman,' Sergios breathed roughly, challenge in the stance of his big powerful body. He stood tall with broad shoulders thrown back and strong legs braced as though he were expecting a blow.

He wanted everything, he wanted too much, she reflected unhappily. He wanted his mistress and he wanted his wife, a combination he evidently believed necessary to his comfort and happiness. Emotion didn't come into it for him. If only it didn't come into it for her either! Her eyes prickled hotly and she kept them very wide, terrified that the tears threatening her would spill over in front of him.

'If we're staying here I could do with lying down for a while,' she said abruptly, desperate for some privacy.

'Of course.' He crossed the room and pressed open a door that led into a corridor. He showed her into the bedroom and startled her by yanking the bedspread off the bed and pulling back the duvet for her. He looked across at her, a dark uncertainty in his eyes that she had never seen before, and for the first time it occurred to her that he was upset as well.

'Thanks,' she said dully, taking off her jacket and kicking off her shoes.

'Would you like a drink?' he enquired without warning.

'A brandy,' she responded, dimly recalling that being recommended for shock in a book she had read. Probably not at all the right remedy for shock in today's world, she thought ruefully. In fact, couldn't alcohol act as a depressant? In the mood she was in, she didn't need that, did she?

Seemingly glad, however, of something to do, Sergios strode out of the room and she sat down on the bed. Time seemed to move on without her noticing, for he reappeared very quickly and handed her a tumbler half full of brandy. 'Are you trying to get me drunk?' she asked in disbelief.

'You look like a ghost, all white and drawn. Drink up,' Sergios urged.

'I can't live like this with you…' she framed, the admission leaping off her tongue before she could stop it.

Sergios came down on his knees at her feet and pushed the tumbler towards her mouth. 'Drink,' he urged again.

'It might make me sick.'

'I don't think so.'

All of a sudden she noticed that the hand he had on the glass was trembling almost infinitesimally. He was behaving as though the drink might be a lifesaver, rather than a pick-me-up. She sipped, shuddering as the alcohol ran like a flame down her throat, making her cough and splutter. She collided with strained dark eyes.

'What the heck is the matter with you?' Bee demanded in sudden frustration. 'You're behaving very oddly.'

Sergios vaulted upright. 'What do you expect? You go and see my former mistress—then you run straight off to stage a private meeting with your ex, who's clearly desperate to get you back!'

he exclaimed wrathfully. 'I mean, it's not exactly been my dream day and I still don't know what the hell is going on!'

Former mistress? Her ears were practically out on stalks. Was he planning to try and lie his way out of the tight corner he was in? Pretend that his relationship with Melita was over? While pondering that salient point, Bee drank deep of the brandy, grateful for the heat spreading and somehow soothing her cold, empty tummy.

'Why did you go and see Melita?' he demanded heavily. 'What the hell made you do such a thing?'

Her brow indented. 'She asked me to come and see her.'

His lean powerful face set granite hard at that claim. '*She* asked...*you*?'

Bee lifted her chin. 'Yes and I was curious. Of course I was. I saw her on the island last week.'

His gaze narrowed. 'Nectarios mentioned it but I hoped you didn't realise who she was.'

Bee rolled her eyes. 'I'm not stupid, Sergios.'

'Not obviously so,' he conceded. 'But if you believed I've been with her since we got married, you are being stupid.'

'According to Melita you've been shagging her every chance you got—that's a direct quote from her,' Bee told him.

Sergios looked astonished. 'I thought better of her. We parted—as I thought—on good terms.'

'When did you last see her?'

'About six weeks ago in Athens. We did not have sex,' Sergios added sardonically. 'I have not slept with her since we got married.'

Bee vented a scornful laugh. 'How am I supposed to believe that about the woman you insisted you had to keep in your life in spite of our marriage?'

'It's the truth. Melita was part of my routine.'

'Routine?' Bee repeated with distaste.

'It wasn't a romantic relationship. I financed her fashion house, she shared my bed. She travelled all round the world to meet up with me. It was easier keeping her as a mistress than having to adapt to different women,' Sergios admitted, his discomfort with the topic obvious. 'I've known her for a long time. I backed her first fashion collection because she was an islander. We ended up in bed after Krista died and I found Melita's casual approach to sex attractive at a time when I didn't want anything heavy.'

'If it was over why did she lie?'

'Presumably because she thought that if she could cause trouble between us I might come back to her,' Sergios suggested grimly. 'I'm furious that she approached you and lied to you. I made a generous settlement on her at the end of our affair and she should've been satisfied with that.'

'She said you were with her on our wedding night.'

Sergios swore only half below his breath, anger burning in his keen gaze. 'I was supposed to see her but I cancelled.'

'You went out.'

'I went to a casino, played the tables and drank.

Going to her didn't feel right. I know our marriage was supposed to be a fake but making a point of being with her that particular night...' Sergios shrugged uncomfortably. 'It would've felt disrespectful, so I didn't do it.'

'Disrespectful,' Bee echoed weakly, her attention nailed to his face, recognising the combination of discomfiture and sincerity she saw there.

'I swear I have not been with Melita,' Sergios growled, his patience taxed almost beyond its limits. 'And if I have to drag her here and make her admit that to your face, I will not shrink from the challenge.'

'She wouldn't come.'

'She would if I threatened to withdraw the settlement I made on her. She signed a legal agreement, promising to be discreet about our past relationship and approaching my wife and lying to her is not, by any stretch of the imagination, discreet!' he bit out thunderously, his anger at what he had learned unconcealed.

Bee recalled how very keen Melita had been

to ensure that Sergios did not know about their meeting, hardly surprising if the money he had given her was dependent on her remaining tactfully silent about their affair. Was it possible that she had simply wanted to cause trouble? Naturally she would blame Bee for Sergios having broken off their relationship.

'I'm starting to believe you,' Bee confided with a frown, worried that she was being ridiculously credulous while at the same time recalling that she had yet to find out that Sergios had ever lied to her about anything. He was much more given to lethal candour than dishonesty.

'Thank God,' he breathed in Greek.

'But I still don't get why you were so determined to retain Melita that you even told me about her before the wedding…only to get rid of her a few weeks later.'

Sergios groaned like a man in torment. 'Obviously because I had you and didn't need her any longer.'

'Oh…' was all Bee could think to say to that.

Was it really that simple for him? Instead of sex with Melita he had discovered sex with his wife and found it a perfectly adequate substitute? Seemingly it *was* that simple on his terms. It was a huge relief to appreciate that he had not betrayed her with Melita. Her head was swimming a little and she thought that perhaps she had had a little too much brandy.

'You're fantastic in bed, *yineka mou.*'

'Am I?' Bee settled big green eyes on him, wide with wonderment at that assurance.

'I haven't even looked at another woman since I married you,' Sergios spelt out forcefully. 'Nor will I in the future. That's a promise. Will you come home with me now?'

A huge smile was tugging the last of the stress from round her ripe mouth. 'You still haven't explained how you knew where I was this afternoon.'

'Your security team know not to listen to you if you try to go anywhere without them in tow. They followed you. What did Townsend want?'

'Me apparently, but after all this time I'm really not interested. I told him that I…er…' Bee hesitated at what she had almost revealed. 'I told Jon that I had become quite attached to you.'

'Attached? Is that a fact?' Sergios prompted softly, sitting down on the bed beside her and tucking her hair back behind one small ear with a gentle hand. 'I'm quite attached to you as well.'

'Sexually speaking,' Bee qualified, a glutton for accuracy.

'Well, I have to admit that you have the most fabulous breasts and I'm ashamed to admit that they are the first thing I noticed about you the night we met,' Sergios confessed with the beginnings of a wicked grin. 'But you've contrived to build whole layers on that initial impression. You're a great listener, marvellous company, very loyal, intelligent and affectionate. When I'm angry or stressed you make me feel calm. When I'm unkind you make me see another viewpoint. I'm not even mentioning how wonderful you are with the children because that's not what you and I are about any more—'

Bee went from hanging on his every flattering word to cutting in with a quick question. 'It's...*not*?'

'Of course, it's not. We started out with a practical marriage.'

'You told Melita that too, didn't you?' Bee recalled unhappily, her brow indenting with a remembered sense of humiliation.

His forefinger smoothed away the tension that had tightened her mouth. 'I'm afraid it slipped out but I really did believe we were going to have a marriage that was like a business deal.'

'And how do you feel now?' she whispered.

'Like I made the killing of a lifetime when I got you to the altar,' Sergios declared, his eyes warmer than she had ever seen them as he studied her intently. 'You've got to know how crazy I am about you. You taught me to love again. You taught me how to trust and you transformed my life.'

Bee stared at him wide-eyed. 'You're crazy about me?'

'I'm hopelessly in love with you.'

Bee wrapped both arms round him as though he were a very large teddy bear and dragged him down to her. 'I was trying to save face when I said I was attached to you.'

'I rather hoped that that was what you were doing, *agape mou.*'

'I love you too but I still don't know why.'

'Don't question it too closely in case you change your mind,' Sergios warned.

'It's just you weren't the most loveable guy around when we got married.'

'But I'm really working at it now,' he pointed out. 'And I won't stop.'

Bee studied him with bemused green eyes. 'You promise?'

'I promise. I love you. All I want is to make you happy.'

The sincerity in his liquid dark gaze went straight to her impressionable heart and tears stung the backs of her eyes. Finally, she believed him. Their marriage was safe. Even better, he was hers in exactly the way she had dreamed. He loved her and love was, she sensed, the only chain that would hold him.

'I should've known I was in trouble when I bought that wedding dress,' Sergios confided with a rueful laugh.

'What were you doing at a fashion show?' As he winced she guessed the answer. 'You were there because of Melita and yet you picked a dress for me?' she prompted in amazement.

'I saw the dress and I couldn't help picturing you wearing it and I know it was high-handed of me but I was determined that you should have it,' Sergios revealed.

She was touched by the admission that even before their wedding he had been attracted to her to that extent. 'Yet we both thought that I was going to be more of an employee than a real wife.'

'Even I can be stupid.'

Bee grinned with appreciation. 'Hold on while I get a microphone and record that statement.'

'Well, I was stupid about you. I was fighting what I felt for you right from the start.'

'Your marriage to Krista hurt you a great deal,' Bee commented softly, understanding that and willing to forgive the time it had taken for him to recognise his feelings for her.

'I thought I would be happier living without a serious relationship in my life. You rewrote everything I thought I knew about myself. I wanted you. I wanted you in my bed, my home, involved in every aspect of my day.' Sergios circled her mouth slowly, gently, with his. 'I know I didn't tell you that I'd finished with Melita but I didn't see the need.'

'I thought that maybe you thought you could still have both of us.'

Unexpectedly, Sergios laughed. 'No, I was never that stupid. I knew that wasn't an option but possibly I felt a little foolish about changing my mind so quickly and wanting the kind of marriage I said I definitely didn't want.'

Bee brushed a high cheekbone with gentle fingertips, loving the new confidence powering her. 'That aspect never occurred to me.'

'It should've done. I thought I had our marriage all worked out and it blew up in my face because I couldn't keep my hands off you.'

'When I saw Melita I decided you only liked blondes…and for just a little while I actually considered getting my hair dyed. It was my lowest moment,' Bee confided with a wince of shame.

Sergios groaned out loud, his long fingers feathering through her glossy dark hair. 'I'm very grateful you didn't do it. I love your hair the way it is—'

'I might grow it longer for you,' Bee proffered, feeling unusually generous.

Sergios pressed her back against the pillows and extracted a kiss that was full of hungry urgency. 'Now that we're here, we might as well take advantage.'

'Oh, yes,' Bee agreed, full pink lips swollen, eyes wide with desire as the tug of arousal pinched low in her tummy.

And the kissing shifted into a fairly wild bout of lovemaking. Afterwards, Bee lay in her husband's arms, feeling loved and secure and boundlessly happy and grateful for what she had.

On the drive back to their London home that evening, Sergios dealt her a slightly embarrassed appraisal and said abruptly, 'I thought that possibly in a few months' time we might consider having a baby.'

'On the grounds that we've got so many children we might as well have another?' Bee prompted very drily.

Sergios grimaced. 'I suppose I deserve that reminder but I've changed. I would like to have a child with you some day in the future.'

'I can agree to that now you've got the right attitude,' Bee told him chirpily and she flung herself into his arms with abandon and snuggled close. 'And now I know that you love me, you had better get used to me doing stuff like this.'

His strong arms enfolded her and dark golden eyes rested on her animated face with tender appreciation. 'And maybe I've even learned to like it, *yineka mou.*'

Bee relaxed and knew she could hug him to her heart's content. From here on in there would be no more boundaries she feared to cross.

EPILOGUE

'How do you feel?' Sergios asked, his anxiety obvious.

'Absolutely fine!' Bee exclaimed, widening her bright eyes in reproach. 'Stop fussing!'

But Bee was less than pleased with her reflection in the mirror. It was Nectarios's eighty-third birthday and they were throwing a big party for the older man at their home on the island. She was wearing a beautiful evening gown in one of her favourite colours but, it had to be said, nothing, not even the fabulous diamonds glittering in her ears and at her throat, could make her elegant in her own eyes while she was heavily pregnant. At almost eight months pregnant with their first child, she felt like a ship in full sail.

Sergios drew her back against him, his hands

splaying gently across her swollen abdomen, his fascination palpable as he felt the slight ripple of movement as their daughter kicked. A little girl, that was what they were having according to the most recent sonogram. Eleni was four years old and she was very excited about the baby sister who would soon be born. Bee had enjoyed furnishing a nursery and had frittered away many a happy hour choosing baby equipment and clothing.

Bee, however, could hardly believe that she and Sergios had been married for going on for three years. They had waited a little longer than they had originally planned to try for a baby but she had conceived quickly. There was not a single cloud in Bee's sky. The previous year, Melita Thiarkis had sold her island property and set up permanent home in Milan with an Italian millionaire. Bee had never got involved with the charity Jon Townsend had worked with because he made her uncomfortable, but she had picked another charity, one that concentrated on disabled adults like her mother. When she was not running round after the children or travelling with Sergios, for they did not like to be kept apart for more than a couple of nights, she put in sterling work seeking out sponsors for the organisation and raising funds.

Bee's mother, Emilia was firmly settled now in her cottage on Orestos. Happier and healthier than she had been for several years, the older woman was fully integrated into island life and a good deal less lonely and bored. She loved living close to her daughter and took great pleasure in Paris, Milo and Eleni running in and out of her house and treating her as an honorary grandmother. Nectarios was a regular visitor to his grandson's home and a very welcome one. He was thrilled that his fourth great-grandchild was on the way.

'You've made so many arrangements for this party. I don't want you to tire yourself out,' Sergios admitted.

The house was full of guests and there was a distant hum, which probably signified the approach of another helicopter ready to drop off more guests.

'I'll be fine.' Bee was wryly amused by the level of his concern, for she had enjoyed a healthy pregnancy that had impinged very little on her usual routine. He was so supportive though, having rigorously attended every medical appointment with her.

Sergios studied the woman he loved and once again worked to suppress his secret fear of the idea of anything ever happening to her. The more he loved her, the more central she became to his world, and the more he worried but the bottom line, the payoff, he had learned, was a level of love and contentment he had never known until she entered his life.

'I love you, *agape mou*,' he murmured gently at the top of the sweeping staircase.

Bee met his stunning dark golden eyes and felt the leap of every sense with happy acceptance.

The world they had made together was a safe cocoon for both them and the children. 'I love you more than I could ever say.'

* * * * *

CABIN
FEVER

ALEX DAHL is a half-American, half-Norwegian author. Born in Oslo, she studied Russian and German linguistics with international studies, then went on to complete an MA in creative writing at Bath Spa University and an MSc in business management at Bath University. A committed Francophile, Alex loves to travel, and has so far lived in Moscow, Paris, Stuttgart, Sandefjord, Switzerland, Bath and London. She is the author of three other thrillers: *Playdate*, *The Heart Keeper*, and *The Boy at the Door*, which was shortlisted for the CWA Debut Dagger.

Also by Alex Dahl

The Boy at the Door

The Heart Keeper

Playdate

CABIN FEVER

Alex Dahl

HEAD
of ZEUS

First published in the UK in 2021 by Head of Zeus Ltd

9 7 5 3 1 2 4 6 8

A catalogue record for this book is available from
the British Library.

ISBN (HB): 9781789544039
ISBN (XTPB): 9781789544046
ISBN (E): 9781789544060

Typeset by Divaddict Publishing Solutions Ltd

Printed and bound in Great Britain by
CPI Group (UK) Ltd, Croydon CR0 4YY

Head of Zeus Ltd
First Floor East
5–8 Hardwick Street
London EC1R 4RG

WWW.HEADOFZEUS.COM

To Fevziye, my favorite Leo, in memory

'Only the wounded healer can truly heal.'

– Irvin D. Yalom

Prologue

You're in the woods. You're alone. You've never known aloneness like this before, but now that you do, it will remain beside you like an unshakable shadow for the rest of your life. So much will be lost in the far recesses of your mind; no life can ever be retained in all of its moments, but you will remember this – the bitter, sickly taste of blood in your mouth, the thousand shades of green enveloping you, the taste, and color, of death. The deafening rumble of your heart echoing through your blood. The sharp-edged leaves knifing your arms and face as you crash through the foliage. Your fear – this vast and uncontrollable fear, as black and deep as a Norwegian forest lake. It will surge through you forever, prompted by big and small triggers entirely unrelated to these moments, and you'll learn to live with it; you'll have to. Sometimes it will roar at you, other times it will whisper. Every breath you take will bear its faint aftertaste. Every forest you walk through will merge with this one. Every sharp sound will take you back here in a split second. And every part of you will be reshaped, contorted into new configurations: like a city rebuilt from ruins.

To save you, your mind will invent escape routes. Your brilliant mind will take your broken heart away from these moments in the only way it knows how – by running.

You run, faster than you've ever run before, and even now, you know you'll be running like this for the rest of your life. You'll run because you don't know that the only way you could ever be free is to stop.

Part I

SUPERNOVA

I

Kristina, October

She's my two o'clock on Fridays, the second last before the weekend. Perhaps this makes me naturally more relaxed and good-humored, but Leah Iverson has always been a client I look forward to seeing. She's reflective and interesting, with a natural ability to tap into my deepest empathy, and genuinely invested in the therapeutic process. In other words, she isn't hard work. That's not to say we haven't done hard work together, at times very hard work. Leah first came to see me almost three years ago, in the aftermath of the publication of her first book, *Nobody*. The book was loosely based on her marriage in the popular Scandinavian trend of autofiction inspired by Karl-Ove Knausgaard, and it was translated into over twenty languages, and so she found herself an unlikely literary celebrity.

At first, she had taken it in her stride, reveling in the unexpected career change from journalist to published author. She traveled the world and spoke of her inspiring

5

healing journey from emotional and physical abuse at various events. But as time went by, Leah began to struggle with the life changes this had brought, and her elevation to 'famous-author' status. Her book remained at number one, and was optioned for a TV-series adaptation. The gossip press preyed on her, speculating over which parts of the book were true, and which parts were fictionalized. Leah made enough money to buy a nice apartment in an upmarket part of town, and a cabin in the mountains of Telemark, too. In spite of all this success, Leah was a nervous, fragile shell of a woman back then, someone who winced when our eyes met or if I asked her a question she didn't know how to answer. Her sentences would begin with, 'I'm sorry,' or, 'I know this is stupid,' or, 'This is so ridiculous, but...'. She didn't trust herself back then, but she came to trust me, and eventually, herself.

As we began to build our therapeutic relationship, a wide array of underlying problems emerged, squirming in the room between us like worms coiling out of the earth. Leah cut herself, and had been doing it since her early teens. She once pulled up the sleeves of her jumper to reveal row upon row of neat incisions, some fresh and pink, many old and white. She had a highly complicated relationship with food, alternating between binging and starving herself, sometimes for weeks on end and until she'd black out. She suffered from debilitating panic attacks and terrifying compulsive thoughts, sometimes suicidal. She was always quick to reassure me that her suicidal thoughts were without intent, and I would point out that they were just thoughts. At the beginning, Leah spent many sessions just staring emptily into the space between us, and I would let her be, without any prompts at all. Occasionally she'd look up, her startled hazel eyes meeting mine before scanning the room, as though she momentarily had no idea where she was.

Over time, I watched as Leah grew stronger. In the therapy room she made great progress, too. It's always incredible when a client comes to therapy at the right time, with the right therapist, and that is what I believe happened for us. Layers of conditioning and trauma and deeply buried pain and untruths peel away, revealing a vulnerable but very strong person underneath – it's powerful to watch and become part of. Though she has significantly battled with writing a follow-up to *Nobody* over the past year, she hasn't regressed to the chaotic, destructive state of when she first came to therapy. She's a very grateful client, one who often makes a point of saying that it's all because of me that things are getting better, but I like to say that I only hold the mirror – she's the one that looks in it.

I boil the water for our tea and rearrange the tea bags fanning out in the dish on the low table. I make sure there are two of each flavor and that they are laid out by color. It's interesting how some clients will choose a different tea each time, whereas some will always have the same one. Leah doesn't always choose one at all, arriving with a takeaway coffee from Kaffebrenneriet across the road. Other times, she chooses a green tea with lemon.

It's five past two, and still no Leah. Unusual – she is extremely punctual, and I actually can't recall a time when she wasn't sitting in the waiting room when I opened the door at two on the dot. I check again, though I would have heard the door open, and the room is still empty. Outside, heavy rain is falling, and slick orange leaves stick to the windowpanes. October always makes me feel both withdrawn and a little wistful, though I've never known why. Perhaps it has to do with the beauty of the decay, how intoxicating it is to observe all the death around us.

This year is worse than ever, so much has changed, so much loss.

All I want for this weekend is to shut myself away in the house with Eirik, lying across from him on the sofas, reading and sipping a rich, dark Malbec, occasionally looking up to meet his eyes and smiling. This weekend is going to be far removed from that gentle domestic dream, and I feel tired in advance just at the thought of it. Tonight I will be supporting my husband at a gala dinner at the prime minister's residence. I feel a nervous ache in my stomach at the thought, but then, who wouldn't? Then, tomorrow, we are visiting my sister and her young family in Drøbak for the rest of the weekend, which is lovely but hardly a relaxing time.

Ten past two, and still no Leah. I bring out my phone to call her – something unexpected must have happened – but just then, I hear the door to the waiting room open. I take a deep breath and entirely clear my mind so that Leah has my full, uncluttered attention for the forty minutes that are left of the session.

But it isn't Leah, not the Leah I've seen every Friday for over nearly three years. This is someone else entirely, a ghost of the woman I know. She's trembling all over and soaked wet. Her right eye is a medley of violet and red and inky blue, swelled shut.

'Jesus, Leah,' I begin, but fall silent at the look in her eyes.

'Can we just begin,' she whispers.

'Okay,' I say, and usher her into the room. My heart is pounding hard and my palms are slick with nervous sweat, as if I'm the client, not the therapist. I've lit a discreet votive candle on the windowsill like I always do, and there are fresh flowers on the table, autumnal amber roses, and I make a point of taking each of them in briefly to center myself. Leah settles into the chair opposite me and fidgets strangely with her jacket sleeves, as though she can't control herself and is at the mercy of a motor running inside her that she can't shut down. Her fingers loop through and around a little hole she's made on the sleeve, making it bigger and bigger. As it recedes, her sweater underneath becomes visible and I see that it is speckled with blood.

'What's happened, Leah?' I ask softly, in spite of my usual habit of letting the client begin the session at their own point of urgency.

'I…' The words seem to catch in her throat.

'Someone has hurt you. Do you think you can tell me about what happened?' I watch as tears drop from her eyes onto her hands, still working away at unraveling the jacket sleeve. 'Leah?'

No answer.

'Have you gone to the police?'

'No.'

I nod, and let the 'no' hang for a while on the tense air between us. 'It's not like they'd do anything much,' she continues in a whisper.

'Maybe it would be good to speak with them anyway,' I say, but she shakes her head curtly. 'Leah, did Anton do this to you?' The abusive and vindictive ex-husband seems like a natural assumption.

Blank stare.

'There is something I have to tell you,' Leah says, her eyes returning to the busy performance of her hands tearing at the jacket sleeve. I remain silent, fully concentrated, ready to receive her words and to help her hold the intense emotions she must be feeling. For a long while, she doesn't speak. She closes her uninjured left eye and I can't help but stare at her now that I know she can't see me. I allow the intense empathy I feel for Leah to wash over me. I hope she can feel that, in these moments, I am all hers, and that I stand beside her witnessing her distress and her pain.

'You know I told you about my cabin? The one I bought in the mountains? Or, the forest really. With mountains nearby.'

'Yes.'

'I want to go there. I just want to go there and collect myself; it's the only place I've really felt at peace. Ever. You know how we've spoken so much about my need for newness all the time? And the need to escape. It's been like an itch, always. As a child, I always wanted to be someone else. It's the same now. I just want to be away. Away. Faster, better, more. Away. I live my life wanting to be somewhere other than where I am. Except for at the cabin. It's like that place is me, but me as a physical place, does that make sense?' I nod. 'It's like it's not only mine, but *me*.'

'That sounds like a very good place to be.'

'Yeah.' She doesn't embellish. I glance at the time, only twenty minutes left.

'You mentioned earlier that there was something you needed to tell me.'

Leah nods. She avoids my gaze, lets her one seeing eye

travel around the room until it comes to rest on the flowers. Then she closes it and tears rush from beneath her thick dark lashes, dropping off her chin and onto her wrung, red hands. I wait.

'I...' she begins, her voice scratchy and raw, like she's been screaming at the top of her lungs. I feel deeply unsettled in her presence, she is so unlike herself, even the way she was at the very beginning. She stands up.

'I'm sorry,' she says, her face twisted and grotesque.

'We have some time left,' I say, but she's already crossing the room and reaching for the door.

'I...' she begins again. 'It's too late,' she whispers.

'What's too late? Leah, talk to me. Tell me what's on your mind.'

'No, it's too late.'

'Why is it too late?'

'Can... Can you come to my cabin?'

I sigh, we've had these kinds of conversations before. 'Leah, you know that the therapy room is our meeting place.'

'Please.'

'I can't come to your cabin. You know this.'

Leah wrenches the door open and turns to look at me. 'I need you to...' she starts, her eyes shining with fresh tears, then she lowers her voice to barely a whisper. 'This is about the truth.'

'Stay a little longer, Leah, please. I have some extra time this afternoon. It's okay. Talk to me.'

She shakes her head forcefully and fumbles around in her jacket pocket with her right hand. She hands me a crumpled envelope with something solid inside.

'Please come.'

'Leah—'

'I'm sorry... I'm so sorry...'

'Wait, sorry for what? Leah, wait.'

But Leah is already running down the stairs, her footsteps echoing up the stairwell. I rush to the window and watch as she bursts onto the street and crosses the road to the royal palace park, where she becomes blurred and distorted in the crashing rain.

2

Kristina

As soon as I get home, I go to the kitchen and pour myself a large glass of Californian red. I walk through each of our large rooms steeped in autumnal darkness even though it is only four o'clock, and enter my walk-in wardrobe, placing the wineglass on a shelf. My reflection is mirrored back at me from several angles, sliver after sliver of Kristina. I look tired and pale. I take a big glug of the wine and run my fingertips across a long row of little black dresses, which are perfectly hung and grouped by fabric. Silk, then chiffon, then satin, cotton, jersey, merino wool, cashmere. Tonight will be formal and I need something special. It's the Conservative Party's annual autumn gala, held at the prime minister's private residence. My husband is second in command of the party and many eyes will be on us this evening. I move toward the jewel-colored dresses, teal maybe, or a deep emerald; those colors tend to offset my dark hair. I select a beautiful ocean-blue silk Bottega Veneta dress and step out of my work clothes. I look at myself for a moment in the full-length mirror and take another big sip of the pinot noir. Woman, thirties, thin and a little drawn-looking, drinking wine in her underwear in a closet – that's me.

I feel unsettled, like something is happening at the back of my mind that I can't quite grasp; it's the feeling of trying to recover a forgotten dream. My thoughts return to this afternoon's session with Leah Iverson. There was something alarming in her level of intensity – in all the time she's been coming to see me, I have never seen her in a state like that before. I know I'll need to return to the session, write up some notes and consider whether to intervene further, but right now, I need to focus on the evening ahead.

I step into the dress and watch myself transform from weary and anonymous-looking to something close to glamorous. Definitely this dress. I choose a cashmere Louis Vuitton scarf to drape across my bare shoulders and a little violet clutch bag with a clasp set with turquoise stones that pick up the color of the dress. From the wall I unhook my trusty skyscraper nude Louboutins and wince at the thought of wearing them all night; my feet are more accustomed to Uggs and sneakers these days. I put the shoes on and go through to the bathroom to do my make-up.

'Black is better,' says a voice from the doorway. I jump, smearing mascara to the side of my right eye. My husband is standing there, smiling bemusedly at me, beads of rainwater studding his jacket, some dripping from his hair onto the tiles.

'Don't you like this?' I ask, turning to face him. He looks me up and down.

'You look beautiful. Ravishing in fact. But on this occasion, definitely black. It's a very formal event.'

'Okay,' I say, and return to the mirror to remove the mascara blob. I feel a pang of disappointment. I wanted Eirik to be impressed with my choice, but my husband is even more of a perfectionist than I am, and this is his work event, so I am happy to choose another dress.

I take a sip of the wine while Eirik gets in the shower, and I watch the outline of his big body through bursts of rising steam, like a skyscraper behind fog. For a moment I consider joining him, slipping my arms around his wet torso from behind, holding him close. I decide against it; Eirik will be fully focused on the evening ahead and most likely needs a little time to himself to get in the right headspace and go over his speech again.

When he emerges from the shower, I've changed and am wearing a foolproof silk-and-taffeta gala dress I bought in Paris several years ago and have only worn once. I've coiled my hair into a high bun, securing a few stray strands to the side in place with discreet diamanté slides. Eirik takes me in, a slow smile spreading across his face.

'Wow,' he says. He wipes himself briskly down with the towel and then throws it into the corner of the bathroom. He sidles up against me where I'm standing at the sink and puts his arms around me from behind, our eyes meeting in the mirror. He pulls me very close and nuzzles my neck, and I can feel his erection nudging against my buttocks. With one hand, Eirik undoes my hair from its clip, sending it flowing around my shoulders, and with the other hand he hoists the dress up around my hips and then he's inside me, moving hard but slow, our eyes still locked on each other's in the mirror.

Though it would be less than a five-minute walk, a black Conservative Party car picks us up and drops us at the residence. Before we step outside onto the pavement, where several reporters and photographers await the arrival of politicians and various celebrities, Eirik gives me a reassuring smile. I lock my eyes on his confident, calm gaze, suddenly feeling nervous. This isn't my world, but if Eirik wins the elections, it will be. I might even live here someday, I think to myself, glancing up at the dramatically lit, imposing residence. It's still raining heavily, and a man swoops in with an umbrella and opens my door, ensuring not a single drop of rain touches me. Eirik and I pose for the photographers under an awning and I feel a deep thrill in my stomach at the surrealness of it; of waking up this morning, seeing clients all day, then coming here and being photographed for newspapers and gossip magazines because I'm married to one of Norway's most popular politicians.

The dinner is exquisite, filet mignon and lobster, and as the last course is cleared away, the speeches begin. I allow myself to drift about on my thoughts, taking in my surroundings and the other guests, making sure to laugh when I hear laughter, and clap when everyone else does. A blonde woman at a table close to the row of windows catches my eye. I feel a sudden jolt – she looks so much like Elisabeth in profile that I lean forward to get a better view. She is craning her neck to see the woman speaking, so I have only a limited view of her face. Her eyes crease as she smiles and her hands are clasped together, as if poised for the next round of applause. Her hair is glinting beautifully; tiny glass beads are woven into her updo, catching the light from the enormous chandeliers overhead. I imagine the woman getting up and walking across the room to me, beaming, her arms outstretched, and for the briefest of moments it's *her*, it really is her, Elisabeth, and none of the terrible things that have happened were real, it was just a dream. Just another bad dream.

I must be staring at her, mesmerized, and as if she realizes she's being watched, the woman turns in my direction. For a second, our eyes meet across the room. I realize that the woman is Mette-Marit, the crown princess, and that she looks nothing like Elisabeth after all. I clear my throat and let my eyes drop to the table in front of me. The palms of my hands are slick, my heart hammering. Will I forever be seeing the ghost of Elisabeth in the faces of strangers? My thoughts dart briefly to Leah Iverson, and I realize that the way she behaved this afternoon in our session also reminded me of Elisabeth. The disjointed sentences, the bruises, the desperation she emanated. I wonder where Leah is right now; I really hope she is safe and taking care of herself tonight.

The woman who was speaking, the minister of education, has stopped and returned to her seat. From every corner, waiters swoop in and refill wine glasses, conscious of the brief lull in proceedings before the next speech. Eirik squeezes my knee lightly.

'I'm on,' he says, winking at me before standing up, the room erupting into an enthusiastic round of applause. He walks to the top of the room and stands still, waiting for the applause to die down, smiling and nodding. There is nothing about his composure that suggests he is even mildly nervous to stand here in a room full of the upper echelons of Norway's society, including the crown prince and princess, about to give a speech. I am mesmerized watching him speak; he comes across as a man entirely in his element – confident, knowledgeable, with a dash of humor thrown in. It's strange to think that this is the same man who sleeps next to me every night, whose most intimate moments are shared with me. I think about the sex earlier, how it felt more like the thrilling sex between strangers than the usual, less adventurous sex we normally have, carefully planned around ovulation cycles and likeliness of conception. For a moment, I allow myself to imagine that tonight of all nights was the time it actually worked, and that in this very moment that much-wanted child is beginning inside me: a single cell breaking into two. I make myself stop this train of thought because it hurts too much. Every month, no matter how hopeful I've felt, no matter how hard I have tried to believe that it will happen for us eventually, the dreaded blood arrives. My heart beats faster. I take a big glug of champagne and return my attention to Eirik's speech. I hear him speak my name and get the sudden sensation of several hundred pairs of eyes on me.

'My wife, Dr Kristina Moss,' he says. 'None of this would have been possible without her.' People smile and clap and a flash goes off somewhere, and it occurs to me, perhaps for the first time, that Eirik needs me as much as I need him.

3

Kristina

I wake to a repetitive muffled sound. Eirik is gone from bed and I sit up, blinking several times, but it feels as though my eyes have been stuck together. My pulse is fast and a vivid headache chases through my skull. I remember last night, all the drinks, the hours of sitting through moderately interesting speeches about political reform, progress, prosperity. For a moment I see the crown princess in my mind, how beautiful she looked with her radiant smile and subtly glinting updo. The neon light from a phone screen moves around from over in the corner, sending roaming shapes across the room.

'Eirik?' I whisper.

'Hey,' he says, shining the light toward me. 'Sorry. Sorry, I didn't mean to wake you.'

'What's happening? What time is it?'

'It's 5.15. I'm going to have to fly to Bergen, unfortunately. A car's waiting outside to take me to the airport.'

'Wait, what? It's Saturday.'

'I know.'

'We're going to spend the night at my sister's, remember?'

'I know. I'm sorry. Look, this is strictly confidential, but there's a situation at the west coast party office. One of the guys I directly oversee has been accused of gross misconduct.'

I feel tears of disappointment pricking my eyes, though I know I'm being dramatic. Eirik's decision to go from international corporate law into politics was a joint decision and I knew full well that it would be demanding on our marriage. Or did I, really? There are so many things in life we can only truly understand once we're actually living and feeling them.

'Okay,' I say.

'I am sorry, Kristina.' Eirik comes over to my side of the bed and squats down beside me. 'Pass on my love to Camilla and the kids. I'll be back tomorrow afternoon. I love you.' He presses his lips to my forehead, and I catch a whiff of his familiar cologne, the same he's used since his student days, when we met: Fahrenheit by Christian Dior, and for some reason this brings more tears to my eyes. He rushes from the room and I imagine him stepping into a shiny party car pulled up outside the building, his mind razor sharp and trained on the day ahead. He has an ability to completely compartmentalize his career from the rest of his life and never lets anything impact his work. I think it is because he lost his mother in childhood and became accustomed to closing off parts of himself and his feelings for protection. For several minutes after he's gone, his scent clings to the air in our bedroom and I close my eyes, though I know I won't get any more sleep.

★ ★ ★

We walk down to the soggy, deserted beach, stopping for the kids to jump in every single puddle. I make myself smile at them and say all the right things when they rush over to where I'm standing with Camilla under a giant oak tree to show us some trinket or another, but inside it feels like I could fall to pieces just looking at my niece and nephew. What hurts so much is taking in their impossible sweetness; it's like being taunted by everything I don't have.

I zone out from the long story Camilla is telling me about the audacity of her awful colleague and try to allow those feelings – they may feel like a numb, impenetrable kind of nothingness, but that is never the case. I remind myself that if I was one of my own clients, I would feel so much empathy for the woman standing on this beach watching those beautiful children play.

Also, I suppose I'm still a little upset that Eirik didn't come with me, though it's nice for Camilla and me to have this rare time together, just the two of us and the kids. Her husband, Mikkel, decided to go on an overnight fishing trip when I explained Eirik couldn't make it, giving Camilla and me some 'sister time'.

'Look!' screams Vilja, holding up a chewed stick triumphantly.

'Wow,' I say.

'Look at this,' shouts Birk, shoving his little sister aside, who responds by throwing the chewed stick hard at the back of his head. Camilla rolls her eyes at me, then intercepts, speaking calmly and diplomatically until the argument dies down and they run back down toward the sand, laughing and shouting. My sister – the perfect mother. She really is. She took to motherhood like a duck to water, like she was born to take care of little people, unlike me. I feel a surge of familiar jealousy toward my older sister, though these days I recognize it instantly and am able to consciously choose to not rise to it. We are fourteen months apart, and as a child, it was hard to be in the shadow of someone always that little bit faster, cleverer, more accomplished. I often felt like a lesser version of her, and it wasn't until I was older that I realized I probably got treated as such. As a teenager, I made a real point out of distancing myself from Camilla, dying my hair blonde and barely acknowledging her at school. As adults, we are extremely close – I'd say Camilla is the person I'm closest to besides Eirik.

Still, our relationship occasionally feels difficult for me – ever since Eirik and I started trying for a baby two years ago. I suppose I took it for granted that I would just get pregnant as soon as I wanted to, like my sister. That I still haven't, in spite of everything, feels like a profound betrayal by my body and these are things I work intently on in my own therapy. I'm not sure I'll ever be able to make my peace with it if we remain unsuccessful, especially if the underlying reason turns out to be the aftermath of trauma. The irony of dedicating my life to healing other people's trauma, while being held back by my own. I swallow hard and turn to my sister.

'Did I tell you that we're taking a break from IVF?'

'No.'

I nod. Our eyes meet; hers are full of kindness. She looks how I hope I look when my clients share something important with me.

'Yeah. Well. My body was literally crumbling from over-stimulation. It's a relief to have a break from all the injections.'

'I can imagine. I'm sorry, Kristina. It will happen.'

'Yeah.' I look at Birk and Vilja chasing each other down the beach, their wellies leaving soggy footprints that moments later get erased by the surging, cold waves.

'It will.'

'Yeah. You know, it sounds a little mad, but I sometimes feel this irrational hope that it could still happen naturally. That if we could just remove ourselves from all the stress, from the invasive procedures, the injections and the carefully timed sex that doesn't feel sexy at all, then it might just happen—'

'And it might.'

I nod and think about last night again, how different and exciting it felt. 'Yeah, it might.' One cell that becomes two that becomes a thousand that becomes a million; it could be happening inside me right now. But I don't dare to believe anymore, and consciously shut down these thoughts – nothing hurts more than false hope.

I move my thoughts away from my own problems and stare out at the raging, gray sea, but feel a flicker of the anxiety I felt after Leah Iverson's session on Friday return. I wonder what she is doing at this moment, whether she is doing better. I think about the envelope she handed me, and its strange contents. I stood watching as she ran across the street after the session, still clutching the little package she'd handed me. Her shape became distorted in the fierce downpour, like a spectre, then it disappeared, merging with the trees and bushes in the park. I opened my hand, then the envelope in it. Inside was a set of old-fashioned keys, like the ones to my grandmother's farmhouse in Valdres. There was also a local area map, with handwritten instructions scribbled on it. A location was marked with an 'x' in the middle of what seemed to be a vast forest. 'Bekkebu', Leah had written above it – the name of her cabin, I recalled. Near a lake called Heivannet, she'd made a second marking – a 'p' for 'park here'. At the top of the map, she'd written 'Please please please come.'

It's not the first time a client has asked me to meet outside the therapy room – it can be very difficult for people to grasp the boundaries between therapist and client, when therapy is necessarily built on emotional intimacy. I've had clients who constantly ask me personal questions, and who have spent significant amounts of time attempting to convince me that we would make great friends in real life. Leah, too, has on a few occasions expressed curiosity about who I am in my personal life. Still, it is definitely out of character for Leah Iverson to behave like this, imploring me to meet with her at a remote cabin – she seemed almost possessed and not at all like herself. I make a mental note to get in touch with her GP tomorrow morning, and to email Leah to suggest she come in for an extra session this week.

'Why don't you stay until tomorrow?' asks Camilla, bringing me back to the blustery beach and my little niece and nephew laughing into the wind, their white-blonde heads thrown back, their hands extended as though they are trying to embrace the whole world.

'I would, but I have a client at eight thirty,' I say. This isn't exactly true – my first is at eleven, but I'd like a couple of hours in my peaceful, bright office before seeing anyone, catching up on emails and case notes like I always do on a Monday morning. Besides, I am exhausted after a full weekend with Camilla, Vilja and Birk and I want to enjoy a long evening at home with Eirik, cooking together and snuggling by the fireplace.

I leave Camilla's at four and start the drive back to Oslo, but get caught up in the painfully slow Sunday-afternoon traffic of weekenders returning to the city from their cabins. At one point it completely stops moving and I put the car in neutral, securing the handbrake. I sit, cocooned, listening to the slam of the rain, which is falling heavily again for the ninth day in a row. I turn the wipers off to better hear the rain and, without them, the world instantly becomes a gray blur. I still feel disconcertingly empty, like I have all weekend. I'm not sure if it's due to how emotional I sometimes get being around my niece and nephew, or a lingering sense of worry for Leah Iverson. I am usually good at switching off from my clients at weekends – I have to be. Or it is because this is the first time I've returned to Oslo on this same road without stopping in to see Elisabeth. And I never will again. Villa Vinternatt is down there, set snug in a leafy forest between the motorway and the sea, less than three minutes' drive away from where the traffic has ground to a standstill. And she isn't there. Of course – that must be why I feel unsettled and a little melancholic.

Still no movement on the road, so I fish my phone from my handbag and glance at the screen. There are two missed calls from a number I don't recognize. And there is a message from Eirik, sent fifteen minutes ago, probably right after I texted him saying I was on my way home.

I thought you'd be home much later. You said Sunday night? I'm with Lars, we thought we'd catch a movie at six.

I feel a stab of annoyance. We hardly ever see each other – why is he making plans with his friend on a Sunday night? And if he really thought I'd be home later, why didn't he cancel with Lars when he received my message saying I was on my way home? I'm not a demanding wife. At least I don't think I am. I just want to feel prioritized by Eirik, and the truth is, much of the time, I don't. Especially lately.

The traffic has started moving again, leaving a wide gap between my car and the one in front, so I put the phone away and nudge the gas. The drive, which usually takes forty minutes, takes over two hours, and by the time I shut the door to the apartment behind me, breathing in its warm, familiar scent, it's six thirty. It's actually rather nice that Eirik is out; I've got used to having the apartment mostly to myself. I throw my weekend bag and handbag onto the sofa and decide to run a bath. I'll pour myself a large glass of red and soak for as long as I want, reading my book or maybe an interiors magazine. I turn on the tap and stand for a while in the bathroom, looking myself in the eye. If I were one of my clients, how would I describe the woman in front of me?

Kristina Moss, thirty-six years old. Married, no kids. A little tired-looking, with harsh blue circles beneath my eyes tonight, thanks to the late night on Friday and last night spent tossing and turning, snatching just a few hours of sleep in the early hours before Birk and Vilja rushed into the room at six like beautiful little hurricanes. My lips are full, my eyes a very dark brown, my chestnut-brown hair is pulled back and fastened in a messy topknot. A long, thin scar runs down my forehead. Strong nose and arched eyebrows from my father. Dimples and straight teeth from my mother, my favorite two things about my face.

A sound separates itself from the flowing water and I stand still, listening. It is a metallic sound, like two components of machinery clashing together, but then I realize it's my new ringtone and the sound is exacerbated against the marble surface of the lounge table where I've left the phone. I reach it before it stops ringing, noticing that it's a different number from the previous missed calls I haven't yet returned.

'Hello?'

There is no response, though I can hear someone is there, breathing into the phone.

'Hello?' Still nothing. I stay on the line for a while, listening to the faint, raspy breathing. This kind of thing doesn't frighten or unsettle me; it has happened quite a few times, and when I've looked up the caller ID on 1881.no it is almost always some client or another, struggling late at night or on a weekend, who couldn't resist calling to just hear the sound of my voice. It comes with the territory, and I never bring the calls up in the subsequent session. They actually make me feel especially empathetic toward a client, and besides, I know the feeling myself, of just needing to hear your therapist's voice when everything feels impossible and pitch black. Tonight, I wonder if it could be Leah Iverson calling. I stay on the line, sitting on the side of the bathtub and watching bubbles pop on the water's surface, for four minutes and thirty-nine seconds, until the line goes dead.

4

Leah, two weeks before

In the small hours, when the sky is still dense with darkness, Leah is jolted from fretful dreams by the sound of a door slamming shut somewhere in the building. There's a doctor on the second floor – he comes and goes at odd hours; it might be him. Or it might be the young girls sharing an apartment on the ground floor – they often come home when others start to wake. There's a cello player across the landing from Leah's own flat, a quiet and skinny man in his forties. She doubts it was him; the only sounds she ever hears from that apartment are mournful rising and falling concertos.

Or... Or it could be Anton. She feels the little hairs on her forearm prickle and stand up at the thought of Anton coming up the stairs and makes herself take several long, deep breaths. *He doesn't know where you live, Leah.* She imagines Kristina's calm, soothing voice speaking the words directly into her ear.

She turns over in bed, wishes she wasn't alone, though

she usually is. She flicks the radio switch and the buzz of voices fills the bedroom. Two men, discussing the situation in the Crimea. She turns the faux-ancient dial on her brand-new radio until soft music fills the room. Cello, in fact – Bach. She closes her eyes but knows she won't sleep again, not tonight.

She'll be exhausted by lunchtime, and feels her stomach tighten with dread at all the long hours in front of the computer awaiting her, trying to find the words she needs to write. They don't come anymore, and she almost can't remember the days when writing was something joyful, when the words seemed to scatter from her fingertips. She'll return to bed in the late afternoon, reading, checking her phone, listening to music, crying, the loneliness and yearning as insistent as bacteria burrowing into her bones. But then sleep does come, and Leah is lulled by dreams. The vision of bacteria inside her body somehow seeps into her dream, a strange world where she's carried through narrow maroon canals as if on a boat, before being expelled into cool air through a purple-edged wound.

5

Kristina

All the jokes about Mondays fall flat on me – I've always liked Mondays, a fresh start every week. In my line of work, I sometimes feel worn down and jaded by the time Friday rolls around and it takes the weekend to process and clear my head. But I love what I do, and by Monday morning, I can't wait to get back to my office. I rent a pleasant, airy space at the pedestrian end of Hegdehaugsveien, in what used to be a large turn-of-the-century apartment, together with two other therapists and an osteopath. We call ourselves Homansbyen Terapisenter and share a kitchen and bathroom. We've become friendly over the years, sometimes heading to Lorry's, the pub on the corner, for a drink after work on Thursdays, and quite frequently passing new clients on to one another when someone isn't quite a match.

On Monday mornings I'm here alone, sometimes for several hours – my colleagues have a policy of not booking clients early on Mondays. So do I, but I still come in early because I love this time to catch up with myself and prepare for the week ahead. It's important to me to always be organized; it prevents so much chaos. Eirik makes fun of me for it sometimes, saying it's almost creepy how one could open any drawer in our house at any time and it would always be immaculately ordered. *Where do you keep the loose ends, the mess, the stuff you want to keep hidden?* he'll ask, laughing. I don't; I go through the mess, and then I get rid of it. I aspire to achieve a mind and a life as transparent as my brightly lit, meticulously ordered closet with neat, instantly recognizable thoughts and feelings sorted like clothes in open shelves.

I get up but almost immediately sit back down – the feeling of restlessness since the weekend hasn't quite left me. I make myself focus on the notes on the screen in front of me. I need to jot down a few notes about today's clients, as well as get in touch with a couple of GPs with regards to clients' medication – I like to stay informed and updated in the cases where someone might be taking mood-altering medication in addition to psychotherapy.

I look up Leah's phone number in my client list, and compare it to the unknown numbers that called me last night. The last one was hers. Where was she when she called? What was she doing in those long minutes she had me on the line? I imagine her in bed, sobbing in the dark, her beautiful face twisted in a grimace of pain, the bruises on her face starting to fade from indigo to pale violet and sickly yellow.

I open my calendar, which is busier than usual, with two new clients starting and a few extra sessions requested by established clients, but I do have a couple of free slots, one this afternoon and one on Wednesday. I hope Leah will take one of them. I redial her number, but it goes straight to voicemail without ringing. I try again, with the same result. It's still early, only just gone 8 a.m. I don't imagine she gets up early, as an author working from home; I don't assume she would have anywhere to be this early. I'll email instead, and she can get in touch when it suits her.

To: liverson@vimeo.no

Subject: Sessions

Hi Leah,

I wanted to check in with you after Friday; you've been on my mind. How are you doing? I know you called me last night; do try again, if you like. I also wanted to let you know that I have a couple of free slots available this week, if you'd like some extra support. I can easily add an extra session or two to your therapy scheme with your GP, so you won't be billed – let me know.

All best,

Kristina

I press 'send' and get up from my desk. I take my delicious Kusmi tea, which I don't offer to clients, from the cupboard and flick the switch on the kettle. While I wait for the water to boil, I draw the scent of the blend deep into my lungs and watch people milling around on the street two floors down. There's a long line at Kaffebrenneriet, snaking all the way outside onto the pavement. A jam-packed blue tram inches past, sandwiched by slow-moving cars heading toward Solli Plass. A blonde woman emerges from the café and dashes across the road. She's wearing wide-leg trousers and impressively high heels, clutching a tall coffee, shielding her bouncy hair from the rain with a document folder.

I hear a ping from my computer, and instantly my thoughts return to Leah – I hope it's her, responding straight away. I realize how worried I am for her by the way I feel a dull ache in my stomach at the thought of her. There was something about the look in her eyes. The way she begged.

The email isn't from Leah but from a woman called Tess who is looking for a therapist to help her 'navigate the worst divorce ever'. I make a mental note to respond to her later, saying I have plenty of experience with divorce, and schedule her in for next week. I open a new email draft and write to Leah's GP, a competent and kindly man called Dr Albert who refers many clients to me and my colleagues for psychotherapy.

I believe there is reason for concern for Leah Iverson's well-being, I write. *She has made repeat mentions of self-harm and suicidal ideation, and while I haven't considered her high-risk previously due to her encouraging response to psychotherapy, I feel concerned that may have changed.*

I have emailed Leah this morning to offer extra support, and I will suggest that she also makes an appointment to see you with a view to discussing more intensive support, and/or further intervention.

* * *

The day passes in a blur, with back-to-back clients, and it isn't until 3 p.m. that I get a chance to check my email again. No response from Leah. The free slot I have is at the end of the day – at 4.30, and I decide to stay until then in case Leah gets in touch and wants to come by. My stomach growls and I realize I haven't had lunch. There's nothing but some dried crackers in my cupboard and I'm not in the mood for prepping something in the communal kitchen; someone will inevitably appear for a chat. I am feeling introspective and restless today, and just want to be in my own space. I message Eirik and ask about dinner plans, and though he reads my WhatsApp straight away, the minutes tick by with no response. I am used to this, but suddenly it makes me angry.

I walk downstairs and out into the misty rain – it's the kind that doesn't seem to dissolve into individual droplets, but that envelops you in a moist sheen. I cross the road to Kaffebrenneriet, which is entirely empty now, and place my order, a tall white Americano and a chicken-and-pesto baguette. My phone vibrates in my pocket and I glance at the message.

What time will you be here? Making butterflied chicken, your favorite! Will Eirik be joining us?

My mother. My heart sinks. I fish my calendar out of my handbag and realize that I had, in fact, written 'Dinner with Mum' on October 26th – today. She gets lonely when my father travels, and he is away this week in Iceland with the geology society he is a founding member of. I vaguely recall speaking to her on the phone last week and making dinner plans, but I completely forgot and don't feel up for it – my mother can talk anyone's head off and I'm simply not in the mood. I think about messaging Eirik again but he's clearly forgotten too so I decide to just go on my own.

The next hour drags past and I'm irritable and unfocused, so I feel relieved when Leah doesn't show up, hoping she'll take the free slot on Wednesday morning instead. At 4.50 on the dot, I leave the office and walk fast alongside the heavily congested road by the royal park to the train station on the other side. Again, I see Leah in my mind, the way she rushed from the session on Friday and outside into the heavy rain. There was something ghostly about how she was swallowed up by the gloomy fog, like she had never existed at all, and I keep my eyes locked to the drenched pavement.

6

Kristina

I open the door without knocking and stand for a long moment in the hallway, drawing in the familiar scent of my childhood home. I run my hand lightly across my father's battered golf bag and smile at a childhood picture of Camilla and me on the wall. I take my drenched parka off and hang it on the wall hook, letting it drip onto the tiles. I remember sitting on this same floor as a child, struggling to get out of my bulky winter boots, loving the warmth from the underfloor heating after coming back inside from playing in the snow for hours. The house smelled exactly the same then – of laundry, food always prepared from scratch, the distinct, chalky smell of the rock samples in my father's office, the orange roses my mother favors: home.

I avoid my gaze in the mirror, the drowned cat look was never a good one, and I need to summon all my energy to get through the evening with my mother when what I want is to just withdraw to the bathtub with a large glass of wine and my own thoughts.

'What are you doing standing there, honey? Oh, gosh, you are absolutely soaked!' My mother has appeared in the doorway without me noticing and pulls me into a close hug. I'm surprised by how good it feels to be held by her and I stay in her embrace for a little longer than I normally would, noticing that she feels slighter and smaller than I think of her. It's a special sorrow, that moment when you realize that your parents have grown old.

'Hey, Mum,' I say.

'Oh, Kristina, you look so...'

'Terrible?'

'No, of course not. Tired and wet. Never terrible, you beautiful, silly girl.' She ushers me into the open-plan living area that she insisted upon a couple of years ago, knocking through the small, cozy rooms of my childhood and creating a 'more modern home'. She presses a glass of white wine into my hand and I take a big, grateful sip and sit down in my usual place at the table.

'It's so good to have you here. I haven't seen you in so long! How long is it?' says my mother, placing two heaped plates on the table, chunks of chicken swimming in watery red-onion gravy.

'It's just a couple of weeks, Mum,' I say, but grant her a smile. It's not her fault that I'm worn out. 'How have you been?'

'Busy. It seems like the petition has a good chance of winning, though if there's one thing I've learned, it's not to take anything for granted. After we were featured in the newspaper, I was invited to speak about the situation on the radio. That raised awareness, as you can imagine.'

'Yes.'

My mother has spent the last year relentlessly campaigning against the council's plan to place a new stretch of the E18 motorway exactly through where my childhood home stands.

'Of course, I now have to do much of the work on my own. After what happened with Elisabeth, Idun just can't face doing what needs to be done, so I'm doing it all. To be honest, she can barely get out of bed in the morning.' I nod, but a visceral dread spreads out in the pit of my stomach and I focus on chewing my food slowly, so I can't be expected to respond. I knew my mother would want to talk about Elisabeth. It's only natural, considering, but I'm still reeling from her loss and find it difficult to manage my emotions when her name is dropped into the conversation without warning. 'I don't think she'll ever get over it,' continues my mother. 'Such a terrible waste. In spite of everything, she didn't see it coming.'

I nod again and look outside to the garden where Elisabeth and I used to play as children. I decide to bring my feelings of guilt and grief over Elisabeth to my own therapy tomorrow, like I already have, over and over, since August.

Elisabeth's family have always lived next to my own, in a house the mirror image of my family's. Our gardens border each other, separated only by a low hedge, which became trampled and mangled over the years as Camilla and I constantly scrambled across it to get to Elisabeth. Because we were friends from before I can remember, I have no recollection of any firsts – the first time we met, the first time we laughed together, our first sleepover. She was just always there. Elisabeth was an only child, which makes her death an even crueler tragedy for her mother and father. As a child, she was jealous of me having an older sister. She used to say that she was the third sister and, well into our teens, she'd introduce me to people as her sister.

Elisabeth was intense, creative, moody, fiercely intelligent. She'd come up with the games we'd play and all the kids in the neighborhood generally followed her lead. I remember her as always having an audience, whether it was just me or many other kids too. It was always *The Elisabeth Show*. We loved her. She'd become famous and celebrated when we grew up; this was accepted among us kids as fact. But she didn't. She died in what should have been her prime, in the most tragic of circumstances.

'I need to get home,' I say, pushing my half-eaten plate of butterflied chicken aside. The dull ache in my stomach from thinking about Elisabeth is spreading outwards and I just want to go home and get an early night. Eirik is working late, I have the apartment to myself.

'But… But you only arrived an hour ago. Why don't you take the eight o'clock train? That will give us a little more time to catch up—'

'I'm sorry, Mum. Really. The food was delicious. I'm just a little tired. It must be the weather. It's so awful; it's like it settles in your bones. And work is stressful at the moment.'

'What about Idun? Aren't you going to pop next door to see her? She'll be expecting you.'

I swallow hard. I can't face Elisabeth's mother, not today. I shake my head, and stand up, avoiding my mother's disapproving gaze.

I decline the offer of a ride to the station, and walk fast through the rain, which is falling sideways now, dragging across the street in bitter columns on a brisk wind. It beats into my face, pummeling it raw. I take the shortcut through the woods, using my special mindfulness technique of focusing purely on the sensation of my physical being in its environment to feel safe. The wet thud of my Nikes on the path scattered with brown pine needles. The sound of rain hitting the crowns of trees and dribbling down their stems. My fingertips turning rigid and red with the cold. The way distant woodsmoke from the suburban neighborhoods surrounding this little patch of woods drifts across on the moist air and settles in my nostrils. The woods give way to a huge parking lot and a gray, huddled building rising from the concrete: the train station; I made it.

On the train, I check my phone. Nothing from Eirik other than he's working late. These days he only rarely arrives home before I go to sleep, and most mornings he's out the door before I wake. And I'm a night owl who gets up early. There's a message from my colleague, Alice, asking if we can share a room at the integrative therapeutic practice conference we're both attending in Tromsø next month. And there is an email from Dr Albert.

From: Walbert@medicus.no

Subject: RE Leah Iverson

Dear Dr Moss,

Thank you for getting in touch with me with regard to Leah Iverson. I, too, am concerned for her well-being, and especially considering her current circumstances. I saw her last week for a routine check-up and she did not appear well. I will get in touch with the borough's psychiatric team as I think Leah may benefit from more support, especially over the coming few months. Could you let me know of any developments after your session/s with Leah later this week? Also, just to confirm – are you aware of Leah's pregnancy (13+3)?

Best wishes,

Dr Wilhelm Albert

7

Leah, two weeks before

It's just gone 4 a.m. and she's still up. It's her favorite time, when almost everyone else is asleep. It's a confirmation of aloneness, a validation – she really is alone then, rather than just feeling alone, like the rest of the time. The words won't come. It is a special kind of pain, waiting for words to form and emerge, perhaps it can be compared to waiting for a baby: it won't come until it's ready.

She stands up and looks over at her bed. Her mind is razor sharp and buzzing. Her body, too, feels like it is throbbing with life and restless energy. She turns to the window and looks out at a dry, crystalline night, shivering slightly with cold she can see but not feel. A thin sheen of ice has formed on the cars parked along the street, making them sparkle in the moonlight. The trees have shed the last of their leaves and stand stripped and resigned to the coming winter. They're more beautiful like this, she thinks, when you can see their underpinnings. Like a woman undressed, supple skin and soft curves glowing in low light. She steps out of her cozy home tracksuit bottoms, and unzips its matching top. She undoes her bra and removes her underwear too.

In bed she relaxes into her own touch, kneading and pushing and rubbing. Her thoughts go from soft to hard; from the gentle curves of a woman to the need to be held by someone bigger than herself, to the exhilarating feel of strong hands closing around her neck, squeezing hard then easing up and stroking her, then squeezing again. Her body responds and she feels herself inch closer, then closer still. She angles the sharp spike on her bracelet against the taut skin of her throat and lets it dig into her flesh. It makes her gasp with pain, and it gives her another surge, closer.

8

Kristina

It's a beautiful morning, the first in a while. It's bitterly cold with ice crystals shimmering on the hoods of cars and the trunks of trees, but the sky is a vivid blue, and a brilliant sun bathes Oslo in a golden autumnal glow.

I leave the house in a daze, the sleepless night lingering like a membrane between me and the cold morning air. For hours and hours, I lay tossing and turning, my mind spinning and my heart aching. I pretended to be sleeping when Eirik came home around ten thirty, but he must have known I was awake because he held me tight in spoons, nuzzling my neck and stroking my arms and stomach lightly. I wanted to cry, but managed to stop myself by focusing on even, deep breathing.

I wish calling my clients and canceling today's sessions was an option – the thought of sitting across from someone, listening intensely, fills me with restlessness. But first, supervision – it will be good to talk to Vera about what's going on.

On the corner of Parkveien, I stop and buy a coffee at Kaffebrenneriet and, stirring the brown sugar granules through my Americano, it occurs to me how absurd it is that I know the most intimate details of my clients' lives, but I have no idea how they take their coffee. I consciously construct an image of Leah in my mind, ordering a coffee at this very same café, which she may well do in real life – she doesn't live far away. I imagine her quick smile for the barista, a moment of deliberation over a pain au chocolat, and her distinctive, quick way of moving as she leaves the café, clutching a paper cup. Almond-milk macchiato, I decide. Leah is someone who makes conscious choices about everything she eats and drinks, and it has more to do with a desire for control than healthy life choices, though she proclaims that is the primary reason. She is most likely even more conscious of her dietary choices at present, considering her circumstances.

It's Tuesday and I still haven't heard from Leah. I am going to have to explain to her in our session on Friday that as our relationship is entirely based on mutual trust, and because our work simply cannot bring change unless that trust is there, we do need to be committed to answering emails, and especially after an episode such as at our last session.

I look around the busy café and make for the door with my coffee, but still an image of Leah lingers on my mind; only now, she is visibly pregnant. She's sitting at one of the tables in the corner, looking out onto the busy street, smiling serenely, drawing the gentle floral scent of a jasmine green tea into her nostrils, resting a hand on a tiny but unmistakable bump. How could I have missed it?

Each time my mind goes to the pregnancy it recoils. I just don't understand why Leah would hide such a thing from me. Or how it is even possible that I have missed the changes that must have been happening in her for a while now – has her skin been particularly radiant and glowing, has a soft swell started to appear on her belly? I run these questions over and over in my mind, but she has been the same all along, I'm sure of it. Did I simply not want to see it? Did I sense it on some level, but subconsciously refuse to acknowledge it since she never mentioned it?

I take a moment to determine whether it still affects me so deeply to learn of another's pregnancy. And – yes. Yes, it does. It hurts like hell; it hits me with the sudden, shocking force of a finger smashed in a doorway – every time. I fill my empty stomach with the hot, bitter coffee and start walking again, chasing away the image of Leah pregnant. The wind is picking up again, tearing at my hair and making my eyes sting.

Kristina, are you aware of Leah's pregnancy?

I open my mouth to speak, but nothing emerges, just a sad little squawk. Vera leans forward, empathy and warmth in her eyes, her mouth set in a commiserating little line.

'You look sad this morning, Kristina.'

'Mmmm.' We sit in silence for a long while – I watch several minutes drain from the digital clock above the door. Vera never prompts me, just sits there like a soothing presence. I often channel her calm, comfortable approach to silence when it comes to my own clients, something which didn't come easy to me early on in my career. I had to fight the urge to fill any prolonged silence with a question or just a sound to indicate I was still listening and soaking up whatever the client brought to the session. Now, I think I have become more like Vera, interested in the silences and able to let them unfold and speak for themselves.

'It's one of my clients,' I say, at last. 'Leah Iverson. You know, the Swedish novelist.'

'I remember.'

'She was very agitated in our session on Friday. She literally ran off before the end of the session, and begged me to meet her outside the therapy room. I explained why that isn't possible, of course. Then she called me late on Sunday evening, but she said nothing. I figured she needed to know I was there so I stayed on the line until it went dead. On Monday I tried to return her call, but it went straight to voicemail. I then emailed her offering extra sessions this week, but she hasn't responded. I felt worried over the weekend. It was as if I couldn't stop thinking about her; it was so out of character for her to behave like that. She's usually quite composed, though in the last year she has increasingly been showing emotions in our sessions, like she is able to connect with them more. I emailed her GP yesterday, saying I felt concerned and that we may need to consider getting Leah some extra support. She's been a self-harmer for years, though nothing very serious. As you know, she's spoken of suicide quite a bit, though more in terms of compulsive thoughts than actual intent.'

'Did she speak of suicide or self-harm on Friday?'

'No. She did say she needed to tell me something, several times. But then she didn't. She asked me to come to her cabin and even gave me a key to it. She seemed very out of it, not at all like herself. Also, her face was bruised but she refused to say what had happened.'

'Yes, it sounds like she was experiencing something very distressing. What did the GP say?'

Again I open my mouth but no sound will come. Tears gather in my eyes, then roll down my face.

'He said he agrees about providing extra support for Leah. And he asked if I was aware of the fact that she's pregnant.'

'I see. And were you?'

'No. She hasn't told me.'

'That must be difficult to understand.'

'Well, I know that she isn't obliged to tell me anything at all and that it's not right of me to expect that of her. It's just, this came out of left field and I suppose it triggers my own experiences.'

'Yes.'

'I've worked with other pregnant women and have a couple of new mothers at the moment, and I'd be lying if I said that it isn't challenging at times, considering the fact that Eirik and I so far haven't managed to get pregnant.' And not for a lack of trying – seven cycles of IVF with nothing to show for it. 'But I think when it comes to Leah, it feels especially unfair and difficult because I know she wouldn't want to be pregnant and is pretty likely to have an abortion. She doesn't have a partner, or a lifestyle suitable for a child. What would she be able to offer it? She's working through some very complex issues which present in ways that would be directly harmful to a child…' I trail off, and wipe at tears, looking out the window at the brilliant blue sky. I can't bear Vera's immense empathy in this moment.

'But Kristina, she hasn't yet spoken to you about her pregnancy. People do change, and perhaps Leah is making changes to her life that would benefit a potential child. It occurs to me that in this case, you don't know what is going on, and perhaps it feels like a rejection that she hasn't chosen to share this with you.'

'Yes.'

'And on a personal level, her presumably unplanned pregnancy feels unfair to you due to your own painful struggle to conceive.'

I nod, not even trying to stop the fresh rush of tears.

'Do you think you will be able to support her through her pregnancy, no matter how it ends?'

'Well, yes. I mean, of course. I'm just shocked, I guess. And grieving.'

'Which are both very natural human emotions.'

'It's just been a bit much recently. I saw my mother last night and she wanted to speak about Elisabeth, and I just need some space from what happened. But it's like she wants to instruct me in how to behave, and how to grieve, acting all disapproving when I won't do what she expects.'

'What do you think she expects?'

'I think she wants me to make big displays of how I'm feeling. To support Elisabeth's mother more, when I can barely handle my own feelings. My mother wants me to share my grief with her – you know, sobbing together and looking through childhood photographs.'

'But that's not what you need?'

'No, it isn't. I need to make my peace with it all. To forgive myself for not saving her.'

'It wasn't your job to save Elisabeth, Kristina.'

I nod, but my throat is constricted by a painful lump. I allow myself a few long moments to breathe through these feelings and feel grateful for Vera's soothing presence.

'I just keep wondering if it could have been different.'

'It sounds as though a lot is on your mind at the moment, both in your personal life and with your clients.'

'Yes.'

'Do you feel confident that you have the tools to process it?'

'I think so. I'm conscious of maintaining my boundaries with my mother. I'm allowing all the stages of grief over Elisabeth and trying to not become stuck in thought patterns. But I see her everywhere, you know? The other night... I was looking at this woman at a party, and it was as though her face briefly became Elisabeth's and it just hit me so hard. And Leah... I think Leah reminds me of her. Last week, there was something so raw and desperate about her, and something about the intensity of her need. I lived with Elisabeth's need for so long. And then, discovering Leah's pregnancy, it just really threw me and triggered my feelings about motherhood. I am going to work on not allowing my feelings to impact my support of Leah; it's crucial that no part of me would judge her for her choices.'

'That sounds very reasonable.' We sit in silence for a while, the softly lit, warm room like a cocoon, and I want it to be Vera who speaks first. 'Kristina, I've been meaning to ask,' she says eventually. 'How are you sleeping at the moment? Any more disturbing flashbacks?'

'No. Well. I've been sleeping quite well.' This is a white lie, but I don't want to get into the sleepless nights today, and besides, they're nothing new. 'I've been really busy. I have quite a few new clients and in the run-up to the elections, my husband needs a lot of support...'

'It doesn't sound like there is a lot of time for you.'

'Well. That might be a good thing. Considering the circumstances.'

'Perhaps you are avoiding thinking about or processing certain things by keeping very busy, and keeping your mind on the surface.'

'Vera. I allow myself to feel and to process.'

'Good.'

'Just. I suppose I have been confused recently. It does feel like I am having a hard time deciphering what exactly my feelings are about stuff. Sometimes I feel so angry I could smash something at the smallest provocation, like if my husband doesn't answer a text message fast enough. Other times I feel like crying, but for no reason.'

'No reason?'

'Well, you know – it seems triggered by the strangest little things. A beautiful, wilting flower. Or a disturbing dream. A song on the radio I'd forgotten, that takes me back to... to the past.'

'What kind of disturbing dreams, Kristina? I thought you said you'd been sleeping well?'

I feel irritated with myself for slipping up and bringing the conversation to my dreams because it will inevitably lead us down a path I don't want to take – not today. 'Mostly well. Occasionally not, I guess.'

'And do you think that coming to terms with what happened to Elisabeth might be bringing some of those old memories and wounds to the surface?'

'Yes. Of course,' I say softly, closing my eyes. I don't

want to go there now, I want a moment's reprieve from the thoughts that chase through my mind like a gathering storm.

'They are, of course, closely linked. I'm just wondering whether new things might appear as a result. Things that have felt intangible or lost.' I nod and look out the window. I'm buying time, trying again to dislodge the lump in my throat.

'I think I need to spend the last ten minutes discussing Natalia Martinussen. She's, uh, very overwhelmed by her family commitments and I want to develop more of a strategy in supporting her.' My voice noticeably trembles as I speak, but Vera doesn't bat an eyelid at my obvious diversion from my own personal circumstances back to my client. I muster all the control I can to discuss Natalia's course of therapy, blocking any other thoughts from entering my mind. After a few moments it becomes easier, and it feels good that I am able to control my thoughts and emotions.

But then, as I leave Vera's snug office at Holbergs Plass and walk the short distance to my own office, slowly, past the park, my control falters and I feel a wild surge of anxiety. Or grief. Or maybe it's a bad premonition, a sense of all the losses still to come, how can I know? I should feel better after supervision, but I don't. I feel unhinged, and unfit to see my first client in less than half an hour. I shut the door to my office and set the timer on my phone to five minutes. Five minutes to cry my eyes out.

9

Kristina

At home, I lean back against the front door as soon as I've shut it behind me. I still feel strangely liquid, like I might dissolve into more tears, or erupt in a rage. Up until this summer, my life was good; predictable, comfortable, stable. It hasn't been without its challenges; like everyone else I have my demons and things to deal with from my past, but in the last few years I have felt as though I am capable of navigating my life, even when it gets really tough. But now, it's as though one thing after another is coming loose from the structures I've built, tearing at the very foundations of my life. I was supposed to be a mother by now. Or pregnant at the very least. *We can't find any reason for it,* say the doctors of my inexplicable infertility. No reason. And yet, there is a reason, there always is; they just can't find it.

And then there's Elisabeth. The way she keeps appearing in my mind constantly, in the face of the crown princess or random women on the street, or even in my own blurred reflection in a shop window as I rush past through the seemingly endless autumn rain. There is an element of obsessive compulsion to these appearances, like my mind is running on a loop and whatever it is I'm actually looking at, it morphs into Elisabeth. I may consider discreetly seeking out some cognitive behavioral therapy from a trusted colleague to address it. But CBT isn't going to change the fact that I will never see Elisabeth again, that I failed her, and I can't bear it.

I walk aimlessly through the dark, hushed apartment. I can't remember where Eirik is or what his excuse was for missing dinner today. I stare at the closed door of the larger of the guest bedrooms, the room in which Elisabeth took her very last breath.

I move my gaze to the second spare bedroom, the one with the lovely outlook into the interior courtyard of our building, with its barbecue spots and sweet little playground. The room we intended for our child. I push the door open and stand for a long while in the sparse, cool space and watch the wind tear at the tarpaulin covering the summer garden furniture three floors below. Raindrops rush down the windowpane and I follow a couple with my fingertips, making myself breathe deeply. *It's just a hard day, Kristina*, I tell myself. This was something my first therapist taught me, back when I had mostly hard days. It doesn't mean that tomorrow, or the next day, or the one after will be hard. *It's just one hard day.*

I shut the door behind me and wander aimlessly into the kitchen. It's five thirty and I suppose I could pour a glass of wine, but it's only Tuesday and I feel a little guilty if I drink during the week, especially if I'm by myself. I consider a coffee but my sleep is broken enough as it is. I settle for a glass of water but pour it out after a couple of sips. I go through to the living room and switch on all the little lamps on each of the three windowsills, casting the big room in a lovely golden glow. I sit on the sofa and pick up an interiors magazine from the pile I haven't gotten to yet. *Elle Interiors*, from April. I'm about to start reading when I realize that I am absentmindedly staring at one of Elisabeth's paintings hung in the next room behind the dining table, visible from where I'm sitting. I look around, and there are another two smaller pieces in this room. And in the spare room, the last room Elisabeth ever saw, there's another. I get up. They have to go. How can I move forward if I'm constantly reminded of the past?

I swiftly unhook the two smaller ones from the wall in this room and leave them face-down on the floor. Then I go through to the next room and run a finger lightly across the largest canvas, which is almost the entire length of the dining table. To think that Elisabeth guided the brush along exactly this same spot just a few months ago is impossible to believe – in a way it's as though she hasn't been alive for many years. It feels as though I lost her that night so many years ago, the darkest of nights, the same night parts of myself were lost, too. With time, those lost and wounded parts began to take on disturbing shadows in the depths of my mind. Though patches of my memory were erased, I could still feel, and the shadows of that night would come back with the force of earthquakes, and with as little warning, shaking me to the core. What had once been one – one girl, one life, one mind – splintered into various broken narratives and personas and coping mechanisms, and it took years to begin to reintegrate those pieces back into a kind of whole. It was intense therapy, followed by my own psychology studies and finally, a doctorate in trauma psychotherapy that brought me to a relative peace with the past. Like Jung said, *I am not what happened to me, I am what I choose to become.*

Just look at me, I think to myself. *How far I've come.* I allow my thoughts to revisit the young woman I was, when I myself first came to therapy. After all these years, the image still packs an emotional punch. I went to therapy against my will at the insistence of my parents. My attitude at the time was that it was a formality before a certain death. A waiting room for the determinedly suicidal. I was skinny and traumatized, my mind and emotions dulled with drugs from my stay at Vinderen psychiatric hospital. I'd spent two months in a residential mental health care program, where the doctors were more interested in medicating away my symptoms than attempting to understand their origins. One day I was unceremoniously released to my bewildered, anxious parents, with the promise that I 'no longer posed a risk to myself'.

But I did. Of course I did. I didn't have a single tool to deal with the images in my head, or the terrifying blank patches, and I've yet to see the pill that can erase the past.

At their wits' end, my parents sent me to a psychotherapist, a woman named Ingvild. I still remember the exact moment I opened the door to her office, which was in the basement of a villa in a residential, leafy street in Bekkestua, watching my mother drive off. I was twenty years old and ready to die. Inside stood Ingvild, a small, slim woman with soft blonde curls, whose presence seemed huge and radiant in the little room in spite of her slight stature. I don't remember what she said, nor what I said in that first session and in the many that followed. But I felt seen, and as though even the very darkest parts of me could be brought out into the light without judgment. Ingvild met me with unwavering empathy and an unconditional presence I had never known before. It was her constancy that became her legacy, and one I always aim to channel into my relationships with my own clients.

Ingvild liked to work with colors in her therapeutic approach and sometimes asked me to describe or draw the colors of my feelings and memories. Back then, when it felt as though I had neither feelings nor memories, only a terrifying void inside, I did manage to ascribe colors to the storms in my mind, and they were invariably the waxy dark greens of forests, and the vivid rich hues of blood, both fresh and dried. I used to pray for a milky white nothingness, the pure, unbroken color of death, silence and release.

I'd tell her I wanted to die and unlike my parents, who'd burst into tears or shame me for being broken, making it all about themselves and their own fears and their expectations of me, Ingvild would listen, unafraid. She'd speak about the lack of language for pain this intense, and how people often say they want to die when what they mean is that they can't live with such torment. I'd insist that it was death I wanted. I couldn't bear to be around Elisabeth, either – I knew that the haunted look in her eyes was mirrored in my own. Ingvild would ask me what the alternative to death might look like, and I said that returning to my old life just wasn't possible. *I wonder whether there could be a middle ground,* she'd say, *not death, and not your old life. A new normal. A life worth living, now.*

I look around my home and realize that I have really made a life worth living, now. I have a home, a stable marriage, purpose. But I don't have Elisabeth and I can't shake off the self-hatred I feel for what I did and didn't do for her. Her life is a closed chapter and she will never find a life worth living, now. The only solace she found was in hard drugs and in her art, and in me, and she was equally devoted to all three, though none of them could save her.

I unhook the huge painting from its mooring on the wall but underestimate its heaviness and it comes crashing to the floor, one sharp corner landing on my bare foot. I scream, so loud I'm sure the neighbors could hear it. The cry of pain just becomes crying and as if I have no control over myself, I grab a bronze candelabra from the table and smash it full force into the painting, effortlessly ripping the canvas. Elisabeth's hypnotic swirls of emerald green and burgundy reds burst open and are swallowed up by great, jagged rips. When there is nothing left of it except the edges that are stapled to the wooden framework, I gather up the strips and chunks of limp canvas that once held the imagery of Elisabeth's inner world and place them into the glass-walled fireplace. I place a couple of logs on top, one wrapped in newspaper, then set it alight. I stand in the middle of the room for a long while, listening to the crackle and hiss of the flames, breathing in the chemical smell of burning paint, practicing a deep, slow breathing pattern to calm my nerves.

When the canvas has entirely been engulfed by the flames, I walk slowly back through the big room to the kitchen, mindful of my bruised foot, the flames still dancing on my retina. I pour a glass of wine from a carton in the fridge and drink it straight down standing at the window, looking across the rooftops at the black bones of trees in the royal park. I hear Eirik's key in the lock. I realize I don't know what time it is or even whether I have had dinner. It feels as though I've just woken up from a nightmare – those stunned, spent moments of blinking in the dark, grateful to emerge into a world more peaceful than the one you just left behind. I move quickly now, and step into my husband's arms as he walks through the door and he lets out a little sound of surprise at this onslaught of affection, but he holds me tight and smooths down my hair at the back of my skull firmly and soothingly, the way you'd stroke a beloved, sleepy dog.

'What's going on?' asks Eirik, finally breaking our embrace and kicking his shoes off. I take his camel jacket and hang it in the cupboard, brushing off a few stray droplets of rain. My husband's face is creased and pale in the low light of the hallway, and he rubs at his eyes and massages his temples.

'I burned Elisabeth's painting,' I say. 'The one in the dining room.'

Eirik stares at me. 'What? Why?'

'I couldn't bear to look at it for another moment.'

'But... I thought you loved that painting?'

'No.'

'Perhaps it would have been a good idea to donate it to her mother? Or to Villa Vinternatt?'

'It was its very existence I couldn't bear. I wanted it gone. It fucked with my head.'

Eirik looks at me carefully, his eyebrows knitting together over the bridge of his nose. 'Kristina. This sounds a little odd.'

'I know. I just thought you should know. There's some, uh, debris in the dining room. I'll clear it up.'

'Look. I know things are still quite raw. And that work is stressful. You've got quite a few new clients at the moment, right? But right now, up until the end of November, we just have to keep it together. I *need* you to keep it together. This is the most important time of our lives. We can't let anything get in the way of this. Think about how hard we've worked, how much we've both sacrificed to get here. Less than a month to go. You have to let go, Kristina. Let it go. You did everything you could possibly have done, you—'

'No. I… I see her everywhere, it's like she's haunting me, she's even in my own goddamn reflection in the mirror, and it's all my fault—'

'Don't you ever say that. It wasn't your fault. None of it was your fault.' Eirik takes both of my hands in his and kisses the top of each tightly clenched fist. He pulls me close to him and raises my chin with his fingertips so I'm forced to look him in the eyes.

'This is not the time for allowing irrational behavior or bad thoughts. I can't afford you falling to pieces now, Kristina. This is the time for focus and graft and control. Okay?'

I nod, but I know more about bad thoughts and the shadowy recesses of the mind than my husband ever will. I nod again, more firmly, and take a deep breath through my nostrils. This is a time for control. *I am not what happened to me, but what I choose to become.*

10

Leah, two weeks before

It's the doorbell that wakes her. It's been one of those rare nights when she just fell asleep, without tears, without rumination, without fear. Her hand instinctively goes to the rounded bump on her lower stomach, as if to reassure herself this pregnancy wasn't just a dream.

She sits up in bed, drawing the cool air of the bedroom deeply into her lungs. It is completely dark and she can't even make out the outline of the door leading to the living room. Outside, the wind rattles down the street, carrying little bits of trash and tearing the last leaves from the trees. She checks her phone, but there are no new messages. She messaged him earlier in the evening, begging. *Please come*, she said. *Please, please, please. I need you.* He didn't respond, as usual. But he's here now, downstairs, on the street, ringing her doorbell.

The doorbell rings again, filling the hushed apartment with its shrill sound, and Leah moves swiftly from the bed, through the living room, to the door.

ll

Kristina, three days later

It's Friday, and I'm feeling much better than earlier in the week. I've mentally reclaimed the driver's seat and will not allow myself to become overwhelmed or terrorized by irrational thoughts. I've committed to taking care of myself this week and feel refreshed. I haven't drunk anything since Tuesday, I've caught up on all my client notes, and Eirik and I have managed a couple of simple but cozy dinners together. All the stress around Elisabeth was triggered by the strange episode with Leah Iverson, but now I'm more aware of it, I'm able to place them into the compartments where they belong in my mind. Elisabeth: tragic, but gone. Eirik is absolutely right, I have to let it go now. And I did what I could. Then there is Leah – a client for whom I hold much hope, and I need to remain committed and focused on supporting her, not letting her behavior or circumstances trigger my own personal reactions.

Arriving at the office, I'm looking forward to the day ahead. I only have three clients today as one called in sick. A fairly new client named Marisa, who struggles with debilitating anxiety and apologizes constantly for absolutely everything, at eleven thirty. Then Leah at two, followed by Siri Engevik, who feels trapped in a bad marriage, but is very obviously herself a wounded woman with a difficult character.

It isn't difficult to access feelings of empathy for Marisa and I listen intently as she painstakingly recounts how she feels like her family take her for granted and don't care about her frazzled nerves. *They don't even ask why my hands are bleeding from the constant handwashing, or why I count under my breath or why I sometimes burst into tears when I'm cleaning.*

When she leaves, I pop down to the coffee shop for a sandwich and a freshly squeezed orange juice, like I sometimes do on a Friday as I have a big gap between Marisa and Leah. When I think about the fact that in just over an hour, Leah will be sitting across from me again, I feel the flutter of trepidation in my gut. Was last week just a dramatic lapse in her emotional well-being, or will she turn up even more unhinged today? I know I will look for signs of pregnancy in her, but I've steeled myself now, and done my work – I know that Leah being pregnant doesn't mean I won't also get pregnant. I just needed to reason with myself. I wonder whether she will tell me or simply never mention it and get rid of the baby. I swallow hard at the thought of Leah's baby, snug and tiny inside the shell of her womb, becoming.

Back in the office I relight the votive candles on the windowsill, still liquid from Marisa's session, and replenish the tea supply. I place each tea bag equidistant from the next on the tray, organized by color. It's incredible how soothing these tiny details can be, and performing them makes me feel like I'm realigning my internal order. Leah usually chooses green tea with lemon, and leaves the teabag in the mug until she's finished, the swollen bag nudging at the tip of her nose for the last few sips. She drinks slowly, unlike some clients who gulp it down and then fuss about with the kettle on the table between us, trying to make another while keeping our conversation going over the screech of the gathering steam.

I make a concerted effort to be very still and very deliberate with my clients. Predictability and transparency is what I try to convey. They will always find the same teas, arranged in precisely the same way. They will always see me drinking plain water, nothing else. I also try to wear minor variations of the same outfits and keep my hair in the same style, swept back in a high ponytail with lightly curled ends. Pretty but professional. I'm the mirror, not the person looking into it, which is where focus needs to lie.

I scroll on my phone for a while, counting down to two o'clock. Instagram offers nothing new, only the usual wistful autumnal posts of children playing in leaves and choosing pumpkins to carve, and typical Norwegian gleeful couple selfies amid stark, rain-lashed mountains. *VG* and *Dagbladet*'s headlines are the usual underwhelming small, peaceful nation ones: *Man Fled Bear in Trøndelag, Real Estate Up 5 % in Oslo, The Five Things You MUST Do to Prepare Your Cabin for Winter.*

I go to the bathroom and reapply my mascara and undereye concealer, and return to the office to pour some fresh water into my glass before Leah arrives. Except she doesn't. The clock strikes 2 p.m., then five past, ten past... I remember last week and how she arrived late, but the minutes tick by and still she doesn't arrive. At two fifteen

I call her, but her phone goes straight to voicemail. I try again with the same result. I also send her a text message asking her to please get in touch. Could it be that Leah has ghosted me? It has happened before, that a client has suddenly terminated a course of ongoing psychotherapy for whatever reason, and not bothered to tell me until weeks later, perhaps feeling guilty or awkward about explaining why. I wouldn't have thought it of Leah – she has always been vocal about the profound effect therapy has had on her life. That said, she has been showing more resistance in recent months and has more aggressively pursued my personal opinion and advice than previously. It could be that she has chosen to go elsewhere if she hasn't felt that she is getting what she needs from my methods. *I need to know what your personal feelings are about this*, I recall her saying to me relatively recently, referring to some situation with whomever she was dating, and I deflected by saying that I found it interesting that she places more weight on my opinion than on how she actually feels about the situation. Could she have grown frustrated with my methods and decided to just stop our sessions? But last week, she insisted she needed to speak to me about something outside this space even though she knows that isn't possible.

I go through all my email folders to make sure I can't possibly have missed a message from her, but there's nothing. I check on 1881.no that her phone number or address haven't changed, but they remain the same. I make a mental note to get back in touch with Dr Albert to see whether he has heard from her. I spend fifteen minutes talking to my colleague, Alice, in the communal kitchen, who is also between clients.

'Sounds like ghosting,' she says, frowning into her milky tea.

'I just don't think she would do that,' I say.

'I never did, either. But then it's often the ones you expect more from who do.'

'Hmmm. Should I call her next of kin or something?'

'No. Kristina, it's not part of your job description. You're the receptacle, not the detective.'

'I know, but—'

'No buts. Okay, back to work, it's almost three. Drinks later?'

'Possibly.'

'It happens again and again,' says Siri Engevik, a middle-aged woman with a deep frown, looking at me from behind thick turquoise glasses. 'He promises he'll change, but he never does. He doesn't even particularly bother to hide the evidence anymore. The other day, a woman called several times when we were having another one of those godawful, silent dinners in an old-fashioned steak restaurant. You know the kind. Unheated plates. Rodeo-style interiors. Laminated menus. Why won't he take me to sushi? I want to go to one of those fancy Asian places in Tjuvholmen. I bet that's the kind of place where you go. With your husband.' She gives me a little wink to let me know she knows very well who my husband is, a tiny triumph.

'Siri, you were saying that a woman rang repeatedly?'

'Yes, his phone was on the table. It kept lighting up and vibrating. Knut glanced at it and I could see the name

"Amanda" flashing across the table. I asked who Amanda is and he just shrugged and kept chewing. I swear, the way he eats drives me crazy. It's like he shovels the food into his big wet mouth and sends it around in circles in there. I wanted to walk out. I really did.'

I glance at the time. Twenty past three. Siri Engevik has been coming for around a year and is quite a demanding client; she becomes easily frustrated with the necessary limitations of the therapeutic relationship and can become agitated if I cut her off to say our time's up, or if I decline to answer a personal question. She frequently finishes her musings with *Don't you think?* and though I point out that what I think isn't necessarily the point, she'll keep pushing and say – *But what do you think? What's your opinion? You must have an opinion.*

'Why didn't you?' I ask, gently.

'Why didn't I what?'

'Walk out. You said you wanted to walk out. And that you feel disrespected by your husband.'

'Well, yes. How would you feel if your husband sat at the dinner table taking calls from another woman, some old bitch called Amanda. Tell me, Dr Moss, how would that make you feel?'

'Siri. Let's focus on how it makes *you* feel. I sense a lot of anger here.'

'Well, wouldn't *you* be angry?'

'I think anger would be a very natural response to the situation you're describing.'

'It's pathetic, though. Getting so angry over little things.'

'Little things?'

'The way he chews. Amanda. His silence. He never asks

me a single question. It's because he doesn't care about the answers. He doesn't care about me. He...' Siri begins to cry softly and I discreetly push the box of tissues closer to her. She doesn't take one, but wipes at her tears with the sleeve of her chunky-knit purple mohair sweater.

'Those things don't sound like little things to me.'

Siri stares at me, then nods, sending more tears streaming down her face. I feel her pain acutely in this moment, and can't help but think how much pain there is in most relationships, layer upon layer of it, even in those relations that on the surface seem harmonious and healthy. A slightly insensitive comment. A rebuff in bed. The silences between partners when there's nothing more to say. Little lies that become big lies.

'So what do you think I should be feeling right now?'

'Only you can answer that.'

'But I don't know. It can't be normal to never know how you're feeling?'

'Not knowing what you feel is a feeling, too, isn't it?'

'Hmm.' She stares out the window for a while and I follow her gaze, watching the brief, gray day fade into a deep, blue afternoon. 'Do you think it's ever okay to stay in a marriage when you're both unhappy?'

'I think every marriage is different and that only the two people in it can know what is right for them.'

'I think I need you to advise me here, Dr Moss. I want to know what the recommended course of action is for this sort of thing.'

'Siri. You know that isn't my role. And I don't think there is a recommended course of action.'

'We've been to couples' therapy before, and that therapist

was quite clear about what the various options were. But you... You won't ever say.'

'My role is to be here for you and to help you understand how you feel, not tell you what to do.'

'We have a house together. A house full of things. A grown-up son. A cabin. An apartment in Antibes. I can't just walk away, I'm trapped—'

'Siri. We are going to have to continue next week.'

'What?' Siri stares at me with a blank expression, as though I were behind a one-way mirror and she only now realized that I'm here.

'Our time is up, I'm afraid.'

She takes me in with an expression of mild disdain, then nods absentmindedly. 'Oh. Right.' She stands up abruptly, gathering her rose-patterned billowing scarf and padded purple velour jacket and pauses at the door for a moment as though there was one more thing she needed to say. I do sometimes wonder what she gets out of these sessions, she seems so in opposition to the therapy structure and the way I work. I make a mental note to ask her about this next time; maybe we should consider referring her on to a colleague with whom she has more personal chemistry. My Fridays are going to be wide open at this rate, if Leah has ghosted me and Siri were to see someone else.

I stand up and walk over to the window. The gloomy morning has given way to a beautiful afternoon with indigo skies streaked by pink gauzy clouds, and I wish I could sit by the sea, looking out over its calm surface, releasing all the nervous energy I feel pulsating beneath my skin. I have the strange sensation that if I were to slice my skin open, tension would flow out of me in thick, black bursts, like tar.

I think about what Siri said, about feeling trapped in a life you don't want, no matter how privileged you might be. I can't imagine a situation in which Eirik and I stayed married merely because we owned property and possessions together, a life in which we'd eat in silence, where we'd stopped caring about each other, or where he'd be courting other women, not even bothering to hide it. I feel a sharp bolt of anger and fear at the thought, followed by gratitude for the things in my life that are good.

I go back to my desk and check my phone and emails. Nothing from Leah, no explanation. It's the start of another weekend, and she'll be on my mind until I know what is going on with her. I go into my contacts list and select 'Leah Iverson', and click on 'next of kin'. Listed is her mother, Linda Iverson, with a Swedish number.

Hi Linda,

I was wondering whether you are in touch with Leah. She's missed a session with me which is unusual for her. I'm concerned for her well-being and wanted to make sure she is okay.

Best wishes, Dr Kristina Moss.

I've barely put the phone back down on my desk when it vibrates. It's Leah's mother.

She's fine. I've spoken to her. Thanks, L.

I sit down and open my client notes. I select Leah's file

and enter 'no show' under today's date. I scroll back up through my own notes from the last few weeks to make sure I haven't overlooked anything of importance, but there's nothing. I still can't quite believe she didn't come today. I feel a pang of sadness at the thought of how unfinished our course of therapy feels. I really believed I could help Leah, and that our bond was strong and transformational, similar to my own bond with Ingvild, when I first came to therapy and found that it had the power to change lives.

Leah is one of those clients I always look forward to seeing, and it's because she's eager to grow, she really wants to learn about herself. She believes in trying to become whole. *Like you,* she'll say. It seems to me like she believed in this possible wholeness all along, that she trusts in therapy, unlike some clients, who resist every step of the way. They question everything, applying their own limited understanding of amateur psychology based on having read one self-help book to everything I say. *Oh, so you are referring to reparenting,* they might randomly ask. *Or, yeah, this is definitely an ego response to underlying rejection issues.* Frankly, it's annoying.

Leah's different. She listens as much as she speaks. She feels the spaces between us and seems to understand the unconditional trust I've tried to build there.

I shut the computer down and make sure everything in the office is in its right place. I feel a need to get out of here so strong it's physical, so I blow out the candle on the windowsill, put my winter jacket on, then shut the door behind me.

12

Kristina

I go the same way as I always do on a Friday afternoon, but today my steps feel leaden, and I know deep down I'm going to turn around before I even get halfway up Bogstadveien, which is busy with schoolkids and those taking an early weekend milling in and out of the shops. Still, I proceed to Rosenborggata, where I turn right. I walk all the way up to the white, immaculately kept turn-of-the-century apartment building and slide my finger down the familiar row of buzzers until it settles on the right one. It wouldn't be so bad to go up. I would be met with nothing but kindness. But it's the kindness I can't bear. Something occurs to me, and I check my phone. No new messages. I open Google maps and enter Leah's address, found and memorized from my client list before I left the office. It's just seven minutes' walk away, across Theresesgate and toward Adamstuen. I glance up at the building in front of me one more time. *Not today,* I say to myself, refusing thoughts of how in this moment the tea will be brewing, the home-made cakes will be meticulously laid out on a tray; they'll be waiting for the buzzer to sound. I walk away.

I head back down Bogstadveien and past my office, and after less than ten minutes, I find myself standing in front of Leah Iverson's apartment building on Benneches Gate. Leah lives in a beautiful yellow-and-white art nouveau apartment building, and I stand for a moment on the pavement looking up at the windows, trying to guess which ones are hers. She's never really spoken to me about her apartment – whenever she speaks about home, she speaks of the apartment where she grew up with her mother, or more recently, her beloved country cabin. She always lights up when she speaks of the peace she feels there, far away from other people and the stresses of city life. I look at the names on the doorbells and find her name at the top. *L.K. Iverson* it reads, and I rest my finger on it for a moment. Without thinking, I press the buzzer down for a long moment and imagine it ringing shrilly in Leah's apartment. Will she be angry with me for coming here? Experience tells me she's more likely to be moved; clients tend to crave feeling important and cared for by the therapist.

Leah has often asked me whether I really care about her, or if I only pretend because I get paid. A lot of clients ask me similar questions and it is one of the more difficult things to address when it comes to therapy – how can they truly trust that I care about their well-being and mental health when we both know I am also there because I am paid? But I care, deeply, about all of my clients. It was something I occasionally worried about during my training, whether I would encounter clients for whom it was impossible to feel empathy and connection. To this day, it's never happened – every single person I have met throughout my years in therapeutic practice has turned out to be fundamentally worthy of empathy.

I press the doorbell again and imagine Leah rising from the sofa and padding across dark hardwood floors to the door on bare feet. I have a feeling she isn't here. But what if she is, only she's hurt herself? Despite Linda's reassuring text, I can't shake off the feeling that something serious is going on with Leah. I feel my stomach sink at the random thought of Leah in her home, thinking about ending her own life, perhaps several days ago. How lonely would those last hours have been; how desperate would she have felt? Still, I don't believe she would take her own life. I press the buzzer again, for longer this time.

Come on, Leah. I care about you. It's why I'm here.

This is about the truth. Those were some of her last words to me. What could she have meant by this? Over the years Leah sat opposite me every Friday afternoon, I became privy to many of her truths. As we began to explore her inner world and she developed the awareness to make increasing sense of it, we discussed conditioning and how the things we are told about ourselves aren't necessarily true.

During her marriage to Anton, Leah was conditioned to believe she was worthless and disgusting, that nobody else would ever want her and that she deserved to be punished. It took us years to begin to untangle these beliefs, in part because it became clear that she'd held them even before her marriage, perhaps results of bullying as a young child and her father's departure. Could this be the misconceived 'truth' she was referring to? Or could it be her pregnancy? Or was she referring to some other truth? I've wondered, sometimes, whether the truth itself had felt central to Leah's suffering, that by writing about it so brutally honestly in *Nobody*, she was left feeling exposed and vulnerable.

'Hello?' says a man's voice, making me jump. I'd been lost in thoughts, momentarily forgetting I'd pressed Leah's buzzer.

'Uh, hello,' I say. 'Who is this?' I feel suddenly deeply embarrassed, turning up on Leah's doorstep when she is probably just cooped up with a new boyfriend, the father of her child. But... Friday. She was hurt. Someone hurt her. There is a long pause.

'Who's asking?'

'My name is Kristina Moss. I'm...'

There is a long pause, and when the man speaks again, his voice is cool.

'I know who you are.' The buzzer sounds and I glance down the street as though someone might appear who could tell me what to do, but there is nobody around, so I push open the door and step inside.

13

Leah, two weeks before

I'm not supposed to be here, he says.

No, says Leah. *And yet. Here you are.*

I can't stay away from you.

Good.

What is this going to cost us? He whispers, tracing light shapes with his fingertips down her bare chest, across her stomach, its swelling barely noticeable, then further down, and draws her even closer, pressing her face into his broad, warm chest. She looks up, makes him meet her eyes.

It's okay, her eyes say.

I miss this so much, he says.

I've missed this my whole life, she thinks. She's tired, but doesn't want to sleep, she wants to be held, to lie here all night just being held, feeling him fill the apartment, the spaces inside her, the night itself. She hadn't seen this coming, this deep and easy feeling of coming home.

14

Kristina

I step into a vast foyer lit by a huge industrial-style wrought-iron lamp. I hear a door unlock higher up in the building and take the stairs slowly, trying to make sense of my racing thoughts. Am I about to come face to face with Leah? Who is the man, and why did he instantly recognize my name? I assume she has met someone fairly recently, and for some reason, didn't want to discuss the relationship with me. But wouldn't Leah have told me? She tells me everything. Or so I thought.

It seems surreal that I am here, climbing the stairs to Leah's apartment. Her apartment is all the way at the top, and the door has been left ajar. To the side of the door is a small bronze doorbell reading 'Iverson', and I imagine her choosing it in a little shop, writing her name down on a scrap of paper, to be engraved.

'Hello?' I say, stepping into a narrow hallway. A man emerges from a room to the right. He looks young, almost like a high school student, and is dressed in navy sweatpants and a hooded sweater with a giant red Ralph Lauren Polo logo. He's a good-looking guy, with dark-blonde hair and light-blue, striking eyes. He looks tired and his clothes are crumpled, as though he was sleeping on a sofa and has just woken up.

'Hi,' he says, stepping forward to shake my hand. His grip is firm, and his hand is cool and dry. 'Anton.'

I can't help a sharp intake of breath at the shock of coming face to face with Anton here, in Leah's apartment. Her ex-husband is an abusive man and Leah had to take out several restraining orders against him. I fight the urge to flee from the apartment, but I need to see Leah and make sure she's okay.

'Hi,' I say. 'I'm Kristina Moss.'

'I know. She talks about you. A lot.'

'She talks about you a lot, too,' I say, my voice trembling with anger, but also fear. I have to tread carefully here. Anton slowly raises an eyebrow and scrutinizes me as though committing me to memory. His jaw clenches.

'Is Leah here?' I ask.

'No, she's not.'

'Do you know where she is?'

Anton releases a sharp little breath, as if to suggest that my presence here asking questions is completely incredulous. 'Why should I tell you?'

'Look, Leah and I have worked together for several years. I have been under the impression that it's been helpful for her, and I want to make sure that she's okay. She didn't turn up for a scheduled session with me this afternoon, and it's left me concerned for her well-being.'

'She's fine.'

'Have you spoken to her?'

'I saw her a couple of days ago.'

'Wait, how?'

'She's at her cabin working on her next book and I went there to see her.'

'I'm sorry, I don't... I find it hard to believe that she's at her cabin and working and that she would have invited you there.'

'She didn't invite me. I went there to check on her as I felt concerned too. She didn't respond to my messages or calls and I felt like I had to see her to...' Anton trails off and I stare at him hard, refusing to break his gaze. I don't believe him.

'I've been trying to call and email her and I feel that it is out of character for her not to respond.'

'There is no reception up there. It's really remote.'

'What was her state of mind when you saw her?'

'She was fine. Focused on the book.'

'Fine?'

'Yeah.'

'I find it hard to believe she was fine. She was extremely distressed when I saw her last Friday. She was also hurt. I'm assuming you might have played a part in that?'

Anton drops his gaze to the ground in the way of the guilty. 'No.'

'May I ask what you're doing here?'

'What *I'm* doing here?'

'Yes.'

'Firstly, I'm not sure how I see that is any of your business. Secondly, I'm in a relationship with Leah.'

A little incredulous laugh escapes me – the sheer nerve

of this man, speaking as though Leah still wanted him. *I would have died if I hadn't escaped from him*, she's said, many times. But what if she's died because she did escape? I swallow hard. He's hurt her, I know it. She must have met someone new and gotten pregnant, and Anton must have found out and tracked her down. I stare at him, more furious than frightened now, and try to determine whether this man could be capable of hurting a pregnant woman.

'I don't believe you.'

'Look, Dr Moss,' he says in a mocking tone, 'I know what a quack you are. Your so-called therapy has done exactly fucking nothing for Leah. The thing that has helped Leah get to a better place in the last few months has been returning to me. To allow herself to be loved fully.'

I'm stunned by his claim. Could it be true that she's gone back to him? It would explain why she hasn't mentioned the pregnancy if she has rekindled something with Anton, after years of sharing her experiences of a very turbulent past with this man. After writing a bestseller about the abuse he subjected her to. How could she have gone back? I feel irrationally angry.

'I don't believe you. Where is she?' I try to look past him and into the apartment, but he's a big guy and he's blocking the doorway.

'I've got to say you've got some nerve, Dr Moss, coming here and accusing me of lying when you clearly don't know a thing.'

'I know what she told me. I know that she was afraid of you. She used to lie awake at night, worrying about you discovering where she lives. And you're standing here saying you are back together and that she is at her cabin, but not responding to calls or emails. How am I supposed to believe that when I know that she had to get a restraining order against you?'

'A restraining order against me?' Anton laughs, and looks genuinely surprised. 'Wait, Leah even lies to her therapist?'

15

Leah, two weeks before

For once, the loneliness she fears and writes about and lives by and even courts, dissipates. He's here. He came back again. Every time, he says this is the last time, it has to be. He holds her, for hours. She curls into him, like a mollusk into its shell.

We need to talk, he says.

I need you to hold me, she says, so he does.

We need to talk, he says, again, later.

No, she says, *not yet*. She places his hand on her left breast so he can hear the thud of her heart and turns around to look into his eyes. He can't resist her like that, he has said that himself many times. She takes his other hand and guides it down, down, and he moans softly when his fingers touch upon her wetness. She's quick to press her lips to his and prize his mouth open with the playful tip of her tongue. He sighs but doesn't, or can't, resist her. He sighs deeper as she gets on top and lowers herself down onto him, rocking back and forth, her tongue probing his mouth, his hands buried in the thick tangle of her hair. She stops, pulls back, looks into his eyes. His mouth is still open as though he hasn't realized the kiss has ended, and she leans back in, closes it with her own.

She gets on all fours, he's behind her, one hand clutching her hip for balance, the other in her hair again, he likes that, and he's gathered it into a thick, glossy rope.

Pull it, she says, and he does. *Harder*, she says. So he does. *I want you to hurt me*. So he does.

I want you to love me, she thinks. But he doesn't.

When she wakes, she's alone. There are bruises on the insides of her thighs, on her arms, along her collarbone, on her wrists, where he pinned her down. A tuft of dark hair he tugged from her scalp is left on the pillow. Her trachea hurts where he squeezed it, and though he didn't actually want to do it, he did it when she insisted.

She gets out of bed and steps under the hissing jet of a hot shower. She turns her face into the rushing water, and rubs the night off her skin with gentle soapy fingers, taking care where it is raised and blue. She allows tears to flow and doesn't get back out until they stop.

She stands a long while in front of the mirror, noticing how the baby has grown since she last did this. She touches her lower belly, gently cradling the tiny, taut bump. The thought of someone hurting the person inside like she herself has been hurt, makes her heart race and her mind run blank with dread.

I love you, she thinks to herself, but has to avert her eyes at the intensity of her own gaze. She knows it's time, now, to do something about the situation.

16

Kristina

'Look. I'm sorry if we got off on the wrong foot. I would appreciate it if perhaps we could talk some more,' I suggest, gauging Anton's reaction – I have to get to the bottom of what's going on here and to do that I need to diffuse the atmosphere between us. I need to make him trust me. He seems agitated below the surface, nervous energy running through him like a frothy river about to break its banks. I don't believe a word he says. 'It seems like there has been a big misunderstanding.'

'Clearly.'

'Why do you think Leah would have told me that she was afraid of you if it weren't true?'

'We have had a difficult relationship in the past. But we love each other. I love her and would do anything for her, I'd fight for her, I'd...' He breaks off and rubs hard at his eyes and I wonder – *would you kill her?*

'I know you've hurt her in the past.'

'You clearly know nothing at all.'

'I'm Leah's therapist, as you know.'

'Yes, well, she clearly lied to you. Like she's lied to everybody. Her life, and her career, all of it, is based on a lie.'

'So, you're saying you never hurt her and she didn't have a restraining order against you?'

'Yes.'

He appears genuine, and despite instinctively not believing him, I can't disregard the possibility that Leah really has gone back to him; abuse victims so often do, over and over, reenacting the only pattern they know. It would explain why Leah was so distressed last Friday and why she was so insistent on wanting to tell me something. I need to change strategy and get Anton to trust me with the truth; it seems like Leah hasn't.

'You seem nervous,' I say, keeping my voice as even and calm as I can manage, trying to convey sympathy, watching his reactions carefully. 'Or upset, perhaps? Do you think you could talk me through what's happened?'

He thinks about it for a moment, then nods reluctantly and indicates a door leading off the hallway with a visibly trembling hand.

'I'll make coffee.'

I follow him through into a small, but beautifully furnished, living room. There are framed posters from Leah's travels – Zanzibar, Havana, Cadiz, Marseille – hung above a shelf on which three curious little trees are lined up. Japanese bonsai trees, I realize. There is a tidy, open-plan kitchen in the corner, with ancient-looking wooden support beams painted gray partially separating the space from the living room. I would have guessed Leah enjoyed cooking, though she's never actually mentioned it, but this is definitely the kitchen of someone who mostly eats out.

There's a beautiful little gilded writing desk by the window and I conjure her up in my mind, sitting there sipping green tea with lemon, humming to herself, writing a little, pausing to look out at the comings and goings in the street below.

I sit on the sofa while Anton makes coffee. He seems familiar with the layout of Leah's apartment and effortlessly locates the coffee pods and the sugar in the cupboards, placing them on a little lacquered tray. He pours milk into a jug and I wonder whether Leah bought it, or if Anton did. Has he hurt her and is he posing as the concerned boyfriend, staying at her apartment and pretending to wait for the woman he claims to love to come home? It wouldn't be the first time a violent, jealous man has done something like that. I feel a dull ache in the pit of my stomach. It's that breathless sensation that follows a punch, before the pain fully sets in.

'When did you last see Leah?' I ask as Anton sits down across from me.

'I told you. A few days ago. Uh, Saturday.'

'When did you see her before then?'

'On Friday morning last week.'

'You were with her on Friday morning?'

'Yes. I stayed over and in the morning we had breakfast, then went for a walk. I left around ten thirty.'

'Right.'

'Look, I took a picture of us.' Anton pulls his phone out from his jeans pocket and scrolls down until he finds what he is looking for. He turns the screen to show me. It's a selfie of himself and Leah posing in front of a fountain I recognize as the one in St Hanshaugen park, drained for the winter season. They are both smiling and Leah is looking slightly off into the distance, as though she didn't know exactly where to look into the phone camera.

'Show me when it was taken,' I say. Anton stares hard at me, visibly annoyed, then seems to decide it's a better idea to continue the conversation. He clicks on the photo settings to show me that the photo was indeed taken last Friday, at 9.20 a.m. Leah's entire face is visible, and without doubt, completely unscathed. Just hours later, she'd turn up for our session, terrified and incoherent, the right side of her face beaten to a pulp. My hand hurts and I realize I've dug my fingernails hard into my palms. I am barely able to contain myself, because I have the terrible suspicion I could be sitting here, sipping coffee with Leah's killer. Then something else occurs to me – what if something happened between them and he attacked her, and she came to my session, disorientated and afraid, trying to tell me she was about to go to her cabin to get away from him? She would still be there, too afraid to return to Oslo, pregnant and vulnerable, trapped with her own thoughts. Leah has told me many times that it's the only place she feels safe. Only, he's gone there, and I find it hard to believe that he just went to check on her. But she could still be there, hiding from him. Waiting for me.

'What happened after this picture was taken? Anton, did you have an argument?'

He stares at me hard and again, I feel a flush of fear spread out in my stomach, there is something unnerving about his ice-blue gaze. He surprises me by nodding.

'Yes,' he whispers. 'That's why I went to the cabin. I couldn't reach her and I wanted to apologize. Which I did. I even called you. Twice, on the Sunday, days before I went there, because I didn't know where she'd gone or why she wasn't responding and I figured you'd know. I thought she told you absolutely everything.' Anton's face creases in a slight grimace, as though it is difficult to think about those days when he was unable to get hold of Leah.

'That was you? On Sunday afternoon?' I recall the two missed calls as I drove home from Camilla's – I looked the number up in the phone registry, but it was unlisted. Hours later Leah called, but said nothing – the last I've heard from her.

'Yes.'

'What was the argument about?'

'Old stuff.'

'Old stuff?'

'I'm sure you know she wrote a fucking book about me. She sold what we had together as though it were a product. Then she fucked off, saying she needed therapy to deal with all the terrible things I did to her? I didn't do terrible things to her, we did terrible things to each other at times. But none of that came out in her so-called autofiction book. Everyone just gobbled it up as truth. How do you think it felt to be cast in that light? Watching her go buy this fancy apartment, a Range Rover and a cabin, too, while I had to move back in with my parents? I even lost my fucking job. I was a radio host and my channel dropped me, saying they couldn't employ a wife-beater. How are you supposed to defend yourself against someone who is apparently being a brave survivor by telling the truth, when actually, it's all lies?

And then she came back, earlier this year, full of promises and regret, saying she still needs me, and that therapy had made her see that so much of what had happened between us went both ways. I believed her. I took her back because I love her, but still, all the while, she was lying to me. I know it. She was fucking someone else.'

'Who? What do you mean? Anton, look at me.' He won't look at me. His knuckles grow pale around the coffee mug and I picture it smashing in his hand, its shards sinking into the soft white skin of his palm, spraying me with his blood. I swallow hard. 'Who, Anton?'

'I don't know. I just know there's someone else.'

'What makes you think that?'

'I found messages from him on her phone. Someone else's cufflink behind the towel rail in the bathroom. Once, I happened to walk past and there was a man in the apartment. I could see his shadow outlined against the wall, from the street.'

'Happened to walk past.'

'Yes.' He won't meet my eyes and I feel a flash of pity for him after all. I remind myself that nobody is all bad, people can't be cast in black and white.

'Anton. That sounds very painful. It's not surprising that you're deeply hurt by this. Anton. Look at me. I need you to tell me the truth. Why would she lie about all of this?'

'She told me recently that it was to punish me. For leaving her. And that she was sorry. She feels trapped by that narrative, now. She says it's stifling and awful to have to maintain that what she wrote in *Nobody* was the truth.'

'Anton. Let me ask you this and please be honest with

me. Have you hurt Leah?' Sometimes a careful but direct question is the best approach.

'No.'

'Never?' He shakes his head curtly and clamps his lips together in a tight line, as though he might say something he doesn't want to if he opens his mouth even a little bit.

I need to extricate myself and get home and call the police. Something is very wrong here and I just can't tell what to believe. I place the coffee cup back down on the table, and focus on keeping my expression open and non-threatening. I glance around the room again, committing it to memory. I feel Anton's eyes on me and clear my throat.

'Never.'

'Okay,' I say. 'Thank you for taking the time to talk to me, and to explain your version of events. I clearly haven't had the full story. The client–therapist relationship is a very unique one. Would you please ask Leah to get in touch with me as soon as she gets home?' Anton nods. 'Did she say anything about when she'd come home?'

'She said she needed to finish something and that she'd most likely come back this weekend.'

'Okay.' I'm about to walk out the door when something occurs to me. 'Oh, hey, Anton, do you happen to know what Leah's new book is about?'

'Uh. New book?'

'The one she's working on?'

'Right. No.'

'Has she not mentioned it to you?'

'Only very briefly.'

'Okay. Thank you. Well, I'll be expecting her call.' I don't believe for a second that Leah, a celebrated author who has struggled for over a year with the process of writing her second book, wouldn't have extensively discussed this with her so-called boyfriend.

Anton nods, and fidgets with the strap of his watch, which has come loose from its leather hoop. I stare at his nimble, strong fingers and wonder if they closed around Leah Iverson's neck.

When I've left the building, I cross the street and can't resist the urge to turn back around and look at the row of windows on the fourth floor belonging to Leah's apartment, but when I do, I catch a glimpse of Anton standing there in the middle window, looking straight at me.

17

Kristina

At home, I close the door to the apartment softly, then lean against it. All the lights are off and the hallway is gloomy, deep shadows stretching across the oak floorboards. I slip my boots off, trying to steady my breathing and calm my racing heart after the brisk, cold walk home.

I walk through to the living room and sit down on the sofa – I need a few moments to center myself and sort my thoughts after the disturbing meeting with Anton. I fix my gaze on the huge canvas hung across from me on the matte charcoal wall – Eirik's favorite. It's a medley of blues and grays and looks like something my nephew might have produced at nursery, and yet, it cost more than my BMW. At least it isn't Elisabeth's – the others are all off the walls now and in the cupboard of the spare bedroom. Eirik says this one represents the storms of the mind and that the tiny slash of white toward the bottom left of the picture apparently represents hope. Sometimes I enjoy the picture and lose myself in the chaotic, hypnotic blur of its swirling brushstrokes, but I feel fundamentally annoyed at the suggestion that this image has an underlying objective meaning that should be apparent to its observer.

I follow a long, dark line running from the center of the painting toward the far-right corner and though I keep my head entirely still, I can't hold the tears back now, and I don't fight them either. I was afraid in Leah's apartment, with Anton. I have an irrational sensation of being watched, and feel the compulsion to rush through the apartment, peering into cupboards and under beds, though I know I'm alone, like I usually am. Still, the fine hairs on my arms stand up at the thought of being watched by someone I can't see, someone I couldn't expose.

If my clients could see me now, what would they think? Anxious and high-strung, unsure of what to do or what to think – nothing like the calm, soothing presence they depend on. I check my emails, but there is nothing new. I try to Google Anton, but as I don't know his last name I get nowhere. I dial the number of the Majorstuen police station. After a series of automated questions, I'm put through to an operator.

'Crime department, Silvia Espensen speaking.'

'Hi, this is Dr Kristina Moss. I'm a doctor of psychology and a practicing psychotherapist at Homansbyen Terapi-senter calling about one of my clients who I believe may have come to harm.'

'Can I take a name?'

'Leah Iverson.' I spell her name out, unusual in Norway, the –on ending making her obviously Swedish.

'Why do you think something may have happened to her?'

'Well, she has missed a session with me, which is very out of character. And she was highly distressed the previous week. She has a history of mental health challenges and an abusive ex-husband.'

'Can I take the name of the ex-husband?'

'Anton.'

'Anton?'

'I don't have his last name, unfortunately. But I've met him. I went to her apartment, and he was there, alone, though she has told me repeatedly she wants nothing to do with him and was even afraid of him finding out where she lives. He says she's at her cabin in Telemark and that he saw her there himself a couple of days ago. I don't believe him. I believe he may have hurt her.'

'What makes you think that?'

'Well, she is not responding to calls or emails. When she came to see me last Friday, her face was badly bruised. She refused to say who had done it, but who is it likely to be, besides the violent ex? Even if he hasn't hurt her, he may have compromised her mental health to such an extent that her life is in danger. She is a vulnerable person with a history of suicidal ideation. Still, I just don't believe this man, or that Leah's just voluntarily disappeared for over a week. I think he's lying and that she's hurt or in real danger.'

'Do you have her address?'

'Yes, and please hurry; you might catch him. I mean, surely there must be reason to apprehend him if he's at her house and she has a restraining order against him—'

'Look. Dr...'

'Moss.'

'Dr Moss, unless the next of kin or her employer has

reported her missing, there isn't very much we can do. We might be able to send a patrol around to the address...'

'Yes, I think you need to get this Anton guy in for questioning. But you need to urgently send someone to her cabin. It's in the mountains somewhere in Telemark – I think it's near Seljord; she's given me the exact coordinates. That's where you need to look for her.'

There's a long silence on the other end.

'I'm sure you can appreciate that we can't send a police car up to some mountain in Telemark to look for someone who may not have been reported missing, but like I said, I'll look into whether we'd be able to send someone around to Iverson's registered address—'

'Hold on, I've got them here, the coordinates for the cabin. It's, uh, fifteen minutes to drive from Seljord in the direction of Notodden, and then—'

'Dr Moss, is this your contact number you're calling from?'

'Yes?'

'I'll make sure someone looks into this and gives you a call back if we have any further questions. Do you know who Iverson's next of kin is?'

'It's her mother. Her name is Linda Iverson and she lives in Årjäng, I think.'

'Thank you for calling, Dr Moss.'

'Wait. Wait just a moment, please. Look, I've already been in touch with her mother, who said she's spoken to her, but that doesn't mean Leah is safe, or well. That she didn't sound worried doesn't mean much at all in this case. I know Leah and I genuinely believe she may be in danger. Listen, Leah is a very vulnerable person. Especially now. She's fourteen weeks pregnant. I believe she could be at risk of violence, or even suicide or serious self-harm. Please. You need to make this a priority and find her, now.'

Another long pause on the other end, and a slow release of breath. 'I'll make a note of this, Dr Moss. And I'll make sure someone looks into it.'

'Thank you.'

I don't know what I expected, but I suppose I thought the police would leap into action and immediately start looking for an unaccounted-for pregnant woman with a provably violent ex. After all, how many calls like that do they get on any given Friday afternoon in this sleepy country? I'm going to have to assume that the policewoman will look Leah up and find the previous reports she made against Anton, prompting them to take real action.

I go through to the kitchen and stand at the sink and look across the rooftops toward the silvery top branches of the trees in the distance. They are the king's trees I'm looking at – we're that close to the royal palace gardens. I wish there was something for me to clean, something dirty needing my attention, so I could spend time rubbing hard at an old piece of food stuck to a plate with the coarse end of the sponge, or rinse some delicate champagne flutes, but there is nothing. All the surfaces are smooth, the gold-veined black marble glinting in the spotlights. My husband always cleans up after himself if he's made a mess or fixed a snack, leaving the scent of disinfectant lingering on the air, even though he knows our cleaner comes twice weekly. Souvenirs of his year in the military, and growing up without a mother, he says.

I need you to— said Leah, interrupting herself, before walking out. But what did she need me to do? *Please please please come*, said her note, followed by the address to her cabin.

This is about the truth. I feel queasy just hearing her words in my head. Her hand was cold and dry when it brushed briefly against mine as she handed me the envelope. Her eyes were already elsewhere, as if she had left long ago and it was just the outline of her that remained there with me in that room.

Could it be that I'm overreacting? What if my mind is running wild and that what happened to Elisabeth is coloring my concern for Leah? Anton may well be telling the truth, and Leah could be at her cabin, just working away on her next book. Perhaps he never hurt her and just went there to apologize for an argument they had, like he said. Perhaps she isn't at any risk from herself, either – after all, suicide is very rare, especially among women, even those with occasional suicidal preoccupation.

I pour some of Eirik's expensive balsamic vinegar into the sink so that there is something to clean, some reason to turn the tap on, the sound of rushing water erasing the silence of the apartment. I look up at the king's trees again and focus in on a particularly impressive one, its branches black and gnarled against the gloomy sky, but now it's like I can see Leah hanging there, close to the trunk as though her body were an extension of it, her neck bent low and at an angle, her thin limbs like drooping branches trailing toward the ground. The palms of her hands are strangely white in the gloomy violet light of the afternoon, and streaked with blood and dirt as though she's fought someone off. The rope is taut and bright blue, reaching upwards into the dense canopy of the fir tree, swaying softly in the gathering wind. I turn away from the window and wipe my wet hands on my jeans, breathing slowly to still my heart.

'Kristina,' says a voice and I jump out of my skin, my heart shuddering in my chest. I spin around and Eirik is standing there, wearing black boxer shorts and a gray T-shirt I don't remember seeing before.

'What...' I start, but my voice breaks and trails off. It's just after five o'clock on a Friday – Eirik rarely comes home before seven, even on a Friday. 'Are you sick?' He does look pale – his face is drawn and deep-blue circles bruise the skin around his eyes.

'No,' he says, whispering into my hair. 'I wanted to come home early to spend some time with you. I feel like I haven't seen you in ages.' I still don't feel quite like myself. I'm aware that I'm trembling and Eirik takes another step forward before enveloping me in a close hug. I close my eyes and let myself be held by him. He smells like soap and wood smoke and fresh rain.

'Have you been out running?'

'Not since yesterday.'

I nod. I open my mouth to speak, to maybe to tell him about Leah, and Anton, but no words will come, only tears, and a flicker of alarm crosses Eirik's face. 'What's the matter, honey?'

'Tough few days at work,' I say, my eyes dropping from his pale face to the floor, and I try to stave off the images of Leah hanging, but it doesn't work – it is as though she has been etched onto my retinas, her limp body swinging back and forth in my mind like a grotesque pendulum. Eirik nods and waits for me to continue, but I don't.

'Come sit with me,' he says, leading me over to the sofa. I let myself relax against him. We fall into a long silence. Eirik gently strokes my hair, then cups my skull in his large, warm hand, kneading tension from my scalp. I love this soft version of my husband – out there, in the world, he comes across as so powerful and self-assured but here, at home with me, he is actually a very gentle man.

'I'm sorry for the other day,' I say.

'What day?'

'You know. The burned painting. It was quite the meltdown.'

'You're going through a hard time, my love. But there is no one in the world I would trust more to get through this time and emerge stronger.'

'It was triggered by some stuff going on at work.'

'What kind of stuff?'

'I…' I can't quite decide whether to tell Eirik about Leah and everything that's been happening; it feels difficult to divulge personal information about a client to anyone, even my husband. I never tell anyone anything about my clients, not even Eirik, no matter what. Besides, I've done everything I could, and my job is to listen, not investigate. It's a police matter now and I have to trust that they will question Anton, if only to find that he's telling the truth. I close my eyes and lean against Eirik's dense shape beside me. But still, all I can see is her, alone in the woods. Hanging.

'I'm worried about a client,' I say, finally, my voice low and trembling. I try to envision something other than the violent images in my head, so I look up at my husband and focus on his smooth skin, his strong jawline and his lovely, slightly puffy lips. I run a fingertip along his bottom lip and he looks at me seriously, waiting for me to continue. 'She's a writer. Quite a well-known one, actually. We've had a very productive relationship, or so I thought. But she's behaving completely out of character.'

'In which way?'

'She came to our session last week, extremely distressed. Someone had assaulted her but she wouldn't say who. She has a history of self-harm and some suicidal preoccupation, as well as an abusive ex-husband.'

'That sounds very worrying.' Eirik's eyes are still locked on mine and I love how he listens so intently, he's able to make people feel like the only person in the world when he turns his full attention to them.

'Yes. And then she missed her session with me yesterday. So I went to her house—'

'Wait. What? You went to her house?'

'Yes.'

'That sounds like an unusual thing for you to do.'

'It's an unusual situation. I have a bad feeling about it. Something has happened to her, something bad.'

'What happened at her house?'

'She wasn't there. Her ex-husband was. My client had a restraining order against the guy; there's a long history of emotional abuse and threatening behavior. So why would he be at her house? But he was nothing like what I would have expected. From what I've heard about the guy, I would've expected some kind of monster. You know, weird and shifty, behaving as though he were guilty of something. But he just seemed quite normal. But if he's telling the truth, that means she's been lying. A lot. He told me she's gone to her cabin, and that she's working on her new book.'

'And why wouldn't that be true?'

'I'm not sure I believe she's there, doing just great, working away on her book, after the state she was in last week.'

'So, you think he's done something to her.'

'Well, I know he's certainly capable of it, at least according to her. And he seemed quite bitter and volatile beneath the surface. He said he was upset about the way she'd written about him in her previous book; he talked about feeling compromised and misrepresented. Said he lost his job and had to go live with his parents as a result. She writes autofiction, you know, in the vein of Knausgaard and Vigdis Hjorth.' Eirik nods thoughtfully, still listening intently. I stroke his hand and uncurl his fist so that my hand fits inside his.

'Is this client Leah Iverson?'

'Yes. I mean, I really shouldn't ever name a client, but I guess it was obvious. So you know of her?' I feel worse now, having spoken of Leah to my husband – I should have known he would have heard of her.

'Well, yes. She's quite high profile, isn't she? Didn't she win a big prize?'

'Yeah. The Nordic Prize for Fiction, a very big deal, I gather.'

'I remember. She was on the cover of several newspapers.'

'Yes.'

'How long have you been seeing her?'

'Almost three years now.'

'Right. And her recent behavior is out of character?'

'Very.'

'Has she said anything that could indicate why?'

'Well, yes. She literally begged me to come to her cabin. I've explained why that isn't possible. She insisted. She said there's something important she has to tell me. I've tried to call and email her, but she hasn't responded. I mean, it's not like it's actually an option for me to go there and speak with her; that would be incredibly inappropriate.'

'Yes. Do you have any idea what it could be? Has she given you any indication at all?'

'No. Well. In the past few months, she has been more assertive with me in our sessions. She's asked quite a few personal questions, like what my thoughts are or how I would react in certain situations, that kind of thing. She seems quite preoccupied with me, which is actually very common – I see it in little things like dressing similarly to me or copying certain mannerisms. I'm confused because it's clear she has been hiding things from me, and I believed she shared everything going on in her life with me – she always gave that impression. The ex told me they'd rekindled their relationship, which is almost impossible to believe after the hell she went through with him.' I take another big glug from the red wine Eirik has poured for me, feeling the alcohol mercifully spreading out in my stomach, loosening my nerves. I focus on taking several deep breaths before continuing, I find it difficult to say what I'm going to say next. 'And then I found out from Leah's doctor that she's pregnant.'

'Oh. Wow.' Eirik looks enraptured, like I'm telling him an exciting story I've made up and he needs to know what happens next.

'But she never told me. And that, to me, feels quite sinister. I'm worried that the ex has hurt her.'

'I'm assuming he's the father?'

'He didn't mention it. Perhaps he doesn't even know. Or perhaps she's gotten pregnant by somebody else and he found out? I could imagine that would make him straight up dangerous.'

'Jesus.'

'Yes. Or he may have caused her to regress so much she might cause herself harm. I mean, you wouldn't believe the state she was in…'

'Poor girl. That's all really shocking. Do you actually think she might be suicidal?'

'I'm not sure. Yes, I think it could be possible, given the circumstances and this strange behavior. But maybe I'm so worried about suicide because of what happened with Elisabeth.'

'Well, she does sound quite desperate.'

'Yes. And I just don't know what to do. It's not my role to pursue this any further. I've done all the right things, I contacted her GP and her mother, and I called the police after I met her ex at her apartment. But after Elisabeth, it's like I just can't let it go. I can't stop thinking about her. I keep thinking that if I just went there like she asked me to, then I could save her—'

'You called the police?'

'Yes. I felt I had to.'

'And what did they say?'

'That they would try to send a car over to her apartment. I explained that she's not there and that they need to go to the cabin and it didn't sound like they would even consider that unless she's reported missing by her next of kin. So what do I do? I can't just do nothing. I can just tell that something bad has happened, or will happen...'

'Kristina. Listen to me. This does all sound very worrying. But you've done all the right things. I think you're letting Elisabeth influence how you are reacting to this. Not every troubled soul will do what she did. Most won't. And even if Leah Iverson did, it wouldn't be your fault. You've done everything you can.'

'I was so shocked to hear that she's pregnant. You can imagine how it made me feel. I completely broke down with Vera. You know, it's made me realize how I'm absolutely not ready to give up. I think we should call the clinic and make plans for a new round of treatment.'

Eirik is quiet and holds himself very still. I can tell he's thinking about how to word his response. 'You're right. It's been a few months now. But we need to wait until after the election.'

I feel suddenly, irrationally angry and turn away from him. Everything needs to wait until after the election.

'Come here, honey,' he says, pulling me closer. I let him hold me because there are tears in my eyes and I don't want him to see.

'I wish you could come with me tomorrow,' he says, after a long while.

'Come with you where?'

'I'm off to Bergen again tomorrow morning, remember? Six thirty flight, nightmare. The campaign? This one is really, really important. If I get the nomination there, I'm likely to win most of the west coast. And then I go on to Trondheim and Tromsø. Back on Thursday.'

'I don't remember hearing about this. I would have written it in my diary...' I untangle myself from Eirik's arms and go to get my diary from my handbag in the hallway. I've been looking forward to this weekend, to us finally having some uninterrupted time together. But there it is – *Eirik Bergen* it says, on Saturday 31st. I can't help the tears that pool in my eyes again, but immediately feel stupid. I feel unsettled and anxious about being here alone for so many days. What if Anton gets questioned by the police but released because of a lack of evidence and comes after me?

'Kristina, I told you about this,' says Eirik, pulling me back toward him. I nod and bury my face in the warm crook of his neck. 'You know it's not for nothing. I hate leaving you, but it's only for a few days. I'll be back before you even realize I'm gone.'

'Sorry. I just want one whole weekend together. It's October and I don't think we've had that this year at all, not once. In over ten months.'

'I know. It should calm down a little soon.'

'When? When you're prime minister?'

Eirik chuckles softly and kisses the inside of my palm.

'I don't want you to go.'

'Shhh. I'm here now. Besides, didn't you tell me you have a boozy brunch with some girlfriends tomorrow? That will keep you busy. And maybe you can go back to see Camilla and the kids.'

He's right, I've made brunch plans with my university friends, and just the thought of it makes me feel exhausted. I'll have to think of an excuse, but for now, I try to relax into his embrace, to enjoy the way his fingers trace shapes across my collarbone and the hollows of my throat, but my thoughts feel disjointed and dense, layered one on top of each other, like the many layers of paint in Elisabeth's artwork, made to look like a single color at first sight.

18

Elisabeth, June

Elisabeth gets up and stands a while at the window. It's a cool, overcast early-summer night, and though she can see no moon or stars, the sky is a pleasant light dove gray, even at midnight. Villa Vinternatt is quiet but it has the comforting hum of sleeping people gathered together. At the end of the vast sweep of garden, a pond. Then thick woods. Beyond the woods, the still and silvery Oslofjord, caught between two narrow headlands like a giant rock pool at low tide.

When she first came here, she couldn't sleep. She lay night after night on top of her bed, sweating and shaking, wracked with sobs, nausea and intense itching. They anticipated this with new arrivals and after dinner, one of the staff members gave her a fistful of pills to take, but she didn't take them; she kept them for a moment in the wet pocket of her cheek until she could spit them out. Nobody checked; Villa Vinternatt isn't that kind of place. She did take the methadone, but it took several weeks before she began to feel better, and several more before Elisabeth started to feel at home. But she still can't sleep.

This is a place to grow and to reconnect, they said when Elisabeth was first introduced to the idea of Villa Vinternatt. A rehabilitation center for artists with addiction issues, which offered progressive treatment for substance abuse, using a combination of methadone, intense group therapy and a chance to contribute to the arts, supposedly giving recovering addicts a sense of purpose and community. Some stay for a few months, some for years, all government funded. Many people want the opportunity to come somewhere like this, Kristina had said, and Elisabeth knew she was lucky. She hadn't had much luck in the years before coming to Villa Vinternatt.

For years, Elisabeth had sold herself for heroin. And if you have sold yourself, what, if anything, of yourself remains yours? She was there, in the little yellow room in the eaves, a woman without doubt. A tired and thin and pale one, but definitely a female human. There were brittle bones and broken veins and some patches of permanently bruised skin and a sweet, youthful face almost untouched by the horrors she'd lived. In her veins rushed blood, and she was often preoccupied with blood; it was in her therapy notes, and it was in her art – repeat mentions of blood, as if it was the source of everything that had happened. Hungry blood, bad blood, blood that needed something injected into its flow to give her body and mind what it craved: she had tried many analogies over the years to describe the notion that what drove her came from her very core, it ran through her veins. But was it always there?

For years, Elisabeth had felt dead inside, as if her internal landscape was a bleak and barren November afternoon. She was stunned by the trauma endured in her teens, and nothing helped; not the care of her family or her friends, or a long succession of various doctors and therapists. Then, in a group therapy session for PTSD sufferers, she met Andreas, who had kind brown eyes, trembling hands that moved her, and a blossoming heroin addiction. He helped, and the heroin helped, too. Those first few years with Andreas were one big high, and the darkness of her early twenties finally faded away in Elisabeth's mind and heart. Elisabeth and Andreas were the sexy kind of addicts, they used to joke; he was heir to a salmon farm fortune and could more than afford to fund them and access quality heroin. They lived in a beautiful apartment in central Oslo, and socialized and went to art school and loved each other deeply, but with time, every aspect of their lives became increasingly dominated by their love affair with the Big H. It began to show. People started to ask questions. Their families grew concerned, then suspicious, then horrified as the scope of their addiction became clear.

Though Elisabeth still doesn't consciously allows herself to return to the icy January morning five years ago when she woke up next to a dead man, the man she loved, those moments are always with her like a backdrop to her mind. Overnight, she was evicted from Andreas' apartment by his family. She had no job and had dropped out of art school several months before. She was thirty-four with nothing to show for it except a body full of broken and bruised veins. Her family tried to help, Kristina tried to help, the welfare office tried to help, but within weeks, Elisabeth was living in a hostel and working the streets, reeling with ever-increasing use to dull the grief. In those days, just *being* felt like falling through endless layers of hot burning air, and every night, lying on the hard hostel bed, coming down from a high, Elisabeth would be bombarded with gruesome images of giant needles plunging into frail veins, blood splattering to the ground, guns pointed in faces, the hairy backs of another faceless client, Andreas dead, his soft brown eyes open and staring straight at her. The only thing that helped, was the only thing that had ever helped – the intensely warm, euphoric lull of a clean, strong hit of smack.

It all feels like a long time ago now, almost two years. Tonight, Elisabeth feels calm and content. If someone were to place a bag of heroin on the table in front of her, Elisabeth wouldn't touch it. She'd be able to hold the memory of its potency in her mind, and still not be tempted. She has too much, now, even though if she were to compare herself to some people she knows, she has nothing at all. But she has a blossoming career as a painter, Kristina – the best friend who'd do anything for her, people she trusts and a sense of purpose. In the group therapy sessions that happen every day of the week except Tuesdays and Sundays, Elisabeth and her fellow residents at Villa Vinternatt explore their pasts, their current experiences, and their wishes for the future – that vague future in which they must leave Villa Vinternatt and reintegrate into society. Someday, she hopes to be ready. In her individual therapy, Elisabeth has begun to address how her family has been affected by her addiction, and ways to hopefully heal those wounds someday. Once a month, her parents visit. Kristina visits, too. And once a month, Elisabeth is released overnight and usually spends the night at Kristina and Eirik's, or her parents' in Bærum.

She looks out at the narrow Drøbak Sound and the wooded headland of Nesodden across the bay. She shivers in the cool breeze coming in through the open window, carrying the scent of Villa Vinternatt's rose garden. She watches the blonde hairs on her arm prickle and stand up, and in the twilight, the fading scars underneath are invisible.

Looking back at her love affair with heroin now, she knows it wasn't love at all, but a very human need for escape. And little wonder, Elisabeth had a lot to wish to escape from. She still does, it is heavy stuff she carries, and it is all the heavier for having to carry it alone. And yet, it has helped to be here and to express herself by returning to painting and being encouraged and supported to do so. Still, she is tired. Elisabeth often thinks of herself as a much older woman, someone who has lived a long life and doesn't yearn for more. Other times, she thinks of herself as an animal, a wild little thing who has exhausted itself just trying to stay alive, and who craves the long, dark months of hibernation, tucking herself away in a tiny cave, giving in to a dreamless, peaceful sleep. Elisabeth leaves the window wide open and returns to bed, tucking herself in tight with the light summer duvet. When the usual images insist themselves upon her and want to keep her up all night in terror, she holds on tight to the image of herself as a wild animal, exhausted but safe in its snug winter den, and it works, she's lulled into a heavy, dreamless sleep.

'Nightmare disorder,' the new therapist says, an attractive woman named Olivia with a faint American accent. Dr Olivia Hudson reads the diploma hung on the wall above her desk. Formal and impressive, thinks Elisabeth, and knows that must be exactly the intention. She studies the other woman's face carefully, trying to decide whether she instinctively likes her or not, if this is someone she could envision speaking to several times a week. Olivia sits opposite her on a blue sofa, casually dressed in jeans and a plain black T-shirt, her face clean of make-up except for a deep red shade of lipstick. Elisabeth is tired: though she fell into an initial, deep sleep, she woke up after less than three hours and the night was short and broken. She didn't want to come here today, running through her therapy notes from her previous shrink with the new one. *Getting to know each other*, Olivia had called it when she entered the room.

'What do you mean?' asks Elisabeth. 'I have bad dreams, so do a lot of addicts. I've read about it. Heroin changes the pathways of the brain and makes them more alive. Comes out at night.'

'Yes, but nightmare disorder, one form of parasomnia, is more than just having bad dreams; it's a disturbed sleeping pattern, being too afraid to fall asleep, to such an extent that it affects you during the day. How does it present itself for you? Are you restless during the night? Do you find that you've kicked the duvet off? Do you sweat? These can all be signs.'

Restless at night, Elisabeth laughs to herself – that would be a rather modest way of describing the full extent of her nocturnal demons.

'Honestly, I don't think there's anything much you can do or medicine you can give me for my nighttime terrors. Besides, I'm a big girl.' Elisabeth stares pointedly at the clock above the door: seven minutes left. She doesn't want to get into a deeper conversation about any of this; if she starts to talk about her dreams she can't be sure she could stop herself building the horrific images in her mind again. It can stay boxed up and maybe touched upon someday.

She leaves Olivia's office on the ground floor and walks down the empty corridors and up the sweeping staircase of Villa Vinternatt back to her room, passing a couple of unknown faces along the way. They look more like visitors than drug addicts, but you never know – Elisabeth knows the same has been said about her. Occasionally new people arrive. Most of them go back to shooting up in a matter of weeks, and Elisabeth can always tell who isn't going to last – she can practically smell the desperation for another hit oozing from their pores. She hasn't made any close friends here – friendships are in fact gently discouraged, as they exponentially increase the risk of setbacks. She is encouraged to think of the other residents at Villa Vinternatt as co-healers. There are a couple of people she prefers to others, but mostly Elisabeth keeps to herself, or speaks to her mother or Kristina on the phone during free time in the afternoon.

In her room stands a wooden easel positioned toward the window to give the best light onto the canvas. It's Italian-designed, a gift from her parents after twelve months clean. She looks out of the window now; the view is beautiful and she never tires of it. The rich green pines of Nordmarka forest in the distance with hundreds of trails for enthusiastic hikers, each path leading to somewhere new. The frothy gray sea, great big rolling waves chasing back and forth in the narrow sound.

She spots a sparrow sitting on the narrow ledge below

her window, cocking its head and chirping merrily, and wants to believe it is the same one she has seen many times before, and painted, too. The sparrow shakes off water droplets from its squat, fluffy body, after taking a bath in a drainpipe. Its movements are so precise and so fast, eyes darting everywhere to make sure it's safe. Another sparrow joins it and they both indulge in splashing about, dunking their beaks into the rainwater dammed in the drain blocked by twigs and leaves from the weekend's summer storms, when lightning and thunder tore at the skies. Elisabeth wishes she could be like the little birds, oblivious to the dangers of what really lies out there.

She takes out her palette and brushes which she keeps meticulously clean and rolled away safely in their canvas sleeves. There is something almost religious about untying the frayed green ribbon and slowly unrolling the fabric to expose the brushes, some so worn the varnish has whittled down to the wood. They're tatty, but they're hers, and they tell a thousand stories of her life when she used them back in art school, when Andreas was alive. She takes the palette knife and starts mixing the colors, always adding dark to light, like she was taught. Maybe that's her problem, she thinks; she always adds dark to light, in life and in her dreams.

Again, she thinks about telling Olivia everything, at least everything that happens in her dreams. She doesn't have to say that the dreams that torture her are real, visceral memories, scorched into the neuropathways of her brain. The irony, Elisabeth thought, when once, years ago, she learned that morphine, the medical derivative of opium, was named after Morpheus, the Greek God of sleep.

Elisabeth places the brush back into the canvas sleeve. Harder than intended, she puts the palette knife down in its holder on the easel, sending the sparrows scrambling into the air. She walks back down the stairs and along the corridors, all empty; it's just minutes until lunch time and most residents will already be waiting in the dining room for the unveiling of the buffet. She sees Olivia through the glass pane on the door, typing away on her computer at the desk. When she knocks on the door, Olivia looks up and smiles when she sees her.

'I'm sorry, you're probably busy. Umm. I could come back another time if that's better, or, like, if you're not the right person to talk to about this, just say, and—'

'Now is fine, Elisabeth. My afternoon is wide open today.'

'Oh. Umm, okay.'

'What's on your mind?'

'I thought maybe I should tell you about what happens in the night. The dreams I have. Or dream, really – it's almost always the same one.' She pauses, trying to find a way to describe what happens to her when Villa Vinternatt settles down for the night, purring with tired, sated humans. Her anxiety at dusk is visceral. Her skin starts to itch, the same way it used to when smack was leaving her body. Her senses bombard her with panic, and she has the sensation of drowning, gasping for air. She's endlessly tried to create a routine to relax, but nothing works; it's the same story, the same recurring nightmare, every single night.

'I'm running though a thick, overgrown jungle. I'm barefoot. Terrified. Wild animals are chasing me, they snap their jaws and tear pieces of flesh from my body, stripping me to the bone. I can feel warm blood running down my face and the metallic taste of it in her mouth. I fall down, I always do, and the animals encircle me, breathing heavily, inching closer; I can see the gnarly, bloodied teeth of wolves, the razor-sharp talons of a white-tailed eagle, and I can smell death in the air. I know that often people wake moments before something dramatic happens in a dream, like falling or being shot. I never do. For me, it is still only the beginning. The animals tear at what remains of my skin, ripping it from the muscle, my eyes are plucked from their sockets. I can feel my lifeless body being pulled in different directions until my remains sink deep into the forest floor, as if the branches and brambles will take whatever is left. When I wake up, I'm always exhausted, like someone has drained my body of blood, and my head spins with dizzying thoughts.'

'What kind of thoughts?' asks Olivia, softly.

'I don't know,' she says, and stands back up, making for the door, avoiding Dr Hudson's eyes. But she does know. These nights make her resent Kristina; it's not like she has night after night of this hell. She'll sleep peacefully, next to her perfect husband in her perfect home. It feels unfair.

19

Kristina

He's gone when I wake up, though it is still dark outside. Tomorrow November will be here, the darkest and dreariest month. Like several of my clients, Leah spoke of the coming winter a few times recently, and expressed anxiety about the dark months looming. Several months of near-constant darkness and cold take their toll on many people here in the north, myself included. It is hard to avoid the feeling of lethargy and melancholy that seems to seep into your very bones when it is dark when you go to work, dark when you come back home and often chucking it down with icy rain to top it off. I've had another one of those nights I often have, struggling to fall asleep, and then when I finally do, I have a terrible nightmare. I wake with a start, heart pounding, my face wet with tears, and no recollection of the dream, other than running away from something. After these episodes, I lie tossing and turning for hours, my mind ruminating over little details from the day, or a client's situation, or the past. By the time I fall asleep again, not even an hour remains until my alarm goes off.

Thankfully, today is Saturday so I've been able to sleep in and feel quite rested. I make the bed perfectly, then remain on top of it for a long while, staring absentmindedly into the walk-in wardrobe through the open door, at the rows and rows of Eirik's expensive shirts. Sometimes living with Eirik is like living with a ghost, one whose presence you can feel but never summon. I try to imagine him in my mind, the way he most likely is in this exact moment; intently focused on winning over a room, or an organization, or an important person sitting across from him.

He'll be smiling and laughing, well aware of his charm, subconsciously mirroring his audience, creating a bond of trust, gesticulating in that rather excessive way of his that makes him occasionally seem more Italian than Norwegian. He chooses his words carefully and isn't afraid of moments of silence, knowing how to use them. It makes him come across as authoritative, self-assured, measured. A leader. When Eirik and I met, fresh out of university, I was the only person who believed him when he said he'd be prime minister someday. Now everybody does. It seems to be only a matter of time.

It's not fake, the charismatic, trustworthy persona my husband projects. He is those things. He is also the sometimes tired, reclusive, spent man who needs calm and quiet at home, who likes to fall asleep with his head held snug between my breasts while I gently tickle the hair at the nape of his neck. And he is still the eager kid I fell in love with: an idealistic, unafraid small-town young man who lights up when he speaks of change and bettering the country. I think of how intently he listened to me last night, how close he held me, and smile to myself in the gloomy room.

I look around the room at the strangely blurred outlines of the furniture – I can't see much without my contact lenses. I switch on the radio and Soft Classics fills the room – perfect for early mornings and perfect for sex, though I certainly have more of the former than the latter these days. I close my eyes again, listening to Einaudi, running through the various options for today in my head. I don't particularly want to go to the brunch, but I have absolutely nothing else to do. My thoughts return to last weekend, to the rainy beach walk in Drøbak with Camilla and the kids – it's where I'd usually go on a weekend when Eirik is away or working. I could go today; it might be fun to tag along with the kids trick-or-treating, it's Halloween. But at the thought of the drive down to Drøbak and back, something tightens in my throat and I swallow hard to dislodge it. Up until August, I would always stop in at Villa Vinternatt on my way home and sit in the rose garden with Elisabeth. I'll never go there again, never again listen to the pleasant rise and fall of her soft voice, or see her fresh, sweet face.

I suppose I could hop on the train out to Sandvika and see my mother again, I felt bad for being abrupt with her earlier in the week. I'd have to pay my dues with Elisabeth's mother, but deep down I know I just can't. Not yet.

I pick up my phone to message the girls, saying I can't make it; the idea of sitting among them at Delicatessen, day-drinking and gossiping and discussing their toddlers' remarkable achievements fills me with instant dread. But maybe it won't be like that, maybe it will actually be fun – something to do that has nothing to do with Elisabeth or Leah or the fact that my marriage and my entire life is on hold until after the elections. Something that might take my mind off the anxiety and persistent dejection I've been feeling. It's been so long since I did something sociable, just for fun, not for Eirik's campaign or a work-related conference. I remember last night and how good it was to speak to Eirik about what's been going on, and I know he's absolutely right – I have to let go now.

I put the phone back down and get out of bed. I have plenty of time to run through my morning routine before meeting the girls at noon – contact lenses, shower, moisturizer, a light touch of make-up. I spend a while studying the pores of my skin close-up – my skin looks coarser than just a few months ago, maybe a result of both the stress of this year and the unusually cold October weather. Perhaps it's time to reconsider the Botox I've always dismissed – it was easier to turn down when my skin was still young and flawless. My thoughts are interrupted by the vibration of my phone on the bedside table. Someone is phoning from a private number.

'Hello?'

'Hi, is that Dr Moss?'

'Speaking.'

'Good morning. This is Hans-Olav Bjerre calling from Majorstuen police station. Can I confirm that you called in a tip yesterday about a potential missing person or domestic violence case to my colleague Officer Espensen?'

'Yes, that's right.'

'We've had a look into the information you provided.

There doesn't seem to be any reason for concern with regard to your client, Miss Iverson.'

'Have you found her?'

'We've been in contact with her mother, Linda Iverson, who confirms communicating with her daughter recently.'

'Yes, I know that.'

'It would seem she has gone away somewhere to finish a book or something. A cabin, it says in the write-up.'

'Yes. I asked your colleague to please send someone there. I believe Leah is in danger.'

'Such a request would need to come from her next of kin, and may be difficult to accommodate as there doesn't seem to be any reason to suspect she is in danger.'

'Did you send someone to her apartment? Her ex, against whom she had a restraining order, was there yesterday. You need to find out why.'

'We did. There was no one there.'

'Did you go in?'

'No. We rang the bell. No one was there.'

'How do you know he wasn't there and just didn't open?'

'Look. We would have needed a search warrant to enter the apartment.'

My mind darts to Anton at the middle window, half of his face cast in shadows, his pale-blue eyes cold and sharp on the street below. I shiver lightly. 'So what happens next?'

'Well, presumably what your client's mother says is correct and Ms Iverson will return to her home when she wishes to do so. Oh, and one more thing – it says that you mentioned to Espensen that your client had a restraining order against her ex-husband, Anton von Thaule.'

'Yes?'

'This is incorrect. It was von Thaule who took out a restraining order against Leah Iverson in 2015, after an assault. She tried to take one out against him, but it was discredited after the discovery of CCTV footage of the alleged incident.'

'What? Are you sure?'

'Absolutely.'

After hanging up, I go back to the bathroom and splash cold water on my face, the recently applied mascara dislodging from my lashes and running down my face in black streaks.

All the evidence suggests she's fine. I should relax now and return to my own life. All the space Leah Iverson has taken up in my mind in the past week needs to be freed up for the things that are actually relevant to my life – my work, my family, my remaining friendships, my marriage. But I'm not going to pretend I'm not a little disappointed in Leah, who, having clearly decided to take a temporary or permanent break from therapy, couldn't even be bothered to let me know. Intellectually I know that she is going through what is no doubt a turbulent time, but I am still human and feel affected by her actions. I make a mental note to take these feelings to my next supervision with Vera in two weeks' time. I am also surprised and disturbed that she has clearly extensively lied to me, both about her present and past relationship with Anton von Thaule.

Lying to therapists is surprisingly common, and in Leah's case, she was most likely ashamed of her own actions during her marriage break-up and reinvented herself as a victim. Then, her book must have exacerbated that false narrative and she got trapped in her own web of lies. This would explain why she was so disturbed and profoundly uncomfortable with her new status as author and well-known abuse victim. Or... Or she told the truth and he played her, perhaps taking out the restraining order to discredit her.

I lie back on the bed for a moment, my head spinning with disjointed, jostling thoughts. In spite of all my training, and all my own therapy work, I am unable to decipher my own feelings in this moment. Restlessness, I think. Underlying anxiety. A sense of unease – it's the feeling of staring at a puzzle and realizing that a piece is missing. But then again, I have had to get used to pieces missing. Since the age of nineteen, when I suffered severe trauma-induced dissociative amnesia, I have known what it feels like to have patches of your life simply erased. And though my own experience with memory loss is limited to one specific incident, I sometimes have the strange feeling in other contexts, of only seeing part of the picture.

Again, my thoughts return to Leah. I instantly grow tense and annoyed with myself for not being able to let it go now. Am I going to plague myself with ruminations about a troubled client for another week until she decides to turn up for our next session, or not?

Please come to my cabin, she said. Why would she beg me to come like that unless it really was important? Why did she lie to me about Anton? It's the lying I feel unsettled by – did Leah not feel enough trust and support in our therapeutic bond that she would be able to divulge the truth about her past to me? And why hasn't she answered any of my calls or emails if she really wanted to speak to me? I do recall her mentioning the exceptional remoteness of the cabin many times, and how she had no phone reception for miles. Still, she has clearly managed to get in touch with her mother.

20

Leah, two weeks before

A magnificent full moon bathes the October night in light. The curtains are open wide, letting a silvery shaft of light into the apartment. She's cross-legged on the floor in the living room, sitting in the moonbeam, like a forest animal resting for a while on a remote stretch of road. In front of her is a box of photographs, some scattered around on the floor. She picks one up, holds it up to the light. It's a photograph of herself as a young child, aged around four. By that age, Leah had already lost her father and was living with her mother, Linda, in a modest apartment in a non-descript suburb of Årjäng. She'd been a beautiful child, her light-brown eyes and dark hair giving her more definition than the classic Scandinavian look of white-blonde hair and ruddy cheeks of her little friends at nursery and in the neighborhood. But even back then, she'd felt different. Worth less. Unlovable.

She picks up a second photograph, this one of a slightly older child. It's Kristina, aged seven. The photo was taken in

Denmark and Kristina is standing on the rails of a wooden fence by the roadside, beaming at the camera. Leah knows this because on the back of the picture, someone has written 'Langeland, August 1993'. Next to Kristina stood her mother and her older sister, but Leah has cut them carefully out of the photograph. Behind Kristina is a rolling field, its late-summer sun-scorched grass having bled out with the passing of time into a faded ochre. A few goats stand in it, randomly captured for all time in the photograph. Leah places the two photos side by side on the floor. To a random observer, the two girls might have passed as the same person a couple of years apart. Kristina has darker-brown eyes than her, a slightly upturned snub nose, a gap between her front teeth and sun-streaked dark-brown hair tied up in a messy ponytail. The main difference between the two girls is the uncomplicated, mischievous joy in Kristina's smile, and the wan, careful expression on Leah's own face. Even back then, Kristina had been like a perfect version of herself.

Was that how it started? An initial sense of similarity between them, followed by a need to get close to it? The beginning is a long time ago now, a lot has happened.

She places both photographs back in the box among the many, many others. She considers trying to write, but decides against it; she can feel that it won't come to her tonight, either, and can't face all those long hours staring at the screen, waiting. She shivers lightly; it's turned suddenly and freakishly cold this past week, though it is still only mid-October. She rubs her upper arms, feeling goosebumps pricking beneath her fingertips. She rests both hands against the tight vault of her belly. In there, she imagines soft pink sludge is hardening and shaping into tiny bones, into a perfect little skull, into a beating heart. The baby will grow and grow until it fills all that empty, dark space inside her and then it will come out, and just by being, it will make her whole.

21

Kristina

I'm in the hallway stepping into my boots when the doorbell rings unexpectedly. I'm struck by a rush of fear, and immediately Anton and his cool blue eyes come to mind. No, it can't be. How would he even find me here? Like most therapists', my address is unlisted. I pick up the receiver and the video monitor flickers to life, revealing the person downstairs. It's a middle-aged woman wearing an oversized black raincoat, its hood obscuring her face. Still, I recognize her instantly – I've known this woman all my life.

'Hi, Idun,' I whisper into the receiver and she looks up, into the camera, and I'm taken aback by how thin she has grown – sharp cheekbones protrude over sunken cheeks, making Elisabeth's mother look bird-like and much older. Her eyes sit deep in her face, surrounded by dark circles. I press the buzzer, because what else can I do? I open the door to her wearing my jackets and boots and she realizes I was on my way out, her mouth tightening into an 'o'.

'I'm sorry. I should have called,' she says, shaking her head.

'You're going out somewhere. You look lovely, Kristina.' I feel guilty for the nice clothes and sophisticated make-up, and wish she'd caught me on any other weekend morning when I'd be in my usual old sweatpants and scruffy T-shirt. Now, I look like I'm going about my best life, just weeks after her only child died here in this apartment.

'Come in, Idun,' I say and decide to not offer an explanation for where I am headed. It's usually best to not over-explain. We hug briefly, and she feels bony and tense in my arms.

'I won't be long. I was just wondering if we could talk a few things through.'

'Of course.' I lead her through the apartment into the living room and only as she sits down on the sofa do I realize that she's facing directly toward the room where her daughter's big canvas used to hang on the wall behind the dining table. Eirik has replaced it temporarily with a Syeed Newham print on canvas and I watch Idun's eyes travel around the room and through the open double doors to the dining room. She's been here many times before for the Christmas drinks Eirik and I host every year, and I'm sure she's noticing the absence of Elisabeth's paintings.

'I was wondering,' she says, 'if you suspected anything in the weeks leading up to the eleventh of August.'

'What do you mean?'

'As a therapist. You must get clients in very dark places. Did you notice those kinds of tendencies with Elisabeth?'

'I see. As I wasn't the therapist treating Elisabeth, that is very difficult to answer. But yes, on a few occasions when we spoke in the summer, I did feel worried for her mental health. I wondered whether it was the start of a regression.'

'Were you aware of any episodes when she broke her sobriety?'

'No.'

'That's what I don't understand. She was so motivated. She spoke about the future. She'd made plans for a trip to Thailand with me in January. And then...'

'It happens quite often, unfortunately. If you want my professional opinion, I believe that many suicides, especially the ones that come as surprises, are impulsive acts in very critical low moments in a person's life, and not the result of longer-term planning.'

'I just can't believe she intended to...' Idun trails off, and her eyes shimmer with tears. She doesn't appear to notice, just blinks hard, sending them scattering onto her jeans.

'I don't think there was much doubt about her intentions. Sometimes, I've seen that it helps the family to know that the person actually did intend to die. Elisabeth wasn't trying to get high, she would have known a dose like that would be fatal. It might be even worse to think of a suicide as an accidental death after a desperate cry for help. In Elisabeth's case, there was little doubt that she, in those moments, truly intended to end her life. It does help me a little bit to think that she is at peace now.'

Idun nods and lets her eyes travel around the room again.

'I've taken some of Elisabeth's artwork down because I thought you might like to have it. It felt like the right thing to do.'

Idun nods, then reaches across and squeezes my hand. 'I'm so grateful for you, Kristina. Won't you come and see me soon? I know I'm not much fun these days, but it would mean a lot to me. Elisabeth was so lucky to have you. And it makes me happy to see you here in this beautiful home, living a meaningful life, still young and beautiful. Your whole life lies ahead of you. You have to live it for both of you now. For all three of you.' I have to look away. I feel a lump in my throat at the mention of Elisabeth, and Trine. It feels surreal that out of the three young girls who once did everything together and embarked on what was supposed to be the adventure of a lifetime, I'm the only one still alive. *You have to live for all three of you.*

'I'll come soon, Idun. I promise. I'm so sorry, but I need to leave in a moment, I'm supposed to be somewhere shortly.'

'Of course. Just one more thing.'

'Sure.'

'Could you show me where it happened?' My heart picks up its pace and I feel suddenly queasy at the thought of standing in that room with Elisabeth's mother.

'Of course,' I say softly, and stand up.

The spare bedroom is immaculately tidy and the bed is freshly made up – our housekeeper must have done it; I can barely bear to be in this room. There is a desk by the window and a big wardrobe used to store winter duvets and cozy throws. Idun takes a visibly deep breath and steps into the room. I follow behind her. She walks over to the bed and strokes the pillow, as though it might still hold the indentation of her daughter's head.

'Oh,' she whispers. I remain by the door, my knuckles tight around the door handle. Her shoulders begin to shudder as she cries, and I feel deeply uncomfortable in a way I never do at work when a client displays intense emotion. 'May I?' she gestures to the bed. I nod.

Idun clambers onto the high bed and lies down atop

the comforter, eyes wide open and staring at the ceiling. From where I'm standing she now uncannily resembles her daughter, the way I found her lying in the exact same place, her eyes also wide open and staring at the ceiling. I swallow hard; it feels as though I'm going to black out.

'I'll give you a minute,' I say, stepping back out into the hallway. I go through to the bathroom and from the highest shelf behind the mirror, I retrieve a tranquilizer from an ibuprofen box. I tuck it underneath my tongue, making sure it's covered with saliva, then swallow it dry. I lean back against the wall, wishing Idun out of my house with all my might, but my eyes fall on the black-and-white photograph on the opposite wall, taken the summer I was nineteen. I'm standing between my two best friends, grinning widely, Trine on my left, and Elisabeth beaming on my right. I force myself to stare at the photo for several long moments until our faces grow fuzzy and blurred.

'What did she look like when you found her?' asks Idun. I hadn't noticed that she'd emerged from the bedroom and is standing directly beside me.

'She looked peaceful,' I whisper, my voice trembling. It's a lie. But sometimes we have to lie.

22

Elisabeth, June

She wakes soaked in sweat. She sits up in bed, letting her eyes get used to the darkness, her head groggy with heavy sleep medication, before picking up her phone. It's only 1 a.m. and she's been asleep for less than an hour. She scrolls through Instagram and likes Kristina's most recent post, a picture of her and Eirik posing poolside in Thailand, sipping from the same drink, a carved-out watermelon cocktail. She stares into the darkness of her room and imagines Kristina in this moment, sleeping close together with Eirik in a languidly hot bungalow, beads of sweat studding her smooth, bronzed skin, her husband's arms flung possessively around her waist.

Elisabeth sometimes wonders whether she'll ever again sleep next to anyone. The idea of letting someone in, all the way in, like Andreas, feels impossible and wrong. She knows she hasn't processed his death yet, and though it's been over five years, she doesn't feel ready to fully take in the fact that he is gone, that he simply doesn't exist, that it could be possible to live in a world where she keeps breathing when he'll never take another breath. It was easier when she was out there, on the streets; at least she'd have a few hours every day when she was high, when everything just felt mellow and possible, even living without Andreas, even living with the carnage and fear of her past, which play in her mind on a never-ending hellish loop. Now, she has to stare reality in the eyes, sober.

Still, she knows she is lucky in many ways, and she especially feels that when she is immersed in her art. She feels overcome with beauty and hope and gratitude when she brings the elegant curve of a bird's wing to the canvas, or when she succeeds in capturing the spill of moonlight on the surface of the fjord in winter, like shattered crystals, or when she pinches a leaf from a branch in the garden and holds it up to the light, exposing its curiously perfect skeleton, later folding it into one of her thick coffee table books to dry.

There is a man here at Villa Vinternatt whose company she enjoys. He's much older than her, at least in his mid-fifties, and they sometimes paint together, positioning their easels side by side in front of the bay windows overlooking the sound. He'll pause his own work for long moments and watch her paint, handing her a color tube she hadn't yet realized she wanted and it's always exactly right. His name is Joel and in another life he was a concert pianist and hobby painter, whose life broke apart after his pregnant wife and his three-year-old son died in a car accident. He succumbed to alcohol addiction and eventually full-blown cocaine and heroin abuse, until he got clean after over a decade and got another chance at life at Villa Vinternatt.

Elisabeth gets up from the bed and sits at her desk in the dark, shivering slightly at the feel of the metal chair against her bare thighs. The huge house is quiet, yet comfortingly humming with the telltale signs of life – a tap running somewhere, footsteps in a corridor downstairs, the unmistakable feeling of a building filled with people.

She opens the selfie mode on the phone camera and studies herself. She still looks young, in spite of everything. She smiles at herself and takes a picture but when she looks at it she realizes she looks so sad it takes her breath away. She tries again, consciously bringing a smile not only to her lips but to her eyes. Better, but still visibly fake. She thinks about padding down the corridor and around the corner to room 21, where Joel lives. She could knock softly and he'd appear, disheveled but awake and he'd smile, happy to see her. They could sneak downstairs, through the big dining hall, onto the covered terrace overlooking the gardens and the fjord, and they could sit together on a bench, sharing a rollie Joel has smuggled into Villa Vinternatt, looking out on the trembling lights from buoys and reef markers on the water.

They could tell each other the stuff that is easier to tell a friend than a therapist or family member or doctor. She smiles at the thought; impossible, but still soothing. The residents aren't allowed to socialize at night. All the doors are locked. No tobacco is allowed on the premises and she doesn't even know if Joel would smoke, but it seems a fair assumption of someone who would shoot up heroin. There are cameras around the house, some no doubt angled straight onto the terrace. She doesn't have the vocabulary to speak to a kind-of friend about the stuff she might have needed to speak of. None of it is ever going to happen.

Elisabeth goes over to the easel by the window. She picks up the paintbrush and holds it suspended over an unfinished white patch of her painting in progress. It's one of her trademark paintings: reds and maroons and watery pinks swirled around and layered onto the canvas in splotches and streaks. This one is called Blood Storms. Some people, probably the ones who go through life mostly with quiet, kind thoughts in their minds, assume Elisabeth's motives are abstract floral references; an experiential interpretation of the virginal, soft inner petals of roses, or swathes of poppies bleeding into each other on a hillside. Others react viscerally to her explicit references to violence and blood and chaos; her favorite was the critic who called her work 'hypnotically grotesque'. To Elisabeth they aren't mutually exclusive interpretations; pain and bloodshed and that which haunts her can surely simultaneously take on a form of beauty?

But tonight she is tired of the evocative but draining imagery. She wants to bring a touch of lightness to the painting, something fun. She smiles at the thought of *fun*, what a luxury fun is. She retrieves a pressed leaf from inside a picture book about Judy Chicago and places it directly onto the canvas. She draws its outline lightly with a charcoal pencil, nudging its outer extremities into the carefully built layers of reds already there, smeared from one corner of the canvas toward the center. She smiles to herself and colors in the outline of the maple leaf in a bright yellow, just because the color makes her smile. The effect is strange, as if a child has walked into the room and taken liberties with her mother's painting in an unsupervised moment, bringing an unstudied, fresh energy to the piece, and maybe on some level that is exactly what has happened. She might kick herself tomorrow for having ruined the painting, one of those she's preparing for Villa Vinternatt's upcoming vernissage, but tonight it feels possible to laugh by herself in the moonlight, filling in the painting's blank spots with happy, bright shades of yellow.

23

Kristina

It takes me over an hour to calm down sufficiently to fully follow the conversation. I order garlic king prawns and chili mayonnaise chicken wings, busying myself with the food and the wine while my friends chatter, the volume steadily increasing with each unit of alcohol. After three glasses of cava, I feel more like myself again. Jenny regales us with one hilarious story after another of her adventures on Tinder – she's the only singleton in our group of friends, and it's pretty obvious that she's the one having the most fun. Carla moans about the relentless pressures of motherhood, and feels that being a stay-at-home mom to her fourteen-month-old twins is a lot harder than her previous high-flying job in management consulting. *I just want to sit on the toilet for five fucking minutes by myself*, she says, taking another greedy glug from her cava. Our eyes meet and I sense a quick apology in the way she looks at me – my friends all feel awkward discussing their children around me. They stopped asking about IVF and how it's all going a long time ago, and I'm glad they did.

'So how's that handsome man of yours?' asks Simone, our impossibly glamorous onetime French-exchange student who ended up staying in Oslo and married Arne, a friend of Eirik's.

'Away, as usual,' I say. 'After the elections, things will presumably calm down. We'll need to get a date in the diary and have you all over for dinner sometime soon. It's been ages.'

Everyone concurs, it has been ages. Over the past year, I've hardly seen my friends at all; Eirik's increasingly demanding career, as well as my own, combined with Elisabeth's tragic death and my own therapy work have all added up to a very busy day-to-day life. It feels unexpectedly good to sit here with my friends, drinking wine as the afternoon darkens into evening, listening to their loud, tipsy laughter, just letting myself grow fully relaxed and mellow, emptying my mind of all the stress and tension.

On my way home, I find myself giggling to myself – it's as though the seven-hour brunch replenished my energy reserves, though I'm sure I'll be sorry tomorrow. I try to call Eirik, I want to hear his deep, soothing voice and tell him I love him, but it goes straight to voicemail. He's probably at some boring dinner, listening to boring speeches by boring people. I giggle again and leave him a voice message on WhatsApp saying I wish he could be waiting for me at home, in bed.

At home, I walk from room to room, switching on all the little lamps, humming to myself under my breath. I used to like to sing, and I was pretty good at it – might it be a good idea to return to it, take some lessons, develop my voice? It would be something to do with the little spare time I have. I make a mental note to Google some options on Monday. I pour another glass of wine and sit down on the sofa. In this moment, nothing seems so bad. All the things that bothered me and made me fearful feel dulled by the warm, glowy feeling I have inside.

I wake with a start, my heart hammering, the remnants of a bad dream disappearing from my mind. I glance at the time, 5.50 a.m. All the lights are on and I'm still wearing my leather pants and silk blouse from the brunch. My mouth tastes terrible and I feel intensely dehydrated. I get up and stumble woozily toward the kitchen. For a moment, I wonder whether I might actually throw up, but feel better after a large glass of San Pellegrino. I realize that two chunky candles have been left burning on the windowsill, though I can't remember lighting them. They're both almost burned out, and one of them has started spitting wax and sending tall flames leaping out of the holder. If I hadn't noticed when I did, it might have set the curtains on fire.

I blow them out and go back to the sofa to lie down. I'm going to give myself ten minutes of scrolling through Instagram before I go back to bed; I want to make sure the nausea disappears completely while staying close to the bathroom. When I unlock my phone, a series of notifications pop up on the screen. A text message from Elisabeth's mother, sent last night, thanking me. *I hope you know that to Elisabeth, you were an angel*, she wrote. Another from my own mother, complaining about my father's inability to plan for their weekend away. And there is an email from Leah Iverson, sent at 10.31 p.m. with the word 'Supernova' in the subject line.

24

Leah, two weeks before

She has the idea one of the many nights when she's alone. The two of them, at Bekkebu. It would be the only way to paint a full picture. All that space, all the time they would have. She would understand. Or eventually, she would come to understand. Leah smiles to herself in the dark. She knows better than anyone that pain, while difficult, is the catalyst for growth. She's just the facilitator.

The doorbell rings. She feels afraid, then angry. She'd told him not to come this week. She wants to be alone, to think and to figure everything out. It rings again. She won't give him a key even though he keeps insisting on one. She glances around the apartment to make sure there's nothing lying around that will trigger suspicion or accusations or fury. She presses the buzzer and stands by the open door, listening to his steps getting closer, centering herself with deep, calm breathing. She places a hand on her lower stomach as if to check the bump, still only noticeable to herself, is still there. It is – a tiny and delicious secret she'd defend with her own life.

For a long while afterward, they lie awake. She feels confused and tense. The familiarity of him used to feel so good, it was worth all the pain, at least she thought so, but now it feels stifling.

I think we should make a baby, he whispers. She's speechless and turns her face away from him so he won't see the tears that appear in her eyes. How is she going to get out of this? He is never going to let her go. Unless…

Her thoughts return to Bekkebu. To the soft glow from the fireplace and the crackle of the flames. To the imagined scene of sitting across from Kristina Moss, telling her everything. She glances over at the man beside her and feels a sharp bolt of dread in her stomach. She realizes that everything that's happened and everything she has done could place her in danger. She needs a plan B. She closes her eyes and brings forth the images that never fail to fill her with awe – two stars colliding and bursting into mesmerizing luminous explosions, so bright they light up entire galaxies, if only for a moment in time.

25

Kristina, November 1st

I sit up fast, stabbing at the screen, waiting for the email to load. It was sent at 10.31 last night, and only a few sentences are written in the body of the email.

Why haven't you come? I've been waiting and waiting for you. All I wanted was to tell you the truth. Something we have in common, you and I, is living a lie. And when you live in the shadow of one lie, you build more and more lies around that lie until nothing is true or real. If you'd come, we could have talked. I just wanted to tell you the truth. And I wanted to talk to you about Carúpano. But now – now it really is too late. Everything is lost. I wrote about you, and I wanted you to have it. I called it *Supernova* because that's the word that comes to mind when it comes to you and me, it's attached.

I look for the attachment, but there is nothing. I reload my email several times to see if it could have been sent after or filtered out of my inbox, but nothing. *Supernova.* I've heard the word before but can't discern its meaning off the top of my mind. I feel suddenly, entirely sober. I sit in the hushed silence of the apartment for a long time, hesitating over the email. The fact that she refers to an attachment and then doesn't attach it seems strange. What if Anton went back there and surprised her, furious after being questioned by the police and killed her? Or what if she's about to end her own life? *Now it really is too late. Everything is lost.* To me, these sound like the words of someone in an agitated state of mind, someone who has planned something.

That she mentioned Carúpano brings me an instant chill, a nervous tremble to my stomach, like the flicker of a tiny bird's wings. Could it be that she has been snooping around in my personal life, and thinks she's uncovered something she wishes to discuss with me. Leah clearly has no concept of how potentially damaging this could be. Or... could it be that she's written about me the way she wrote about Anton, isn't that what she's implying? I feel a wild surge of fury. How dare she?

I open Chrome on my browser and type 'Supernova'. After ten minutes of scrolling through websites from NASA to Wikipedia, I have learned that a supernova is the phenomenon of a star exploding spectacularly. The images of dying stars are beautiful and intriguing, their brightness sometimes reaching a billion times that of the sun. *A supernova is the biggest explosion humans have ever seen,* says NASA. *The original star is completely destroyed,* says Wikipedia. In obliteration, supernovae can outshine an entire galaxy, according to space.com. *A beautiful death,* I think to myself, picturing luminous, technicolor destruction drenching the dark corners of space with its light. I study the images, trying to still my racing heart and figure out why Leah referred to this phenomenon. Is this what she was getting at, comparing herself to a star whose death is both powerful and awe-inducing?

I called it *Supernova* because that's the word that comes to mind when it comes to you and me...

I consciously calm myself down slightly by reminding myself that the event she is referring to – Carúpano – is hardly a secret, there is nothing she could find out about me or my past that isn't a click away on the internet. And Elisabeth is dead.

But Leah is a novelist and a famous one at that – she is someone who is in a position to draw public attention to things that could ruin my life. I need to know what Leah is playing at; I can't sit around my house waiting for the phone to ring or something else to happen. *Have it your way, Leah*, I think to myself. I'm going to find her. And I'm going to shut her up.

26

Kristina

It's still early morning. If I leave now, I could feasibly be back home by late this evening. I grab a black leather weekend holdall from the closet and place a spare pair of contact lenses into it, as well as some underwear and a thick sweater. I'll be back tonight, but you never know what might happen and I like to come prepared. I get a torch from the kitchen drawer and throw in some chocolate chip cookies and a large bottle of San Pellegrino too. I grab the car keys from the key holder on the wall by the front door, then step outside into the foyer. I can't immediately recall when I last drove my car – living so centrally in Oslo, I never have to. All our groceries are delivered to the door, and both Eirik and I walk to work, and yet we keep both a BMW SUV and a Tesla.

As I lock the door, I have a sudden and violent conviction that I am doing it for the last time, that I will never again see these gray turn-of-the-century floor tiles, never again stand in this exact spot, resting my hand on the smooth wooden door handle, never again walk down these black stone steps, or open this door onto Incognito Gate, letting the blustery air rush into my face. I stop for a moment and look back up the sweeping communal staircase toward our apartment. What I am doing is clearly in breach of professional conduct and perhaps a little crazy, but I have the sensation that I don't quite know what I'm dealing with here. Could it also be dangerous?

27

Kristina

It's almost three hours to drive from central Oslo to Seljord, the nearest settlement to Leah's cabin, according to the coordinates on her note. Thankfully I've set off early, so I should get there before it gets dark. Hopefully, whatever I find, I can get this strange situation out of my head, arriving back home again before evening. It feels good, actually, to be on the road, driving fast and listening to the radio, doing something other than sitting across from a client or moving around in the hushed, oppressive silence of our apartment. Besides, if nothing else, someone needs to go and check on Leah since the police won't.

In the aftermath of difficult times in my life I have always been able to find some peace on the road, just letting all the hard stuff drop away from me, leaving it behind on the road dwindling away behind me. In my twenties I sometimes felt that going for a long drive alone was the only way to process, but in recent years I haven't turned to it in the same way. I guess I've been consumed by work and by my marriage. And it has finally been quieter inside my head. Until now.

I listen to the weather report: heavy snow this afternoon. Hopefully I'll have time to head back to the city before it sets in. I switch to a channel playing old hits and this makes me feel young again, like I might yet discover new things about myself or make decisions that would set my life onto a different path. This is of course true for everybody, but not many people live like that once the central pillars in life are in place; life partner, career, home. And yet. I could, technically speaking, retrain to do something else, just like I did once before, and live somewhere else, with another man. None of the things that feel fixed and set in stone truly are. This is something I try to convey to my clients in the therapy room, too – that, for better or worse, change is the one constant, and even if life feels unmanageable and impossibly dark in the present moment, it will change, if you can find a way to hang in there.

I pull into a picnic area by the roadside a few miles past Kongsberg. There is nobody here and the sky is an oppressive slate gray. Patches of dirty snow line the roadside. I feel profoundly troubled by Leah's words. I get out of the car to stretch my legs for a moment. Dark pines tower over the little parking lot, veils of mist twisting between their crowns, rising toward the low-hanging clouds. A bitter wind sweeps across the road, tearing at me. I can feel more snow in the air, and it occurs to me that I still have summer tires on the car.

What am I doing here, by the roadside in the depths of the woods, on my way to Leah's mountain cabin? Am I regressing into irrational behavior after having come so far?

Nobody knows that I am here, not even Eirik. I think it's because of Eirik that I've come here. Doing something out of character like driving halfway across Norway to check on Leah feels like a little rebellion against my husband's relentless recent travel schedule. Though I am fully aware of the demands of Eirik's political career, I sometimes can't help but feel this isn't what I signed up for. I worry about the toll on our marriage as his public profile grows, and that an ever-increasing distance will open up between us. There are times when I wake in the night and listen to Eirik's soft, even breathing in the dark, and it feels like being in bed with a stranger. But there are also the times that he pulls me close and looks me in the eyes and strokes me all over, and I feel close to him again.

I get back in the car, rubbing my icy hands together, but wait a moment to start the engine. I feel a deep trepidation in my gut that isn't entirely unpleasant. As disturbing and worrying as the developments of the past ten days have been, Leah's dramatic exit from the therapy room and apparent disappearance have dominated my thoughts, giving me something other than Elisabeth's suicide to think about. Like with Leah, I was the last person to see Elisabeth alive. Like Leah, Elisabeth trusted me with her innermost thoughts. Or so I believed.

I don't want to think about Elisabeth, not now; I want to just block her life and death from my thoughts and my heart, but I know better than anybody that it doesn't work like that. Elisabeth will always be on my mind. Elisabeth, whose talent for self-destruction overshadowed everything else — how wonderful she was, how intelligent, how good at her beautiful art she was, how very loved. But like most lifelong addicts, no matter how functional at times, she ultimately loved the needle more than anything else, including herself. And it killed her.

Tears again. Jesus, I'm not going to go there now. I have spoken about Elisabeth constantly in my own therapy sessions; about how it felt like she was a part of me – a shadow with a penchant for darkness. I am wracked with guilt over how her life ended. It came after a long period when she had showed so much promise and improvement. I wish, so deeply, that things could have been different. That she could have made better choices. I take a few deep breaths and center myself in the moment. This isn't about Elisabeth, or me; it's about Leah.

It's been nine days since I last saw her. She was afraid. And hurt. She lied to me about Anton. What else did she lie about? She didn't tell me she was pregnant, a kind of lie in itself. But why? And why did she say she wanted to speak to me about Carúpano? Every time I think about the way she casually threw that into her email I feel consumed by rage. And what will I find once I arrive at her cabin?

I start driving again, slower now – I feel a little tender, and the dual carriageway has narrowed into a small, windy district road as I head into the mountainous forests of Buskerud county. The forests become even denser after I pass into Telemark county, the sky briefly clearing and weakening into a gorgeous pink-streaked indigo as the sun lowers itself down towards the rounded, snow-capped mountains in the distance. Close to Seljord I stop in another lay-by and peer at the map on my phone. The forests crowd in on the car, like the road is a wound that the forest is trying to heal.

Leah's cabin seems to sit entirely on its own, high up against the crest of a hill overlooking Heivannet Lake. She wouldn't be within earshot nor easy walking distance of any other cabins, and I wonder whether she ever even meets anyone else up there.

I take several wrong turns before I manage to find the right forest track – they all look the same and they all inevitably end in a locked barrier. On my fourth attempt to find the right track, which is supposed to run alongside the lake, then rise to climb into the hills on its north shore, I'm successful. One of the two keys Leah gave me slots into the rusty padlock of the road barrier and the gate swings open. I drive through, then stop, leaving the engine idle while I return to lock the barrier behind me. Only the residents of a given area have the keys to the barriers on these remote forest roads, avoiding through-traffic and burglaries in scarcely populated areas. I feel a sudden irrational panic rise in me as I return to the car; for a moment I am dragged back in time to another forest, another car, another me. I slam the door hard and breathe calmly, focusing on the narrow road unfolding ahead, caught in the headlights. I urge the gas, my heart hammering wildly. *Stop, Kristina*, I tell myself. *The only thing to fear here is your own mind if you can't control it.*

The sky is changing again in the East – from frosty white to a dark charcoal. Thin wisps of fog drift between the trees, giving them an eerie, milky glow. Leah would have driven down this exact same track not long ago. Did she intensely commit all of this to memory like I am: the dripping spruces, the brown-black pines, the meek, steely skies, the black lake at the bottom of the valley, occasionally glimpsed through the dense crowd of trees?

The phone vibrates and a voice says: 'Your destination is on the left.'

There is nothing to the left except a wall of trees, but then I spot a wooden sign nailed to a trunk that reads 'Bekkebu' and next to it an even smaller track. I turn onto it and quickly realize I'm going to have to leave the car and continue on foot. Light snow begins to fall. There is a cleared, car-sized grassy area to the side of the track and a white Range Rover Evoque is parked there, tucked in neatly from the track, surrounded by mounds of hardened snow. I assume it is Leah's car, and as there are no visible tire tracks in the patches of snow surrounding it, it would seem it has sat here for days. It looks as though it has been placed here from above by the hand of a giant, like a Lego car.

I turn off the engine and the lights and sit for a long moment in the deep silence of the woods. I feel a nervous flutter in my stomach, but refuse to indulge this kind of irrational fear. Walking alone at night in central Oslo is much more dangerous than being out here in these remote, untouched forests, though it doesn't feel like that.

My phone vibrates in my hand.

Hey babe, all set up and ready to smash it, reads a WhatsApp from Eirik, accompanied by a selfie of my husband against the picturesque backdrop of Bergen harbor, a line of Høyre Conservative Party campaign flags snapping in the wind behind him. I smile at the goofy expression on his handsome face. It occurs to me that I haven't actually let Eirik know that I've come here on my own. I open the camera and take a selfie, angling the phone to catch the snow falling against a backdrop of thick forest outside.

Impulsive road trip, I write. *I've gone to Telemark to find Leah Iverson, long story. Turns out she wrote about me (!) so I've decided I need to speak with her and get her some intervention. Couldn't make it up. Good luck & call me later.*

I only have one bar of phone reception and have to press 'resend' three times before the message finally goes through. *You're not in Frogner anymore, that's for sure*, I think to myself and ready myself to step outside into the cold.

I grab a flashlight from the emergency pack Eirik insists I keep in the glove compartment and fasten the strap of my handbag across my chest. I shine the flashlight into Leah's car, but there's nothing unusual there – just a pair of iPhone headphones and a chewing gum wrapper on the passenger seat. I take a couple of steps back and am about to start walking when I let my eyes rest on the tires of the car. I can't help but release a shocked sound when I see that both tires on this side of the car are flat, clearly slashed. My pulse rising, I walk around the other side. These too, are flat.

I stare up the narrow, steep slope of the track. Again, I think about my sensation of danger as I left the apartment in Oslo. What am I going to find at the end of this track? I decide to leave the holdall in the car – I'm just going to do a quick sweep of the cabin. Hopefully Leah is there, safe and willing to have a real conversation about what's going on. We can talk in the car on the way back, no reason to remain in a remote cabin. No wonder she hasn't returned home if her car has been deliberately damaged and she has no phone reception. I get a sudden, terrifying picture in my head of Anton slashing her tires, angry with her for refusing to return to the city with him because she was still waiting for me. I have no intention of staying for longer than to convince Leah to come back to Oslo with me, but I simply have to get to the bottom of this. I glance at the crude map Leah drew for me, and walk for a good ten minutes, and my legs start to ache as the track's incline gets ever steeper. The snow is still falling in tiny flakes from a dull white sky, and as I turn and look back down the way I came, I see much darker, lower clouds encroaching, closer now. They're the kind that carry heavy, wet snowflakes capable of covering the landscape in a swift whiteout.

I reach the top of the hill and pause for a minute to catch my breath. The track flattens out and I emerge from a dense clutch of trees; I'm standing on the shoulder of the mountain. Far below me a jet-black lake spreads out in full view, its water held beneath a fragile lid of sparkling ice. I look around for signs of Leah's cabin, but can't see anything man-made at all. I notice a smudge of blue paint on a birch tree a few meters away, and realize it's a trail marker. I consult the map again, it seems I need to find a much smaller path winding further into the woods from the clearing. When I start walking again, I see a little hand-carved wooden sign strung from a tree that reads 'Bekkebu', with a pointed arrow in the direction I'm heading. I wonder if she made it herself; it seems like the kind of thing Leah might do.

How does she even bring groceries up here? I can't imagine wanting to stay in a cabin so remote you have to walk for twenty minutes from the parking spot up a steep, slippery track through the woods, but each to their own, I guess, and it is fairly common among Scandinavians to seek out this kind of very basic back-to-nature experience.

I stop for a minute and have to control another onslaught of sudden fierce fear of being here in the woods, so utterly alone, so far from my real life, but there is something rather exhilarating about it, too. I'm able to control my thoughts and dispel the anxiety. I feel proud of myself for being able to be somewhere like this, in the thick forest, alone, and not succumb to an irrational, blind panic.

I look at my phone, but as I suspected, I have lost reception. I'm about to keep walking when I glimpse a slash of wan white sky beyond the trees just ahead of where I'm standing. It must be another clearing, and I push my way through the trees and spot what looks like the low grass-topped roof of a cabin, noticeably straighter than the craggy clearing it edges on, nestled up against the woods, overlooking the lake and the valley. The snow, already falling thicker and faster, settles onto the roof and I imagine it's only hours until the cabin will merge with the surrounding terrain in a cloak of pristine white.

I walk toward it, slowing down as I approach because my heart is beating so hard. A light is on inside. I imagine Leah in there, sitting at an old wooden desk by the fireplace, typing quickly, her beautiful face glowing golden in the light from the snapping, lively flames. I approach the door and glance around for footsteps around the cabin, but the snow has already started to settle on the ground around the cabin, erasing whatever might have been there.

I knock on the door and listen, but can't make out anything other than the soft rustle of branches. I knock again. I could just turn back around and hurry to my car and call for help once I have reception. I have the sudden conviction that if I use the key Leah gave me I'll find her dead inside. Perhaps that's what she wanted, and why she tried to get me to come here in the first place. I don't want to find her dead. It's been less than three months since I walked into our spare bedroom and found Elisabeth on the bed, staring straight at me, unseeing, her sweet face already eerily different.

I knock for the third time, harder, then instinctively try the door handle. The door is unlocked and swings open inward.

28

Leah, one week before

She closes the door to the cabin behind her and draws its familiar scent deep into her lungs. No matter how the future plays out, at least she has this sweet, beloved place. She moves without fear through the silent, dark space and twists the knobs on the oil lamps lined up along the windowsill. She stares out at the impossible beauty of the valley, its trees shimmering in autumnal shades of gold, bronze and ochre in the last of the afternoon light. Already, the long, exhausting Friday-night drive from the capital is forgotten. She steps back from the window and her face is reflected back at her. Her expression is haunted and her left eye is still swollen shut. She runs a fingertip alongside the broken and bruised patch on her face, prodding gently for signs of broken bones.

In the kitchen she unpacks her one small bag of groceries. Minced meat, shredded cheese, cucumber, taco spices, corn tortillas – Leah has come to love the Norwegian obsession with Friday-night tacos. There is also a bottle of wine, some milk and a pizza for tomorrow. She pours herself a small glass of wine, they say just one doesn't hurt the baby, and sits on the sofa, just listening to the deep silence. She touches her hand to her belly and is filled with the most unbearable dread. She would give anything for this to be different. How is she supposed to forgive him for what happened in Oslo? But she knows she will, if only he'll come back.

In the meantime, there is nothing to do but wait; she has to believe that Kristina will come. *Please come*, she whispers into the air. *Please.*

She picks her favorite book off the shelf and sits down on the sofa. She opens *The Bell Jar*, flicking through it to where she last marked it by folding down the page.

> *What I want back is what I was*
> *Before the bed, before the knife,*
> *Before the brooch-pin and the salve*
> *Fixed me in this parenthesis;*
> *Horses fluent in the wind,*
> *A place, a time gone out of mind.*

It's this that finally brings tears to her eyes. Not the words, or the strike, or the devastating kindness on Kristina's face, nor the long, lonely drive on winding roads into the hills, then the mountains. It's Sylvia Plath who unleashes the storm of emotion Leah has held back, suppressed, and it's Sylvia who makes her lean into the pain, pushing herself deeper and deeper into it until she emerges into the still, black eye of the storm. From there she invites it all and observes its devastating rampage through her mind from the safe vantage point at its very core.

She gets up, suddenly filled with conviction about what to write. For so long, she's tried to force the words, though anyone who's ever tried to write knows words won't be forced.

As she starts to type, she fights the urge to both laugh and cry, consciously maintaining her focus on the screen. *I can't believe I didn't realize it before*, she begins, *that what I really wanted all along was to write to you. So that's what I'm going to do. A memoir, perhaps. No. A confession.*

And finally, the words flow, so fast that Leah can barely keep up, and by the time she takes a break, it's already past midnight and she is several thousand words in. It felt good, even though they were hard words to write. She still can't be sure whether this confession, or whatever it will be, is a work of love or a work of hatred; the two always seemed intrinsically linked, like we can only hate that which we also love and crave. She gets up and stands a while in front of the bathroom mirror, taking in her bruises; purple and blue and yellow, spreading across her face like supernovae shockwaves across the black velvet universe.

29

Kristina

'Leah?' I say, first gently and then louder. There is no answer. I'm in a dark entranceway and I fumble around for a light switch, but realize there isn't one. The cabin doesn't appear to have electricity – there are no visible wires or switches anywhere. I grab my torch, shining it around, trying to get my bearings. There are three doors leading from this tiny space. I try the first one. It's a large, empty bathroom, its timber walls painted a beautiful deep shade of aqua blue. A round gilded mirror hangs above a stone sink, and under the window stands an antique brass bathtub, big enough for two. I shine the beam from the torch into it as though Leah might be lying at the bottom.

I try the second door but it's a deep airing cupboard used to store linen and towels, as well as a thick down winter duvet. The third door leads into the cabin's main room and I quickly scan the space, but it's empty. Still, I call her name while shining the beam into all the nooks and crannies. I stand in the middle of the room for a long moment, deciding what to do. She's not here, that much is obvious. Maybe she's gone outside for some reason, a walk around the lake perhaps, though with heavy snow forecast I'd imagine she'd want to stay close to the cabin. Perhaps I'll wait for her for an hour or so; I can still make it back to the car before it's fully dark. There is also the possibility that she has been picked up by someone, and could be anywhere by now. Or, Anton really has hurt her and has had several days to cover up his crime.

I swallow hard and glance around the room for any sign of what could have happened to Leah. The cabin is made up of one large, open-plan room, with a built-in sleeping alcove in the far corner by the hearth. There is a cozy timbered kitchen nook held up by low, original beams painted a dusky gray. I take in Leah's space, the space she loves. *It's as if the cabin is a physical incarnation of my soul*, she once said, and with this in mind, it seems inevitable that this is Leah's space. Unfussy and sweet, unconventionally beautiful and a little cluttered, like its owner. There are books everywhere, crammed onto shelves, piled on the floor, stacked on windowsills and a couple splayed face-down on the coffee table.

There's a strange little stuffed animal sitting in a chair – it looks like a child's toy. I pick it up and quickly place it back in its seat – it feels wrong to snoop around and touch Leah's possessions. I walk into the kitchen and stand by the sink. The workbench is beneath a window, looking out at the empty valley, the lake and the white-capped mountains beyond. A chipped mug stands to the side of the sink and I pick it up. It bears a faded crest from Stanford University and I recall that Leah went there for a semester on an exchange program. It occurs to me that even as her therapist, there is so much I don't know about Leah and her life. In this moment she could be anywhere and with anyone, and there is a real chance I'll never see her again or learn what brought about her abrupt change in behavior.

Finding myself standing here, in her space, in the place she loves, looking at a quirky hand-made key holder and a framed poster for her first novel hung side by side on the wall, her walking boots carefully placed under a wooden bench, and a lingering scent of what I now realize is Leah's perfume, intensely familiar to me, I feel her absence acutely and just want to get to the bottom of this.

It's easy to understand why she loves coming here. *The cabin is my oasis*, she often says, and this makes perfect sense. And yet, it's quite a radical thing to do, for a lone woman to come somewhere like this on a regular basis. What, exactly, does she do here? I feel a strange jealousy of Leah's bravery, of her obvious connection to nature and commitment to this simple life – it's very far removed from the comfortable life I lead in central Oslo.

The cabin is miles away from the nearest dwelling, set in woods so thick I doubt one would be able to pick out the house from above. It has no modern amenities. What it does have is beautiful wood carvings, lovely rounded blonde timber walls that I imagine would take on a golden glow from the hearth when lit, and books everywhere, leaving the sweet, subtle scent of well-thumbed pages and firewood on the air.

I pick a random book off a heavily laden shelf – Dostoyevsky – and run my finger lightly across the cover.

I pick up another, Arundhati Roy's first, one of my own favorites, and feel pleased to see that it is well-thumbed and dog-eared. I let my eyes roam and everywhere they go, they find something beautiful and comforting. Books. Small, carefully curated paintings in the same warm hues as the timber walls themselves. A little black Chinese antique lacquered cupboard with fine crystal glasses lined up on its shelves. I lift one and hold it up to the weak light from the oil lamp I've lit, its intricate carvings glinting in rainbows. Leah clearly loves beautiful things.

And then it's like something in the air shifts, like she's here with me, having sidled up beside me, becoming clearer and clearer as I begin to sense her and now I can practically see her. She's sitting on the stone ledge next to the hearth, feet drawn up, beneath a collection of ancient copper pots and pans strung from a metal railing.

She's singing out loud, softly, rubbing her arms trying to get more warmth into her body. She's almost childlike in the way she's sitting, hugging herself, staring into the leaping flames, willing their heat to spread faster around the little room. Her beautiful face is red and glowing, like she's run here through heavy snow.

Sometimes in our sessions, she came across as almost childlike, too, displaying unusual mannerisms for an adult: picking at her jacket sleeve until it frayed, a constantly jerking foot, or an unusual choice of words. She dressed young, too, especially at the beginning, and I wouldn't have been surprised if she still wears items from her midteens, though she's over thirty. This is something I see quite often, and can be seen as a desire to hold onto youth and freedom, a subtle rejection of the demands of adult life. I see it particularly often in the very wounded, those clients who come to therapy with life-altering trauma. It's natural to seek out those feelings of security and protection we felt in childhood when we have had the experience of living entirely unprotected in the world and suffering deep wounds as a result.

A strange sound snaps me out of my reverie, and I hold myself entirely still, suddenly irrationally fearful. I hear it again, a long and exaggerated murmur, like an old animal exhaling slowly, sending air through obstructed passages. There is a series of splutters, like a throaty cough, then silence. Could an injured animal have gotten into the cabin, now dying in a dark corner? I feel the hair on my arms stand up and begin to shiver. I move slowly toward the kitchen nook, peering into corners, but see nothing unusual. I light another oil lamp and turn the torch back on to boost the light.

In the kitchen nook the noise starts up again and it turns out to be coming from a small refrigerator on the countertop, seemingly running off a generator placed on an open shelf near the floor.

I open the refrigerator and there is a bottle of white wine and a pint of milk, both open. There is a plate of cooked margherita pizza, but it has patches of mold on it. There are a couple of browning, shrunken limes and a wilting bunch of coriander. At the back, I find an unopened packet of minced meat, which expired two days ago. Another sound insists itself into the cocoon space of Leah's cabin. It is the wind chasing up the mountainsides from the lake in the valley, and it carries with it a smattering of snow, tiny perfect snowflakes kissing the diamond-gridded windows.

I close the refrigerator and stand for a while looking out into the main room; its hushed, peaceful atmosphere is intoxicating and instantly soothing, like standing inside a hug. And yet, there is something not right about this place and Leah's absence. Then I notice something I missed on my first sweep of the room. Next to the sofa is a small, low table on top of which sits a MacBook Air, exactly the size of the tabletop. I stare at it and have the disturbing feeling I often get when I try to reach back in time through my own life and come up against that blank wall of nothingness that shrouds significant chunks of my experiences. I know that something dark is there beneath the ominous white haze, like the charred bones of a burned-out house beneath deep snow, but I can't quite grasp it. Now, I feel as though I am looking straight at the missing piece of the puzzle, but still can't make out what the bigger picture is.

I move toward the laptop but feel a headache coming on, so I sit down on the sofa and press my fingers against my eyes, and I see Leah so clearly in my mind, as if she was stamped on my retinas like the blurred shadows that roam across my field of vision. That last session, her last day. Pleading with me, eyes wild. *Come to my cabin. Please, please, please.* I open the computer and it instantly lights up to the home screen, its backdrop a beautiful photograph of the valley below Bekkebu in summer, the hillsides draped in heather and the lake reflecting a bruised evening sky. The desktop is empty besides a document titled with a single word: 'Supernova'. I shiver lightly at the memory of her disturbing words.

This is about the truth.

I wrote about you.

I called it Supernova *because that's the word that comes to mind when it comes to you and me.*

And I want to talk to you about Carúpano.

30

Supernova

I can't believe I didn't realize it before, that what I really wanted all along was to write to you. So that's what I'm going to do. A memoir, perhaps. No. A confession.

Kristina, I'm waiting for you. I pray that you'll come. I'm alone and I'm afraid for the future and I want to use this time to put everything I want to say to you into some kind of coherent account. I want to tell you everything myself, I have it all planned out in my head – you'll come here and you'll sit across from me and we'll light the fire and I will start from the beginning and I won't stop talking until there is absolutely nothing unsaid between us. If you can't or won't come or if something outside of my control happens to me, you'll find what you need here. Either way, I need you to know the truth.

Let's imagine that the story of our relationship was a novel. Writing a novel is like constructing a body from severed chunks of flesh and then magically breathing it to life, sending themes coursing through its inner framework like blood through veins. Love, empathy, obsession, jealousy, fear, grief, memory, betrayal, redemption. Which would be the main themes in our story, Kristina? I think by the time I've said everything I want to say, we'll see that all of the above will jostle for space in a complex narrative in which past and present are as entwined as a body with its soul.

And which genre might such a novel fit into? My first instinct might have been that it was an unusual kind of love story, one that explores connection and vulnerability rather than romance and sex, but the boundaries between them became blurred a while ago and now they have come to seem increasingly indiscernible from one another. On second thought, just a few weeks ago, before I began to see the lines, the ones that link each occurrence in a person's life to the next and the next, I would have called it a nihilistic reverie of sorts; meaningless fragments of lives and experiences, souped together and brought to the boil. Now, I'd be inclined to call such a novel a psychological thriller. It would contain all of the components of the genre's best offerings – unreliable narrators, a missing woman, the dangers of love and desire, the past looming at the edges – more potent than ever, a dash of amnesia, murder. This is, of course, not a novel, though I'm finding it an interesting comparison. Like I said, it's a confession.

I'm calling it *Supernova* because it's the word I could never let go of. It's what I think of when I think of you. I can't let go of the images, either. Did you know that a supernova is a result of two stars colliding and they both end up dead? A big star and a little one, together in a celestial dance. The little white dwarf star steals material from the big one until it has too much, too much to carry and to hold, drawing both stars into a gigantic thermonuclear explosion so bright it can light up anything, anything at all. And afterward, a black hole, a rip in the lining of the heavens.

It's late at night and it feels as though I am the only person left in a cold and deserted world, but as you know, I have often felt like that in my life, and not only in the dead of a freezing October night. I have felt like that on hot afternoons in summer when the air is clammy and the stench of barbecue smoke drifts across the city, walking down streets and through parks aimlessly, surrounded by throngs of laughing people, unseen. I have felt like that in bed with lovers, feeling their touch travel across my skin, but actually being light-years away, shut away inside myself. I have felt like that in my family, as though nothing of me could have come from anything of them; at best I was like a ball of phlegm – expelled and forgotten about, certainly not loved or missed.

But I didn't feel like that with you. You changed everything and you don't need me to tell you what that kind of shift can mean to someone. It was seismic. And it was dangerous. It made me believe that I could be like you, and that I, too, could have everything. Those can be dangerous thoughts and in this moment, alone and waiting for you, I wish I could have learned to be content with what I *did* have: health, a home, people reading my words, you. But people always want more, don't they?

I am sitting here trying to imagine you reading these words, but can't imagine a world in which that would be possible, simply because I know what it would mean. It would mean that you never came. Or that I've been hurt. Or perhaps it would just mean that after writing everything

I want to say to you I'll come to the conclusion that I'd rather send it to you than speak these words out loud. Any way, I can't envision us ever sitting across from each other again, in that dear little room in Homansbyen that came to mean so much to me.

We need to go back to the beginning, though beginning in itself is a relative term – there are many story threads here and each one of them has a beginning – we'll get to each one of them in turn.

You were chosen for me, and I think of that with a measure of awe now. That a psychotherapist was assigned me and it just happened to be you; it seems almost impossible to grasp that the most important person in my life would be delivered to me by random allocation. *Fridays at two*, my GP said. *Dr Kristina Moss will see you. A very impressive psychotherapist. Fifty minutes.*

It was all paid for, all I needed to do was show up.

You know, you fully had me from the very first session. I became yours in a way I'd never been anybody's before, just by really being seen. Our sessions were my first meeting with being taken seriously and being fully listened to. You were the first person I ever met who offered me an unconditional relationship without judgment. My mother loves me, as we've discussed in depth, but her love was always conditional. She drilled into me that I was free to be whatever I wanted, but really, it was only true when I was little enough for her to still believe that I'd want to be like her. She celebrated my achievements, but only when she could take credit for them. She commiserated when I failed, too, but wouldn't want any credit for that.

You were just *there*, regardless of what I brought to

therapy. You made me feel like there was space for all of me. That it was okay to be sad and angry and empty, that none of that took away from my worth in your eyes. I hadn't anticipated the effect that would have on me, nor how deep the grief it triggered would be, to realize that I'd never had it before.

I know that to you, I'm nothing. Or at best, I'm a number on a list, just another name in your professional diary. To me, you're everything. Don't think that I simply idolize you; I know you better than you think, I see a whole person, and at first it was difficult for me to accept you were actually real, flaws and all. People inevitably change when light is cast upon them; they seldom turn out to be the beautiful, perfect holograms you saw when you first looked. They crumble or grow distorted because nothing in life is pure enough to withstand real scrutiny – people and places and objects equally. Take the supernova. What looks so beautiful, like the moment something precious is created, is actually the moment of violent destruction. Nothing is ever how it looks at first, it's just how it is, and it was the same with you. And me.

When I try to determine what exactly you know of me, I draw a blank. I can't be sure. Once, I thought you knew and intrinsically understood everything about me, that you had preemptive powers to discern my every need before I could even begin to identify them myself. I was wrong, of course. But you know about the way I think. You know that emotion comes at me thick and fast. You know that I've been burned. You know that I don't love myself and that it leads to others taking what shouldn't be given away. And yet, you only know what I've told you. This is where we differ, you and I. You have told me exactly nothing about yourself, and yet I know – dare I say – everything. Even things you yourself don't know.

Let me explain. Beginnings.

It all started very innocently, and entirely by chance. I'd been coming to see you for a few months by then, so it must have been around Easter time. I was settling into therapy and found that it had become a lifeline. The sessions made me ask myself questions I wouldn't otherwise have raised. My awareness increased. What was my response in a given situation, and why? Could it be different in the future? It was exhilarating to realize that I may have a choice in the matter. But most of all, the thing that brought real change was the bond built between you and me. I trusted you. You showed me what I could do in a million little ways. You were never late, never distracted, always focused on whatever I brought to the room and for the first time, it made me feel like I actually mattered, that my feelings should be listened to and valued. By pretending you cared (and it *is* pretending) you made *me* care.

Back to that Easter. It was a beautiful Friday and we had a good session. I remember it clearly – I asked you lots of questions about yourself, which you gently deflected. I wanted to know about you because as the sessions increasingly began to have an effect on me, I felt intensely attached to you. I still do. Those feelings have played along the whole spectrum of human emotion, from neediness to admiration to attraction to love to dislike and even hatred.

To obsession.

After our session that day, I felt strangely liquid inside, like you'd torched me with your careful questions, setting fire to the long-held beliefs about myself that no longer served me. *Leah, could it be that you deserve your own kindness? That sounds like a very distressing experience, Leah. Even if he said you deserved it and you believed him in that moment, does it mean it was actually true? Could it be that you deserve to be loved?*

I walked the few meters from your office to Kaffebrenneriet on the corner of Parkveien and Bogstadveien, ordered a cortado and sat in the corner by the large windows, my back to the counter. It was loud in there, the baristas banging the portafilters against the countertops to empty the espresso grits, a steady chatter of the afternoon coffee crowd from nearby offices, and the occasional blue tram rambling past outside, heading uptown. I saw a flash of orange pass by the window as I raised the cortado to my nostrils, drawing its perfect bitter and burned scent into me, then the door opened, bringing a cool draft. Then I heard your voice.

A double tall white Americano, you said. I turned my head slowly, to double-check that it really was you. You stood, unaware, scrolling on your phone, waiting. When your coffee was ready you flashed a quick smile at the barista and it made me irrationally angry for a moment, watching you smile at someone as inconsequential as a random café worker when I was used to having your undivided attention. Your smile also prompted another wave of that liquid heat in my stomach. This was back when I sometimes felt confused by overwhelming attraction to you.

You took your coffee to go, and before I knew it, I'd left my cortado half-drunk on the narrow window table and scrambled after you out onto the street, struggling to get my jacket on. It was only March and the air was crisp, but the sky was a deep indigo blue and the days were getting longer. The promise of spring had changed the atmosphere of the town and even the facial expressions of the people. You walked slowly up Bogstadveien, easy to spot in your orange parka, and I hung back at a little distance, yet close enough to observe you. You stopped to look in a few windows, sipping at your coffee, and several times you checked your phone. About halfway up Bogstadveien, you crossed over to the other side. I followed. You turned down Rosenborggata, a quiet residential street, and I wondered whether it was where you lived – I didn't know anything about you back then. I hovered at the corner of the main street, pretending to look at my phone, and watched you approach a white, turn-of-the-century apartment building.

You stood looking up at the building for a long while, as if psyching yourself up to meet whoever was inside. You raised your finger to the panel of doorbells on the side wall, and it hovered there a while. I couldn't tell from where I stood whether you'd actually pressed one, and if so, which one. You glanced down the street in my direction, but wouldn't have been able to pick me out; I stood partially hidden in a wide doorway opposite the Peak Performance shop. Your face had changed, and you looked troubled and nervous. Suddenly you seemed to change your mind and came walking back down the street toward me, drawing your parka tight, burying the lower part of your face in the faux-fur hood. You walked straight past me and into the throng of shoppers and people taking an early Friday, heading home from work downtown. I let you out of sight and remained in the doorway for a long while. Then I headed back down in the direction we'd come, until I arrived back at Kaffebrenneriet.

The line was longer now, but I didn't mind waiting. My head was spinning with what I'd done and seen. It had been exhilarating seeing you out of the therapy room, and I knew even that first day, that I'd do it again. I couldn't have known then what I would find and what processes the slow discovery of Kristina Moss would bring about. Back then, you were still perfect to me, the way I wanted you to be. I wish I'd stopped there and then so you could have remained a shiny, flawless hologram. If I had, I wouldn't be writing these words. But equally, it is the imperfect, real Kristina I came to discover that has brought true empathy and a deep desire to be there for you like you've been there for me.

A double tall white Americano, I said when it was my turn to order, flashing the same barista who'd taken your order a quick smile.

31

Kristina

I slam the MacBook shut so hard the sharp sound makes me jump. I take a few moments to recenter myself in my unfamiliar surroundings. *It's okay*, I tell myself, but my heart is pounding and my hands tremble. In the minutes it took me to read Leah's words, everything I believed about our relationship and our journey into therapy, have come undone. She's betrayed me in the most fundamental way. The relationship between therapist and client necessarily has to be confined to the therapy room, and the therapist's personal life and preferences need to remain unavailable to the client. This is difficult for a lot of people, as the bonds forged are so deep and the intimacies shared so life-changing. To think that Leah blatantly disregarded the explicitly stated boundaries of our relationship and followed me around is profoundly disturbing. Had I known, I would likely have had to end our working relationship.

I try to determine whether there were any signs of her becoming unusually preoccupied with me, or especially interested in my personal life. She asked a few questions here and there; most people do. Right at the beginning, she would sometimes blush deeply and become visibly embarrassed by some of the things she'd tell me, especially if they were of a sexual nature. But there wasn't anything she did that set off any alarm bells or gave me any cause for real concern, at least not in terms of our therapeutic relationship.

I try to channel my feelings of empathy for Leah Iverson, for the person she is, a client I have always looked forward to seeing, and though it doesn't come easily, this situation is clearly complicated and Leah is very disturbed, significantly more than I was aware, it would seem.

Still, she betrayed me. I have the sensation that the relationship between us, the single most important aspect of the therapeutic process, has not only been irrevocably compromised, but also that it might have always been different altogether than how I subjectively perceived it.

I get up, still unsteady on my feet, but my mind is razor sharp. It seems to mean that Leah intended me to read *Supernova*, whatever this is, only in the event of something happening to her. But what did she think might happen to her?

I know that I won't be able to rest until I know what she meant. The strange thing I was left with in the years after my own traumatic experience was a heightened sense of danger. It's easy enough to explain in medical terms – my body and brain remained on high alert, resulting in PTSD and anxiety issues which I have been able to resolve. And yet I have been left with an ability to sense danger, and I sense it now, that Leah's words aren't just the ramblings of someone in a compromised state of mind, but rather, something potentially dangerous. To herself, but also to me. What did she intend with *Supernova? You have told me exactly nothing about yourself, and yet I know – dare I say – everything,* she wrote.

No one knows everything about me, not even myself. Not even now, after all the work I have done. All the years in therapy. So straight off, her statement is categorically untrue. She doesn't know anything about me, let alone everything, and I'm starting to feel I didn't know anything about her either.

I have to keep reading. I glance around, and the cabin is entirely silent, like a cocoon. I open Leah's Mac again.

32

Supernova

I'm hoping we can agree that it started pretty innocently, that day you happened to walk into Kaffebrenneriet to order a tall white Americano and I trailed you up Bogstadveien. It was a spur-of-the-moment kind of thing. It was such a rush to watch you when you didn't know that you were being watched. Back then, at that stage of therapy when it had become a focal point in my life, you were constantly on my mind. An hour on Friday just wasn't quite enough. Our sessions churned in my mind all week and I was always trying to conjure you up in my mind – your calm, encouraging way of being when I faltered, your gentle and unwavering support. I'd started to feel that you were like an invisible best friend I could carry around inside me, someone who'd always have my back even if you weren't physically there in that moment.

I'm not making excuses for my behavior; I don't feel like I've done anything wrong. I've come to understand what my role is in your life – it's not the poor, downtrodden client;

it's being your helper, your closest ally. Your savior, even. Of all the things you taught me, the most important thing was the realization that you can't ever outrun the past. You have to process it, to use your own jargon. Integrate it into the narrative of your life. And I'm going to help you.

It was an unseasonably warm spring, do you remember? Seen in the context of the autumns and winter we've had since, I don't think it's unreasonable to say that we're witnessing a shift in the climate in which every season presents itself more extremely. Hotter, wetter, drier, colder, darker. And that spring came upon us so suddenly after a relentlessly wet and stormy winter, giving us day after day of glorious sunshine and temperatures in the early twenties in mid-April. It breathed everything back to life, even me. It was like the whole city was buzzing with new love.

I did it again, two weeks after the first time. I waited for you at Kaffebrenneriet after our session, sipping a tall white Americano in the window seat. I'd gotten used to drinking my coffee just like yours by then. You didn't come into the café, but after an hour or so, you emerged from your office and walked past on the other side of the street. That day, you wore dark-blue jeans and a white and navy striped sweater with gold buttons on the sleeves. You looked young and carefree, more like a student than a Doctor of Psychology. You were so impressive to me back then – it was like I needed to drink in every last part of you so I could retrieve them later in my mind, and emulate them. North Face orange parkas? I got one, too, but was careful to never wear it on a Friday. White and navy maritime sweater? Check. These things made me feel close to you, like if I wore them, something of you would rub off on me.

Back to that day. You headed up Bogstadveien, like the last time. I followed at a distance, keeping your glossy, high ponytail in sight. If you'd suddenly turned around and noticed me walking in the same direction some distance behind you, it wouldn't be weird at all. I'd merely stopped at a café after our session and happened to also be walking up one of Oslo's busiest shopping streets. You took a right at the corner of Rosenborggata, like last time. That really caught my attention. You stopped at number 11 and hesitated by the doorbells. You stood looking up at the building for a long moment, as if psyching yourself up for meeting whoever was inside. I remembered the last time, when you'd suddenly turned back around and walked away, and I had to press myself into that doorway and hope you didn't see me.

You pressed the buzzer and disappeared inside. A couple of minutes later I went up to the door and read the names on the doorbells, but none of them gave me any clues.

Christiansen. Mikkelsrud. Tanum. Siemens. Olsen-Hoff. Rickards. Thiske. Ellingsen.

A lover? That was my first thought. It struck me like a bolt of lightening; the idea of you doing something sordid was totally irreconcilable with what I needed you to be. At the same time, I was intensely jealous at the thought of you having an illicit affair, and confused by those feelings. I knew you were married from the simple gold ring on your finger, and Google easily uncovered that your marriage was rather high profile. I'll return to it, of course. But back then, it wasn't Mr Moss who most held my attention. It was the suspicion that you were something other than I'd thought.

I fell into a routine of sitting at that café several afternoons a week, keeping an eye on the door to your office building across the road, waiting for you. Sometimes I'd get up and follow you for a while; other times I'd just watch you, committing what you wore to memory. After those first couple of weeks of sheepishly following you around, my fascination with you grew drastically. You might think that observing another person's day-to-day life might reveal them to be as underwhelming and boring as most people probably are, but oh, no – not you. Some parts of your life were as shiny and perfect as I'd previously imagined them to be. Your house, for example. Your husband. Your marriage. Your friends. (But only your new ones, right?) I'll return to all of those things.

The thing I hadn't anticipated was the fact that you clearly had some problems. Secrets. In our sessions, you'd encourage me to look where it hurt, to try to describe painful experiences, insisting that to process them, they must be brought out into the light. But what about yours?

The following Friday we had another tough session.

That day, you asked me to speak directly to myself as a child, to reconnect with that inherent goodness all children have and to consider whether I could find empathy with the little girl I once was. It didn't work like that for me because the little girl I saw was worthless and dirty, like a thieving street urchin. You were moved by the way I spoke of myself and you asked whether I would be willing to consider from whose point of view I was observing myself as a child. Could it be that it wasn't my own perception at all? What child perceives herself as inherently bad and unlovable?

Could it be that this was how I imagined my father saw me, as a way to comprehend the profound rejection of his departure? And if so, could it be that my interpretation of this was simply wrong and entirely unrooted in reality?

Your words hit me so hard it felt as though you prodded me with a searing prong, as though you knew me better than I could ever know myself. I felt at your mercy. But back then I felt at everyone's mercy. And now, here we are; the tables have turned, and it is you who are at my mercy, and it is me using all of myself and everything you've taught me, to help you. You see, Kristina, nothing is as it seems. Sometimes our worlds, which look beautiful, are actually on fire.

After the session I deliberated over whether to just go home. I had plans that evening, with an old friend from Karlstad who was in town. I felt torn – a part of me wanted to go home and relax for a few hours before getting ready for dinner. We were going to Sawan, the kind of fancy place I imagined you'd go to eat, and I wanted to try out a new look inspired by you. High ponytail, gold stud earrings, a whimsical flick of liquid liner. Another part of me wanted to indulge in my guilty pleasure of trailing you up Bogstadveien to Rosenborggata and observing you agonize over whatever it was that awaited you there. I decided on the latter. I felt unsettled and blue after our session and it helped a little to process while drinking a coffee as I waited for you to finish for the day. You appeared in the doorway, your face guarded and drawn. You looked a little sad, perhaps affected by the fact that you'd spent your day going deep into dark places with people like me. You walked slower than usual, stopping several times to look at your phone. You frowned, typed a response, checked your phone again, typed some more. You crossed the street absentmindedly and a car had to brake hard to avoid you. Its driver shouted at you but you didn't respond with aggression, or at all, really; you just stood there in the middle of the road, blinking. You raised a hand in apology, or surrender, and stumbled back onto the crowded pavement.

I wanted to swoop in and pull you into a hug. I wanted to take you home with me and make you tea and sit across from you, me listening to you, for once. I wanted to know what was on your mind. In hindsight, I wondered whether it could have been me. I would have liked to know whether I ever really affected you, Kristina. Whether you brought occasional thoughts of me home with you, into your real life.

That day, you didn't go up. You stood a while outside number 11, staring up at the building. Your finger hovered at one of the buzzers, then you changed your mind and rushed away, passing just meters from where I stood on the other side of the road, partially hidden by a white van. Tears were streaming down your face, and when you'd crossed Bogstadveien, you headed down a less-crowded side street and broke into a run, your hair flowing behind you on the soft breeze like contrails from a jet.

That evening, I began to understand that something had shifted in me. Something big. I could barely follow the conversation with my girlfriend at dinner; I had the sensation of sitting there trapped in my body, but my mind was far away. It was with you. All I wanted was to see you and talk to you and talk about you – it was as though anything other than you had just faded into uninteresting shades of gray. I was so worried about you and what I'd observed that afternoon. I was also feeling the first stirrings of anger, though I didn't recognize it as such at the time. It was like a dull ache in my stomach, that feeling you get when you've eaten something you know disagrees with you and you have no choice but to wait and see what happens. I was angry that you were more than what you showed to me, that you had a life outside of the therapy room, that you were affected by the highs and lows of life, like everybody else. It made me feel so anxious that someone who emanated such calm, such gentle compassion, was actually as intensely vulnerable as me. I'm over it now and that anger grew into an even deeper love, and a fierce need to protect you, and ultimately, to set you free.

33

Kristina

I want to howl and throw the laptop across the room. My face is wet with tears. I feel tired to the bone and highly agitated; it's as though an electric feeling of nervous energy rushes through me. I remember that day she's referring to. Elisabeth had taken another overdose and had just been released from hospital to another bleak women's shelter, and I was desperately trying to get in contact with the director at Villa Vinternatt, an old colleague of mine from when I did my psychology doctorate residency at a private hospital specializing in treating addicts like Elisabeth. He'd gone on to found Villa Vinternatt, and I believed its progressive arts program could be exactly the kind of thing that could bring lasting change to Elisabeth's life, so I tried to convince him to take her on the program. Instead, it led to her death.

I couldn't bear to sit across from the Rickards that day in their clammy overheated apartment, eating dry cakes and sipping sherry, which they always insist upon. I couldn't bear to listen to their reminiscing, their exaggerated stories of their only child's remarkable achievements, their musings about all the ways she'd be changing the world, if only she'd lived. I couldn't bear to sit there and look at the framed pictures the Rickards keep everywhere, on the walls, on the windowsills, on the kitchen counter, even on a shelf in the bathroom. Everywhere you'd look, Trine Rickards would look back at you, suspended in time, young and alive. Sometimes it feels good to be there with them, and speak of their beloved daughter as though she had only just left the room, even though she'd been dead for almost two decades. But that day I just couldn't bear it.

Out of the three of us, Trine, Elisabeth and me, I was the lucky one. I've had years of trauma therapy and built a good life for myself. My traumatized brain shielded me from reliving what happened and I have made my peace with it. Elisabeth wasn't so lucky – though she escaped, she didn't really; she was held hostage by trauma, and instead of facing it, Elisabeth tried to run from it through her addictions until she couldn't outrun it anymore and it ultimately cost her her life.

And Trine… No. I'm not going there. I never do.

So much grief, so many dark corners, so many things lost forever. I allow myself a few thoughts that never fail to center me. The view of the royal palace gardens from our kitchen windows, and the way being in my home makes me feel so held and so safe. The feeling of my husband's arms closing around my waist from behind, drawing me close. These are mindfulness techniques I use to select the thoughts I allow – I see my thoughts as floating past in little boats on a river. It's up to me which ones I pick up. If there are too many dark ones, I remain patient until a good thought comes floating downstream. It doesn't mean that dark thoughts are suppressed; it means that they are observed, acknowledged and released. I do it now, and it takes me a long while to build the image, because tonight the river runs red with blood and all the little boats are overflowing and jostling each other, snapping this way and that on a churning current. When my mind is finally calm, I keep reading.

34

Supernova

There was a day I remember later that spring when I felt particularly unhinged. I already lived for Fridays by then, but it was increasingly obvious that one hour a week just wasn't enough. I wanted more. It was midweek, and like I had started to do on a few occasions, I made my way over to Kaffebrenneriet when I took a break for lunch. I stood outside your office for a while, feeling numb with jealousy at the thought of someone else up there with you, bathing in your irresistibly soothing presence. I wished I could go up there and shove that person out of the door so I could sit across from you. Standing there, I felt tinged with bitterness – the more I knew about you, and the more I saw, the more I wanted. It's normal to get attached to your therapist; I've read all about it. But I knew that what I was doing wasn't normal. I knew it, but I couldn't stop.

I went across the street and bought a coffee. I sat in the window seat and waited for you to appear. I'd learned by then that you finish at four on Wednesdays. Four o'clock came and went and you didn't appear. Maybe a client had canceled and you'd left early and I'd missed you. I could have screamed. All I wanted was a quick glimpse. But in that moment, I had an idea. I would try to find out why you kept going to Rosenborggata, it would be like uncovering a mystery. And I would go to your house.

35

Kristina

My blood runs cold at Leah's mention of my house. My home is my sanctuary, the physical container for my life, the hub of my marriage. To think that she repeatedly followed me on Fridays to Rosenborggata, observing me as I weighed up whether or not I could face going up that day, is bad enough. The idea that she could have gone to my home is unthinkable, that she might have stood in my living space among my personal photographs and possessions, drinking them in and storing them in her illicit bank of information about me.

My head is throbbing and my stomach feels liquid and strange. I have to fight the urge to just flee from this disturbing place and Leah's increasingly insane narrative, but the need to read just one more section is too powerful. I have to know what she's done. And what she knows.

36

Supernova

A few days before I went to your house, on a Tuesday, I waited at Kaffebrenneriet from three thirty. I'd finished my tall white Americano by the time you arrived, just after four. By then, I knew that Tuesdays were exhausting for you, with clients back-to-back from ten until four, which is why I chose that day because I knew that you always stopped for a coffee after work, drinking it in the café instead of taking it to go like you normally do. It was a beautiful, hot day in late spring and I worried that you'd choose to sit outside on one of the little wrought-iron tables; one was free, but you didn't – you chose your usual seat at the back of the café, a barstool facing the wall. Your face was peaceful, serene, unsuspecting. I had a watertight plan I'd run through in my head over and over in the event of you suddenly glancing over to where I sat at a table just behind you. I'd simply smile shyly and say, 'Hi'. After all, why would it be strange that we should bump into each other there, at a popular café equidistant between your office and my house? It would only seem strange if I made it seem strange.

You didn't look over. Not then, nor any of the other times I observed you from less than two meters away at that same coffee shop. As far as I'm aware, you only ever saw me once outside of the therapy room, an episode I'm sure you'll recall. And even then, it didn't seem like you were remotely suspicious; you acted discreet and professional, like I knew you would, most likely assuming that us both being in that particular place was just a coincidence, albeit a big one.

You read the previous week's *A-Magasinet* and ate an oat cookie alongside your coffee. On the floor, next to your barstool, stood your Louis Vuitton Neverfull bag. It was exactly identical to my own, purchased especially for that reason. Extreme, I know. But I'm sure I'm not the first client who has tried to emulate your style; after all, it's quite the conformist Oslo West look you go for – inoffensive, quietly expensive, discreet. Like you. Tailored Prada, classic Louis, a glimpse of Hermès on your wrist.

Back to those moments. You'd placed your bag on the floor. Who would do such a thing, some might ask, but that's Oslo West for you. Nobody would steal your Louis Vuitton bag, because they all have their own. Lol. I pushed my identical bag close to yours very slowly. I'd endlessly rehearsed what I would do if I got caught, of course. It would be very obvious that I hadn't taken your bag on purpose, it was an honest mistake.

You seemed engrossed in an article, and I watched your back for a long while. You were close enough for me to be able to see the rise and fall of your chest as you breathed.

And I copied even that, syncing my own breath to yours. I got up to leave, while scrolling through Instagram on my phone, no doubt appearing distracted if anyone happened to be watching. I looped my hand through the straps of the Neverfull bag, yours, not mine, of course. Then I walked out. My heart thundered in my chest and my mind raced as I stepped outside into brilliant sunshine. No one said anything. Why would they?

I'd taken the car that day to ensure a swift getaway, and I reached it within seconds – I'd driven around the block at least ten times when I arrived to snare a parking space on Grønnegata, a stone's throw away from Kaffebrenneriet. My hands were slick with sweat on the steering wheel. I wanted to roll down the window and sing at the top of my lungs. It suddenly made sense to me in those moments why some people choose a life of crime. I fought the urge to laugh hysterically but settled for a smug smile at my own reflection in the rearview. The bag stood on the passenger seat next to me, just like its doppelgänger had done earlier that afternoon as I drove the few hundred meters home. Nothing appeared different, and yet everything was. Before I drove off, I fished your phone out of the bag. It had several notifications – WhatsApp, Messenger and Outlook, but Face ID was activated and there was no way I could access it, as I'd anticipated. I turned it off, and then I dropped it into a storm drain on the street.

At home, I carried the bag sagely and nonchalantly up the stairs like I had done every day for a couple of weeks. When I first bought the bag, the annoying flat-sharing girls on the ground floor had cooed over it when I bumped into them in the entrance hallway. *Oh, my God*, they'd chanted, *it is, like, soooo cool*. So, nothing new if I bumped into them again, but I didn't. I made myself wait for my cup of tea to brew, ginger and turmeric, what I imagined you'd choose. I took the bag through to the bedroom and upended it onto the bedsheet. Your keys, bingo. Your wallet. Louis Vuitton, too. Nice. And predictable. Like you, I thought, back then.

I slipped your driving license out and studied your photo for a long time. Like most people's, your expression was serious and unsmiling, like you feared they wouldn't let you drive otherwise. I took a picture of the photo with my phone; back then, I didn't have many pictures of you and I thought it would help to look at it when I craved your closeness between sessions. It did, for a while, but I assume you are familiar with the law of diminishing returns and how, once you get what you want, you always want more? I wanted more.

The bottom of the bag was surprisingly messy – I didn't have you down as a messy lady and I felt a stab of annoyance at this discovery. I had to scramble around amid old receipts, loose change, parking slips and empty chewing gum wrappers to reach the last few objects underneath. But, oh boy, it was worth it. There was a small, burnished-orange leather-bound journal. I opened it, assuming it was a calendar, so imagine my delight when I realized it was much more personal than that. It was almost full – page after page of your innermost thoughts and musings. I swear, my heart somersaulted. I put it aside, knowing I'd spend my evening drinking in your words, and that I'd cherish the little book forever. I was right about that.

I also found a Dior lip gloss, which I instantly applied to my own lips, and this, too, was an intensely satisfying moment. Several times, I ran the little wand up and down the length of my lips, thinking about how it had also touched yours. I closed my eyes and allowed myself an imagined scene in which you kissed me passionately, your lips slick with that same gloss, passing it from your lips to mine. You'd slip your tongue into my mouth and hold me close, so close I could feel the beat of your heart and the soft contour of your breasts. Back then, I often had fantasies like that, when the only language I had to describe feeling that close to someone was sexual or romantic.

With time, my attachment to you grew from the perceived sexual to the frenzied, obsessive friendship feelings of young girls, and then it deepened into a gentle, parental kind of bond, and that's when things really went wrong. In my mind and heart you were the very incarnation of perfection, though, like I've said, I knew you were human just like everyone else. But to the child inside, to little Leah who craved a stable, predictable, unconditional adult, you were perfect. So it hurt like hell to discover that you were its very opposite. That you were as hollow as Swiss cheese, vast parts of what makes a whole person, just gone. The rage I felt at first wasn't rational, I know that. But I feel it, still, when I revisit the memory of your persona disintegrating before my very eyes. I didn't stop loving you, in my basic childlike way. I never will. Now, I'm telling you this because I want you to know that there was a reason for my behavior, for all the questions I asked, for everything I did.

It was selfish at first, this need for you to be like a perfect hologram, so that I could feel safe. Naturally I felt angry when the bubble burst, but then as things progressed, I realized that you need me as much as I need you and the real healing, for both of us, will happen when all the cards are on the table. Mine, and yours. I need to fix you to fix me.

37

Kristina

I hold myself entirely still. There's a throbbing pain in my temple that burns and insists itself into my very brain. I steel myself to let in one thought at a time. It was Leah that took my bag and I try to take in the enormity of that fact. The lengths she went to. The depths of betrayal of the bond between us. At the time, I had no choice but to write the missing bag off as an honest mistake, the one that was left behind on the floor next to my chair was exactly identical to my own. There was no phone in the bag, no credit cards or any other identification. There was a generic set of keys and a cheap wallet with a couple of hundred-kroner bills, and some make-up. I handed the whole thing in to the police, and assumed that the person who'd taken my bag by mistake would do the same thing. But they never did. I bought another Neverfull bag with the insurance money and eventually forgot about the whole strange incident.

★ ★ ★

To think that Leah sat that close to me, close enough to smoothly exchange the bags, and I didn't notice her, is profoundly disturbing. But I know all too well that we don't often see what we're not looking for. I try to recall whether I ever felt like I was being watched or like someone was following me. I do remember the episode she referred to, and it is the only time I can remember ever seeing Leah outside of the therapy room. It was during the winter, months after the episode with the handbag, so by then, she must have been playing this game for close to a year. Eirik and I went skiing in Geilo, a rare weekend away together, and treated ourselves to a stay at Dr Holm's Hotel. On the second evening, we were at the after-ski hotel bar, drinking champagne and reminiscing about how we used to go away like that together all the time. We vowed to do it more often. We were just about to start our third round of IVF and were in that phase of really believing it was going to work this time. *Third time lucky*, we said and gently touched our thin champagne flutes together and smiled at each other in the soft light from the fireplace. Eirik had just been elected second in command in his party and the demands of a political career at that level were beginning to show. But I remember how close I felt to my husband that evening, how I noticed the new sprinkles of gray in his hair and how it only made him more handsome.

At one point in the evening, I realized I'd left my phone upstairs in the hotel room and went to get it – I wanted to take a few pictures of Eirik and me. I bumped into Leah in the corridor leading to our room and at first I couldn't instantly place her – this happens to me often when I see a client out of context. Then I matched the woman in front of me with the pretty Swedish writer I see every Friday at two. I smiled at her as she came toward me and as always, allowed the client to decide whether or not to acknowledge me. Leah looked shocked to see me there, but smiled shyly and whispered, 'Hi', and then she disappeared around the corner. I didn't give the episode another thought. I would have just assumed that she was there for the weekend like us; there wasn't anything particularly strange about that – Dr Holm's is a very popular weekend destination for the Oslo West crowds.

Thinking back, I realize she must have followed us there. That whole weekend, she must have lurked in the shadows, watching.

38

Supernova

Four days later, on the Saturday, I went to your house. I'd looked at your husband's party's event calendar and he was listed as attending a rally in Kristiansand that weekend. It said that there would be a gala dinner on the Saturday evening with local stakeholders and politicians, and I knew that you would be accompanying him to that, like you usually do.

On the Friday in my session, we had a moment when we were talking through some particularly difficult stuff I'd been dealing with, to do with compulsive thoughts of suicide and self-harming, when your eyes filled with tears. I asked you why you were crying, and you said you felt so moved by what I'd said and so empathetic toward me for having to deal with it. Your display of emotion, and the validation it brought, moved me so much, Kristina. It was in moments like that that I believed what we were doing in that room really had the power to heal me.

I walked out of there and straight home, not even

considering hanging around Kaffebrenneriet in the hope that you'd stop in. I lay on my bed and stared at the ceiling, tears rushing from my eyes. I felt so bad, then, for everything I'd done. For a moment, I considered calling you and confessing, laying it all bare so we could start over. But I knew it was already too late. I was in too deep. I promised myself that I would go to your house, satisfy my curiosity and then stop. I cried harder because I knew that even if I actually managed to walk away after that, there would always be these secrets between us now. I cried with confusion and jealousy, because in your diary I had read page after page about the worrying blanks in your mind, and about someone called Elisabeth, who sounded like another client, but not a single word about me.

I cried myself to sleep in the middle of the afternoon, and when I woke up it was close to midnight. I poured myself some wine and sat on the floor, letting the warm summer night into the room through the wide-open windows. I looked at your solemn face in your driving license picture and then I spent a long while reading through your journal again and looking at the strange drawings you'd made. I looked at the calculations too, and though math wasn't my strongest subject at school; it seemed to me like they were some kind of probability equations, page after page after page of them. I had to know more, Kristina.

I arrived early in the morning, around eight. I'd planned it very carefully, as you can imagine. I wore gray sweatpants and a baseball cap, and with me I had a bucket and a mop. The bucket was filled to the brim with various cleaning products. My face was scrubbed clean and not made-up and my hair was tied into a severe ponytail that emerged from the back of the baseball hat. I felt confident that if I bumped into a neighbor, they would just assume I was there to clean one of the apartments in the building.

I prayed you hadn't changed the locks after the incident with the bag, but the key slipped easily into the lock and I entered the communal hallway, which was much fancier than my building's, with soaring ceilings and ornate, freshly painted stucco. I didn't know which floor you lived on, so I crept upstairs and checked the doorbells until I found the one that read 'E & K Moss' on the second floor. I pressed it briefly, just to be totally sure that I wouldn't get a nasty surprise, such as a houseguest or an angry dog, when I unlocked the door. The apartment emanated the silence of a large, abandoned space. I slipped a key into the lock, and when it didn't work, another. This one unlocked the door with a smooth click.

I stepped inside, and couldn't help but take a sharp, stunned breath. Your home is exquisite, Kristina. The kind of home one would expect to see in interiors magazines, not a single detail left to chance. Your expensive handbags hung proudly from a series of hooks along the wall – Gucci, Givenchy, Hermès, Louis Vuitton – and it occurred to me then that you clearly have much more money than I'd thought, that you live inside an impenetrable bubble of serious wealth. I suppose I'd thought we were on the same level in that respect – I make a very good living, and I too, own a nice apartment in a snazzy part of town. But this – this was a different level. A huge gold mirror hung above an antique table on top of which stood an incredibly beautiful porcelain vase filled with peonies. I stepped closer to it, but felt afraid to meet my own gaze in the mirror – I think I irrationally craved that the person looking back at me would be you, and didn't want the disappointment of my own reflection.

The floor was laid with a warm, matte oakwood and I slipped my shoes off, feeling its smooth surface against my bare feet. On the wall of the corridor leading to the other rooms were several black-and-white, professionally-shot photographs, blown up big and placed in identical brushed-bronze colonial-style frames. I moved from one to the next slowly, taking in each one carefully, stopping to take pictures of them all on my phone. The picture of your niece and nephew is so beautiful. I wanted to know their names. And the one with you and Eirik on your wedding day. Everyone always says that a bride was radiant on her wedding day, but never was it more true than for you. I could have cried just looking at you, and maybe I did. He's a handsome guy, Eirik, but from a purely physical attractiveness perspective he pales next to you. Still, he has the self-satisfied smile of a man who believes he deserves you and knows he can afford to spoil you. Does he treat you like a trophy, Kristina? Does he make you feel like just another piece on the chessboard of his life? A queen perhaps, but a piece, nonetheless.

I liked the picture of you, Trine and Elisabeth, too. Back then, I didn't know what I know now, so I thought it was just a cute shot of three cute teenagers posing together, smiling innocently at the camera, arms flung around each other's shoulders. You're in the middle, of course. Now, I want to know how you can walk past that photograph every day of your life. Doesn't looking at those young, smiling faces fill you with dread and with the images of what was to come? Or do you think of yourself as so thoroughly healed that looking at them fails to provoke any emotional response? Then why do you cry on the street in Rosenborggata? Why do you fill your diary with all those detailed nightmares of crashing through forests echoing with laughing voices and the sound of gunshots? Why do you write out all those calculations, trying to work out if the outcome could have been different?

See, I get all agitated putting all of this on the page. It isn't easy, that's for sure. My mind is like a storm. I didn't know then what I know now. I didn't yet know what you'd been through or how much what happened to those three young girls would take from all of you. But even now, when I know everything, more than you, I still want to know how you can bear to look at all that innocence, every single day.

Are you ready to go back, further back, all the way back? Shall we go back to Carúpano? Yes, Kristina, I know. I know all about Carúpano.

39

Kristina

I pause, gauging whether I can actually handle this. I have naturally encountered a lot of people with serious mental health challenges over the years and have always been of the school that believes that even the most extreme manifestations of dissociation and emotional disturbance can be countered and healed with long-term psychotherapy. To be witnessed and tolerated in their most challenging incarnations can bring the broken pieces inside someone back together in the most miraculous ways; I've seen it over and over. In others, and in myself. I thought I saw it in Leah Iverson, too, but now I am forced to consider whether the healing I believed I saw was in fact just misguided preoccupation with me. I'm afraid of her now, of what she wants from me, and almost hope that she is dead – at least that way I never have to see her again.

It's obvious that these are the words of an extremely damaged individual. To break into the home of your therapist and steal her diary and take pictures of her personal photographs, and repeatedly follow her around – you'd have to suffer highly compromised mental faculties. What else could she have done? I'm not only furious, but afraid – I can only imagine how dangerous this might get if certain elements of the past become subject to the interpretation of a disturbed person such as Leah Iverson.

I suddenly understand Anton's rage and feelings of powerlessness. I tell myself that nothing she did or claims to know about me can hurt me, but I need to find out what she's playing at. And then I am going to return to my life and my husband and my work and all of this will fade away into a shocking, unsavory episode. But where is she?

I return to the document. There are over eighteen thousand words, over seventy pages. I don't want to know what more she wrote, or why; I just want to know where Leah is so I can leave all this behind. Wherever she is, she is clearly in need of psychiatric intervention, and I will make sure to get back in touch with her GP when I get back to Oslo to recommend exactly that.

I certainly won't let her invade my life any further. I will take this experience to my own therapy and attempt to learn from it. I will move on. Eirik will win the election. We'll get our baby. All of this will eventually feel distant and impotent. I have to believe that.

I look around Leah's cabin again and this time it doesn't feel like a comforting cocoon, but cramped and claustrophobic, rather. She'd clearly come here to write this stuff, all these weird and disturbing things about me, and fantasized about me reading her words. The space itself feels sullied, as though I'd stumbled upon the sinister lair of a twisted criminal.

I need to leave; coming here was clearly not a good idea. The sky is blustery and dark gray now and the snow is falling more heavily, not instantly melting as it touches the windowpanes, but settling in clusters across them, like iced spiderwebs. I bet the heavy clouds hide a most magnificent evening sky, far away from the glare of lights from the big city, and I wish I could see the stars when they appear, that they would light up the way back down to the car. I think about Leah's mentions of supernovae, especially the obliteration of the larger, brighter star by a little dwarf star stealing its matter, prompting them both to explode, as she described. Why did she choose it as the title for this strange and disturbing account? I close my eyes and imagine those thermonuclear explosions, the white heat, the rainbow fires of destruction shredding the blackness when stars collide.

I check my phone. No reception, unsurprisingly. It's just past 5 p.m. and I still have a headache from all the wine yesterday. My stomach growls with hunger, but I've left the cookies in the car.

I peer out of the window at the flurries of snow churning on the darkening air like static on an old television. I am dreading the walk back to the car through the woods. What if Leah comes back and I bump into her on the forest track? I realize I am afraid of coming face to face with her now. She lured me here and could come back at any time. She is clearly unhinged, and has not only extensively lied to me, but also stalked me in my personal time. She even had a restraining order out against her for assault. I need to get out of here right now. I choke the flame on the oil lamp, steeping the vaulted room in a deep twilight, a chill spreading through my bones.

I use the torch to get back to the front door without bumping into anything, pausing for a quick moment to listen before I step back outside – a visceral fear is taking hold of me but I have to find a way to control it and get myself safely back to the car. I place the phone on the floor for a second and shove my feet back into my boots, which I'd graciously left by the door like a polite guest, and the torch beam falls on something high up on the wall that I hadn't noticed before.

It's a long glass cabinet designed for a hunting rifle; its door is open, the weapon is gone. *Enough, Kristina, enough.* I hear the voice inside me as clearly as though it were spoken out loud. I grab the door handle and pull the door open toward me, but as I do, I can't help but unleash a scream of sheer shock – my hand comes back wet with something thick, sticky and cold, and even before I manage to direct the torch beam straight into my right palm, I know that it's blood.

40

Leah, days before

She can't stop shaking at the sight of him hammering on the cabin's door. Light snow is falling, settling in his hair. He's shouting her name, sending bursts of frozen air from his mouth. She watches from the window, and he suddenly realizes she's standing there. He stops knocking and shouting and holds her gaze. She turns her face so that the swollen, injured skin is clearly visible. He looks down at the ground, somber and sorry.

Hours later, when she's finally managed to get rid of him and the bright sky has faded to a dark ocean blue, she decides to go home. She finds her way easily enough back down to the car; the path is lit up by the moon and the walk through the woods soothes her after the stressful afternoon. She still feels wounded, somehow, by the way he screamed at her. But out here, she feels like a part of everything, unlike in her life among other people. She sits in the driver's seat and rubs her hands together hard a few times, breathing icy steam into the cold, dark space, then she starts the engine.

Several lamps flash on the dashboard and when she tries to inch back in reverse, a terrible crunching sound makes her realize something is really wrong with the car. She puts it in park and leaves the engine idling while stepping outside to take a look. All four tires are slashed.

She walks briskly back up to the cabin, but when she's almost at the first clearing, her foot catches on something and Leah comes crashing to the ground. For a long moment, she lies still, waiting for pain to crash over her, but it doesn't happen, only mild discomfort and the shock of actually falling over. When she sits back up, she feels a deep twinge to the left of her abdomen; she must have pulled a muscle trying to catch her fall. As she starts walking again, she feels a trickle of blood run down the side of her face and realizes the fall has opened a cut that was already there. She also feels a couple of achy spots on her legs and hips; she'll have even more bruises. She has no choice but to stay another day and tomorrow she can walk to the spot in the valley by the lake, where her phone usually picks up reception and call for help.

The afternoon is deepening into evening when she returns to *Supernova*, overcome by an almost feverish energy, like she has been every night since she got to Bekkebu, and the act of writing to Kristina instantly transports her away from her own circumstances. The day slips away as she delves deeper into her narrative; the shock of Anton hammering on the door, the slashed tires, the fall.

It's past midnight when she goes to the bathroom and runs a bath. There is a second door that runs from the corner of the bathroom to a more recent bedroom wing extension, and Leah goes through to her bedroom and lies down on the freshly made bed while she waits for the bathwater to fill the tub from the little cistern outside. After next week, the cabin won't have hot water again until the spring and Leah will have to heat big cauldrons of melted snow over the fire to take a bath.

In the bath, she closes her eyes and breathes the rising steam deep into her. She runs a natural sponge across her bruised collarbone, across her suddenly much-larger breasts, over the tight drum of her stomach, avoiding the tender points and the little cuts and grazes. She'll run disinfectant over the wounds, then sink into bed, hoping for a restful night and more clarity tomorrow. Maybe she will wake up to the sound of Kristina knocking on the door; she still can't help but hope it might happen. Since she started writing *Supernova*, the connection between them seems even stronger, like an umbilical cord of sheer energy.

She feels her eyelids growing heavy and the side of her face is throbbing; it's time to get up and go to bed. As she steps from the bathtub onto the bathmat, she has the strange sensation of a sharp twinge from within her womb. She feels woozy and holds onto the side of the bath for support. A dark drop of blood splashes onto the bath mat. Then another.

41

Kristina

It is the most disgusting, terrifying sensation and I instinctively wipe my hand down the front of my jeans, streaking them maroon. I shine the beam onto the door and its handle, and both are streaked with dried blood. The handle has significantly more blood on it, and some has dripped onto the floor below. There are also several patches of it on the floor, almost indistinguishable against the slate floor tiles, and I didn't notice it in the meager light of the little vestibule when I arrived – you'd have to direct the beam of a torch straight at it. There seems to be a trail leading to the bathroom. I step inside the bathroom and, shining the torch around, I spot another few small drops alongside the sink. There's a bio compost toilet I am familiar with from other trips to similar cabins. There's a bloody fingerprint on its closed lid and I shudder at the sight of it. There is also another door in the far corner of the room, impossible to see from where I stood before in the doorway of the vestibule.

I open it and realize that the cabin has been extended and is bigger than I thought. There is a pine-clad corridor with a door on either side and a floor-to-ceiling window at its end, with sweeping valley views. I shine the light onto the door on the left, which is ajar. I push it open with my foot to reveal a small but cozy bedroom with a built-in triple bunk, presumably for visiting children. I climb onto the bottom bunk and shine the light into the middle and top bunks in turn, but they are empty and neatly made up. There is a cupboard, also empty, and there are no signs of bloodstains anywhere in this room.

I go back out into the corridor and shine the light onto the second door, the one on the right. There is a rusty smudge on its door handle and I cover my hand with my sweater sleeve before grabbing it. The door doesn't open easily, I have to lean against it to get it to budge inwards into the room, as if something is blocking it on the other side. Is she in there, dead? I pause for a brief moment, but find that I am strangely freed from fear or hesitation in this moment and know that it's because I am high on the adrenaline surging through my veins.

The door gives enough for me to squeeze through and as I send the torch light around the room to get my bearings, I can't suppress a cry – it is as though the sound is torn from my insides and will now remain an eternal echo in the room.

42

Leah, days before

The blood stops as suddenly as it started. She has heard of sporadic bleeding in pregnancy; it doesn't have to mean anything at all. She prays; she doesn't know what else to do, and though she's never done it before, she knows how to ask for mercy.

Please, please let the baby live.

She conjures up the baby in her mind the way she constructed the characters in her book; she gives it little details that make it feel more real – a fuzzy little patch of strawberry blonde hair atop a soft pink skull, tiny fingernails, a slightly upturned nose, slim, almost see-through wrists. She breathes life into the imagined child, until she has a vivid image of it there inside her womb, fingers and toes moving, heart fluttering.

Please, please live.

She's in bed, with her legs elevated on a tall stack of pillows. She's waiting, for Kristina, for morning, for the dull ache in her stomach to stop. She brings her phone out, and realizes there is, unusually, a single bar of reception. She does something she has never done before: she dials Kristina's number, which she knows by heart. It rings for a long while before she picks up, and when she does, tears begin to flow from Leah's eyes at the sound of her voice. There was a time when Leah believed that Kristina could fix everything, and a part of her must still believe it, and maybe it's true, because there is something so soothing in the silence that unfolds between them on the crackly line that Leah feels her heart resume its normal beat. In the end, she puts the phone down and lies back against the pillows. She prays again, feeling new hope and energy flow through her after hearing Kristina's voice. Maybe now she'll come.

She falls asleep. When she wakes again, she feels strange, as though her limbs are weighted down, and she has the sensation of being submerged in water. She blinks in the dark, getting her bearings, taking in the outlines of her surroundings; Bekkebu, she's at Bekkebu. Fragments of the day before return to her. The screaming, the slashed tires, the fall, the blood, the email. It is completely dark outside but she can make out the glow of the moon through the gauze curtains. She tries to sit up but a searing pain across her abdomen stops her. Then she realizes she is bleeding again.

43

Kristina

At first I can't makes sense of what it is I'm looking at. The bedroom is small, but neat, with pine walls and a big double bed with a white padded headboard and white bedsheets, gathered into twisted piles. There's blood on the bed, as well as traces of it on the floor, half cleaned up with a big pile of bath towels. The door nudged against these when I tried to push it open. The bedsheets are gathered in a mound on the bed, and I give them a little tug to make sure she isn't under them, though there is nothing there, only some streaky, brown bloodstains. I push a large cupboard open with my foot but there is nothing but towels and sheets and a couple of ski jackets inside it.

There is no sign of her but I think about the empty gun cabinet in the vestibule; whoever has killed or injured Leah is armed and still on the loose.

'Jesus,' I whisper. I'm about to turn around and leave the room when I notice something sticking out from under one of the pillows. I unfold it and recognize Leah's handwriting from the note she pressed into my hand in our last session. I read it, and it's instantly clear who killed Leah Iverson.

44

Kristina

It wasn't going to be like this.

I've fought and fought so hard to find a way to be me. To be someone else. To be anyone at all. But I can't. Even my own child couldn't bear to remain inside me. And I can't do this. I can't bear it anymore because the thing is I just don't get any breaks I don't get a breather or a break or just peace it never ever stops. It's like I'm roadkill, ripped open and exposed and bleeding to death in the road and my dark thoughts are vultures, feasting before my pebble-sized racoon heart has even stopped beating. The thoughts the images the words the pain and the endless black aloneness which is different from loneliness because it isn't a perception, it's a statement of fact. The only time it ever stopped was when I tried to be different, to undo me, and become someone else, someone sane and beautiful and whole and worthy but no one is really like that, even if it looks like it; the shiny perfection we see is just another symptom of the darkness inside isn't it and anyway we can't ever be anyone other than who we are, can we – not really

I felt the exact moment when the baby died

It was like the flip of the smallest switch

I knew it even if I couldn't bear to know it

Lights out

I wanted the pain to come, then. I needed to see the blood and the evidence of it but now I wish I hadn't. I wish away the inevitability of what will happen next. The darkness. The simple, simple answer. The shame. I am so sorry I'm so very sorry

I want Kristina to know about Supernova, I want people to read it, for Elisabeth, for Kristina, for me, for Trine, for all of us, could it be that if people did it could turn all of that destruction into something beautiful?

Even now it's the word I can't let go of. The images. A big star and a little one, together in a celestial dance. The little white dwarf star stealing material from the big one until it has too much, too much to carry and to hold, drawing both stars into a gigantic thermonuclear explosion so bright it can light up anything, anything at all.

And afterward, a black hole, a rip in the lining of the heavens.

Lights out

I'm going to the lake, it's so beautiful, there is nowhere more beautiful in this world, not to me, so I'm going there and I will stay there forever until I become part of it, disintegrating into its deep, cold water, infusing it with the very essence of me.

Ask Linda and Anton and Kristina to forgive me. Most of all Kristina. It wasn't meant to happen like this, none of it

***

I crush the note in my hand, then smooth it back out – I'll need to hand it over to the police. I glance around the sad room one last time and immediately wish I hadn't – I know I'll never forget this.

I rush back down the pine corridor and through the bathroom and the vestibule with the empty gun cabinet; I've seen enough and I need to get out of here. I burst from the cabin into frozen air, bustling and wet with thick, swirling snowflakes. I'm crying with shock and the horror of the afternoon and the tragedy of Leah's last hours – all those hours she waited for me before she went to the lake. To think that she wrote those words after losing her baby, and waiting, hoping, that I'd come help her – I can't bear it, in spite of everything.

My cries holler into the blizzard, settling against the wall of trees, against the iced lid of the lake deep in the valley. She's down there, below the surface. Jesus Christ, the poor woman is in it. I didn't help her, just like I didn't help Elisabeth, in fact. I might as well have shoved her into the icy, black water. I haven't cried like this in years. Like a trapped animal. Like a hurricane gathering wild speed, screeching through the night. I scream until my voice bleeds dry, until I start to cough and splutter. I take a few stumbling steps away from the cabin and turn around to look at it, but already it is almost swallowed up by the snowstorm, only a dim haze from one forgotten oil lamp still lit on the windowsill discernible through columns of whirling snowflakes. I've left it burning – will it catch fire and raze the cabin to the ground? I decide I don't care, I just keep stumbling through the snowstorm. I need to get away from this place more than I have needed anything in my life. Now.

I try to remember the direction I came from but my mind is in overdrive, throwing random thoughts and images at me, and my heart is pounding. *Which way?* I scream the words out loud, but this time my voice doesn't carry; instead it peters out mid-holler to a pitiful squawk. The cabin lay to my left as I approached, on the edge of a rocky promontory overlooking the lake. No. It lay to my right. Or did it? The air is murky gray, with particles of pure white rushing at me on a bitter wind like confetti, and there is just no way of making out the path that leads back down the hill to my car.

I'm shaking with cold and sheer dread, and I spin around on my heels, rubbing at my arms; I'm not dressed for a dash through deserted, mountainous woods in a blizzard.

I grab my phone from my parka pocket, but there is still no reception. I find the compass function and though I am only just able to make out the hazy green glare of the screen, I begin to follow the needle north – I am certain I headed south on my way up here – I have a vague memory of the opaque sky being brighter to my left as I emerged from the clutch of the woods into the cabin's little clearing. I want to run as fast as I can away from the horror of Leah's cabin and her terrible words, but I have no choice but to inch forward slowly, until I reach what must be the path, a sliver of space between towering rows of pine trees. I can see more clearly here – the snowstorm is hampered by the density of the trees – so I pick up my pace and rush down, down, away from that place and the terrifying reality of what I've just read.

I'm in a forest in the foothills of a long range of mountains that stretch from Skien in the south across much of Telemark to Kongsberg and into central Norway beyond, in the middle of a blizzard on the first day of November. *Stay sharp, Kristina. Just get out of here and get home and all of this will eventually fade away into just another bad memory.* The wind is bitterly cold and carries the scent of deep lakes and mulchy earth and ancient trees.

I stop for a moment, pressing my fingers to my eyes, before looking around at more static whiteness, more blurred outlines of trees. The path has opened out into another snow-drenched clearing. I am breathing so hard I feel as though I might black out. I can feel the downward slope of the path and its uneven surface of slippery roots and jagged rocks poking out of the earth, concealed by fresh snow, but can't see anything. How much further? I'm about to keep walking when I notice something beside me, breaking the almost complete whiteout of the hillside clearing. It's the blonde wood and charcoal metal barrel of a rifle, emerging from the snow like the mast of a sailing boat rising on the horizon. I reach for it, then decide against it: it could go off in my hands. Next to it is a huddled mound; at first glance I assume it's a fallen tree. But it isn't a tree; this is instantly clear when I kick it with my foot, revealing the outline of a hand, a sickly shade of ice blue, then a shock of long brown hair atop a rusty patch of blood-stained snow. It's Leah.

Part II

EXPOSURE THERAPY

45

Leah, days before

It had always been the words that saved her. They gave her something to hold onto when she felt too little and too weak to go on. But they can't save her now, nothing can. The violent contractions stopped a long while ago, and the blood, too. She is empty again, emptier than ever before.

She runs through everything in her mind, but her mind doesn't work the way it usually does, there are vast chunks of nothingness, like black holes thoughts get sucked into and disappear. Is that what it feels like for Kristina? It makes sense that the brain would simply erase what it can't bear to contain. *Supernova*. Yes. The big star and the little one, locked together in destruction. The beauty of them burning each other out.

She wants everyone to see these fires. She wants them to watch her burn.

Since the baby went, since she realized what the blatantly obvious answer to everything was, she has read back through everything, all the way up to the end of *Supernova*, and only the silent blackness of the night ahead remains. It's time. She'll send *Supernova* to Kristina and then she will go to the lake.

Supernova, back to *Supernova*, she needs to be quick, now. But how? There is no reception, though she has very occasionally been able to catch a faint signal in this newer part of the cabin. She composes the email, using all her remaining strength to sound vaguely coherent. But the document won't attach, even when she moves around the room, painfully slowly, holding the phone up in the hope of a single bar of reception. By the lake, there's a patch of occasional reception near the jetty, which is anchored to the surface now by ice. She'll bring the phone, send the email, then take it with her into the lake.

Just one more thing to write, to be read by whoever comes to Bekkebu next and finds her gone. She starts writing, but keeps stopping, erasing, trying again; the words don't come out right. Some words she crosses out because she doesn't mean them.

I'm sorry.

She imagines the dark water of the lake closing over her head like the velvet blackness of the night sky and maybe when she really gives in to the lake and death, the glimmer of stars will reach her all the way down at its bottom. Maybe it will be like a supernova, when death itself is more beautiful than anything in life. She doesn't want to die, she wants to live, but not this life, the life that can now never be separated from that other life, the lost life.

But what if there is a message waiting for her when the phone recovers reception? Maybe Kristina has left her a message. Maybe she is on her way, maybe she will come tomorrow. Would it make a difference now? She thinks about the phone call, days ago now; how she still didn't come.

Leah gets up and stands a while at the window. She's still a little unsteady on her feet after days in bed drifting in and out of dreamless sleep, and she feels a deep ache in her womb that travels all the way up to her heart. Her reflection is mirrored in the little grid window and Leah studies her sad, bruised face and its mournful expression. She finds it easy in this moment to access the empathy for herself that Kristina always speaks of.

She stands at the window a long while looking out at the beautiful night with crystal clear skies awash with billions of stars. She's about to put clothes on and get ready to go when she hears a sound. Footsteps approaching. A muffled cough. A series of firm knocks on the door as knuckles strike the thick timber.

46

Kristina

She's buried in fresh snow which I brush easily away from her face, but the back of her body is welded to the ground by older layers of snow that have hardened into solid ice. There is nothing but a fleshy crater where the left side of her sweet, familiar face was. Her right eye is intact but grotesquely rolled back in her skull. The rifle points its cruel black mouth straight at her.

On impulse, I touch her hand with my own, as though my touch might make her leap back to life, but she's cold as ice and as hard. I scream, and it is my screams that suck me from these impossible moments, back in time and into the blank patches of my consciousness. It isn't Leah I'm looking at, it isn't Leah at all anymore, there's nothing Leah about these mangled remains. I can smell the bitter, rotting-egg smell of gunpowder trapped in the pit of my brain – it must have been there all along, stored away. I can see the strange maroons and grays and purples hidden inside skulls, blasted open and exposed, like the vivid wet cores of smashed melons. I know these images; they were just removed from my consciousness like words with correction fluid, invisible but nonetheless still there underneath, black on white.

I become aware of my own high-pitched, uncontrollable screams ripping through the air and force myself to physically clamp my mouth shut with my left hand. Whoever did this to Leah could still be roaming the woods. But she did it herself. She wrote that. No, she said she was going to the lake. She must have changed her mind. Or someone must have hurt her after she'd already written the note. Anton – it must be him. And he could be on his way back up here, right now.

I have to get help. The snow is still falling heavily, and there is nothing visible to mark the spot where Leah lies; she'll be covered again by the time anyone can get here. How am I going to direct the police or emergency services to the exact place? I point the phone to the grotesque remains of Leah, my hand shaking violently, and open the camera function. I take several pictures, but have to stop and retch, spitting mouthfuls of bile into the snow at the harrowing sight of Leah's shattered face, even more brutal in the light of the flash. *It's not her, it's not her*, I tell myself out loud, fighting the urge to start screaming again – *it's not her. This isn't real.*

I can't control the wild gallop of my heart or my shallow, panicked breath, and I begin to run, hurtling down the steep incline of the narrow path, stumbling over slippery rocks and partially buried roots coiling from the earth, and it must be under one of the bulbous roots my right foot slips and catches, bringing me crashing to the ground, and it must be against one of those sharp rocks my head strikes because in an instant the white night is replaced by solid blackness.

47

Kristina

I'm in space. Silent technicolor explosions tear into the velvet backdrop of the universe, sending soundwaves across light-years, tearing my skin clean off and melting my insides. My consciousness drifts into vast clusters of swirling green gas. It goes from green to ocean blue, then deep indigo, before it gathers again, drawing together into bulbous clouds of electric blues and pinks and neon orange that collide and burst into white flames, streaking and pulsating across the black.

No. I'm not in space. This isn't air, it's water. The water is black and so cold that my limbs have grown stiff and numb and I sink slowly, slowly, like a statue thrown into the deepest part of the ocean. I try to move my hands and feet but they are entirely unresponsive to my commands. I hear something, a muffled sound traveling slowly through the water, but can't discern what it is or where it is coming from. It grows louder and then louder still, and it seems to be a siren, with prolonged wails followed by silence, but then I realize it is music. Rising and falling, closer and closer, until it is crystal clear, a warm, trembling vibrato, produced by an expert hand. I feel overcome by emotion listening to the cello, and just then, it seems as if I reach the bottom of the sea, my body settling onto something firm after all the falling. Like the water, it's cold and dark. The bottom is entirely smooth so this must be a pool rather than a lake or an ocean.

I'm aware of something foreign in my mouth – a pebble, a rock, a snail, a fragment of metal? I try to spit it out but my mouth is filled with water. I push whatever it is away with my tongue, and it finally slips from my mouth. Slowly, I feel about the bottom of the pool, and my right hand seems to regain some of its movement and I realize I'm not in water at all, but on the ground. I'm so cold, colder than I've been in all my life, the kind of cold I know to be dangerous. Some life and movement seeps back into other parts of me. I wave the toes of my right foot and they move. I try the left but a wild pain crashes over me, like I've been struck by an ax. I clench the muscles in my jaw and they tighten. I try to open my eyes, but they won't. I touch a hand to my face and the right side feels almost normal, but the left is a swollen, unfamiliar landscape of tender bumps and stinging cuts. I rub my right eye gently and after, I'm able to open it a little to look around.

I'm face-down on the ground, shrouded by a layer of fresh snow. I vaguely recall stumbling through a snowstorm, my foot catching on something, falling. The terrible reality of the afternoon returns to me – *Supernova*, the remote cabin, finding her note, then Leah herself. I remember the terrible gaping mouth of the gun. Leah's one rolled-back eye, her violet lips peeled back, the meaty hole in her face.

How long have I been unconscious? It's unlikely to be more than a few minutes, but the snow is still coming down heavily. I pull myself up and feel around for my phone, but it's nowhere to be found; all I can make out in the meager light is the unbroken shroud of bone-white snow, except for a spray of blood above where my head landed. I turn my head slowly and now I can make out the mound I mistook for a fallen tree, I've clearly been unconscious for long enough for the snow to cover her again. I shudder at the thought of the two of us out here in the night, side by side in the clearing, struck still, snow falling silently onto us until we are entirely covered and one with the landscape.

There is a strange feeling in my mouth and I run my tongue around it. A tooth toward the back of my lower left jaw is missing; this must be what I spat out when coming to. In its place is a disturbing hole and fresh blood surges to its surface as I probe it with my tongue.

A searing pain tears into me, shooting up my leg when I try to flex my left foot gently. My ankle is broken, without doubt. If I hadn't regained consciousness when I did, I don't think I would have lasted a half hour in this cold. I'll die out here if I can't get back to the car, but how? I remember the long walk up to the cabin through the woods from where I parked; it took me at least fifteen minutes of brisk walking to reach it, on uneven terrain, and that was before the snowfall. There is simply no way I could make it back, not with a broken ankle, in the dark, in an unfamiliar place. I could fall again, or get impossibly lost, and either way, I'd freeze to death before morning, my body entombed in ice like Leah's. I don't want to die.

'I don't want to die,' I whisper out loud, and even my voice hurts. I begin to cry because the pain in my foot is so intense. My mind darts to a wild animal caught in a trap and left to die. I bring my hand to the racoon trim of my parka jacket and cry even more. My head spins.

I very slowly drag myself up so I am standing on my right foot, using an upended tree trunk for support. I run my hands across my torso and over my head and find everything more or less in its usual place, with the exception of some very sore points at the left side of my skull and jaw, and quite possibly a broken rib. I can't help but cry out loud as my fingers travel across the bruised side of my face. My fingers are so stiff with cold, their tips are numbed beyond any real sensation. With the exception of the broken ankle, I don't think I am dangerously injured, though the state of the left side of my face is worrying. An image of Leah that last day comes to mind – how I must resemble her now, eyes bruised shut, covered in bloody scratches, terror etched on my face.

I have no choice but to try to return to the cabin. Maybe I'll be able to find some bandages and something to splint my left leg with, and tomorrow morning I might be able to drag myself back down to the car in the daylight. Or at least find my phone and call an ambulance. I'll light a fire and eat whatever I can find in Leah's cupboards, then I'll sleep. Everything will be better tomorrow; I have to believe that.

I burst into tears again at the thought of my own bed at home, and how every night I fall asleep next to my husband, drawn close into his warm embrace. But not tonight. How could I have been so stupid to come to a remote cabin by myself? Telemark is a big county, with thousands of cabins scattered across remote and mountainous terrain. Nobody can find me here.

I try to hop up the slippery path in the direction I came, but I can't place any weight at all on my left foot, and after less than a couple of meters, I fall back down. I scream with the pain; it is unlike anything I've felt in all my life. I make myself get halfway back up so I'm on my hands and knees and begin to drag myself up the path. My hands claw at the slushy snow and the sharp rocks underneath, tearing at my skin, and I also have a nosebleed, making droplets of blood drip onto the snow as I inch forward. The snowstorm has momentarily eased up and the dense clouds have parted to reveal patches of inky black sky. Pinprick stars twinkle merrily and it feels as though they are taunting me – a lone, broken woman crawling on her hands and knees across snow-covered rocks, up an inaccessible forest track to an isolated cabin.

I keep going. I have to, or I die.

'I don't want to die,' I whisper, over and over. I really don't want to die, not here, like an animal, no, not at all, and the truth of that makes me want to both cry and laugh at the same time, because nothing could be a stronger sign of how far I've really come. How incredibly far I've succeeded in removing myself from the rock-bottom hell of my life as it once was, how I've turned trauma into triumph, building a valued life for myself with my husband who adores me. I think of my husband and my home every inch of the way.

The white porcelain Jonathan Adler vase Eirik bought for my birthday, filled with a riot of tulips. Five inches forward. The antique hand-painted silk lamps we bought in a tiny shop on a back street of Montmartre many years ago, casting our living room in a cozy, homely glow. Another five inches, the sickly taste of blood at the back of my throat. Our deep bathtub, big enough for two, the feel of the mosaic wall tiles beneath my fingertips as I soak, eyes closed, a glass of red on the shelf to my right. Ten inches forward, a wave of pain. The way it feels to be pleasantly trapped beneath my husband in bed, his skin on my skin, his hands in my hair, his voice murmuring into my ear. Five inches more.

I become aware of a strange sound, a low, animal-like grunting echoing up and down the narrow shaft of the path, slicing through the trees. It rises into a wail, then a high-pitched keening, and I realize that it is coming from me – the pain tearing through me manifested in sound. I don't want to die, but in this moment I am convinced that I will. I have no strength left in my hands, my fingertips are raw and feelingless, my head is pounding and strangely light, like everything that normally fills the conscious mind has seeped out into the white night. What I want now is to lie down. To give my body to the earth. To be cocooned in dark silence, to feel some peace.

'I don't want to die I don't want to die I don't want to die,' I try to keep whispering out loud but the words die on my lips. *Come on, Kristina. Come on.* I can feel a voice speaking to me inside; it's so strong, it's physical, like the rush of blood through my veins. In my mind, I see a girl. A young girl. She's in the woods, like the broken woman on the snowy hillside in Telemark. She's going to die, and she knows it. But she doesn't. She is going to get out of there and build a beautiful life. She will leave those woods. But still, the woods won't ever really leave her.

I inch forward. I follow the girl. She's crashing through the forests, screaming. She doesn't want to die. She wants to become whatever it is she'll become, if only she lives. She wants to see her parents again. She wants to lie in the narrow bed in her childhood room, following the slight tear in the wallpaper with her eyes in the soft darkness, just one more time. I follow her desperate sprint in between impenetrable patches of shrubbery, across clearings, across streams, alongside a dirt track, into a tiny hamlet with a single meandering mud track alongside which sit squat gray brick houses with tin roofs and black gashes for windows. She screams. People come, rubbing sleep from eyes, muttering in a foreign language.

She lives. She goes home. I open my eyes.

The cabin is there, just yards away, its middle window still lit up invitingly by the oil lamp I forgot. I drag myself over to it, then through the door, collapsing on the floor, shaking and retching. The gray slate tiles feel warm and smooth beneath my fingertips. Fresh blood rushes from my nose onto the tiles, dripping onto the dried blood stains already there. I close my eyes. I thank the girl that was me in my head for showing me how to live.

48

Kristina

I drag myself into the bathroom and crawl onto a turquoise Berber rug between the bathtub and the compost toilet. Its lid is shut and I manage to pull myself up onto it. I'm shaking uncontrollably and my fingers are a strange shade of gray-blue. I blow on them repeatedly and after a while I feel some warmth return to them. I manage to slowly peel off my jeans, though the pain as I graze my left ankle is so intense it momentarily takes my breath away.

I inspect my ankle and foot in the faint light from the oil lamp on the shelf above me. The skin is unbroken, but grotesquely swollen and bruised. I very gently run my fingers across where the fracture seems to be, and even the lightest touch provokes an onslaught of pain. I open the bathroom cabinet where I discover that Leah thankfully kept an impressive supply of painkillers. There's ibuprofen, paracetamol, codeine and, impressively, oxycodone. I take two dry – there's no water in the tap – Leah must have a summer cistern or get it delivered in tanks for the warm season. Cabins like this one often don't have water in the winter – the pipes would freeze. In the cupboard I also find sterile compresses and bandages. I manage to stand up for a moment, catching sight of myself in the small mirror. My face is swollen and almost unrecognizable. The skin is broken in several places, with mud and pine needles pressed into the cuts and scratches. I spit on my finger and rub the dirt away gently before sticking the compress over the entire side of my face. I hold my own gaze for a long moment, almost mesmerized by the terror in my own eyes. *It's okay*, I tell myself. *It's going to be okay.*

I lower myself very gently to the ground and crawl into the main living space, and when I take infinite care to not brush against anything with my ankle, the pain is just about manageable. Like I thought I remembered, there are some scraps of kindling in the wood basket by the hearth. I choose the longest and firmest pieces and press them gently in place to support my ankle in a splint, while winding the bandage tight. When I finish, the pain has softened somewhat, probably a combination of the bandage and the Oxycodone. I sit by the side of the hearth, in the exact place I imagined Leah before, singing to herself and drawing warmth into her body. I layer four logs with kindling in between and place some scraps of old newspaper into the gaps between them. When I strike a match it takes immediately, sending big flames leaping into the chimney.

I sit here for a long while, feeling warmth return to my limbs. Occasionally I look across the room through the little grid windows at the dark night beyond. All the clouds have disappeared now, leaving a huge moon hanging high in the sky. The snow has stayed on the ground and the little clearing sparkles in the moonlight. It must be getting late, though how late, I can't tell without my phone. Nine o'clock maybe? Eirik might be back at his hotel after dinner. Maybe he's trying to call me. My phone will ring from under a thick cloak of snow, if it even works still.

The shock and fear have given way to numbness and an almost overpowering fatigue. I decide to look for coffee. I need to think, and I don't feel ready to lie down to sleep in this place, among Leah's possessions. The very thought of it makes my skin prickle into goosebumps on my arm.

Once I have fully regained my warmth, I make my way over to the kitchen nook, supporting myself on bookshelves, backs of chairs and the side of the little Chinese cabinet as I go. There is instant coffee and a kettle, but I don't understand how to make it work without electricity. I follow the cord from the little countertop refrigerator down to the floor, where it disappears into the large, humming generator, almost as big as the appliance itself. I realize there are plug holes around its sides and connect the kettle. In a cupboard I remember seeing several bottles of Imsdal bottled mineral water, and pour half of one into the kettle.

I drink my coffee black by the side of the hearth, gazing into the flames. It is utterly delicious, and for a long moment I feel a strange calm, considering the circumstances. It could be even worse, I suppose. I made it back to the cabin. I have firewood and coffee. I won't die from these injuries. All I have to do is get through the night. But what if whoever killed Leah comes back for me? Or did Leah kill Leah? My mind is spinning. She left a suicide note saying she'd drown in the lake, and yet she ended up shot on a hillside. I take several deep breaths. *Control yourself, Kristina*, I say to myself. I am safer here than anywhere else in this moment, no one knows I am here. All you have to do is get through this night.

I let my eyes travel again across the numerous books that dominate the room. Several copies of Leah's own novel are displayed on a shelf, I hadn't noticed them before, in Norwegian, Swedish, English, French, Portuguese and Italian. I could choose any one of them and make my way to the windowless, cozy sleeping alcove tucked away in the corner of the room, reading until I am able to fall asleep. And tomorrow will bring light, hope and rescue – I have to believe that.

And yet, inside, I know what I crave. I try to resist, because I decided I couldn't bear to read another word she wrote, and don't want to know of any more ways Leah might have infiltrated my life. None of it matters now – she's dead in the most tragic of circumstances and her misguided actions will have no further impact on my life.

What did she hope to achieve by following me around and writing about my life? I try to run through all the possible scenarios, but my brain is dull and uncooperative. It also feels impossible to spend the long night here alone, and choose not to know what she was trying to tell me. I inch across the room to the sofa and settle myself into it before opening Leah's MacBook and opening the document. She would have been pleased to know she has my full attention now – that's what she wanted.

49

Supernova

You'll be familiar with exposure therapy. It may come as a surprise to you that, so am I. According to *Psychiatric Times*, exposure therapy is defined as, 'any treatment that encourages the systematic confrontation of feared stimuli, which can be external, such as feared objects, activities and situations, or internal, such as feared thoughts or physical sensations'. Consider this entire account exposure therapy, Kristina.

I'm getting ahead of myself. I've mentioned Carúpano. I bet it horrified you. I'm not doing this to torture you, I only want your life to be perfect. Selfishly, I suppose I need you to be perfect, and the only way you can be perfect is if you're whole.

What we're going to do here is to rewrite the stories you tell yourself. You see, like any good journalist, I've done some research and some fact-checking, and it would seem things aren't quite how they looked at first glance. Your dissociative amnesia came as a surprise to me. A trauma therapist marred by trauma; you couldn't make it up. A doctor of psychology dedicating her life to the extensive exploration of the inner life, and yet your own remains steeped in shadows.

I've been thinking about how to best do this, and came up with the idea of a 'guided walk through the mind' approach. Bear with me, I've actually done a lot of research into this. It'll be a bit like that meditation bit in yoga; I know you like a bit of vinyasa flow, you told me yourself in your diary. See, I pay attention.

Let's start off with the mental image of a large, beautiful house. It's modern and sleek, in a good part of town. The house is your life. Your marriage is one room, your friendships another, your career a third. Your past is downstairs, and behind one of several doors is Carúpano. But you've nailed that door shut and plastered over it, making it indistinguishable from the smooth white walls. We're going to open it.

How? And why? I can almost feel your questions, across whatever time lapse separates us. How did I know? It wasn't that hard. It's pretty public knowledge if you know where to look. But I know more than them. More than everyone, including you, it would seem. Why, is arguably more interesting. I want to put you back together. I believe that if we build a picture and reconstruct what happened, then the white patches in your mind will become colored in, and you'll be able to move on. Here goes.

Your mother is a delight, isn't she? Not sure I understand why you're cold toward her; at least that's how she feels.

She told me herself. It was easy to get her to talk. I must say she's a talker, unlike you. It was difficult to find my angle of approach; you can't just turn up on someone's doorstep and get them to divulge intimate details about their family members without rousing suspicion. You need to establish a connection over something they care about, build a sense of trust. Finding out where she lives was obviously easy; I must say I love how almost everyone in Norway's address is listed on 1881.no, from the moderately famous to the very wealthy. Bærum, huh? I suppose I should have guessed you'd grown up somewhere fancy. You have that rich-girl privilege; that's the thing about you I find hard to acquire as my own. As you know, I didn't grow up like that and it's hard to fake when you don't know all the nuances and cues of privilege.

Your house wasn't fancy, though, and that's where I lucked out. I spent some time on Google and discovered that the row of semi-detached houses where you grew up were scheduled to be demolished by the council to allow the new E18 motorway extension to bypass Sandvika. Most of the residents had accepted this and taken the generous payoff, but a few refused to budge, delaying the expansion of the new road. Your mother was pictured on the cover of *Bærum Budstikke* with two neighbors, holding a poster reading 'E18 over my dead body'. Passion and fury – great. I had my angle. All I had to do was call her and tell her the truth – that I was a journalist freelancing for several national newspapers interested in speaking with her. She may have mentioned it to you – I even succeeded in getting them some coverage.

We got on well, your mother and I. So well that she quite

happily chattered on about her family and her kids when I prompted her about what a fantastic place it must have been to raise a family. She told me of your father's impressive career as a leading geologist and that it had been hard, sometimes, to be married to a man who is more interested in rocks than in sex and conversation. This made me laugh, genuinely, and it made me wish I could laugh with my own mother like that. Yours is very different from mine, though you've probably already concluded that a long time ago based on what I've told you in our sessions. Yours is funny, a little scatter-brained, full of energy and with tons of plans for the future. She's trusting, too trusting, but I guess that is not so strange when you've been married to a man more interested in rocks than sex or conversation for over forty years. Everyone needs someone to talk to, and someone to feel close to.

She told me all about your impressive and exhausted sister, both surgeon and supermom, fighting tirelessly on that battlefield of career and children. Then she told me about you.

She is, in fact, practically a hero, said your mother. She lowered her voice when she spoke of the terrible trauma you'd endured in your late teens, and of how you'd turned your life around and become a highly respected psychotherapist who contributes to international research and has made a name for herself, specifically in the field of trauma. I gently encouraged her; I know how to make people talk. She made more coffee, reassured herself that I wouldn't speak of this to anyone, and of course I reassured her – the empty promises of a stranger. She dropped her voice as though you were there somewhere in the house and might walk in to learn of your mother telling a stranger the things you don't even talk to your friends about. Or your husband.

Her hair dropped out, she said. *Her skin broke out in scales. She lost her period and it never returned to normal. Personally, I believe that it was the trauma that robbed her of the chance to have children.* I asked, carefully, about the trauma, and she told me that you and your two friends were held at gunpoint in Venezuela. *She went there with her two best friends, Elisabeth Eliassen and Trine Rickard.* This rang an instant bell and I felt exhilarated; it was the feeling of discovering a crucial piece of a puzzle. Rickard – it was one of the names on the doorbells of the building in Rosenborggata 11, where you go on Fridays after seeing me. And Elisabeth – the name in your diary. *They thought they had to travel across the world to that dangerous country to find themselves. Only Elisabeth and Kristina came back, but they didn't come back as themselves.*

She spoke for a long time; it was clear that she needed to get something off her chest.

Everything she told me became part of the backdrop. I didn't yet know what to do with it, or where I was going with any of it – I just wanted to be close to you. At that point, I was driven by needing to prove my illusion of you as perfect, because if it was possible for you, then it might be possible for me. I didn't know, then, that it would be up to me to piece you back together.

It was your mother who first told me about Elisabeth. She spoke of a sensitive and beautiful little girl with natural charisma and a love of the arts who'd lived just next door – she pointed to the left, and my eyes traveled through the windows into the gardens outside, yours and Elisabeth's separated only by a low hedge, and it was almost like I could see two little girls out there, running through sprinklers, chasing a ball, playing hopscotch.

She turned out badly, said your mother, her face grief-stricken.

After, I went home and hit Google, as one naturally would. It wasn't hard to find the old articles about the three girls from Bærum who were held hostage in Venezuela back in 2003.

'The Trine Rickards Tragedy,' read *Aftenposten*'s headline. 'The nineteen-year-old aspiring vet was traveling around South America with close schoolfriends, Elisabeth Eliassen and Kristina Hellerud, when she was shot at point-blank at a private address on the outskirts of Carúpano on August 24th. *It was, quite simply, an execution*, says Jorge Aruelo, police chief in the Eastern Venezuelan region of Sucre. A local man with an already extensive criminal record, including several drug-charges as well as assault, Xavier Miguel Rodriguez, was apprehended at the scene and will face trial for first-degree murder.'

'The murder of innocence,' read *VG*, dated three days after the attack. 'One life lost, another two shattered. The surviving girls of the Carúpano shooting, Elisabeth Eliassen and Kristina Hellerud, of Sandvika, Bærum, are receiving trauma therapy in Caracas after Thursday's brutal attack. They are receiving support from the Norwegian foreign office in Venezuela, and are expected to return to Norway later this week.'

I opened a third article, this one in *Dagsavisen*. 'Rickards, who recently turned nineteen and was a graduate of Sandvika Gymnasium, had spent most of the summer working at 7-Eleven in Bekkestua to save money for the trip of a lifetime, traveling around South America for six months. Excitement turned to tragedy just two weeks into the trip, when the Norwegian trio decided to hitchhike in the notoriously dangerous northern Sucre region, after several scheduled buses failed to showed up. The girls were picked up by Rodriguez, who brought them to a house party at a private home near Carúpano. According to the witness statement of Elisabeth Eliassen, they stayed for several hours, taking drugs and drinking alcohol with Rodriguez, his brother and several others. At one point in the evening, Rodriguez, an unidentified second man and the three Norwegian girls retreated to a gazebo in the grounds of the house, bordering the surrounding jungle. It was here Rodriguez brought out the weapon and threatened the girls when they refused to perform a sexual act on himself and the other man. The girls tried to run, but Rodriguez fired the gun straight at Trine Rickards, who was killed instantly. Elisabeth Eliassen and Kristina Hellerud managed to run off into the jungle in the commotion that followed.

'Hellerud was recovered several hours later, disorientated and dehydrated, a few miles away in the Macarapana area. She remains in hospital care and is said to suffer from cognitive impairment as a result of the incident. Elisabeth Eliassen managed to reach the main road and flagged down a vehicle. She was brought to the Hospital General de Carúpano, where she was reunited with Hellerud the following day, before being transferred to Caracas at the insistence of the Norwegian Consul General, Einar Johannessen.'

I was so shocked to learn what you'd been through. It changed everything. I had to know more. I suppose I wanted to know how it had affected you and how you could have survived something like that and gone on to seem so whole. I pored over the images of teenage you and your two tragic friends. Blonde-haired, blue-eyed Trine, tiny next to you and Elisabeth who are both so tall, smiling in every picture. Trine was obviously the goofy one, unable to resist a peace sign behind your head, or crossing her eyes, or sticking her tongue out.

What kind of monster could point a gun at her head and pull the trigger?

Elisabeth seemed more concerned with striking a pose; she was probably quite aware that she was the most physically striking out of the three of you. You seem insecure and more anonymous than your friends in the pictures, and in more than one, you were looking at Elisabeth in the moment the flash went off, as if to gauge how to pose, whether to smile.

I spent a lot of time thinking about what your mother said, and what happened to you. I thought about it so much that it almost felt like I, too, was there and that I'd shared the experience with you. I could practically feel the fear you must have felt crashing through that terrifying forest, all alone, the sound of the gunshot reverberating in your head. I saw what you must have seen – the girl crumpling to the ground, a spray of blood lingering for a moment on the air that had held her, fragments of her skull landing on your skin. I could smell the sweet scent of rot on the air, the sulfur of the gunpowder, the cruel murderer's rancid body odor. I built these images in my mind obsessively, not really understanding that my preoccupation with them was just another of my brain's escape fantasies.

I was even jealous of your trauma, Kristina. It's true. I think what I mean by that is that I craved a tragic story of my own, something as big and shocking as the Carúpano shooting, that would explain why I have spent so much of my life feeling so empty, so ravaged by grief, so utterly alone. I had an absent father and a self-obsessed mother who doesn't like me very much, and a failed marriage to a man who rejected me in myriad little ways every day, but those things aren't exactly reasons to feel so broken. Or are they? You always made me feel like my feelings were valid, whatever they were. When I think back at how you used to make me feel, I miss you so intensely that it takes my breath away. I wish we could go back to that time when I'd sit across from you in our sessions and drink in your kind, attentive presence, when you were all I needed, and entirely mine for fifty minutes each week. I wish I hadn't done what I've done.

For a while, knowing about Carúpano made me even more obsessed with you. It was so moving and impressive that you'd moved on from a tragedy of such magnitude and built a good life for yourself, a life in which you managed to offer support to others who suffered trauma. I put two and two together and realized that you paid a weekly visit to Trine Rickards' parents, presumably out of the kindness of your heart. It wasn't hard to understand the conflicting emotions around those visits, and why you clearly sometimes couldn't face going. I assumed that you'd be haunted by impressions and memories of that terrible night all those years ago, the images that came so easily and convincingly to my own mind when I thought about it.

What I didn't know back then was that I'd conjured up memories you yourself don't have. Cognitive impairment, said *Dagsavisen*, but what did it mean?

I'm getting ahead of myself. I was overwhelmed by sympathy for you and your plight; I couldn't stop thinking about what your mother said. That your hair fell out, that you couldn't have children, that you had basically hauled yourself out of the flames and soared into the sky like a phoenix, like a hero: those were her exact words. I also thought about the other survivor, charismatic and beautiful Elisabeth Eliassen, clearly the ringleader out of the three of you, and wondered what her life might be like now. *She turned out badly*, your mother said, and when I thought back to that conversation, her choice of words made me angry, because it was exactly the kind of thing my mother might have said about me. *She turned out badly*, meaning – *she turned out different to me*.

I became curious about this woman who, like you, had survived unimaginable trauma but 'turned out badly'. I made a mental note to find her.

50

Elisabeth, June

The group has fallen silent without Elisabeth noticing. She's been lost in thought, staring at the strange imagery of the painting in front of her. She realizes that Arne, Villa Vinternatt's visual arts therapist, has stopped in front of her and has clearly asked a question.

'What?' she whispers.

'Do you want to share something about your painting with the group?'

'Um.'

Arne watches her carefully. His face is kind and open, but when he turns to study her newest picture, done during the morning's two-hour session in watercolor, his eyes change expression and he frowns.

'What do you think this picture is trying to tell you?' he asks.

'Umm.' She stands up, takes a couple of steps back and stands shoulder to shoulder with Arne, considering her work. She glances around the room, at her fellow residents craning their heads to get a clear view, and catches Joel's eye. He raises an eyebrow slowly and gives her a little encouraging smile.

'It seems to me that this picture is quite different from most of the images you've produced here in these sessions, Elisabeth,' says Arne.

'Different how?'

'Does anyone else want to contribute? Does anyone have an idea why I believe this picture is a clear departure from Elisabeth's general style?'

'It's certainly more explicit,' says Gina, an older woman with scraggly black hair and teeth stained an impressive shade of yellow.

'Continue,' says Arne.

'Well. In most of Elisabeth's pictures, the themes seem to be pretty abstract. You might see bloodstains, I might see the inside of a jam jar, Joel might see something else entirely. But this... This is, like, obvious.'

'What do you see, Gina?'

'Well. A river. Of blood. A dark, busy forest. Uh. Lots of life somehow. Bugs, bats, those faces among the trees.'

'Faces?' Elisabeth blurts it out, her eyes returning to the painting, and only then does she see them: faces indeed, distinctly human, and ghoulishly twisted into terrifying grimaces that bleed into the dense foliage of the forest.

'Elisabeth?' says Arne. 'You sound surprised.'

'No. No, just I didn't realize that they were so obvious, that's all.'

'Can you tell me about this?' Arne points his finger to the top right-hand side of the picture, where a little brown bird, painted meticulously and in more sophisticated detail than the rest of the scene, flies in between deliberately childishly drawn, yellow five-point stars.

'Um... No.' She has rarely felt this tongue-tied in a group therapy session; usually Arne's art sessions are her favorites, but today she feels strangely discombobulated and dissociated, entirely unable to decipher any meaning in her own imagery. The task they were given was to 'paint yourself in nature'.

'Would I be correct in assuming the bird represents you?'

'Yes. Yes, maybe.'

'It looks like a happy bird.'

'Yeah.'

'And yet, the scene it flies over is very disturbing.'

'Yeah. Yes, I guess it is.'

'A blood-red river, threatening faces among dense trees, a real sense of danger.'

'Mmmm.'

'But the bird is free.'

'Yeah,' says Elisabeth, blinking at sudden tears in her eyes.

51

Kristina

I shiver lightly at her words. My mother. I can't believe Leah has really gone that far, seeking out people in my life and striking up contact with them, but she clearly has. The problem is, Leah is certainly mistaken if she thinks that she could uncover some deep, dark secrets about me by speaking to my mother. There are no deep, dark secrets to uncover. It's all right there, on the internet, like Leah herself says.

Could she really have gotten to Elisabeth, too? I can't imagine it would be possible; Elisabeth spent the last eighteen months of her life in a rehabilitation facility with limited visitor access. I think she would have mentioned it to me if someone had come around asking about me, no doubt about that. But what if she didn't?

Leah was clearly completely destabilized, and I have truly failed at picking up the signs of how disturbed she really was, but how much damage has she managed to do? Leah speaks of missing pieces of puzzles, of unlocking the doors to the past, as if my life was some fucking story to be reconstructed for her twisted entertainment. I hate her smug, misinformed voice and find it impossible to reconcile with the Leah Iverson I thought I knew. The reality of what she has done is shocking: she sought out my mother, who, like Leah said, likes the sound of her own voice, and possibly poor Elisabeth too. It explains a lot. Everything, in fact.

I don't know why Leah became obsessed with what happened to us in Carúpano, but I think she's right about the preoccupation with someone else's tragic experience being a way for the mind to escape its own reality. I see it sometimes in clients who become unusually preoccupied with events that ultimately have nothing to do with them, such as a plane crash or a terrorist attack.

What happened to us in Venezuela was a terrible tragedy, one that has defined my life in many ways, but still, I have built a life beyond it. I committed to my own healing and I was able to move on past trauma by accepting its presence and integrating it into my experience. It's true that I was more fortunate than Elisabeth in the way my mind and body processed the attack – I haven't been forced to endlessly relive what happened or been haunted day and night by what that man did to us.

Why is Leah hell-bent on dragging this back out into the light? I feel sick at the thought of her seeking out Elisabeth; she was a very vulnerable woman, and especially in the last months of her life. She would have been easily won over by someone as devious and convincing as Leah. She might have told her things that were untrue, or irrelevant, or dangerous, or all of those.

Elisabeth was confused and unreliable in the months before she died in August. More than once, she relapsed with both alcohol and marijuana, and I had to use my professional relationship with Villa Vinternatt's founder for leverage to allow her to stay on the program after breaking the strict policy on total sobriety. She also showed worrying signs of distorted memory and reality perception. She'd ruminate over her relationship with Andreas and make it sound like it was the greatest love story in the history of the world, when in reality it was a disastrous five-year descent into hell, defined by an endless cycle of co-dependency, addiction and chaos. She'd paint and draw obsessively, and her incredible talent was clear for everyone to see, but her art gave an insight into the turbulence of her mind – she'd paint blood and violence and that jungle she wasn't ever able to leave behind.

She began to say worrying things, and at times she took her underlying anger out on me. One of the last times I saw her, she called me a 'Fucking golden girl who lives in a fucking golden bubble with my fucking golden husband,' and I had to work hard, then, at controlling my own reactions to her. I knew that what she said really had nothing to do with me or my life, and everything to do with how deeply disappointed and ashamed she was about the mess she'd made of her own life. I knew that it wasn't my fault that she couldn't find healing and peace.

Loving Elisabeth in those last days required merging friendship with therapy, but I loved Elisabeth; she was my best friend in spite of everything, and I tried everything in my power to save her. I really did.

I feel overwhelmed with dread thinking about Elisabeth

and how she ended her life, and the thought of Leah insinuating herself into her life is unbearable. Highly unstable herself, she might have directly contributed to the way things turned out for Elisabeth. Looking back, I can see how she might have influenced Elisabeth; toward the end, she went from being seemingly content and more at peace than she had been for many years, to becoming so angry and so bitter. At the time I suspected that her treatment at Villa Vinternatt was making her question everything and that her new pursuit of art had brought all those feelings to the surface. I tried to redirect her focus to the future, to everything she could still become. But she refused to let go.

My head and the bruised side of my face throb with increasing intensity. My fingers hurt and still feel strangely numb. My stomach aches and growls. And my ankle hurts so badly the sensation of it almost goes beyond pain, like if you put your hand into a flame and watch the skin burn but feel a wild heat rather than pain. It must be late in the evening by now, but it's hard to tell because the moon is hidden behind thick clouds and I can see from where I'm lying on the sofa that the snow is falling heavily again. I close the computer to preserve the battery; it's just gone into power-saving mode and I doubt I have more than another half hour of power. I haven't seen the charger anywhere, and it's not like I can easily move about to search for it. I need the bathroom and it takes me at least ten minutes to get there. I find that the easiest way to move around is to sit on the floor and very gently push my way backward.

Still, I cry with the intensity of the pain and by the time I return to the sofa, I'm trembling with exhaustion. How will I ever make it back down to the car? And how will I get through the night, with nothing but Leah's insane account for company?

52

Supernova

Many days have passed since I wrote this account up until this point. In the meantime, terrible things have happened. When I first started this, it felt powerful and exhilarating, like all the pieces just magically slotted into place. It just flowed, at long last. Night after starry night, the words came rushing out, just how I intended them, like a piece of music masterfully coaxed from an ancient instrument. For every day that passed I lost hope that you might come, that we might sit across from each other here in this room, like I'd envisioned, finally united in truth. But for every day that passed, it mattered less, and a slight hope began to grow, that writing this account of the truth might come to matter just the same. But then the baby left me, Kristina. I can't bear it. It made me realize the outcome will be different now. There will be no happy ending. I can't, won't, can't, stay. But I decided to finish this, first. Why? Because I wanted someone to know the whole truth. My truth. We're arriving at a crucial point here, something I've been staving off and also building up in my head. Perhaps what's happened to me in the meantime can bring the right rawness to what happened to you.

Someone once told me that when it comes to writing, you start off with an earthquake and then work your way up to the climax. It's strange, how something seemed to loosen inside me once I started writing to you, and on some level, I must have known all along that we'd end up here. Back there. I meant what I said about exposure therapy, that it will help you, so I've tried to rebuild what happened. I feel I know these scenes so intimately it's as though I was there myself. I wish I could see your face as you read my words. I wish I could know if I got it right. If I helped.

You run excitedly towards the dirty grey Mazda sedan purring impatiently by the side of the deserted road, exhaust rising into the night sky. You scoot across the back seat and try to get a glimpse of the man behind the wheel, but you can only make out a smooth brown neck and longish black hair curling at the tips. You feel a wave of trepidation and fight the urge to slip back into the night, but you immediately feel silly – after all, there are three of you. Elisabeth and Trine rush into the car, giggling and breathing exaggeratedly after the little dash up the cracked tarmac towards the car. Trine's bare legs squeak against the leather seats. Elisabeth mutters, 'Hola,' and, 'Gracias,' and then all three of you giggle again, a hollow nervousness creeping into your voices. The man steps on the gas and the car surges off, fast.

When someone had finally stopped, you'd squealed and clapped your hands, it felt like you'd been standing there for hours in the hot, dusty air. You know that hitchhiking in Venezuela is a bad idea, but you also know that you need to free yourself from the over-protectiveness of your parents back home, and that young people need to have adventures. Wild adventures – that was the whole point of this. Besides, Elisabeth and Trine are convincing co-travelers and you know better than to question their plans. Mostly, you just do what they say.

You glance at them now, watching shadows chase across their faces as the car speeds north towards the coast, bringing those sandy palm-fringed beaches you've been dreaming of closer.

Carúpano, Elisabeth had said as she got in the car, and the man had nodded, so presumably he'd understood. It isn't far, less than thirty minutes, but the bus you'd planned on taking never came. While you waited, you drank tequila from a roadside shack and danced in the violet twilight with your best friends, well aware of the stares from the men populating the plastic chairs to the side of the makeshift bar. You smoked cigarette after cigarette, stubbing them out with the heel of your flip-flop. After a long while, feeling warm and woozy, you started walking, leaving the few lights dotting the steep hillsides of the little crossroads town behind. Then it got dark. Elisabeth and Trine had stuck their thumbs out every time a pair of headlights appeared in the distance, but not a single car had even slowed down, before this one.

The car stops. The jungle has grown denser and stands like mountainsides on either side of the road. A long sliver of moonlight spills down the empty road, making it appear liquid, like a river snaking through the forest. You glance down at your hands, held gingerly in your lap. A childhood memory flashes through your brain, random but clear;

those same hands gripping the handlebars of your first bicycle, purple and white streamers flying behind you as you tore down the streets. You look at Trine and Elisabeth, but they are both quiet and serious, now, like you. Your eyes have adjusted to the darkness and you can make out a narrow dirt track disappearing into the forest from the patchily asphalted main road.

The man turns around and only now do you finally see his face. It is a beautiful face, with soulful black eyes set beneath thick brows, and full lips spreading out in a slow smile at the sight of you. His cheeks are sweetly dimpled, and a long scar runs from the outer corner of his eye all the way down to his stubbled jaw, as though a tiger had clawed him. A small snake is tattooed on his throat, its red serpent tongue flicking upwards to the man's chin. You can't help but take a stunned, sharp breath of air. He'll come back, this man, in your dreams and in your waking moments, and maybe you know already now that you'll never be free of him. You'll write about him in your diary in twenty years' time, when you'll be a respectable, married woman with a beautiful home and a rewarding career. You'll write about that first moment. About desire coursing through you like a white heat. You won't feel desire like it again, not ever, not with anybody. Is it even real, such a sudden and uncontrollable explosion in the synapses, at the mere sight of a stranger? In your own words – *an instant surrender of everything I knew, everything I thought I was?*

I'm on my way to a party, he says, in almost fluent English, nodding towards the dirt track. *It's an awesome house. Overlooking Playa Hernan Vasquez. My brother and a couple of friends are there. Come and have a few drinks with us.*

Trine shakes her head almost imperceptively. Elisabeth says nothing, but looks at you for direction. A glance passes between you, and she *knows*, she'll always remember the look in your eyes. At the time, she would have called it the look of desire, or love, even, but much later, she'll realize it was the thrill of danger.

Yes, says Elisabeth. You coyly break the man's glance; you know instinctively to leave him wanting more.

How does it make you feel, how *his* life turned out?

53

Kristina

I close my eyes. I have to. I feel myself disappearing down into the empty spaces inside myself, back in time, back to the place I never allow into my thoughts, there is no point anyway – there's nothing but a milky nothingness there.

But now it is as though the scene Leah describes colors in the white patches in my memory. Where my brain has always drawn a blank when it comes to *him*, I now suddenly and distinctly remember the serpent tattoo on his throat, his soulful eyes and deep dimples, the scar on his cheek like a river on a map. In spite of Leah's extremely limited understanding of dissociative amnesia, it's true that huge patches of my memory were simply erased. I spent my early twenties in intense therapy to heal and to try to retrieve the memories of what happened in Venezuela – like Leah, I believed back then that remembering would be the only way to move on. In the end, Ingvild taught me that acceptance was more important than full recollection, and besides, we knew what happened because Elisabeth was there.

I open my eyes briefly and they flood with tears. I close them again and now I see *him* clearly in my mind's eye. I can't recall the rest of the scene – the car ride and the words he spoke, what we were wearing and what thoughts might have run through my head, but Leah has succeeded in sending me back there, to Carúpano. The forest that surrounded the futuristic beach house set high above a pristine bay we were brought to was as dense and ancient as the one surrounding this cabin. Instead of being snow-covered and silent, the jungle of Carúpano was sticky warm and buzzing with a plethora of sounds. The sounds of lives lived in the undergrowth, in the trees, in the air above them, a ceaseless chattering of a thousand species. This I remember. And the deafening gunshot.

'Why?' I whisper into the cool air of the silent cabin. 'Why are you doing this to me?' I have to know why. And, Elisabeth – what have you done?

54

Elisabeth, July

The dining room looks and feels very different. No longer witness to the chattering of residents and clinking of cutlery, the commissary tables and long benches are gone and replaced with row upon row of white sheets like sails awaiting their ships. The exhibition, titled 'Recovery Reframed', is the first of its kind in Norway and seen as a groundbreaking attempt to rehabilitate some of the country's most prolific drug addicts by restoring their art careers left in ruins by addiction. Similar programs have already met with great success in New York and London, and Oslo is keen to follow suit.

The management of Villa Vinternatt is busy organizing the installation, and the stress of it all is etched on their faces. Carpenters are still busily constructing the gallery while staff meticulously pin small white description cards to each piece in an attempt to make some sense of what the artist is trying to convey. The media has taken quite an interest in the story and several journalists are expected to attend the vernissage, hoping to speak to the artists themselves.

Elisabeth is one of the most high-profile artists in the group and her series of five paintings all center on the recurrent theme of blood. She smiles to herself as she stands back and looks at her work, knowing that a part of her is on the canvas, her blood, guided by the brush strokes of her memories. Memories so dark that the only way she feels she can survive sometimes is to get them out of her physically. Nobody knows that she cuts herself. The inside of her mouth hides the lacerations; it's one of her many secrets and it brings her a strange thrill to know that her blood is there, unhidden, on the canvas for everyone to see. Her haunting imagery sees wild animals, scared, trapped and abandoned, fused against a bleak swirling landscape of rich earthy tones. Bloodshot eyes, bloodied mouths, bleeding wounds, blood-emptied open bellies.

Her thoughts are interrupted by a junior counselor asking her to change as the guests will be arriving in the next thirty minutes. Elisabeth makes her way back to her room and rifles through the few items of clothing in her wardrobe. It actually hasn't occurred to her that it might be nice to wear something special on a night like tonight. She throws on a navy chiffon blouse and the only pair of trousers she owns that aren't sweatpants, adding a flick of mascara and a touch of lipstick. Perfume is banned at Villa Vinternatt because it contains alcohol, as if she would glug her favorite Chanel, and the thought makes her smile impulsively at herself in the mirror. Her palms start to sweat as she heads back to the dining room, the hum of voices rising up the stairwell from the formal reception rooms downstairs.

All the artists are asked to stand next to their work, like schoolchildren awkwardly showing their finger-painting skills at parents' evening. Elisabeth guesses it is mainly so that the press and members of the local community can more easily tell the druggies from the staff. Elisabeth wishes Kristina were here tonight. It feels almost impossible that she isn't – all these years later, Kristina remains her main source of support and comfort, more so than her elderly mother. But Kristina is in Hamburg at a conference about rapid eye movement therapy. Elisabeth asked her if there was any way she could move it around or even not go so that she could be there tonight, but Kristina had to go. Elisabeth understands, of course she does, but glancing toward the wide double doors at the throng of people waiting to be let in, she has to swallow hard at the thought of Kristina not being among them.

The members of the local community hover at the entrance, like vultures circling high above carrion; nothing like ogling the inner thoughts of a bunch of junkies. It was only a few years ago, under the old management, that the residents were nicknamed the Vintanutters, a term that still endures many years later.

Elisabeth goes through the motion of explaining her pictures and answering the usual questions from well-meaning people who have no ability to understand what she's been through.

'What made you take heroin?'

'It looks like real blood; well done. How did you manage that?'

'Why don't you paint happy themes?'

'Do you think you'll return to drugs?'

'Do they lock the doors at night here?'

'You don't look like a drug addict.'

'I suppose prostitution must have been part of that whole life, eh?'

She turns away from the man asking the question mid-sentence and walks out of the room. In the next room, where the larger sculptures of some of the residents are displayed, she catches the eye of a young woman, a tall, attractive woman in white jeans and a blue-and-white striped blouse. The woman smiles at her, and she smiles back in passing; she's on her way to the bathroom to splash some cold water on her face and get a moment's peace.

'Hey. Hey, wait,' says the woman and Elisabeth turns back around to face her. When she does she is struck by a sudden familiarity, and then it occurs to her that the stranger in front of her bears a slight resemblance to Kristina. It's something to do with the smooth bronzed skin, the understated style, the gold stud earrings and the chocolate-brown, expensively highlighted high ponytail. 'Are you Elisabeth Eliassen?'

'Uh, yes?'

'I'm familiar with your work. I really wanted to speak with you. My name is Ella Victor, I'm a journalist at *Dagbladet*.' Elisabeth shakes the woman's hand and lets herself be gently led by the elbow back through the throng of people to her canvases in the next room.

'Your work is fantastic,' says Ella Victor, looking past Elisabeth and gazing to the pieces strung from the ceiling, focusing intently on each one in turn. 'You've really captured the essence of something quite frightening here.'

'Thank you,' Elisabeth replies, blushing slightly at the praise. Sometimes she thinks her work is so dark that nobody could ever see past the darkness and see beauty there, too. She looks at Ella again and there is something about the way she stares at her that makes her suddenly afraid – it's not Kristina she reminds her of now, but one of the animals circling her in her dreams. She takes a big sip from her glass of orange juice and feels like laughing out loud at her own ridiculousness.

'Shall I tell you about this one?' she says, pointing to the middle canvas and Ella nods enthusiastically, any trace of imagined threat gone from her eyes.

55

Supernova

You moved on. You healed. I get it. It's what people do. You did your own long years in therapy and it made you reflective and aware of your own reactions and contributions – I suppose those are the things we all hope for when coming to therapy. Your training taught you real insight into yourself, I imagine, to the point where your inner life became subject to understanding and empathy, and perhaps this was one of the things I sensed and which so drew me to you. You know how to forgive yourself. You believe that you deserve it. I want that for myself. Especially now, as you will come to understand.

Let's move on, so much ground to cover. Another thing that impressed me about you was your obvious ability to maintain, and thrive in, a long-term partnership. As you know, this isn't an ability we share. It feels as though whatever I do and whomever I do it with, I leave nothing but pain and destruction in my wake. Take Emil, for example, that guy I dated last year; you might remember him. A good man, and someone who was endlessly patient with all my whims and insecurities and issues. I dropped him over and over, until he was so bruised by me that he'd lost all sense of himself. Still, he'd come back for more. Like a dog.

I guess it was just me replicating the behavior I'd learned from Anton, and even earlier, from my father, hooked on the emotional rollercoaster ride of loving men who have nothing to give you except rejection and abandonment.

I lied to you about Anton. I lied to the whole world about Anton, didn't I? We hurt each other; it went both ways, that's the truth. Before I came to therapy, it was me who hurt him. But last Friday, before our session, it was Anton who hit me. It was him who did it. He punched me in the face and that was actually the first time he ever physically laid hands on me. By doing it, he actually turned my lies to truth.

And because of my book, I got trapped in a web of lies about what happened between us. Much of that book was made up; it was partially fiction, after all, but everyone thought it was a precise account of our relationship and hailed me as a domestic abuse survivor, when the truth was a lot more nuanced and rather more boring.

So I let everyone believe that I left Anton in the end, that he attacked me and left me in fear of my life. I adopted the persona of the brave but downtrodden abuse victim because I just couldn't bear the truth that sat beneath the surface of my skin like a never-ending itch, impossible to escape. It's what I told you, even. *I realized that I had to leave to survive*, I'd say, smug as fuck. I lied because I was too ashamed to tell the truth, even to you. In the book I preached about self-love and the need to protect the flame burning inside myself when I had no fucking concept of either of those things. I still don't. But they sounded good, and they were what people wanted to hear.

Who would want to read a story about a cold marriage from which the main protagonist actually doesn't want to leave, where she deep down welcomes constant rejection and cruel ridicule because they are the only things that confirm what she believes to be true about herself? People want happy endings, stories of strong women who overcome abuse and build shiny, wholesome lives.

But it was Anton who left me and I'd suppose you would say that it triggered that underlying wound of my father leaving me. It unleashed a wild, primal grief. He'd been indifferent and cold toward me throughout our marriage, occasionally throwing me an intoxicating little bone of affection. I was obsessed with really winning him over and mistook my hurt over the fact that he had one foot out the door for excitement. I bent over backward trying to make him stay, compromising myself more and more; I couldn't bear another man walking out on me. I begged him to stay, but he didn't even react, just looked the other way. I would have preferred being hit to his indifference. I'd never known shame like that. Or anger. I can still see his look of surprise when I slammed my fist into his face, breaking his nose. I clawed at his skin and pummeled him and pushed him down the stairs. Then I threw myself down them, too, breaking my collarbone and giving myself severe concussion. I told everyone I got a restraining order against him, so nobody would suspect that the actual story was rather different.

Nobody believed Anton's version of events, especially after the book came out. We didn't speak for years. But

I'd go by his apartment sometimes at night and watch the shadows of his flickering television from across the street. I'd lie in bed and dream of him holding me, making love to me, hurting me even. I just wanted to be held, Kristina.

Then I got what I wanted. He came back last year. Because I'd lied about Anton being physically abusive, I couldn't exactly tell you that I was seeing him again. I was in therapy then, of course, and I just couldn't find a way to tell you. I'm still not quite sure why I lied to you about this, but I had fallen in love with the victim role and wanted you to feel sorry for me. And I guess it was hard to admit that I was so pathetic. I couldn't tell you that the more therapy I had and the more I began to grasp the underlying patterns that led to my behavior, the more I lost interest in Anton. A man suddenly committed to staying was unfamiliar and uninteresting to someone as messed up as me. I began to seek thrills elsewhere. I began to sleep with men who were willing to act into the never-ending cycle of hurting me and leaving me – it's what I know.

And now, it's all over. So much is lost. I'm afraid of myself.

But for you, it's different. You don't court drama and pain and rejection and abandonment. You have a solid marriage. And you've held onto it. Without drama, and with what appears to be an above-average level of happiness. Just look at all those interviews your impressive husband gives. He never fails to mention you. It's like he thinks he's married to a saint. His rock, he calls you. His inspiration. *I'd be lost without her*, he said recently. *Me too*, I thought, scrutinizing the photograph of the two of you – a classic Norwegian shot of an outdoorsy couple climbing some mountain or other, beaming at each other, a broody and barren valley rolling away behind you.

It must be nice to be loved like that.

Someday, your husband will be prime minister if he has his way. And it seems to me that this guy mostly has his way. You'll be propelled to the forefront of our society then; the intriguing other half of Norway's leader. The media and the public will be interested in you – you're rather different from those who have gone before you. Much younger, with a fresh look and a rock-solid education, a respectable career and a winning, unassuming way of being. You have made yourself so inoffensive, so inconspicuous. You've built a life so ordinary, but so beautiful.

They'll find out about your past, of course. It's not like it's a secret anyway – a simple Google search will give it away. It's a long time ago now, but your past will without doubt be brought back out into the light when your husband ascends to the very top of the political hierarchy. Perhaps you'll give a tell-all interview to avoid any rumors and to elicit even more sympathy. People will cry for you. You will cry for yourself, too, like I already know you do. At night. Right now, probably. Sometimes when you're driving. On Friday evenings, walking back home, your eyes locked hard on the blur of pavement, not noticing your surroundings, or me, twenty yards behind you.

You'll realize by now that I've done quite a bit of homework. Learned to talk your talk. According to betterhealth.com, dissociation is, 'a mental process of disconnecting from one's thoughts, feelings, memories or sense of identity. The dissociative disorders that need professional treatment include dissociative amnesia, dissociative fugue, depersonalization disorder and dissociative identity disorder.'

I want you to understand that you were the victim. To really understand it. I believe that you blame yourself. That's where the anger comes from. And the control issues. Did you think I didn't notice them? The way you arrange the tea bags is a dead giveaway. The way the photographs were hung at your house, I just know you obsessed about the distance between them. The calculations in your diary move me to think that you're trying to work out the mathematical probability of what happened to Trine Rickards.

I've wondered whether you really can't remember, or if you have become so good at control that you don't allow your mind to be whole? Either way, it must be lonely. Especially now that Elisabeth is dead. It must be so hard to not know why *she* died. I imagine you believe she committed suicide because of the endless cycle of addiction. That she just couldn't stand it anymore. Except that wasn't why. I tried to tell you. I tried to talk to you about it. I wanted to be there for you. Haven't you always said to me that the truth is never ugly, unlike lies, and that we will live better if we live by it? She committed suicide because of you. Elisabeth died to protect you. She loved you so much because you're worth that much love. But before she died, she told me what she'd been carrying for so long. And I need you to know, because otherwise it will keep hurting you in myriad ways – you need to know and then you can be free. This freedom is my parting gift to you.

56

Kristina

take a break here. I'm sick of Leah Iverson playing some fucking cat-and-mouse game with me. My mind is spinning and I don't know what to think or feel about anything anymore. In spite of everything, I feel sorry for her; it's terrible to think of her sitting here in this cabin, losing her baby and clearly having some very dark thoughts and, by all accounts, a serious mental breakdown that resulted in the delusions that make up *Supernova*, only for Anton to return to kill her. I know he did, and either he made her write that note or she wrote it before he got to her. I glance out the window at the black night. Could it be that he'll come here again? He could turn up here tonight, and might try to cover up what he's done to really make sure it looks like suicide.

I shiver violently and my pulse is so high I keep bringing my hand to my throat to feel it. I feel strangely light-headed. A part of me wants to try to get to the kitchen nook and drink the bottle of wine in the fridge. I'm desperate to numb my mind but I equally know I need to stay sharp to get out of here alive.

I reread the last few sentences over and over again. I almost want to laugh. *She committed suicide because of you. Elisabeth died trying to protect you.*

For a moment there, I was getting worried about where she was going with all this. Now, it's merely laughable. *Oh, Leah, how could you have got it so wrong?*

57

Elisabeth, July

She loves many things about being here and this surprises her every day because she hadn't anticipated relaxing into her surroundings or feeling at home. She can't recall summer ever being more beautiful than here – the vast neon-green lawns rolling down toward the steely water of Drøbaksundet, which in turn leads to the inner Oslofjord. So close to the capital, but light-years away. The incredible orange and pink roses growing on scraggly bushes alongside the path leading to the beach. The emerald forests climbing the hills behind Villa Vinternatt, unmistakably stern and Nordic, nothing at all like the dense, humid jungles that haunt her.

In the afternoons, after lunch, she likes to sit out in the garden, sketching, even when it is chilly like today. Just basic charcoal sketches on plain notepaper, depictions that don't need to carry any meaning at all. She especially likes to capture the elegant line of a bird wing caught in flight, or held close to a little bony body, or touching its tips against the surface of the sea. Today, she is drawing a small sparrow perched on a bird feeder hanging from one of Villa Vinternatt's enormous oak trees. It twitches its wings, draws them close around a fat, fluffy belly, stares at her with its black pinprick eyes. She spends a long time on the texture of the feathers; it's hard to capture their lightness and near-translucency in contrast to the sturdier, coarse feathers underneath.

When she moves her gaze from the bird to the path running from the terrace at the back of the house through the garden toward the beach, she notices that a woman is walking to her. There is something familiar about her, and Elisabeth narrows her eyes trying to place her. One of the new members of the rehabilitation team? The woman stops in front of Elisabeth and she turns the drawing over: she's self-conscious about her work until it has matured. The bird scrambles up into the upper branches of the tree.

'Elisabeth?' asks the woman. Elisabeth nods, still unable to place her. She doesn't think they've met before, but the woman reminds her of someone. She is tall, though not as tall as Elisabeth, and has thick chestnut-brown hair streaked through with lighter strands piled on top of her head in a deliberately messy bun. Her skin is a beautiful, smooth, sun-kissed brown, and she has wide-set hazel eyes realizes that it is Kristina the way she carries herself, *bohemian artist witch*, Kristina sometimes jokes. *But that's what I am*, Elisabeth would respond.

'Yeah?'

'My name is Ella Victor. We met briefly the other day. At the vernissage.'

She remembers, then. Of course. The journalist; they'd spoken for a while and she feels stupid now for not remembering, but all the years of drug use have taken their toll on her brain.

'Ah. Yes. I do remember.'

'I wanted to stop by and speak with you again, if that's okay. I really loved your work. I've never seen anything quite like it before. Such emotive pieces.'

'Thank you.'

Ella sits down on the bench next to Elisabeth and for a long moment they sit in a comfortable silence.

'What were you drawing earlier?'

'A bird.'

'Could I see it?' Elisabeth looks over at Ella and there is something about the warmth in her eyes and her kind smile that makes her trust her. She nods and flips the notebook over to reveal the unfinished sketch of the bird.

She glances down at it and sees it as if for the first time; it's really good. 'Wow,' says Ella. 'I was wondering how I could support you.'

'Well, you could buy a ꜰ. guess. If you wanted. T⸍

at re⸍

'I'm sorry, Elisabeth. I should have explained. freelance at the moment, and I'm thinking about wri. non-fiction book. About art therapy and trauma.'

'Oh.'

'When I saw your work, I wondered if you might be interested in contributing to the project.'

'Oh.'

'I'm thinking of choosing ten or so promising artists who have experience with trauma and who incorporate it into their art as part of their healing process.'

'Oh.' Elisabeth feels her cheeks redden, she always feels numb and speechless when asked about her past or her artistic process. 'I don't know... I don't think...'

'You could be anonymous if you wanted.'

'Umm.'

'It would be my goal for the book itself to be cathartic for the participants.'

'I'm not sure I'd fit that description. About, uh, trauma and using it for healing...'

'Oh. Okay. Well, of course no pressure whatsoever.' She's going to get up and politely bid this woman goodbye, but maybe because she seems so gentle and trustworthy, or maybe it is because she reminds her of her best friend, Elisabeth surprises herself by speaking of the things she never speaks of anymore.

'I paint a lot of blood,' she whispers. 'The way it is such a symbol of death and destruction, but really it is the very essence of life. The other day... I painted actual blood into one of the paintings. One of the ones in the vernissage. Watching it merge and darken with the paint and become part of a thing of beauty – it made me feel good. Like

...ng ugly could become beautiful someday.' When ...ops speaking, she's surprised and also moved to see a ...een of tears in Ella's eyes.

'That's the picture I want to buy,' she says.

Later, in the night, she sits on the windowsill and looks out at the shimmering, moonlit sea. She considers painting, or maybe finishing the bird sketch, until she gets tired enough to hope for sleep. She'd felt light after speaking with Ella, and it took her by surprise. It had felt good to speak to someone not paid to care for her, someone who knows nothing about her history, other than that she is obviously a recovering heroin addict.

Though Elisabeth has spent years in therapy and various rehabilitation programs, it is different speaking to a friend, and most of her friends have dropped away by now. Many have died of overdoses, a few have managed to stay clean and understandably have to cut out everyone from that old, dark life of using and abusing, and then there's Kristina. Where Kristina comes across as so infuriatingly perfect and calm and centered, Ella seemed a little rougher around the edges, a little more real. Still, Elisabeth misses Kristina and cherishes her monthly overnight stay away from Villa Vinternatt at Kristina and Eirik's house.

It's just hard, sometimes, to be around Kristina. The two of them started life side by side with very similar family backgrounds, and they went through the same school system and moved in the same circle of friends. They went through the same traumatic experience in Venezuela. And yet Elisabeth spiraled downwards, all the way to rock bottom, and stayed there. Kristina found a way back up, and though Elisabeth is happy for her, and impressed with the success she's made of her life, she can't help but feel a little bitter and jealous. Kristina Moss, the mind doctor who was saved by the dysfunction of her own mind. If she could remember what really happened in Carúpano, she'd be on her fucking knees. Elisabeth remembers, and keeping it secret is like bleeding slowly to death from an invisible wound.

58

Supernova

Everything that has happened is because I love you and wanted to be like you and wanted to keep feeling what being near you made me feel. It doesn't excuse what I've done. I've done bad things.

The image in my mind when I think of you and the way you live is this: a charmed, honed life, nothing left to chance. An inner life picked to pieces and analyzed inside out. Back to the house analogy – I want to take it even further. If you were a house, you'd be a sleek modern one with symmetrical lines and huge floor-to-ceiling windows looking out at an equally unblemished landscape. The house would have carefully arranged sections of expensive furniture – glass tables, flattering mirrors under warm lighting, soft leather chaise longues, never-sat-on white sofas. Other than that it would be empty. But under the house, where its foundations should sit on impermeable rock, is a vast, black space. The house sits precariously on a couple of wobbly stones, and far below the world you pretend to live in is another world. A dark one.

Now, we need to move forward. I'm so tired, so empty, wrung inside out. I can't know what you will do with these words. Perhaps you've already abandoned them. In a way it wouldn't surprise me if you had, I could imagine you might simply walk away and never look back if you suspected that something might compromise you in any way. It's not a bad thing to be self-protective but I'm not going to lie, I hope you're still reading. And listening carefully. We are going to be covering a lot of ground here, both past and present, and you will come to see that your life is enmeshed with mine in many more ways than one.

Onto the next thing. The big thing. Kristina, we need to talk about your husband.

59

Kristina

I can feel Leah's hands reaching for me through time and space, closing around my throat and squeezing tight. She's like a determined little dwarf star that sidles up to its unsuspecting neighbor and sabotages it until they both go up in flames. I can barely breathe. *Onto the next thing. The big thing.* I don't want to know what she is going to say about Eirik; I can't bear the thought of Leah having uncovered something sordid that will destroy my marriage. Because she's right about one thing – my life is built on unstable foundations, like most people's lives, and I need my husband.

My head is literally spinning with an onslaught of thoughts. My mother, Elisabeth, Venezuela. And now, Eirik. I realize that the dread I felt as I got deeper into the *Supernova* document is precisely this – that Leah would stop at nothing, that she'd go from my mother and Elisabeth to Eirik, bringing my whole life crashing down in some misguided attempt to get close to me.

I move a little, positioning the MacBook more comfortably across my lap, taking care not to graze my left ankle against anything, and yet a terrible pain chases up and down my leg. The battery is down to nineteen percent. It's still relatively early and I'm nearing the end of the document; I should be able to get through it before the battery runs out. The question is whether I can bear to read another word. It is profoundly disturbing how wrong I got it with Leah Iverson. I look out the window at the sky, still opaque with white clouds.

I'm still staring at the frozen, white world outside, about to return to the screen, when a peculiar blueish light sweeps across the snow outside. A comet? I push myself back up against the cushions to a more upright sitting position but the shift hurts my ankle so badly I cry out loud. The light appears again, bouncing across the dark shapes of trees at the edges of the clearing, then shining straight into the window. It remains there, held in place, its unbearably bright light projected directly onto the timber wall behind me. It is, without doubt, the beam of a very powerful flashlight.

60

Kristina

'm a calm person. I'm calm even now. I'm not someone who
gives into wild panic or irrational thoughts. This isn't true.
I'm terrified. *Calm down, Kristina*, I tell myself, slipping
quietly from the sofa and onto the floor. The beam of the
flashlight is roaming the little cabin, as though whoever is
holding it is inspecting it from every angle before deciding
what to do. I push Leah's MacBook under the sofa and
begin to crawl toward the entrance. When I first came here,
I noticed an ancient pickax hung in the space between the
bathroom and the front door. It could be there for decorative
purposes, or it could actually be that Leah used it to split
firewood – either way, I'm glad it's there.

Stop, I tell myself. Whoever it is, they're way more likely
to help me than to hurt me. Unless it's Anton. He might
have just come out of police custody and headed straight
here to cover his tracks before the police realize what he's
done. I'm in no doubt he'll kill me in cold blood if it's him,
and in my current state that won't be difficult.

The beam from the flashlight is being moved alongside the length of the wall as if whoever is holding it is walking slowly around, inspecting the cabin. I drag myself across the floor, trying hard not to cry with the pain from my ankle. Whoever is outside seems to be moving toward the front door. I am obviously unable to outrun anyone, so what do I do? What part of a normal life might prepare you for something like this? Do I unhook the pickax and hold it in my hand just in case, risking looking utterly insane in the event it's just a random neighbor who may have heard my screams earlier or seen the unfamiliar car parked at the head of the track leading to the cabin? But there are no neighbors. The track is used only for Leah's cabin.

If not Anton, who? Who else might have known Leah was here and come looking for her? Her mother? Could it really be Linda, unsettled after being contacted by the police about Leah's whereabouts? From what I've heard about Leah's mother, she is primarily concerned with her own pursuits and would be unlikely to get in her car in Årjäng and drive for hours and hours just to check whether her daughter is okay.

My heart shudders in my chest and I pause for a long while, listening. There are no sounds coming from outside, not even the gentle rustle of swaying trees. I pull myself up by the door frame and unhook the pickax from the wall.

Calm down, Kristina, I tell myself. Surely a crazed killer wouldn't announce his arrival by shining a powerful flashlight in front of him? And surely the odds of encountering a murderer the one time you find yourself trapped in a remote cabin in the middle of the woods are fairly slim. I turn around and look back into the living room, but the roaming beam is gone and only the murky night lies beyond the windows. Could I have imagined it? Is this the beginning of a total loss of my faculties? My head, like my heart, is throbbing; I hit it badly when I fell and could be concussed.

I hear something. A sharp cough. A man's voice muttering. Then the muffled thud of footsteps on snow, approaching. I tighten my grip on the pickax's wooden handle, biting into my bottom lip to stop myself from crying out loud. Then someone grabs the door handle and shoves it hard without knocking, and because I must have forgotten to lock it when I dragged myself into the cabin earlier, it shoots open inward, bringing a surge of icy air.

Part III

POINT-BLANK

61

Kristina

The pickax is wrenched from my hand by someone much stronger than me and dropped to the floor. I am picked up, gently, and carried. I am held. I am rocked back and forth, my face pressed into a broad chest, the sound of a hammering heart beating directly into my right ear.

'Jesus Christ, Kristina,' says my husband, over and over. 'Jesus Christ.'

Eirik has placed me on the floor by the hearth on top of a sheepskin rug and a thick down duvet taken from Leah's bed. He swiftly and expertly examines me, running his fingertips across my bruises and my bones. I watch him, feeling a flood of love rush into me, as if it were being injected directly into my veins. His hair, still wet from the snowstorm, glows in shades of chocolate and amber and coffee in the flickering light of the flames. His face is serious and concerned and I have to fight the urge to laugh. It must be shock. He found me. Eirik found me here against all the odds. I'm not going to die up here by myself.

'Broken,' I hear him say.

'What?'

'The ankle is broken, in two different places. I think your cheekbone is fractured, too.' My husband's eyes shimmer with tears and he looks around the cabin. He runs his hand through his hair and presses his thumbs into his eyes. He must have driven straight here after I messaged him. I feel giddy with love for him, this man of mine who drove through the night to my rescue, like a hero.

'Happened.' I see his mouth forming words and I hear them without being able to understand what he says. It's as though I am separated from Eirik by an invisible membrane, like hearing him speak through water.

'What?' I whisper. My voice is raw and painful. He says something again and I can't quite make it out. I close my eyes. Eirik kisses my neck, my face, my hands, and I sense his warmth. *Don't leave me*, I want to say, but I can't get the words to come. 'Please,' I whisper.

'Jesus Christ, Kristina.'

'Please...' *Please just hold me*, I want to say, but still, the words won't come, but it doesn't matter now, because my husband understands, and very gently lies down behind me, enveloping my body in spoons. I close my eyes for a long while, and my mind feels blurry and strange, as though it has simply crumbled now I'm safe and don't have to stay on high alert. I clutch Eirik's big, impossibly warm hand at my waist. I feel dizzy and nauseated.

After a very long time, I open my eyes. Where we're lying, we're facing into the living room. I can make out the outline of Leah's MacBook on the floor underneath the sofa, and just then, I remember her words, the terrible words I read just before the flashlight shone into the cabin.

Onto the next thing. The big thing. Kristina, we need to talk about your husband.

I need to think. And I need to know what Leah wrote next.

'Water,' I whisper. I need Eirik to get up off the floor so he doesn't happen to catch sight of the laptop. 'Please can you get me some water?'

He places me gently on the sofa, then sits down and places my head on a pillow in his lap. He strokes my hair, kneading out knots with his fingertips, tracing patterns on my scalp. I try to muster all my focus to gather my thoughts, but the fuzzy dense feeling remains. I sip water and watch the flames still dancing in the hearth. I think about Leah's MacBook on the floor, just centimeters from my body.

'What time is it?' I ask. Eirik pulls his phone from his pocket.

'Eleven forty,' he says. 'No reception up here. In fact, not since I parked, next to your car.'

'How did you find me? I don't understand?'

'Honey, we need to talk.' I turn around so I can see his face. He smiles gently at me, his fingers still buried deep in my hair. 'Something very strange happened earlier this evening. When you messaged me, I had just walked through the door at home – my last two meetings and the dinner got canceled, so I caught the four o'clock flight back to Oslo. I figured I could always fly back to Bergen on Tuesday morning and I was going to surprise you. I knew you have had a lot on your plate recently and I knew you were feeling stressed about the situation with Leah Iverson, after everything you told me on Friday night. I was really worried for you. I was standing in the hallway, quite shocked to read that you'd set off to find Leah, and that she'd written about you, when the doorbell rang. It was a man, asking for you, and when I said you were out, he grew really agitated and so I went down to street level to speak to him. He seemed completely out of it. A young, kind of squat guy with these light-blue eyes. Quite a scary-looking guy. He said his name was Anton. I'm assuming that's the ex-husband?'

I nod. 'Yes,' I whisper.

'Okay. Seemed totally nuts.'

'What did he say?'

'He said… He said he was going to fuck you up since you'd called the police on him.'

'Uh. I don't. I don't understand…' I am trying to get my mind to compute that Anton came to my house.

'Then he literally ran off. Krissy, I was terrified for you. I called and called and called and you didn't pick up. I called the police, but without any other information there wasn't much they could do. I didn't know if he might have guessed you'd have come here to look for Leah, so I decided I had to find you before he did. Now, where is this woman? Leah.'

'She's dead.'

'What? How do you know?'

'I found her, outside. He's killed her.'

'Oh my God. How do you know?'

'I— she's shot. When I came here, I thought she'd committed suicide. She left a note…'

We stare at each other for a long moment.

'Wait. What? She left a suicide note?'

'Yes.'

'So she shot herself?'

'No. I don't think it would be possible. It was a big hunting rifle; she wouldn't have been able to turn a weapon like that on herself. Besides, she wrote that she was going to drown herself in the lake.'

'Wait, are you sure?'

'Yes. It's so tragic and shocking. She lost her baby. I think the shock of it massively destabilized her, and…' I have to pause for a moment, my voice is raspy and weak.

'Where is the note? Can I see it?'

'Yeah. Of course. But Eirik, there is something I just don't understand… How did you find me?'

'I found you on Find My iPhone.'

'Ah.'

'Clever, huh? When I'd got the coordinates, I went on Google Earth and screenshotted the map so I'd be able to find it even if reception was bad. There was only one cabin, so I knew this must be where you were. But Jesus Christ, how remote is this place? Why did you come here alone? I need to know what's happened. I've been so afraid.'

'I'm sorry, honey,' I whisper. And I *am* sorry. Eirik must have been terrified.

'Where did you find the note? And why did you she write about you?' I think of *Supernova* and the MacBook on the floor under where we are sitting. I don't know why, but I know I must keep its existence from Eirik for now. *We need to talk about your husband.*

His hands have stopped moving in my hair; he's waiting for me to answer. My heart is hammering so loudly it feels like he'd hear it if I open my mouth to speak. I take several deep breaths, calm my mind down, and tell myself that I have the tools to handle this.

'That guy. Anton. He told me that she was unnaturally preoccupied with me. And that she'd been writing about me,' I say. 'Like she wrote about him. I decided that I wanted to speak to her about it.'

'Why didn't you tell me this on Friday?'

'I don't know. I guess I forgot.' *Because I didn't know about* Supernova *yet.*

'And had she?'

'What?'

'Written about you?'

'I don't know. I've looked around but there's nothing. Just the note. And my diary.'

'Your diary? How did she get hold of that?'

'Honestly, I just don't understand it. She must have taken it from my office during one of our sessions.'

'Jesus, that's so creepy.'

'Yes.'

'You shouldn't have come here by yourself. You could have died out there.'

'I know.'

'So what happened after you found the note?'

'Well, first I found some bloodstains. In the bathroom and in her bed, and the note was on the pillow. She said she couldn't face the rest of her life after she'd lost the baby. By then, I was shocked and afraid; it had started snowing heavily and I worried I wouldn't find my way back down to the car. Then I found her, shot. It was so horrifying and

I couldn't help running away and then I fell badly on the steep part of the track. I was knocked unconscious.'

'Oh, baby.'

'I'm sorry. I'm sorry for everything...'

'Shhh. I'm here now.'

'Do you think you should go out there and do something? Bring her inside, or—'

'Honey, I can't bring her inside. It's best for the forensic team to be the ones to move her. But you're right, I should go out there. Is the weapon still out there? Did you see it?'

'Yeah.'

'I'll go out there and secure it, and cover her with tarpaulin.' I nod, trying not to think of the gruesome task Eirik has ahead of him, but when I close my eyes I see her, outlined beneath a shroud of snow, one hand curled like a claw. 'And tomorrow morning I'll go for help first thing, it's going to take at least two men to get you out of here. It would be straight-up dangerous for me to try to get you down to the road in the middle of the night in a snowstorm. The safest place until tomorrow morning, is right here,' he says, and his fingers start moving again, gently tracing little shapes on the skin behind my ears, before moving down to my throat and collarbone, pressing his fingers against the soft and firm parts of me under his fingertips.

Eirik detangles himself from me and places my head gently back down on the sofa.

'If I don't go deal with her right now, I'll talk myself out of it,' he says, stretching his limbs and staring out the window at the stormy night.

'Be careful,' I whisper. He nods and listens intently as I explain where I found her.

When he has gone I have to fight the urge to get the MacBook back out and quickly read the next section – I have to know what Leah was about to say about Eirik but I don't want to risk him bursting back into the cabin and asking questions about what I'm reading. I'm glad I don't because he returns after less than ten minutes carrying the rifle, his face pale and twisted into a terrorized grimace. He places the rifle back in its cabinet, then I hear him in the bathroom, retching.

'She did this herself,' he says, when he emerges from the bathroom after a long while.

'What? Why do you think that?'

'She removed the shoe and sock on her right foot and pulled the trigger with her toe.' I try to picture this scenario. Leah, so desperate she got the hunting rifle from its cabinet, took it outside, selected an apparently random spot on the hillside just off the path, and fired it straight into her own face. But I can't.

'Are you sure?'

'Completely. Jesus, what a sight. That poor woman. I saw something similar once, when I was in the military. A guy in my barracks blew his brains out with a rifle. Same thing, used his toe.'

'I… I just can't even—'

'Shh, my love. You're safe now. You need to sleep. Everything will be better tomorrow.'

62

Kristina

I fell asleep easily moments after settling closely against
Eirik in the comfortable, deep sleigh bed in the sleeping
alcove, my whole body heavy and aching. In the middle of
the night I wake with a start and the sudden movement
sends waves of pain up my leg and I have to bite my lip not
to scream out loud. Eirik shifts slightly beside me. I push
myself up against the pillows into a half-sitting position and
feel about on the nightstand for the painkillers he laid out
for me before we went to sleep. I take two ibuprofen and
an oxycodone. I can make out a faint milky glow from the
window high up on the wall, and realize it is still snowing.

This sleeping alcove seems to have been made by
integrating a storage space into the cabin, and not originally
intended for sleeping. I don't understand how it could be
possible to get this bed here, then I realize it must have been
built in place. I lie back down and close my eyes, waiting
for sleep to carry me away, but it doesn't. My mind is racing
with disjointed, strange thoughts. I keep seeing myself

running through the forest, the snowflakes biting my skin, those last terrifying moments before I fell to the ground, my screams hollering down the hillsides. This image bleeds into the other image, and I'm *her* again, the kid running for her life in the Venezuelan jungle.

The familiar nausea rises in me, the way it always does when I can't control my thoughts and they go to where I can't allow them to go, not ever, if I'm going to stay alive, if I'm going to stay Kristina; success story, survivor, wife, psychotherapist.

The contours of what Leah has actually done are becoming clearer. But did her snooping around kill Elisabeth? It was as if one of the blank patches in my mind disappeared when I read her words, rebuilding the scenes in Venezuela. The dirty Mazda. The clifftop house. Xavier, with the bottomless eyes and the slashed cheek and the warm hands and the rough stubble deliciously turning the skin around my mouth raw as he kissed me. The gun glinting in the moonlight.

Of course they will find out about your past, Leah wrote, *it's a simple Google search away.* Except it isn't. It's true that if you were to look, you'd find old media coverage of what happened in Carúpano; it was all over the newspapers for weeks. You might find some quotes from the witness statements I gave at the time, though my name was Kristina Hellerud then, not Kristina Moss, so you'd probably only make the connection if you were specifically looking. You might see the picture of me arriving at Gardermoen Airport, being met by my parents and the foreign secretary at the aircraft steps.

Do you ever think about how his *life turned out?*

He, too, must return to that night. For the first time, I try to imagine what his life might be like, and find that I can't. Another blank. What game is Leah trying to play?

Tears are flowing down my face and I snuggle closer to Eirik. I'm facing him now and though the light is dim, my eyes are used to the dark and I can make out the outlines of his peaceful face. His hair is cut shorter than usual, and I realize I haven't noticed this until now. His eyelashes are long and fluttering slightly as his eyes shuttle back and forth beneath his closed eyelids. His jawline, which was always strong and clearly defined, has softened slightly, and this makes me feel a flush of empathy for him. All those late nights at the office, too many dinners out of a delivery box. And all the while, I've been at home, waiting and waiting with dinner, until I inevitably give up and eat alone, scrolling on my phone. I don't mind so much most of the time, I'm used to it by now, but lying here like this, next to my husband in the dark, I am filled with such conflicting emotions.

I am overwhelmed by relief and gratitude that he managed to find me and came straight here. What would this night have been like without him? I also feel that deep, constant love for him that I've been able to hold on to throughout the years of our relationship and marriage – fourteen now. And I feel something else, something new and frightening. Looking at my sleeping husband, I feel a sliver of fear run through me for how little we actually know of another person, how little we can ever know of what goes on inside their head. Life, and love, are like therapy sessions at the end of the day – we only know what someone says and shows. But what about the things they choose to hide, and go to great lengths to keep hidden?

What have you done? I mouth the words in the dark. Could Leah have followed Eirik around like she followed me and found something out about him that she now wants to tell me about? She was jealous, that much is obvious. Obsessive. And yet, I felt that she and I had a good therapeutic relationship and that we made solid progress over the years she came to see me. Was it all fake? Did Leah play a role in our sessions while attempting to inch ever closer to me, motivated by obsession, or is it more complex than that? I wish I could go through to the living room and read the rest of *Supernova*. I *have* to know, but more than that, I have to tread carefully. There is something about the measured tone and the controlled patience of Leah's revelations that make me take her extremely seriously.

I very gently run my index finger across Eirik's thick eyebrow, smoothing the wiry hairs into place as I go. He barely stirs but purses his lips. *I love you*, I think. And – *I need you.* And – *What have you done?*

63

Kristina

'Honey? Honey, wake up.' His words reach me, but slowly and buffered through a dream. I try to open my eyes but it is as though they've been glued shut. 'Krissy, can you hear me?'

'Mmm.'

'Wake up.'

'Mmmm.' My right eye cracks open. My husband is sitting on the side of the bed, eyes puffy from sleep, dark stubble chasing up his neck, face serious.

'Jesus, Kristina. You had me really worried there. You wouldn't wake up.'

'Sorry. I... My head hurts. Uh. What time is it?'

'Just gone nine. I didn't realize it was morning; it's almost completely dark in here. Look, sit up. Bit of a problem.' Eirik helps me to sit up, positioning me carefully against the pillows and the wooden headboard.

'Ow.' The pain is significantly worse today than yesterday.

It feels as though I have been pummeled and then run over by a freight train.

'Look,' says Eirik and points across the living room to the windows facing out to the valley and the little lake far below. But we can't see any of that, in fact we can't see anything at all, because we are snowed in. When I was a child, we'd stay at my grandparents' cabin in Valdres and we'd get snowed in fairly often, waking up in a muffled, hushed cocoon. My father would have to dig us out and sometimes Camilla and I would toboggan off the roof of the cabin, which would only be a meter or so above the ground. I didn't realize it could happen as far south as Telemark, and especially this early on in the season – it's only just November.

'It's fucking crazy out there. I'll have to dig us out.'

Eirik half carries me as I limp over to the sofa. He places a large mug of freshly brewed coffee on the table in front of me.

'My poor girl,' he says, leaning in to plant a kiss on my cheek. Then he goes back to the front door and begins the slow and cold task of getting us out of here. He is wearing light jeans, a cashmere jumper and a lightweight down jacket, hardly the attire for unearthing an entire building devoured by snow, but it's not like he thought he'd have to do that when he set off from Oslo yesterday. As the cabin is built on a slight slope, the snow will be deeper at the back of the building where the door is, so the windows facing onto the valley might be a better bet.

'Try the windows, babe,' I say. I sip my coffee and focus on taking deep, even breaths. The combination of the strange, unsettling situation we're in and the terrible pain in my ankle is making my anxiety, which I have managed well for over a decade now, rear its ugly head. It's like the bubble of boiling water in the pit of my stomach. And it's like that moment after you realize you've seriously hurt yourself, before the pain crashes over you. A prolonged wince. I am itching to get back to *Supernova*, but I have to wait until Eirik has managed to get outside.

'Did you tell anyone you're here?' I ask. 'As in, is there anyone who might come and look for us if we don't return?'

'Like who?'

'I don't know? A friend? Bjørn?' Bjørn is Eirik's older brother, and they're close enough to speak several times a week.

'Nope. After that weirdo came to the house and I couldn't get hold of you, I just got in the car.'

'Thank God you did.'

We smile at each other and in this moment, I am overwhelmed by my love for this man. I know in my heart what a good man he is, and I'm furious with Leah for planting even a sliver of doubt about my marriage in my head.

'But babe, how are you even going to get back down to the car? It must be, what, two meters deep?'

'Yeah. Jesus. You're right.'

'You'll have to make your way out through a window and then dig the front door free from the outside. Then we'll have to focus on how to get you to the car or at least somewhere with phone reception.' Eirik nods and pulls his iPhone from his jeans pocket as though he might suddenly have reception in this most remote of places.

'Fuck, I only have twenty-six percent battery.'

'Where's the charger?'

'In the car.' We stare at each other. For a moment I almost feel the urge to laugh.

'You couldn't make this up.'

'Nope. Okay, no time to waste. Operation window leading to operation evacuate invalid wife imminently commencing.'

I smile at him and he smiles back, and in spite of everything it feels good to be here, alone with my husband.

It was his determination that won me over. Back then, when we met at the student union bar at Oslo University, he wasn't so special. He didn't yet possess that easy authority that he does now – that came with money and power and age, but he embodied a grittiness I hadn't seen before in a Norwegian boy my age. When you grow up in one of the richest countries in the world, where the school system is rather relaxed, and you're statistically speaking unlikely to have faced any real challenges in your early life, it's perhaps understandable that Norwegians often seem to be unusually laid back. Some might call it lazy, but it isn't that, exactly; it's more an ingrained belief that life doesn't have to be a struggle and so why sweat it? It's an easy enough attitude to cultivate in a country that has organized itself in a way that means life isn't too much of a struggle for most people. A lot has been achieved in terms of gender equality and bridging the class divide. People are fairly compensated for the work they do, there is little unemployment and a livable minimum wage. We leave work at four on the dot and most people have access to nature and use it frequently for recreation.

There is no reason to be fiercely ambitious, or work into the early hours – those qualities aren't expected or particularly celebrated. And yet, that is what my husband is like.

He needs to be top dog and best at everything. Those qualities could have impacted Eirik's likability but the reason they don't, at least not in my eyes, is that he only compares himself against himself. He doesn't gloat or make unfavorable comparisons to others, he merely acknowledges his victory and moves on. I wonder what he will do once he breaks through the ceiling of his own ambitions. Will he be able to just enjoy it and not chase the next achievement, or will he always be chasing the next thing?

He pursued me with the same quiet determination he goes about getting whatever he has decided he wants. He isn't forceful or flamboyant or overtly persuasive. But he's patient and secure in his own offerings. *It's a long game, Krissy*, he often says, and I think he means everything: life, and love, and his career. He seems to have been able to settle into our marriage without growing restless after a few years, and has always made a point out of idolizing me. This is something I have struggled with at times, because by repeatedly claiming that I am 'perfect', and 'the ideal woman', and 'ridiculously clever', he is actually subtly stating his expectations of me. I know he doesn't do it consciously but we have had many talks over the years about how I feel that those kinds of definitions feel like attempts at control. And yet I am lucky, because I have never had to doubt my husband's love or devotion. He has never given me any reason to grow suspicious of his actions or motives. But what if I haven't been looking in the right places? What if he has grown bored and unfulfilled in our marriage and started chasing the next thing, as is his tendency otherwise in life?

I swallow hard several times, trying to dislodge the raw hoarseness at the back of my throat. I watch Eirik unhook the window clasps carefully, running his palm against the blueish, densely packed snow outside. One window thankfully opens inwards, and I assume this must be intentional in the event of getting snowed in. Eirik begins to dig, using a metal mixing bowl from the kitchen, emptying the snow into the kitchen sink as he goes along. It is slow and painstaking work. He shrugs his jacket off, having grown hot from the physical effort of the digging and when I complain that I'm getting colder, he comes over and puts it on me, gently slipping my arms into the armholes as if he were dressing a child.

The last of the firewood is gone and to get more, we'd need to access the woodshed to the side of the front door. It occurs to me that if Eirik hadn't come to my rescue when he did, I would likely have died here, even though I made it back to the cabin. I wouldn't have been able to dig my way out of a window, climb through, and make my way down to the car in shoulder-height snow – I can barely stand up. I shiver at the thought that if I hadn't had the sense to message Eirik when I did, mentioning that I'd gone to Leah's cabin, he wouldn't have found me. I would have gone through all the firewood and when it was gone I may actually have frozen to death in my sleep. If that had happened, how long would it have taken for someone to find me? It could have been years. We've all read the stories here in Norway, of dead bodies found in the beds of abandoned and remote cabins.

What would my parents and Eirik and the police have concluded happened to me in the absence of a body? Would Anton perhaps have been investigated, considering I called the police expressing concern about him just before I came here? And what would have happened to my clients? Some of them may have experienced real shock and substantial setbacks at my sudden disappearance. Several tell me they live for our sessions; at least that's how it feels for them, that our weekly hour is the one place they feel seen and heard.

'Look, honey!' shouts Eirik. I follow his pointed finger out the window where he has succeeded in making a narrow tunnel through the snow, at the top of which is a sliver of blue sky.

64

Elisabeth, August

'Thank you for coming all the way out again this week.' Elisabeth smiles at Kristina, who looks tired and a little pale, and pours two mugs of steaming black coffee from the thermos. They're sitting on a blanket on the beach below Villa Vinternatt. The huge Color Line passenger ferry, bound for Kiel, fills the narrow sound between Drøbak and Hurumlandet, and many smaller leisure boats float languidly on the water. It's a beautiful day, and Elisabeth is glad; it feels easier having this conversation out here rather than inside one of Villa Vinternatt's austere common rooms.

'That's okay. It's good to get out of the city for the afternoon.'

'How have you been?'

'Yeah, good. A little tired. This summer has been quite full-on. Eirik has worked nonstop and I've been keeping busy with the research paper I'm submitting in September. But, you know, I guess I would have liked to get away for a couple of weeks. We talked about going to Cannes, but then he had to work. What about you?'

'I'm good. Better and better,' says Elisabeth.

'You look and sound good, sweetie.' Kristina places a hand on Elisabeth's and smiles at her. 'The work you are doing for yourself will serve you for the rest of your life. So many people would have given up, but you're a fighter.'

'Uh-huh.' Elisabeth looks out at the deep-blue water, sunlight trapped on little wavelets.

'Is everything okay, Elisabeth? You know I can speak to them if there is something you need that you're not getting here. Are the therapy sessions working out okay? Is it just once a week? Maybe twice would be—'

'I don't need any more therapy.' Elisabeth speaks more firmly than she intended and feels Kristina's surprise at being cut off. 'Sorry. Just that I've had a lot of it.'

'Sure.' Kristina takes a sip of coffee and her eyes follow Elisabeth's out on the water. She waits for Elisabeth to speak and Elisabeth is envious of her ability to just sit in loaded silence.

'I was wondering if we could speak about what happened. In Venezuela.' Elisabeth speaks quickly, then wishes she hadn't thrown it in there quite so bluntly. She glances quickly at Kristina, who looks as calm and composed as ever, but Elisabeth has known her all her life and can tell by the vein pulsating visibly on Kristina's neck that she is agitated beneath the surface.

It's no doubt a surprise to Kristina that Elisabeth has chosen to bring up the shooting. They haven't spoken about it in over a decade; there didn't seem like anything more to be said, and Kristina never recovered her full memory and made her peace with that. She moved on. Why would Elisabeth drag the terrible tragedy back out into the light, when it would change nothing? Trine was dead and gone forever. In the last few weeks, since the vernissage and since the meetings with Ella Victor, who has visited twice more, Elisabeth has begun to question her decision to not speak up about certain things. After all, she put an innocent man in prison, where he remains to this day. How is she supposed to carry that for the rest of her life? She is starting to wonder whether by keeping secrets, they are what eat away at her and stop her from being really free.

'You know you can talk to me about whatever you want, Elisabeth.' Kristina is looking straight at her now, and her brown eyes don't flinch or give away even slight anxiety.

'I suppose I feel that we never talk about it, though.'

'I suppose we don't. I'm not sure I personally feel that anything can be gained by going over it again now, but if you need to talk about it, of course we can.'

'Well, the thing is, since I've been here and really returned to the art, I've realized how much what happened influences me. It is the backdrop of my mind. The images are always there. I paint them sometimes, like all the pictures with swirls of red that are meant to look like bloodstains. They encourage that here, to bring what we see in our minds to the paintings.'

'That sounds like a very healthy approach.'

'Yes, but... The thing is, I think I need to speak about Carúpano differently. I've come to realize that it is harming me not to talk about it more explicitly. In my art. And in my life. I've been asked to contribute to an art book about trauma. You know, the experience written about and chronicled in writing on one side of the page, then depicted on the other side. I want to be more explicit in my image-building. I don't want to just paint blood patterns and frightening foliage forever.'

'I'm not sure I follow.'

'I can't move on until I tell you what really happened back there.'

'Elisabeth, what do you mean? We know what happened. Everyone knows—'

'Nobody knows.'

'What? You know, you were there. I know, I was there, too.'

'You don't.'

'I can't recover those memories, Elisabeth, God knows I've tried. I wanted to process them fully to recover but came to understand that accepting I won't regain full recollection is enough. I live with it now, in peace. But I *know* what happened.'

'There are things I never told you. I didn't tell anyone.'

'What are you talking about?'

'What really happened.'

'Elisabeth, you're worrying me. We know what really happened. We've been over it endlessly...'

'But it wasn't the full story. When I saw you there, in Caracas, in the hospital, that first time, *afterward*, when I saw how frail and broken you were, and realized that you actually had no recollection of what had just happened, I made the decision to tell the story a certain way. But it wasn't the whole truth...'

'Elisabeth, listen to me.' Kristina's voice is crystal clear and controlled, and Elisabeth can see how hard she has to work to control the anger and fear running through her. 'Stop, please stop. Jesus, Elisabeth, please just stop. You have to let it go now; we're thirty-six years old. Hashing out some minor detail you haven't told me about isn't going to help me, or you. What happened has dominated your life for almost twenty years. You have to let it go.'

'Let it go? That's surprising advice coming from a psychotherapist, a Doctor of Psychology, especially one who specializes in trauma. Don't you think I have read about this stuff? Don't you think I know all about integrating trauma to process it properly?'

'Of course. I'm just saying that going over and over what happened in Venezuela isn't serving you. Look at your life, Elisabeth. You are in the process of rebuilding it. I love you and want you to get better. I think the way to do that is accept that what happened can't be changed. It can never be changed. We can only attempt to move on.'

'But it wasn't what happened.'

'Elisabeth. Please, please stop.' Elisabeth can tell that Kristina is about to get up and walk away, and she might never get another chance to broach the subject with her.

'I can't carry this anymore.'

'What... What is it?' Kristina looks alarmed at the tears rushing down Elisabeth's face, but she can tell she is listening intently now.

'I only did it to protect you,' she whispers. Then she speaks of Carúpano, slowly at first, stumbling for words, then faster and faster as the images leap back to life, the images she has never spoken of and when she stops, Kristina gets up and walks away, straight into the water, soaking the hems of her white jeans. It is several minutes before she returns, tears streaming down her face, which bears a strange expression; pinched and pained, like she's just bitten down hard on her tongue and is trying hard to not scream out loud.

'Can I ask you something?' asks Kristina.

'Of course.'

'Have you spoken about this to anyone? Your therapist here, or your mother, or—'

'Never. And I think that is the problem. I need to speak the truth, and then maybe I can really let it go. Can you imagine carrying something like that for almost twenty years?'

'Well, yes I can, because even though I can't recall the events in a coherent way, I certainly carry them, too. And I don't think there is anything to be gained by coming out with this now. It would crush the Rickards. That kind of shock could actually kill someone, and it would massively compromise me—'

'Wait, what? Of course it won't.'

'It would most definitely compromise me. And Eirik. Can you imagine the effect on his political career? You have to understand that you can't just suddenly drop a bomb like that on my life.'

'But why would it compromise anything? We were the victims, we were just kids,—'

'Exactly. And we are going to leave it at that, Elisabeth.'

'No.'

'No?' repeats Kristina, incredulously, and Elisabeth sees something ugly then, in her eyes.

'You don't get to decide how I talk about my own trauma.'

'It directly affects me.'

'Yes.'

Kristina stares hard at Elisabeth for several long moments, and it occurs to Elisabeth that her friend doesn't recognize this Elisabeth who answers back and challenges her after so many years of being a downtrodden mess, pathetically grateful for the smallest of charities. *I did it for you*, she thinks. *Now I'm going to put me first.* Perhaps Kristina senses how serious she is, and how steely her resolve is, because she subtly changes her approach. Kristina begins to cry again, and doesn't attempt to wipe away the tears that run down her face and hover at her chin before dropping onto her jeans.

'I'm sorry,' she whispers. 'What you've told me is obviously a very big shock. I think I just need to process this.'

'Of course.'

'Elisabeth, could you please do something for me? Could you please hold off a little bit before speaking about this? Just so I get a chance to really take it on board. I think that's only fair – this does primarily affect me.'

'Okay.'

'Just a little while, okay? Can you promise me that? Of course you deserve to speak your truth and I can only imagine how hard it must have been to hold all of this for so long to protect me. I was just thinking that maybe you and I could do some processing exercises together at the weekend when you come to ours. Eirik is away again. It could be really healing for both of us.'

'Really? Uh. Are you sure you still want me to come?'

'Of course, Elisabeth. This doesn't change anything at

all. But please just promise me that for now, you and I will work through this together, just the two of us, in the first instance.'

Elisabeth nods, and returns her gaze to the water, but the sun has disappeared behind a cloud and the pretty deep blues of the sea have turned steely gray and obscure.

65

Kristina

He stands on a chair positioned underneath the window and scrapes furiously at the mouth of the tunnel, dislodging big lumps of snow that come crashing into the cabin. The slash of blue sky grows wider, casting a patch of brilliant sunshine on the floorboards. He whoops like a kid. I can't help but laugh. I watch his look of triumph as he judges the tunnel wide enough for him to pass through, and he instantly clambers onto the chair and hauls himself onto the window ledge. My husband disappears through the hole and sticks his head back down into it from the top.

'I made it!' he shouts. His face is red and elated, and though he is forty, he looks about fourteen in this moment. He squints in the sudden bright sunlight and pumps the pickax up and down, like an actor who just received an Academy Award. 'Are you okay? This is going to take a while. Just stay where you are on the sofa, I

should get through the door in an hour or so. Maybe two.'
He shouts.

'Okay,' I say and smile up at him from my icy tomb. I'm
huddled underneath a duvet and two woolen blankets and
still, I can't help but tremble with cold.

'I love you,' shouts Eirik, and then he disappears from
sight. I wait for several minutes, until I can hear the faint
repetitive thud of the scooping bowl hitting the top layer
of snow outside the front door. Then I turn over onto my
stomach slowly to not prompt another onslaught of pain,
and slide Leah's MacBook back out from underneath
the sofa.

I hesitate for a long moment, trying to breathe calmly,
trying to maintain my composure in case Eirik suddenly
reaches the front door – I'd only have a second to slip the
laptop back under the sofa and face my husband. I'd need
to make sure nothing about me would betray what I've
read. And I fear what I'm about to read; I fear Leah will set
about reducing Eirik to something other than what he has
been to me for almost fifteen years, in just a few devastating
sentences. I can hear him outside, but the digging still
sounds distant, so I can assume I have a little more time. I
have to know where she is going with this – I have the eerie
image in my mind of Leah as my executioner, dropping
an acrylic rope around my neck and pulling it tighter and
tighter, watching me. And then – the moment that changes
everything. Because sometimes it is a single moment that
changes everything.

I just happened, for the briefest of moments, to let my
eyes roam around the cabin, and perhaps it is because the

room is now brilliantly lit up by the sunlight streaming through the hole Eirik made that I notice it – it would have been harder to spot last night or this morning in the meager light. On a top shelf, close to the hand-carved, exposed supporting beams, several small picture frames are lined up. From what I can see from here, a couple are photographs from nature, places I don't recognize – a beach, a mountain, a forest-fringed lake. One is a drawing of a middle-aged woman leaning her face against the palm of her hand and staring into the distance – Leah's mother? The last is a little oil painting, an abstract in beautiful shades of vermilion, maroon, scarlet. And it is unmistakably one of Elisabeth's paintings, not dissimilar to the one I have at home.

I have to swallow a scream and fight the urge to launch myself from the sofa and grab the picture, but I'd have to climb onto a chest of drawers to reach it, and it's not like I'd be able to do that, let alone move over there.

It is like finding another piece of a puzzle and realizing that it alters the whole picture in every single way. I feel like I am looking right at the answers but can't decipher them. This casts *Supernova* in an even more sinister light. She stalked me. She claimed to know things about me that seem impossible for her to have found out about. She infers that she knew things about my marriage and my husband. But could it be that Leah Iverson somehow also directly contributed to Elisabeth's death? Elisabeth was my best friend, and now she's dead. I get a sense, in this moment of what she has done, and how.

I'm so worked up that I can no longer feel the pain in my leg or the icy cold air of the cabin. I'm running out of patience, and battery, and time. I feel a strange sensation in my left hand and realize I've dug my nails into my skin so hard I've pierced it, making dark beads of blood appear. I suck at the cut and return to *Supernova*.

66

Elisabeth, August

Elisabeth feels strange to be somewhere other than the ordered, predictable world of Villa Vinternatt, even though she comes here overnight once every month. Kristina picked her up in the late afternoon after spending the day in Drøbak with Camilla and the kids, and they got stuck in unusually heavy traffic heading into Oslo on the E6. They talked about what had happened since they'd last seen each other less than a week before, but Elisabeth fell silent as Oslo came into view, a gray blur in a wide valley, held in between dark pine forests on one side and the shimmering fjord on the other. She spent her whole life in this city and its outskirts, but since what happened with Andreas and getting sober and living at Villa Vinternatt, Elisabeth feels trepidation at returning, as if bad memories will spring forth from Oslo's streets, chasing her down.

At Kristina's house, she slips her shoes off and places her weekend bag down on the gently heated wooden floorboards of the impressive hallway, and stands a moment looking at the familiar pictures on the walls. Elisabeth is always momentarily taken aback by just how grand Kristina's apartment is, but then again, she is married to a wealthy politician and has a successful career in her own right. She remembers living in a similar apartment just down the road when Andreas was alive, though the circumstances were certainly different. Theirs had been a world of painting, passion and wild drug parties.

Elisabeth stops for a moment in front of the black-and-white photograph of herself, Trine and Kristina, taken at graduation from high school, just weeks before they set off for South America. Kristina comes back into the hallway, having gone ahead into the kitchen.

'Look at us,' says Elisabeth, softly.

'Yeah,' says Kristina. 'Come.'

Elisabeth follows her back into the kitchen. On the granite countertop is an opened bottle of red wine, an Italian amarone. Outside it's raining lightly, a relief after a relentlessly hot August. Elisabeth feels suddenly excited about the coming fall and what it might bring. The vernissage at Villa Vinternatt had gone beyond all expectations, and many of her paintings were sold that same evening. She'd had several additional commissions in the months since, as well as an interview request from one of Norway's major newspapers, *Dagbladet*. Elisabeth also can't wait to get properly started with the art book curated by Ella Victor. Ella had been to see her twice more at Villa Vinternatt since the first time and on both occasions they'd ended up talking for hours and hours, and it had felt like a beginning friendship. It was nice to laugh with someone and to discover common ground. It was fun, Elisabeth realized. Such an easy, light word – fun, but how important and difficult, too.

She'd been in contact with Ella again by email just days before about the book. Elisabeth found it easier to talk that way, and Ella had been so pleased to hear that Elisabeth would be willing to take part in the project and her preliminary thoughts. She glances at Kristina, who is placing pieces of cheese and fat olives and serrano ham on a metal Alessi tray. She feels momentarily guilty for having agreed to do the book and for having decided that the only way she can really move on is to deal with the full truth in the only way she knows how – through her art, and with real honesty. Kristina was very clear about her feelings when they spoke on the beach below Villa Vinternatt, and while Elisabeth understands and wants to protect her and please her, she can't do it forever at such a high cost.

She watches Kristina pour two large glasses from the bottle – strange: she knows Elisabeth is required to stay totally sober at all times, including when on leave like now, to continue to be eligible for Villa Vinternatt's residency program. Elisabeth remembers how angry Kristina was last winter when she was caught drinking smuggled whiskey with Joel and one of the other guys. *I put my professional reputation on the fucking line for you*, she said, a vivid red stress rash appearing on her neck.

'Is Eirik home?' she asks, looking around as though he might suddenly appear. Elisabeth assumed he wouldn't be; in the past five years she's only seen him a handful of times as his political career has skyrocketed. It's strange to her that the undeniably charismatic but rather immature man Kristina met at university has morphed into this political powerhouse often on the cover of Norway's major newspapers.

'No.'

'Oh. Yeah, I thought you said he was traveling for work. Is someone else joining us?'

'No.' Kristina smiles, a warm, carefully honed smile, the kind Elisabeth imagines she gives her clients when they say something particularly disturbing and she wants to make them feel secure. She slides one glass across the countertop to where Elisabeth sits on a bar stool.

'But... You know I can't drink. Obviously.'

'Well, I was thinking to myself this morning how far you've come. It isn't at all obvious, actually, at this point, that you shouldn't be allowed to unwind and have some fun with your best friend.' Fun, that word again. Light. Dangerous.

'I...' Elisabeth begins to respond but is so surprised she actually has no words.

'Look. I work with this stuff. On a daily basis I see clients struggling with grief and addiction and trauma. I know about these things, probably more than anyone else you'll ever meet. And I know you. I know your personal strengths and weaknesses and in the past year I have seen, firsthand, your incredible strength and ability to pick yourself back up. You should be proud of yourself and feel free to celebrate.'

'By breaking my sobriety? Kristina, I'm sorry but this has really thrown me.'

'Obviously no pressure. It was just a suggestion. I think it is also important to take steps back to normality when it comes to sobriety. I don't believe that complete abstention is necessary forever; true healing can only come when you find balance.'

'But the rules...'

'You're right, Elisabeth. Maybe this was preemptive of me. Just, I've had a tough week at work. I've been looking forward to seeing you. I just wanted us to have some fun. Like in the old days. You know, a couple of girlfriends on the sofa, watching *Sex and the City* reruns, eating crazy amounts of cheese and enjoying a couple of glasses of nice red wine.'

Elisabeth feels a warm, cozy feeling spread out in the pit of her stomach at the description – she knows that is how they could have been, in another life. She looks at Kristina, noticing the way she emanates calm and trustworthiness, as always. Maybe she's right. If someone as knowledgeable and experienced as Kristina says that balance is the goal and that occasionally allowing yourself a little bit of fun is necessary, then why shouldn't she?

No, she thinks, and realizes that this thought came from deep within her, as though spoken by her very core self.

'No,' she says, her voice low and trembling. 'No. Thank you, but I'm not ready for that. Let's do all that, but I'll stick to iced tea.' In the past, whenever Elisabeth has come to stay at Kristina and Eirik's, Kristina has gone out of her way to prepare delicious non-alcoholic alternatives for her. Home-brewed iced Kusmi tea with fresh blackberries and mint leaves, or decaf espresso tonics with juicy, thick wedges of lime.

'I don't have any, I'm afraid,' says Kristina, and retracts the offered wine, pouring it into her own glass, filling it all the way to the brim. She takes a sip from it and laughs. 'Why don't you take this through to the dining room and I'll see if I can rustle up something yummy.' Kristina hands her the tray and takes another big gulp of the wine.

Elisabeth takes it and heads to the dining room, passing through two other huge, spotlessly clean rooms – a drawing room with heavy damask sash curtains and impressive modern art, and a library with custom-built color-coordinated shelves and a French marble fireplace with a gaping black mouth.

She sits down where she usually sits and waits for Kristina. She's a little different today, she noticed it when they were driving – she seems preoccupied and jittery, though she is good at summoning a calm presence. But not that good; Elisabeth has known her since they were three years old. *I've had a tough week at work*, Kristina said and this comment makes Elisabeth suddenly angry. *You've had a tough week at work? You should try to take a walk in my shoes, golden girl.* She instantly feels guilty for these thoughts; Kristina has done more for her than anyone else, and they are bound together by so much shared history. Kristina walks into the room, carrying her own wine glass and a beautiful non-alcoholic cocktail laden with fruit and ice and fresh mint.

Elisabeth smiles at her, hoping that Kristina will eventually forgive her for what she is going to do and say in Ella Victor's book. She also hopes that someday they will sit across from each other like this, on even terms, not as addict and her friend-slash-therapist-slash-savior, but just as friends.

'Try this,' says Kristina, placing the berry-red drink on a jade-veined marble coaster in front of her.

67

Supernova

We're coming up to a really important part. I know why Elisabeth committed suicide. It wasn't your fault. And I know how much guilt you must feel. Elisabeth never blamed you, I know she didn't. But I think you blame yourself and that's why you will always be haunted by it. I worry that you will have stopped reading, that all of these revelations coming at you hard and fast will have scared you off. Somehow I think you're still here, all ears. I wonder what will shock you the most, the truth about Carúpano and Trine and Elisabeth, or the truth about your beloved Eirik and what he's done. Don't worry, we'll get to all counts soon.

So. We've done your mother. We've done Elisabeth. We've talked about exposure therapy and now we're going to take all of this to the next level.

Okay. Carúpano. Not going to lie, this part packs a fucking punch.

★ ★ ★

Like Xavier said, the house is stunning. Built into the cliffs above the sheltered bay at the eastern fringes of Carúpano, the villa has several levels, with two separate rooftop pools. There are people everywhere, dancing, laughing, openly doing coke. One couple is clearly making love in a dark corner of the main living space. You walk through the room on Xavier's arm and take the beer he hands you. You begin to sway to the music when you reach the dancefloor outside. You've never been anywhere like this before. This is what you dreamed of, all those long months dragging past during your final year of school in a safe, underwhelming suburb of Oslo. You look at Xavier. You smile. You get high.

Occasionally, you scan the crowd for Elisabeth and Trine and spot them both on the dancefloor, moving energetically with a couple of guys, the usually reserved Trine pumping her fist in the air. You laugh and Xavier closes your mouth with his own, playfully touching the tip of his tongue against yours.

After a while, you edge towards the edge of the crowd, time for a break. Xavier takes your hand and leads you through the main space, down a flight of stairs, then another, along a long corridor, to a bedroom. The crowd is thinning, some must have left, some might have retreated to the bedrooms on the lower levels. The heavy bass throbs through the house like a pulse. You don't need me to tell you what happens next. When you emerge from the bedroom, your hair messy and your eyeliner dragging sweetly upwards at the corners of your eyes from laughing so much, you seamlessly rejoin the others on the dancefloor and they pretend like you'd been there all along. Elisabeth and Trine are red-faced from all the dancing, beads of sweat running down the sides of their faces glinting in the white light of a high, full moon.

Let me show you somewhere special, says Xavier. *Come.* The three of you walk behind Xavier and one of the other guys who'd danced with Elisabeth and Trine, away from the house, away from the beach, into the jungle on a narrow track. Perhaps he senses a change in atmosphere, a charged current of beginning fear, because Xavier turns around and smiles widely, pointing up at the hillside, clearly visible now after a sharp turn. Up there, nestled in verdant forest, is a wrought-iron gazebo. It's beautiful, like something out of a fairytale. You step inside and settle in a circle on the floor, around a large round mirrored table. The other man, Xavier's friend, plays tinny hip-hop music on his phone. You look out over the gently rippling Caribbean, then back at Xavier. You can't stop smiling. The other man pulls a little Ziploc bag from his pocket and cuts five long lines of coke on the table clearly intended for this purpose.

Puro, he says, and winks at you.

Muy puro, adds Xavier.

After another hour in the gazebo, laughing and chatting, Trine grows quiet and visibly tired, and Elisabeth whispers straight into your ear.

We need to get going. It's the middle of the night, she says. *Our hostel might not even let us in.*

Soon, says Xavier, when you nuzzle his neck and ask him if he can take you to Carúpano.

The three of you confer quickly in Norwegian and agree that you need to be a little more forceful with Xavier, it really is time to go.

Let's play a game first, says Xavier's friend. He's a scrawny guy with a blandly handsome face, and although he's quite a bit older than the rest of them, Trine had seemed quite taken with him on the dancefloor, though nothing seems to have happened between them. Xavier pulls you down gently next to him on the dirt floor and you let yourself be drawn close. Xavier laughs and pokes you playfully in the soft hollow between your breasts, so you laugh, too. But then the man pulls out a gun and places it on the stone slab with a loud clang.

Let's go, says Elisabeth and stands up, but you tug gently at the hem of her dress and she sits back down.

None of you have ever seen a gun before. And why would you have? Naïve, spoilt, sheltered little girls from average families in the richest and safest country in the world usually haven't and never will. Later, much later, you'll be asked to identify the weapon. They'll show you image after image of handguns; small ones, big ones, black, bronze, silver, guns with wooden details, guns with silencers and guns without. You won't be able to take more than a single glance at them without starting to sweat and shake. Which one? They'll ask, and you'll close your eyes and shake your head lightly. Your mind will be blank, entirely empty, like the still surface of a lake.

The man, who will never resurface after this night, and whose name you'll never recover, removes something from the back pocket of his low-slung, mud-splattered jeans and holds his palm out for you to see. The bullet glints in the incandescent light of the full moon. A single golden cylinder, an object of beauty, like an amulet. He flicks the hand holding the gun, and the weapon splits open to reveal the chamber with six empty holes. You can't help a sharp, audible intake of breath at the sight.

Hey, chill out, Xavier says. *He'll go first.*

The man slots the bullet into the chamber and stares at you all in turn with small, strangely burning eyes, buried in the folds of heavy eyelids. He spins the barrel dramatically and it hurtles around its axis until it suddenly stops with a soft 'click'. Then he hands the gun to you, the ringleader. (Yes, you were the ringleader, Kristina, even though you might have claimed it was Elisabeth. It was always you, the others revered your natural authority, your calm, centered way of being.)

No, says the man. *She chooses.*

You hold the weapon entirely still in your hands. You'd have felt power, trepidation, fear, exhilaration. A heavy silence settles over all of you. Did you try, in those moments, to work out the probability of a bullet burying itself in your brain if you were to raise the gun to your head and pull the trigger? It was one of the most moving things I discovered about you, back when I was discovering everything about you – your meticulous penciled probability calculations. You turn the gun over in your hand, its dangerous body cool against your sweaty palm. You hand it to Xavier.

You go, you whisper, taking in his handsome face as his expression goes from suspenseful to shocked, then quietly impressed. He takes the gun from you, slowly, and laughs softly under his breath. You can see a thick vein pulsate on his neck. You can still taste him in your mouth. Never was anyone more alive than Xavier in those moments (your own words, again). You glance around and your eyes meet Elisabeth and Trine's terrified ones. They are both enraptured and horrified. You raise an eyebrow and Xavier takes it as his cue. With his right hand he lifts the handgun and presses its mouth to the soft hollow at his temple. He places his left hand in yours, his gaze not leaving yours for a second. Then he smiles slowly, that same smile he gave you when he first looked at you in the car, a smile that seems to wash his face in light, making a tough-looking guy look soft and easy to love. He raises an eyebrow almost imperceptively and everyone holds their breath. You give the faintest nod and Xavier pulls the trigger.

A soft click. A collective whoosh of released air from five pairs of lungs. Laughter. The sharp sting of tears in the corners of your eyes, quickly dismissed. Xavier's tongue probing your mouth, the cheers of the others, another round of cocaine.

Just one more time, says Xavier. *Come on, ladies, seems only fair.* Elisabeth wants to leave. Trine is too tired, too high, to protest.

Yes, you say. *Just one more. Then you take us home.*

Xavier nods. The other man picks the gun up off the dirt floor where Xavier dropped it after the first roulette. He flicks the barrel open and shows it to the four of you, as if to prove the bullet is still there. Then he spins it, and it turns rapidly around itself with a soft whirr that merges with the murmur of the waves far below you, until it audibly clicks into place.

You choose again, says Xavier, placing the gun back in your hands. Did you ever feel more alive than in that moment, Kristina? I doubt it. Do you think you ever will again? I'll never know why you chose her. A crystal-clear demonstration of the hierarchy in your trio, perhaps. An attempt of showing off to Xavier. After all, you could have handed the gun to the second man, a random stranger. But you don't. You hand it to Trine.

It's not even real, you whisper. *It's just a game.*

Trine emerges from her coke-haze to find her eyes locked on yours. She can't quite decipher your words. Elisabeth says something. *Let's go*, probably. Trine tries to do as she's told, to lift the gun, but she's started to shake uncontrollably, the sound of her teeth chattering audible to the others.

Stop, says Elisabeth and tries to stand up, but Xavier gently and firmly pulls her back down.

Come on, ladies. We have to finish what we started. Last round. You laugh, but your voice sounds hollow and strange.

If you want to play this game, you should go next, says Elisabeth. Everyone falls silent. A long moment unfolds between you.

You're right, you say. You reach for the gun, which lies nestled in the space between Trine's jittery, trembling knees.

No, whispers Trine. *You chose me. But you hold it.*

You glance at Elisabeth, then at Xavier, their faces are unreadable. Suddenly none of it seems funny or exciting and you fight the urge to just get up and bolt into the clutch of the jungle, merely inches away. Finally, you look at Trine. She has stopped shaking and appears strangely calm. You can make out the beat of her pulse on her throat. A slight smile plays on her pink, full lips and she gives a little nod as your hand closes around the gun.

Another collective intake of breath. Metal and moonlight. You struggle to lift the weapon to Trine's temple, it feels impossibly heavy, and you press it very hard against her temple to stop your hand from trembling violently. A wince. Then, another little nod.

68

Kristina

'Kristina? Honey, what's happening? Kristina, what the fuck? What's going on... what are you doing? I don't understand? What are you reading?'

I needed to stay composed. I needed to keep this from my husband, but I have entirely lost control of myself. I am racked with sobs, waves of grief shooting to the surface like molten chunks of lava erupting from a volcano.

'Babe,' he says and sits down next to where I am crumpled on the floor by the sofa. He reaches out to take the laptop from my hands, but I'm clutching it tight. 'What's happening? Why are you on the floor?'

'I'm sorry,' I whisper, trying to come up with some kind of explanation for this meltdown. Eirik has never seen me like this in all the years we've been together – I pride myself on having found the perfect balance between showing emotions and controlling them.

'Whose laptop is that?' asks Eirik and when our eyes meet, I notice something cold in the way he's looking at me.

'It's mine,' I say.

'Yours is at home. On the kitchen table. I used it to find your iPhone before I left – they're synced.'

'This is my work laptop. I… I'm feeling so overwhelmed because I just read through my patient notes for Leah Iverson. It's just so sad, what happened to her. I think I just needed to cry it out.'

'Can I see?'

'No.'

'Kristina.'

'No.' Eirik reaches for the laptop again, more forcefully this time, but I wrench it away from him and try to move away, but he's so much stronger than me, and the movement brings another crash of pain and I cry even harder. 'Eirik, you're hurting me. Please. Let go.' When I speak calmly and slowly to him, he snaps back into himself, realizing what a strange thing it is to do, to try to wrestle your badly injured wife to read her professional notes.

'Sorry. I'm sorry, Krissy. Just, I guess I felt suddenly irrationally suspicious of you when you said it was your laptop when your laptop is definitely at home.'

'You know I have two.' Thank God everyone seems to have the same MacBook.

'Yes. Look. I'm sorry. You look… Terrible. Can I do anything? Shall I make you a coffee?'

'Yes, please.'

Eirik goes over to the kitchen nook and I place the laptop on the table. I don't know what I would have done if he hadn't bought my lie about it being my work laptop and insisting on seeing it. I watch him make the coffee and we sit in silence, the air filled with the loud whine from the kettle as the water gets closer and closer to boiling, and the groan of the refrigerator too. Eirik kicks the side of the refrigerator and it instantly stops. The kettle boils and snaps off. It's totally quiet except for the sound of Eirik stirring milk into my coffee, the spoon scraping against the porcelain mug. He looks up and realizes I'm staring at him. When our eyes meet, I suddenly grasp hold of a vague sensation I had moments ago – there was something about the way he nudged Leah's refrigerator and knew how to make it stop. Something familiar.

69

Kristina

Eirik hands me the coffee. I blow on it, sending ripples onto its surface.

'What is it?' asks Eirik, and again, I catch sight of something cool in the way he is looking at me, as though he is trying to analyze my thoughts. I remind myself that he can't and focus on making my face soft and relaxed. I feel uncomfortable holding his gaze, it suddenly feels like the gaze of a stranger. I glance around the room, careful to avoid Elisabeth's picture – I don't want Eirik to notice it. I'm wondering how he got through the barrier from the main road to the private track leading to the parking space for Bekkebu; I locked it behind me.

'Nothing,' I say and wince exaggeratedly. 'I'm in quite a bit of pain.' This is true. But also, I'm afraid. For the first time in my life, I'm afraid of my husband.

70

Kristina

Eirik returns to the digging, and for a long while I just sit in silence, staring at the timber walls, at Elisabeth's picture, at the laptop on the table in front of me. I know that what Leah wrote is true. I already know what happened; Elisabeth told me before she died, but I don't remember it. I don't want to remember, that's the truth. I can build the images Leah describes in my mind, like any reader could, but still it is as though they are being constructed by her descriptions, rather than drawn from my own memories. I don't have any memories of my own from those moments, the last of Trine Rickard's life. Until now, because Leah unleashed them.

The thing she said about the single bullet glinting in the moonlight like something beautiful. I can see it. The feeling of the gun's barrel, snug in my hand, so heavy. I can feel it. The sound it made, tearing the night to shreds. I can hear it. The moments after, when I opened my eyes. There was nothing there. I saw nothing at all. A black hole, a white patch, a cloak of nothingness.

I hear a sound. It's Eirik, standing right in front of me, speaking.

'What?' I whisper, my whole body feeling weak and strangely numb.

'Look, I've managed to free the front door. It's just after noon. I was thinking I'd get some more firewood out of the shed, and once I've got the fire going, I'll try to make my way down to the car. I should have phone reception there. At least now the door is free.'

'Okay,' I say. I think about the strange moments that passed between us before. I was afraid of him. But am I just disorientated and in shock? This is my husband. I've known him inside out for fourteen years. I smile at Eirik and he smiles back. Still, something is different about him, in the way he watches me. He places a glass of water on the table in front of me, next to the laptop, and kisses the top of my head lightly.

'Kristina?' he calls from over by the front door.

'Yeah,' I say, leaning forward to see past the doorway. He pushes the door open to show me the tunnel he's dug outside. In his right hand is the pickax. I feel another surge of fear. *What have you done?* I think, looking at him.

'I'm getting the firewood, okay? Do you need anything?'

'No. I... Actually, I wondered about something.'

'What?' He's halfway out the door but turns back to look at me.

'Did you ever meet Leah?' I've spoken without properly thinking through the consequences, unusual for me – my impulse control is good. Her name hovers in the air between us. I watch Eirik very carefully. There is no reaction other than a very slight clench of his jaw.

'Leah Iverson?' He repeats her name, as though I might be referring to some other Leah than the Leah who owned this cabin, who stalked me, who killed herself, who set in motion a devastating chain of events, who insinuated that there could be some juicy stories in store about the man in front of me.

'Yes.'

'No, of course not.'

'Okay.'

'Why? Did she ask about me or something? She might have been aware of who you were married to.'

'No. No she didn't.'

'I knew who she was, like I said. I imagine most people would. She was pretty high profile, wasn't she?'

'I guess.'

'Okay. Well, see you in a minute.' Eirik holds the pickax up and waves at me, then he disappears outside.

Eirik drags the sofa with me on it closer to the hearth, as close as it will go. If I reach my hands out, the heat from the flames is so hot I have to retract them after a moment. He carries me to the bathroom and waits outside while I go, then back to the sofa.

'The fire won't go out for a long time; I'll be back way before it does. But do you think you can manage to toss a few more logs on if it starts to die?'

'Yeah. I don't even have to get up.'

'I think the nearest hospital is in Notodden, they might choose to send an air ambulance.'

I ponder this for a moment, the surreal thought of being

airlifted away from Leah's cabin. 'The moment I have reception, I'll call the hospital and the police.'

'She'll be buried completely by now,' I say, and imagine what would have happened if Eirik and I hadn't come to the cabin – she would most likely have stayed underneath the snow through the winter. She might have been found in the spring, or not at all, and eventually she'd be nothing but a few bones, scattered across the hillsides by the wind, where wild animals roam, picking up what were once parts of her and putting them back down somewhere else.

He nods and looks stricken.

'I covered her well. She, uh, they'll remove her by tonight, I imagine. I'm going now; hopefully, I won't be long.'

'Just hurry, okay?' I say, though in spite of the pain I am in, I hope he takes a good long while.

71

Supernova

It is my hope that you'll come to understand why I've done what I've done with Carúpano. I just wanted to set you free. I want to set you free in more ways than just one, though, and this is where Eirik comes into it. The thing is, Kristina, I've failed. I've fucked up big time. I know you'll have been freaking out at the mention of your darling beloved husband, and at the suspicion of where this is heading. The perfect man – your golden guy in the middle of your golden world. You'd do anything to hold onto him; maybe because deep down, you know you can't – not really.

He's the type that does what he wants and takes what he can, and you know it. We're alike in that way, you and me – successful and beautiful and accomplished by most people's standards, but fundamentally always at the mercy of some man who loves himself more than he could ever love someone else. Maybe you should ask yourself how far he'd go for you and whether he really matches your devotion. You've said it to me before and it always felt like a sucker punch in the gut, so now I'll say it to you – do you think, perhaps, that you deserve better?

For what it's worth, I think you deserve everything.

But this wasn't about him, at least not to begin with. It was all about you. I got close to him because I wanted to get close to you, or as close as I could to actually being you. I laughed with your mother. I spent time with your best friend, and gained her trust so much that she finally felt able to release what she'd kept for herself for so long. You may not believe me when I say that with Eirik, my intentions were entirely innocent. I wanted to know if he deserved you. He doesn't.

You remind me of someone, he said that first night I approached him at the bar, wanting to gauge how easily he could be led astray. Easily, is your answer. The someone, of course, was you. The thing I didn't factor in, Kristina, is that he reminded me of someone, too. It has taken me a while to figure out who it was, and I'm sure you will use all your impressive psychology credentials to arrive at the same conclusion. This is my excuse; I don't have a better one. I just didn't see it coming, that I'd love him. Or that my attention would be wrenched from you to him. I didn't mean to create a situation that will no doubt bring you deep hurt. I believed him when he said that he'd never loved anyone like he loved me. He knew what to say to the fatherless little girl who lives inside of me, the girl who just wants to be taken care of. He made me feel taken care of. I believed him when he said he would leave you, and for a while, I saw myself stepping into your shoes, living your life, for real. I talked myself out of my persistent feelings of guilt by thinking that if that was truly how he felt about me, then you'd be better off without him. I suppose I felt that he and I deserved each other and that neither of us deserved you. Still, I felt bad, terrible, doing what I did, and I have no other excuse than that I love him, even now.

72

Kristina

In the same moment I read her last words, the MacBook shuts down. The fire has gone out inexplicably, and the logs are still intact, only flame-licked on one side. I am shaking so hard that my fingers fumble with the matches, lighting one after another, then dropping them to the floor where they extinguish. My fingertips are still raw and sore from last night's crawl through the snowdrifts to the cabin, but after several attempts I finally manage to relight the fire. In less than twenty-four hours my life has been left in ruins. I try to think but now it is as though my entire brain has gone blank, not just the parts I lost after Carúpano.

Eirik has betrayed me. He's come here with her before, how else would he have known how to silence the refrigerator or gotten past the barrier? They've all betrayed me: Elisabeth, my mother, everyone I love. And now, Leah is dead. Elisabeth is dead. Thank God.

I'm still alive and Eirik is still alive and Leah and Elisabeth are both dead. If I could find a way to let it all go, if I can lock all this away somewhere inside me, I can still have everything. My home and my work and my family and my calm, controlled mind. My husband. But do I still want him? *I just didn't see it coming, that I'd love him.* Leah didn't have the faintest concept of love. And just because she thought she loved him, it sure as hell doesn't mean he loved her. So he bought her a few drinks, he fucked her, maybe he came here with her for a faux-romantic weekend to fuck her some more, but Eirik loves me. That much I know. And I don't know any of the rest of it; it's all speculation, I don't ever have to know. I can live with blank patches.

I want to throw the MacBook into the leaping flames, destroying Leah's insane words. What I would give to never have come here, to never have read her words. To not have found her dead. She would just remain where she is until nothing would remain of her at all.

I hear a sound, footsteps approaching. Eirik appears in the doorway, his face red with exertion and the biting cold. In his right hand is a thick coil of blue rope, in his left the pickax. I try to smile at my husband, because I am terrified by the look in his eyes. I want him to look at me the way he usually does, with adoration and awe. *You're my crown jewel*, he always says. He loves me so deeply; he always says it and shows it in a million ways, but could it be that Leah was right, that he treats me like a queen, but a queen in a game of chess? Is his love about him and how it makes him look and feel, not about me? Could it be that she was right, that I deserve better? His eyes are empty of love now. They are distant and haunted, like he's been pursued all the way back up the hillside. I realize again that I'm afraid of him.

He watches me from the doorway with those cold eyes.

'Hey you,' I say, shrinking back into the sofa, making myself look vulnerable, which of course I am. He doesn't answer. 'Is something wrong? Did you manage to reach the car?'

Eirik nods. He places the pickax on the floor in the vestibule and takes a few steps toward me, leaving lumps of tightly packed snow from his shoes in his wake. He's still holding the rope and I recognize it vaguely as one he keeps in the boot, coiled inside the spare tire, in case of an emergency. *In case of an emergency.*

I swallow hard. 'What's happened?' I ask, careful to keep my voice soft and calm. It's like the Eirik I know and love isn't really here, that this man standing in front of me is a stranger, living a separate narrative playing out inside his head. I have to connect with him, to bring him back around to this moment with me. 'Eirik. Did you get reception on the phone?'

He gives a faint nod, a brief flick of the head, but it's as if the movement isn't in response to my question but rather in response to whatever is happening in his mind. Eirik stops a couple of steps away from where I'm lying on the sofa, my splintered and aching leg propped up high. He is clutching the coil of rope so tightly his knuckles have turned white. He stares at me and I'm shocked to see tears pooling in his eyes; in all these years, I've never seen Eirik cry.

'You haven't called anyone, have you?' I whisper.

'No.'

'Can you please talk to me and tell me what is happening for you in this moment?'

'I—' He begins to speak but interrupts himself. He stares at the floor and at the rope, sending tears flowing down his face. 'I didn't want to have to do this,' says Eirik.

'Do what, honey?'

'Get rid of you.'

73

Leah, two days before

He was the only one, out of all of the men, she'd brought to this cabin. The only one she'd wanted to. Inviting him here was the same as inviting him into the inner chambers of her heart, she knew that. She hadn't seen it coming, and what started as a way of getting closer to Kristina, or closer to being Kristina, perhaps, had turned into something else entirely. It had brought so much joy but also remorse and heartache.

But now, seeing him at the door, face cast in shadows and hair whipped up on the fierce wind chasing down the hillsides to the clearing, she feels none of the feelings that caught her by surprise. She feels fear. She should have known that he might have come for her here – he's the only one that could. Except...

We need to talk, he says.

No, she says.

You always say no.

There's nothing more to talk about.

He pushes past her into the tiny vestibule and in the faint glow from the oil lamps in the next room.

I'm sorry for Friday.

Sorry?

Yes.

You screamed at me. You threatened me to abort our baby.

Leah... I'm sorry.

Fuck you. You'll be pleased to know that there's no baby anymore. You'll have it your way.

Her face is deathly pale and her hair is stuck to her skull in greasy strings.

What... what have you done? And what happened to your face?

What have I done? She screams the words, and they burst from her empty insides with such force he actually takes a step back. *What have you done, you mean? Everyone is going to hear about this. I'll make sure they all know about the promises you made, the way you said you love me, how you lied to your wife night after night, how you got me pregnant and then threatened me to get rid of the baby we made, how you said you'd ruin my life if I didn't. No, wait, you said you'd hunt me down and fucking kill me like an animal if I didn't. Well, I bet you're pleased now. But let me be very clear with you – you're going down, you fucking asshole!*

Wait, wait, baby, listen to me, I came here because I was so worried about you. I wanted us to talk more, better, properly, I can't live with what I said to you the last time I saw you.

I was confused and upset and what happened should never have happened, Leah please listen to me, please, please.

But she's already outside, running fast down the hill. And Eirik's behind her.

74

Kristina

'Get up,' says Eirik. His eyes are wild, far away in the recesses of his own mind. I need to find out what he sees there, or I am never going to get out of here alive.

'I can't,' I whisper.

He comes over to me and yanks me hard by the arm. 'I said get up!' I move slowly, pulling myself up to an awkward standing position, placing all my weight on my right leg and holding on to the low table in front of me, avoiding his eyes.

'Eirik—'

'Shut up!'

Eirik pulls something from his pocket, some kind of little book, and flicks through it before throwing it onto the table in front of me. It's my diary, the orange leather-bound one that was in my Neverfull bag that Leah stole.

'You know, I meant what I said. I really didn't want to have to do this. Can you even begin to fucking imagine what the last few days have been like for me?'

'For *you*?' I scream it out loud, without thinking, and for a long moment, Eirik and I stand staring furiously at each other. I need to defuse the situation here or I'll end up dead like Leah. Dead like Elisabeth. 'Eirik, wait. Listen to me. We need to talk, not get all crazy with each other. A lot has happened here. But first, we need to focus on getting out of here. We need to get home.'

'Home!' Eirik begins to laugh incredulously. 'What, you think we're going to leave here and go home like nothing happened?'

'Eirik, please help me home. I'm in so much pain.'

'Soon you won't be.'

'What—'

'Write.' Eirik fishes a Montblanc pen from his jacket pocket and slams it onto the table in front of me.

'Write what?'

'A note.'

I can't stand up for a moment longer and sink back down onto the sofa, my leg hurting beyond anything I've ever felt before, wave after wave of crashing pain, my heart hollering in my chest. I can't stop the tears that begin to flow, and don't try to wipe them away; I just keep my eyes trained on my hands folded in my lap. I hear a huge crash and when I look up I realize Eirik has smashed a chair against the timber wall, splintering both the chair and the wall with the force. He lets out a wild cry and bursts into tears. I have never seen Eirik, or anyone for that matter, like this before. He's muttering to himself, his eyes roaming the room as if trying to find a cue to his next move.

'What the fuck?' he screams suddenly and scrambles past where I'm sitting. He climbs onto a chair and reaches for

Elisabeth's painting on the wall. 'What the fuck,' he says again, over and over. 'How—'

'Eirik,' I say, keeping my voice low, 'You and I have both been the victims of a very twisted individual. Leah Iverson—'

'Shut up!' he screams at the top of his lungs. 'I don't understand! I don't understand...'

'Listen to me,' I say. 'You haven't done anything wrong. You're in shock. We need to get out of here. Eirik, please. Think about the elections. Think about our home. Think about our baby. The baby we're going to have. You and me. When we get out of here. We just need to get out of here.' He falls silent and sinks down on the floor in front of me, crying quietly now. It's several minutes before he speaks again, and when he does, his voice is strangely controlled.

'I can't bear it any longer, I'll never get over what happened. Venezuela. Then Elisabeth committed suicide. And then my client, Leah Iverson, committed suicide, too, not even two months later. I love you, Eirik. Please find a way to move on without me,' says my husband in that strange, low voice.

'What—'

'Write it,' he hisses. 'Write what I just said. Along those lines. In your own words.' He picks the pen off the table again and throws it at me. 'I didn't want to have to do this, Kristina,' he whispers, burying his face in his hands. 'When you told me on Friday that she was your client, my world just fell to pieces. It had never occurred to me, not for a moment. But it was pretty obvious that you genuinely had no idea about what had happened, or about the pregnancy. It meant nothing, I swear on my life, it meant nothing at all, and I made it really fucking clear to her that I wanted her to get rid of it. I think she lived in some crazy fantasy world where she thought I'd leave you for her and we'd shack up together and play happy families. She threatened me and said she would tell you, and everyone else, the truth about me. Then she just disappeared. I assumed she'd come here, so I drove here but when I got here, the sleazy ex's car was parked next to hers so I went straight back home.'

'Wait, last Saturday? When I was at Camilla's? That's why you didn't come?'

Eirik nods. 'The week passed in a blur and I was consumed with work. Every goddamned minute of my days were filled until late in the evening and I had no chance to get back here, so I decided to just wait until she got back to Oslo to try to reason with her again, or pay her off or something. But then, on Friday, when you told me she was one of your clients, and that she'd begged you to come here so she could tell you the so-called truth, I realized I had to get rid of her. So I did.'

'The Saturday when I was at brunch.'

'I came up here again. She was a fucking mess. I only did what she would have done herself. She'd clearly even planned it. You said so.'

'So you came up here and found Leah alone, having lost her baby. And you shot her.'

He stares at me hard.

The enormity of what Eirik has just said dawns on me and my mouth must drop open, and it's as if my husband suddenly notices me again after being lost in his own moments of confession. 'Write it, I said. I can't bear it any—'

'No.'

'What do you mean, no? I said, fucking write it. You know, I still didn't think I'd have to do this, even after you came here and I came after you. She was dead by then, after all, and I didn't have to worry that she'd talk. It would get ruled a suicide for sure, especially after you told me about the note. So I told you she'd taken her shoe off and fired the weapon with her toe. That could have been that, Kristina. Leah's therapist testifying she was suicidal, the note, all of it. It wasn't until this morning when I came back inside and saw you with her laptop that I realized it was too late. You'd have to go. Look. On the side, there. Yeah, that little dent. I recognized it. I knew you were lying when you said the laptop was yours and when I saw how hysterical you were. I'd feared that she would write something to you, especially when you said she'd begged you to come here, but I assumed I'd shut her up in time.'

'She actually tried to email me what she wrote on Saturday, when I was still at home. But it never came through, only her email.'

'Wait. What? There is no phone reception here.'

'Where is her phone?'

'I took it with me. When I got to the main road, I messaged her mother. Then I threw the phone into one of the lakes I passed on my way to Bergen.'

'She must have tried to send it to me earlier and when you brought the phone from here it picked up reception and processed her outbox, sending it.' We stare at each other again, the shock of the past week hanging on the air between us.

'If only you hadn't read it. If only...'

'You know, what she wrote was all about me and her

and how she was obsessed with me. Whatever happened between you and her wasn't the focus of what she wrote.' I'm acutely aware of talking Eirik down here; there is no doubt in my mind that he is set on silencing me.

'She threatened to ruin my career, my marriage, everything. My whole life. I won't let her. It didn't mean a thing, she was just some girl. She reminded me of you when we were young, you know? That was all. She was a diversion. And she's fucking cost me everything. Now just do as you're told and write what I said.'

'What are you going to do? Get rid of me and tell everyone that you came up here to look for your wife and found me dead, having killed myself like Elisabeth and Leah?'

'Precisely. Now write it.' Eirik grabs my arm hard with one hand, and holds me by the back of the neck with crushing force with his other hand. It feels as though I am going to black out. I think fast. I can get out of this, I know I can. I pick up the pen.

I can't bear it any longer, I write. *I've failed as a friend and as a therapist. And as a wife. I love you, Eirik, more than life itself.* I push the little book over to my husband and as he reads the words, fresh tears gather in his eyes.

'Come,' he says.

'Where?'

'Outside.' He picks up the coil of blue rope from where he dropped it on the floor and then he stoops down and gently picks me up from the sofa. It's his gentleness that breaks my heart, he thinks he has no choice in this moment other than to kill the woman he loves. I need to give him a choice.

'It was me who killed Trine Rickards,' I say, straight into

his ear, as he carries me toward the door. 'I shot her. Point-blank. Like you shot Leah. We played Russian Roulette and it was me who pulled the trigger. I saw her go from everything – every beautiful, living, irreplaceable thing, to nothing at all. I didn't have a choice, Eirik. My mind blanked it out and Elisabeth told everyone that it was the man, Rodriguez, who just randomly shot her, but it wasn't, it was me. He's still doing time, for fuck's sake. And all those years, Elisabeth kept the truth quiet, trying to protect me and it killed her, really. No, actually, that's not true; it was basically Leah who killed her.'

'What are you talking about?'

'Leah. You and I are both Leah's victims, Eirik. She set you up, and me. None of this is your fault. None of it. You have to listen to me. She infiltrated my life, holding the twisted beliefs that she was somehow freeing me by telling me the so-called truth. But her truths were all lies. Can't you see? It's all Leah's fault. She went and found Elisabeth at Villa Vinternatt and convinced her that she should speak out about what happened to Trine, that it was me who shot her. Elisabeth then came to me, wanting to speak about Carúpano, saying she couldn't bear to carry it alone anymore. She left me no choice, Eirik. And it was all because of Leah. It's her fault.'

'What do you mean, she left you no choice?'

'I couldn't let Elisabeth use the most personal, painful thing that has ever happened to me, a terrible trauma that's ruined so many lives, as some kind of entertainment. And fucking stupid Leah got it all wrong. She thought that Elisabeth killed herself because she couldn't bear keeping Carúpano secret any longer and wanted to protect me from knowing the truth. But she *did* tell me, and that's why she died, not because she didn't. And she was going to tell everyone else, splashing it out for all to see in some lurid art house picture book. Think about it. It would have cost you the elections, Eirik. Imagine the headlines – Conservative Party's PM candidate's wife is a teenage murderer? And think about the poor Rickards; it would have killed them. She left me no choice.'

'No choice for what.'

'I got rid of her, Eirik.' He stares at me, sheer shock etched on his face. 'I killed her. For us. Just like you killed Leah for us.'

'Shut up, Kristina,' he says, kicking the cabin's door open, letting a gust of icy air inside. 'Shut up. I need to think. I don't... I don't believe you.' Eirik steps outside and begins to drag me toward the trench he's dug in the snow, up toward an inky black night sky throbbing with stars. I bite my lip to stop myself from screaming out loud from the pain in my leg; I don't want to antagonize him more than I have to.

I glance at the rifle cabinet on the wall in the hallway and notice that it is still open and empty. Where is the rifle? Last night when Eirik came back inside the cabin from inspecting Leah's body, he said he'd brought the weapon back with him and secured it in the cabinet. Smart – that would justify to the police why his fingerprints are on it. So where is the rifle? Is he planning on giving me the same ending as Leah – a shattered skull, a bared ice-blue toe on the trigger, a spray of blood in the snow?

'I killed her, Eirik,' I say, my voice trembling, then breaking as I speak the words out loud. 'I killed them both.'

'You're fucking with my head, Kristina. I know you are. You're trying to manipulate me, just like you always manipulate everyone, knowing full well that your calm demeanor falsely makes everyone trust you, but it doesn't work on me, not anymore—'

'I killed Elisabeth, Eirik,' I say again, louder this time, practically shouting the words, letting all the horror of that night loose into the night air. Her sweet face. The way she spoke about the future. She looked forward to it. The way she tried to fight me off, but couldn't – she didn't stand a chance. 'I fucking killed her,' I scream. 'I killed my best friend for us, and you need to listen to me, right now! I know why you did what you did. I know that you fucked Leah and I believe you when you say it meant nothing. But you and I, Eirik, we are so much more than that. So I don't give a flying fuck that you screwed her. She's dead, and can't hurt us now. We have a life together, a whole, beautiful life in Incognito Gata, and soon we'll have an even better one in the prime minister's residence. With our baby. Think about that, goddammit! Are you going to let all of this be for nothing? Think about it, Eirik. Even if you get away with it – a wife who kills herself in the middle of your electoral campaign? It's not going to look good. I'm telling you right now, I'm no better than you. I've done the same, if not worse. And I can keep my mouth shut if you can. We can get off this mountain together. We can go home. Eirik, Jesus Christ, no, stop it, what are you doing, don't, baby, please don't.'

I pause for breath for a brief moment, adrenaline coursing through my blood at the sight of my husband looping the blue acrylic rope around a tree branch at the edge of the clearing. I remember the vivid vision I had of Leah hanging, of her twisted and stiff body swinging slowly back and forth on the breeze, her neck at a strange angle, the milky white palms of her hands turned outwards. Perhaps it was myself I saw there all along, hanging beneath the branches.

Eirik moves slowly toward where I'm lying in a heap on the ground, gathering the other end of the rope into a noose, expertly tying strong, unbreakable knots. I'm running out of time. Is this really what the last few minutes of my life will be like? No. I won't allow it.

'Your mother would be so ashamed of you,' I say, using the last of my strength to keep my voice strong and unfaltering.

'Shut up,' he hisses, a look of surprise and pain washing over his face.

'She wouldn't believe that you could do this to me. That you'd be able to. She just wouldn't believe it. It's not too late, Eirik, it's not too late to make Juliane proud of you still. Think about it. You've spent your whole life trying to make her proud. Did you think I didn't know that about you? But it's not too late. It's up to—'

'Shut up, Kristina, Jesus Christ.'

'Juliane would have been the proudest mother on Earth to see you as prime minister. With me by your side. It's why you chose me, isn't it? Because I'm the kind of woman your mother would have chosen for you. If only she'd lived. But she lives on in you, and you're right to honor her in everything you do. If you do this to me, it will all be for nothing. All of it. Her life, and yours, and mine. All of our sacrifices. Think about the promise eleven-year-old Eirik made to himself that night, on her deathbed. You would make her proud. You promised. It was the last thing she ever heard...'

My desperate words are having the right effect; Eirik is sobbing openly now and has dropped the rope to the ground, but just then a gunshot tears through the night and my husband falls to the ground.

75

Elisabeth, August

'Look what I got you,' she says, pressing the bag into Elisabeth's fist. The words sound distorted and far away, blurred with all the alcohol. Elisabeth doesn't understand at first, but she recognizes the feel of the smack in the palm of her hand, the fine powder taking the shape of her hand as she grips it through the plastic.

'No,' she whispers.

'Yes,' whispers Kristina. 'It's okay.'

'No.'

'Let me help you.' Kristina takes the little plastic bag back, zips it open, sets about preparing the hit. The room is swimming and Elisabeth is face-down on the bed, trying to focus on the chair in the corner to regain control of herself and the situation. How does Kristina know how to do this? Elisabeth turns toward her, but the movement makes the room lurch, vodka-vomit splashing from her mouth and onto the bedsheet. She can't fully focus, but she registers Kristina's fluid movements as she holds the flame under the

374

spoon and she hears the hiss of the smack as it crystallizes, then runs clear. It's as though all her senses are heightened; she can even hear the little sound as the heroin is sucked into the syringe – it sounds like a kiss.

'No,' she whispers again, but her tongue feels thick and foreign in her mouth and the word comes out distorted and faint. 'Please.'

But Kristina doesn't look at her or pause for a single moment. She flicks her fingernail against the syringe, dislodging air bubbles, Elisabeth can hear the tap tap tap. She picks Elisabeth's arm off the bed where it lies flung, immobile. Elisabeth tries to retract it, but finds she can't. Kristina looks for a vein, prodding her skin hard, angling the arm into the light from the hallway. When she doesn't find one, she tries the other arm. Elisabeth writhes in pain, but the movement causes more vomit to flow into her mouth, making her splutter and choke.

The other arm is examined, twisted toward the light, hard, but there isn't a single viable vein; they've all collapsed too many times, leaving the arm a strange overall shade of light blue, but with no discernible veins. Kristina swears under her breath. Elisabeth tries again to move and to speak, to fight, to do something, anything. But her limbs are dead and heavy, so heavy she can't even move her toes. Still, she can feel it when Kristina pulls her left shoe off, then the sock, and when she finds what she's looking for – that one, big, clear vein that travels straight from Elisabeth's foot to her heart. She can feel it when the syringe goes in, when the heroin rushes hotly through her blood, so much of it she's dead in less than a minute.

76

Kristina

My screams bounce across the clearing and return in echoes. I can't move or get away or defend myself; all I can do is wait for a volley of bullets to hit me. I hear the crunch of the gunman's shoes on the snow as he comes closer, but I'm face-down and can't muster the strength I'd need to roll over and face him. Eirik is whimpering and muttering to himself somewhere nearby. I feel about me in an attempt to touch him and comfort him and reassure him that I meant every word I said, I wasn't just saying it to save myself. *Hang in there*, I want to say, but no words will come.

I hear a crackling sound followed by several loud voices shouting. I try to turn my head to discern where they are coming from, but even the slightest movement brings another onslaught of terrible pain. *Five oh one*, says someone. Or am I imagining it? Could it be that I've already died, that these moments are just the remnants of a life already over? Crackle, crackle. *Five oh one, Dragonfire has a visual. Copy.*

There is a kind of chopping noise, as though someone were drilling holes in the earth.

'You fucking psycho,' I hear someone say close to my ear. I follow the sound with my eyes and look into the mouth of the rifle, and at the other end of it, Anton's icy, cool eyes. For a long while, he holds the weapon trained straight at my face and I make myself look him in the eye, daring him to pull the trigger, knowing he won't. Behind him, the nimble body of a black-and-white police helicopter comes into view, lowering itself into the clearing.

Epilogue

Anton, hours earlier

He feels a growing restlessness every day when he wakes up, gasping for air, feeling as though he is emerging from a dream in which someone was trying to drown him. Today is no different. It's already past midday and he can taste yesterday's booze in his mouth. The bed is empty next to him and he runs his hand across the cool sheets.

He's been waiting for many days now. He considers going back up there to Bekkebu, but after the last time, the day after he lost it completely and hit her, finally turning her lie about him into truth, he's not sure it's a good idea. When she opened the door to him she held her head high, letting the golden rays of the autumn sun settle on her deep violet skin, and he realized that his apologies just wouldn't cut it. Still, she let him in and they talked. He had the sensation of having driven down a dead-end road – that there really would be no more going back this time. *I'm sorry*, he kept saying. She kept nodding, but her eyes were miles away. *What are you doing here?* he asked, looking around the sweet, familiar cabin. *Writing*, she said. *Waiting.* She wouldn't say what for, or for whom. *I'll be back on Thursday*, she said. *I'm going to need you to be out of the apartment when I come.*

No.

Yes.

He doesn't like to think about what happened next. He can't fully remember, anyway, besides screaming at her so loud his voice broke. He's still hoarse now, several days later, that's how loudly he screamed at the woman in front of him. She doesn't get to do the leaving. It's not how it works between them. He leaves, she begs for him to return, he hates her for being so pathetic, but he misses her too, and he's learned to call those emotions love. So he returns to her and they have a few weeks of relative peace after whichever drama came before. They do this again and again. Until now.

She didn't come back on Thursday like she said she would. Anton didn't leave her apartment like she asked him to, because he doesn't have anywhere to go. He doesn't know that after he left Leah at Bekkebu, she felt liquid and unsettled, as if Anton's voice were still hollering inside her head, so she decided to go home. Only she couldn't, because Eirik Moss had slashed the tires of her car while Anton was at the cabin. He doesn't know that she slipped on a wet root looping from the earth on her way back up to the cabin, or that she fell hard to the ground and while she was able to get back up and return to the cabin, the impact caused a small rupture in the developing placenta. He doesn't know that she began to bleed that evening.

Anton doesn't know any of this. It's been a week and he

is growing increasingly restless. Maybe he really was right about there being someone else; maybe they weren't just empty accusations to undermine and humiliate her.

He's sitting on Leah's sofa, looking out into the living room at her possessions, wishing for her presence. He wants to stay here and to make a life with her. He can do better, be a better man for Leah, he knows he's capable of it. He tries to call her yet again, but like every other time he's tried, it goes straight to voicemail. He goes into the bathroom and splashes cold water on his face. He looks at himself in the mirror and wishes it was Leah's warm, hazel eyes that were looking back at him. He opens the bathroom cabinet and rummages around for a painkiller; a vicious headache sits at the base of his skull, like a claw. He finally finds some in an old washbag at the back of the cupboard and in addition to the paracetamol, there's an elongated white object at the bottom. A pregnancy test. Anton's heart leaps in his chest and he holds it up to the light; it reveals two clear, strong lines.

It's his natural instinct to smash something, to wield destruction on physical objects in response to his feelings; whatever they are, he can't tell. A baby. Leah is carrying his baby. Anton bursts from the bathroom into the apartment's corridor. It feels as though his mind is on fire. He stands there for a long while as if paralyzed. Then he tears some clothes from his single shelf in Leah's closet and puts them on quickly. He glances around the apartment one last time, shellshocked, before grabbing his car key and rushing through the door.

Five months later

Dagsposten, article by Selma Eriksen.

There was a record turnout for the *Supernova* vernissage at Villa Vinternatt last night. Tragic novelist, Leah Iverson's unfinished work was displayed alongside paintings and illustrations by Elisabeth Eliassen, a previous resident of Villa Vinternatt. The event was the latest development in the Iverson Eliassen case, which has received worldwide attention since last November. The artist and the novelist were murdered a couple of months apart in a case that has shocked the nation and indeed, the world. The onetime strongest contender for the Conservative Party's highest appointment, Eirik Moss, and his wife, Dr Kristina Moss, once a highly respected Doctor of Psychology, were convicted of the crimes. The couple have been dubbed the 'sociopathic socialites' and both husband and wife are facing imminent trial for the first-degree murders of Iverson and Eliassen.

But last night wasn't about Mr and Dr Moss; last

night was very much a celebration of the remarkable achievements of their victims. *Supernova* is, 'an evocative and visceral account of the descent into madness', according to *Aftenposten*. *Publisher's Weekly* calls it, 'a multi-layered psychological study, chilling to the bone'. 'Terrifying and well-crafted,' says *Stockholmsposten*. 'The work of a writer in her most brutal and uncompromising prime' – *Deutsche Zeitung*.

Ms Eliassen was met with similar praise for her haunting depictions of trauma and its effects on the human psyche. It is safe to say that this undefined work, though most likely not intended for publication, written in the style of autofiction, like Iverson's previous *Nobody* (2018), is already causing major waves both internationally and in Norway, no doubt exacerbated by the extraordinary circumstances of its author's and illustrator's shocking killings, which have shaken the very foundations of Norwegian high society. *Dagsposten* will be running an in-depth headline review of *Supernova* for Saturday's special literary supplement magazine.

Acknowledgements

Cabin Fever was written during the pandemic and provided a refuge from everything going on in the world; a therapeutic pursuit about friendship, betrayal, and therapy itself. I already miss its universe and the escape it provided. This novel would not, could not, exist without the work, support and guidance of so many wonderful people.

A very big thank you is due to my agent, Laura Longrigg – I enjoy working with you so much and am so grateful for your sound advice and support over the years. Thank you also to the whole team at MBA Literary Agents, and especially to Tim Webb and Andrea Michell. Louisa Pritchard, I know how enthusiastically you champion my work in the foreign territories and appreciate it so much.

To my editors at Head of Zeus – Madeleine O'Shea and Laura Palmer – your insights and expert knowledge on all things books have hugely benefitted *Cabin Fever*. I love our often insane and creepy chats about plots and timelines and baddies and odd Norwegian customs. Thank you both for being a true joy to work with. Thank you also to the whole team at Head of Zeus, working with you is always a pleasure. A big thank you is also due to Louis Greenberg, for your pitch-perfect insights into *Cabin Fever*. Also, you managed to make me laugh out loud repeatedly during the rather stressful final stages of edits – so thank you.

I'd like to thank my writing group – I just can't wait for our next retreat together. Thank you to Tricia Wastvedt; as always you are such a gift in my life, both personal and professional. A very big thank you is due to Kristina Takashina, for longevity, loyalty, love and laughter. You helped me so much in creating Dr. Kristina Moss in this book. Martin Philips also helped me so much in understanding the therapeutic process and the psychotherapist's role, thank you so much. Rhonda Guttulsrod – I don't know how I got so lucky! You (and your family) are truly family to me (and my family), and I am so very grateful for you. Thank you, a million times over, for everything.

Thank you to Trine Bretteville, who kindly lent her name to one of the tragic protagonists in this novel. I absolutely adore you – thank you for all the years and maybe especially this past year. Our 8 A.M phone calls never fail to make me laugh and I can't wait for our next Paris adventure. Thank you to Elisabeth Hersoug, who lent her name to another tragic protagonist in this book; I appreciate our friendship so much. A special thank you to Olivia Foster who contributed to the preservation of (some kind of) sanity with our fantastic coronawinus sessions over the past year and whose presence in my life is much appreciated. Thank you also to my lovely ladies in Wimbledon – I can't wait to paint the town red and the air Chanel with you guys soon.

Thank you to Fevziye Kaya Sørebø, for all the good times, I so wish there would be more.

To all my other friends – I am very fortunate to be surrounded by such awesome people, so thank you.

To Lisa L – thank you for holding the mirror with the steadiest of hands. I promise I'm not as creepy as the events in this book!

As with every novel, the music is hugely important to me in the writing process. For *Cabin Fever*, I was in excellent company with Lana del Rey, Birdy, Eminem and Ane Brun, so thank you for the music.

A final, and very big thank you to my family, for putting up with me and allowing me this life as a writer. Thank you to my mother, Marianne, for always instilling in me that this would be possible. Thank you to my grandmother, Karianne – I know how much you would have loved to hold my books in your hands. Thank you to Chris and Judy. Thank you to Oscar, Anastasia and Louison for choosing me as your Maman. Thank you to Laura, for believing, for always fighting my corner, and for everything you are to me.